TROUBLE
IS WHAT I DO

ALSO BY ROB KANTNER

NOVELS

THE BACK-DOOR MAN
THE HARDER THEY HIT
DIRTY WORK
HELL'S ONLY HALF FULL
MADE IN DETROIT
THE THOUSAND YARD STARE
THE QUICK AND THE DEAD
THE RED, WHITE AND BLUES
CONCRETE HERO

TROUBLE
IS WHAT I DO

ROB KANTNER

POINT*BLANK*

TROUBLE IS WHAT I DO

Set in Sabon

POINT*BLANK*
www.pointblankpress.com
an imprint of Wildside Press
www.wildsidepress.com

edited by Kathleen Martin

For more information contact Wildside Press

0-8095-1156-8 (tpb)
0-8095-1157-6 (hc)

Table of Contents

Publishing Credits

"C Is for Cookie" first appeared in *Alfred Hitchcock's Mystery Magazine* Sep., 1982.

"Duck Work" first appeared in *Alfred Hitchcock's Mystery Magazine* Feb., 1988.

"Dynamite Park" first appeared in *Mike Shayne Mystery Magazine* Dec., 1984.

"The Eye Went By" first appeared in *Alfred Hitchcock's Mystery Magazine* Dec., 1986.

"Fly Away Home" first appeared in *Mean Streets* (Robert J. Randisi, Ed.); Mysterious Press 1986.

"The Forever Trip" first appeared in *Alfred Hitchcock's Mystery Magazine* Sep., 1985.

"Left for Dead" first appeared in *An Eye for Justice*; ed. Robert J. Randisi; Mysterious Press 1988.

"Libby's Luck" first appeared in *Alfred Hitchcock's Mystery Magazine* Jun., 1983.

"The Man Who Called from Tomorrow" first appeared in *Alfred Hitchcock's Mystery Magazine* Sep., 1986.

"My Best Fred MacMurray" first appeared in *Alfred Hitchcock's Mystery Magazine* Oct., 2000.

"My Brother's Wife" first appeared in *Alfred Hitchcock's Mystery Magazine* Feb., 1985.

"Perfect Pitch" first appeared in *Alfred Hitchcock's Mystery Magazine* July., 1985.

"The Rat Line" first appeared in *The Eyes Have It*; ed. Robert J. Randisi; Mysterious Press 1984.

"Sex and Violins" first appeared in *Trouble Is What I Do: Collected Ben Perkins*. PointBlank Press, 2005.

"Sleeping Dog Lies" first appeared in *Alfred Hitchcock's Mystery Magazine* Feb., 2000.

"Something Simple" first appeared in *Alfred Hitchcock's Mystery Magazine* Jun., 1999.

"Tall Boys" first appeared in *Alfred Hitchcock's Mystery Magazine* Mar.,1990.

"Unfinished Business" first appeared in *Deadly Allies* - ed. Robert J. Randisi & Marilyn Wallace; Doubleday Perfect Crime, 1992.

Acknowledgments

Thanks and a tip of the hat to colleagues Joe Konrath, Kevin Burton Smith, and Jim Winter, for the encouragement.

Many thanks and a big hug to my brilliant and able daughter Meaghan Kantner, for her hard and diligent work in digitizing the stories.

Thanks also to Carolyn Marino, and requiescat in pacem to Cathleen Jordan, the best publishing-world friends a fledgling writer could ever have.

And forever-thanks to my lovely, kind, and endlessly patient wife Deanna Heath. I love you, sweetie.

The Importance of Being Perkins
by J.A. Konrath

Ben Perkins is back!

It feels so good to say that.

Twenty-three years ago, when Rob Kantner introduced his Detroit PI in the short story "C Is for Cookie," he probably had no idea he was heralding in a new era of mystery fiction.

Before Rob, the private eye genre was glutted with down-in-their-luck losers who wore trench coats and talked like Bogart. Stereotypes ruled the paperback racks, and a revamp was sorely needed.

Rob's genius was to give his hero something more than clichéd one-liners and a drinking problem.

Namely, a life.

In hindsight, this seems obvious. These days, modern mystery writers weave intricate back-stories and relationships for their protagonists. The personal lives of Matthew Scudder and Kinsey Millhone are just as important to readers as catching the bad guy, and a continuing cast of characters is *de rigueur* for mystery fans. Watching the hero develop as a person, throughout the course of a series, has become more important to editors than a high concept story idea.

Ben Perkins was one of the first to do this.

Not to say Ben doesn't have his two-fisted moments—he does, and many of them are included in this collection. Ben is as smart as Lew Archer, as tough as Mike Hammer, and proudly carries on the tradition of the great private eyes that came before him.

And not to say that these stories lack plot. Rob is a mystery writer, and his stories are prime examples of how tightly woven a narrative can be. Some of the shorts in this volume are so tight, they squeak.

But Rob took it to the next level. He makes sure that his characters aren't simply pawns pushed around by the plot. Rob cares about his hero. As a result, so do we.

Ben Perkins has a detailed past, and a constantly changing future. In this collection, as in the novels, Ben proves himself to be dynamic; he changes as a character, as he matures. Ben's motivation isn't always correct, and it isn't always pure, but it's always *real*.

In Ben Perkins, Rob Kantner created a walking, talking, three-dimensional person, who also happens to be a private detective. Ben is the main character *in spite* of his profession, not *because* of his profession.

What a bizarre idea that must have been back in 1982.

Throughout these twenty-plus years, we've witnessed Ben grow. We've been privy to his home life, his childhood, his thoughts and dreams. Unlike Robert Parker's Spenser, whose past is mostly unknown and who ages one year for every ten he's in print, Rob Kantner allows us to get to know Ben as intimately as a member of our own family.

This odd approach apparently caught on. Not only did Rob nab four Shamus Awards from the Private Eye Writers of America, he inadvertently spearheaded the modern mystery movement, revived interest in the series character, and influenced a whole new generation of young writers, myself included.

The extraordinary thing about this collection, other than the fact that this is the first time all of these wonderful stories have been brought together, is that it reads very much like a novel.

This book is a time line. We start with Ben as a teenager back in 60s Motor City, and end up with him in the present. We meet Ben's longtime girlfriend, Carole Somers, and her son, Will, for the first time, and then watch them grow along with Ben. We get to spend quality time with all of the regulars— State Policeman Elvin Dance, Detroit cop Dick Dennehy, Ben's estranged sister Libby, his Uncle Dan, and even Ben's parents. We also get to see Ben Perkins's Detroit, which ages and matures just like a member of the cast.

In between novels, there was no downtime for Ben. He remained working and active, and some of these cases rival, and even surpass, his book-length adventures.

With *Trouble Is What I Do*, Perkins fans finally get the *whole story.*

It's important to mention a side note here. In 1994, despite awards, accolades, and a growing fan base, Rob Kantner took a break from fiction. He had the opportunity to start his own business-consulting firm, and as his children neared college age, he nobly put family ahead of Ben's exploits.

I'm thrilled to report that Rob's business has been successful, and Rob has once again picked up the pen. Besides this anthology, which contains a brand new Perkins story, Rob is also busily writing *My Eyes Keep Me in Trouble*, the 10th Ben Perkins novel.

The 10th Ben Perkins novel!

It feels so good to say that.

J.A. Konrath
Schaumburg, Illinois
June 2003

Foreword

Down the years, I've done just about every kind of writing there is.

Some decent, much acceptable, the occasional bits dreadful.

(Like ugly little trolls, the dreadful bits still pop up. I've just gotten better at not letting them out of the building.)

And like many who practice what Mailer calls this "spooky" craft, my emotions about it are mixed. I do not subscribe to the "I hate the act of writing" school, because for me there are times when the act of writing is a release, an escape, an activity that provides moments sometimes extended ones of transport. As a craftsman-in-training, nothing pleases me more than achieving a sentence that's the best I can make it, that gives me not even an ounce of uneasiness, that just plain works. And for me, aside from the company of my children or the smile of my wife Deanna, nothing feels as good as having laid down on a printed page a piece of fiction that comes even close to living up to the feel of it in my head.

Though I put my all into my fiction, I do not consider myself to be different or special, just because I write and have been lucky enough to be published. I'm no authority on the writing process, I barely understand it myself. (There are only two rules that always work for me: 1. Start as close to the end as you can, and 2. When in doubt, leave it out.) I have no Magic Key to Life, or Big Message to beat over readers' heads. My aim is simple. I write to divert, to entertain, to provide the reader with a world to escape into for perhaps just a few minutes, and, God willing, feel better afterward.

In this I think I've been most successful with short fiction. It's where I started, forty-odd years ago. It's what I gravitate to, whatever else comes along. It's what I've stuck with, despite the marketplace realities. I like the challenge: writing a decent novel is pretty hard; writing a short story that actually works is borderline miraculous. I like the quick gratification: a short takes me two months; a novel more like a year. And I like the chances short fiction affords me to innovate.

Ben Perkins started out in a novel, a dollop of derivative dreck called The Killing Path, written when I was 23 going on 16. But Ben's first real breath came in a short story called "The Long Slow Dive," and he first met his audience in another short called "C is for Cookie," which is in this collection.

Though Ben has starred in 9 novels so far, I believe he has lived and developed more fully and satisfactorily in the 20-odd short stories in which he's appeared to this point.

In used-book stores, rummage sales, and the odd auction, the novels still get a certain amount of underground attention. The shorts are (pardon the pun) another story. Though an occasional Ben story has been anthologized here and there, most of the them vanished quickly into dusty stacks of back issues of the various magazines, some of which no longer exist. I'm sure that, outside the library of my mother, no complete set exists. Even my own inventory had gaps, I found to my chagrin when starting work on this collection. Since starting www.RobKantner.com, I've had many requests for some sort of anthology or collection of Ben Perkins short fiction.

So here it is.

Not all of them are here. I could not do that and keep the length reasonable. So I chose what I consider to be the most decent, down through the years. "Tall Boys" leads off because, though it's a later work, it's set early in Ben's life. As it happens, it concerns his sister Libby, so it seemed sensible to follow with "Libby's Luck," a very early story, that features Libby in adulthood. Then, with "C is for Cookie," the stories appear in the order written, and in the order Ben lived them. The collection ends with "Sex and Violins," a very recent work and never before published anywhere.

In re-reading these stories (some of which I had not looked at in a decade or more), I wasn't as tempted as I thought I'd be to tinker and edit. Not that the work is perfect - far from it. These stories were never really finished; they were abandoned. But I confess to having made three very minor changes. In "C is for Cookie," I've restored Kate's original nickname for her ex-husband. Similarly, the contents of the "sack" Raeanne mentions in "My Best Fred MacMurray" have been restored to their original iteration. And from one of the stories I peeled off the original concluding 3 or 4 paragraphs, finding them now to be extraneous, and knowing I could never live with myself if I inflicted them on you now.

If you have half the fun reading these as I've had editing them, I'm sure you're in for a good time. That's my earnest wish for you: to have fun with good old Ben Perkins, spanning some 20 years of his career. And thanks to you and to all the readers for your support.

Rob Kantner
Blanchard, Michigan
May, 2005

Tall Boys

Daddy was dying. Not from the emphysema; that was three years from grabbing him. No: Daddy was dying because it looked like come November he'd have to vote for a Republican—or a Catholic.

"Even Truman don't want him in there!" Daddy ranted, waving his forkful of smother-broil chicken in the air. "He said Kinnedy ain't ready to be president yet, and I agree with him."

"Now there's a surprise," Ma said as she spooned a double helping of mashed potatoes onto my plate.

Daddy's lips whitened as he glared at her. "I always took a shine to President Truman," he said dangerously.

Ma stopped serving my brother Bill, straightened and stared at Daddy. "For heaven's sake, Lewis! Back when he was in, you said men under five eight shouldn't be dog catcher, let alone president!"

Daddy looked angrily perplexed. Across from me, Uncle Dan cleared his throat. I was hoping he'd point out that Daddy himself was only five seven. But Uncle Dan was just as gun-shy of Daddy as the rest of us. Ironic, since he was the only person I ever knew for whom Daddy had a grudging respect, bordering on awe. He observed dryly, "Well, Truman should know 'not ready to be president' when he sees it."

I snickered. "Let's eat!" Ma said, pointedly ending the political discourse as she sat down at the end of the table to my left. "Libby will just have to take supper cold. Say the blessing, please, Benjy?"

We linked hands around the table and I closed my eyes, trying to think of the words. Fortunately, I was saved by the scuffing of footsteps on our porch outside and the squeal of the screen door hinges. "Hi, everybody!" my sister Libby called from the door. "I want you to meet somebody."

She walked at a bounce toward the dining area, accompanied by a boy/ man wearing a small respectful smile. Even to my unschooled eyes, he looked older than Libby. Than me, even.

Libby's black hair was parted in the middle and combed smooth, cut at ear lobe level all the way around. Bangs curved down her forehead, arching over her dark eyes. She more than adequately filled her black sleeveless blouse and white striped shorts. A perky girl with a secret smile; my baby sister but suddenly no little girl anymore.

Ma was looking at Libby. Uncle Dan, having sized things up, was examining his clasped hands. Daddy, leaning back in his chair with feigned casualness, studied Libby's friend with his smoky blue eyes, the kind of eyes that terrorized Union troops a hundred years before. "Where you been, Elizabeth?" he asked softly.

"A carnival out in Nankin Mills. Jill's brother took us. That's where I met Jimmy. He works in the carnival." She beamed at her friend. "Jimmy Herndon, meet my family. That's Daddy and Mama. This is my brother Bill, that's my brother Benjy, and over there's my uncle Dan Perkins."

Herndon was a big beefy razor-cut blond wearing a yellow sport shirt, dark slacks, and pointy-toed shoes. He stepped toward Daddy, big paw outstretched. "So nice to meet you, Mr. Perkins. Say, what a great house you have here! You know, I've seen a lot of the Midwest, but Detroit is—"

"How old are you, son?" Daddy asked. There was nothing but interest in his voice. He was relaxed there in his chair, head tipped back, the hard planes of his face benign. The hairs rose on the back of my neck.

"Twenty-four," Herndon said, dropping his untouched hand.

"Daddy—" Libby began.

"Did you know," Daddy said, "that Elizabeth just turned fifteen?"

Herndon grinned crookedly. "Well, we hadn't really—"

Libby threw an imploring look at Ma as Daddy said in a whiplike voice, "Fifteen years old! What kind of skunk did your folks raise you to be, courtin' a fifteen-year-old little girl?"

Herndon held up both hands. "Courting? I'm not—"

Daddy leaped to his feet, his chair crashing to the floor behind him. "Get out!" he shrieked, face purpling. His fury demanded more oxygen than his ruined lungs could possibly provide; he exhaled in hard puffs between phrases. "Get out! Get *out* of my house! You *son* of a bitch! Get out!"

Libby began to cry. Herndon, twice Daddy's size and well under half his age, took one step back, gave Libby an unreadable glance then turned and strode out of the house.

My sister's round face was wet and white. "Thanks an awful lot!" she shouted to the room at large then ran away into the living room.

My big brother Bill stared grimly into his lap. Uncle Dan looked levelly at me. My heart pounded as if I was the object of my daddy's wrath instead of a bystander. Ma had risen and now, as Libby's footsteps echoed up the stairs, she went to Daddy and put her strong arms around his thin shoulders. "Now sit down, Lewis," she said brusquely. "Sit down and rest and take some supper."

"Son of a bitch," Daddy muttered, the words punctuated by puffs. But he sat.

Ma looked all right, but in her own way she was as upset as Daddy, as indicated by the fact that she clean forgot about grace. "Come on, let's eat," she said, spearing her chicken. "Libby will just have to take hers cold."

†††

I surely do look forward to these Wednesday night suppers with your family, Ben," Uncle Dan said dryly.

"Daddy's been real poorly lately," I said. "And that dopey sister of mine must have a death wish or something, dropping that guy on Daddy like that. I mean, she ain't even officially allowed to single-date yet. You really think he's twenty-four, Uncle?"

"Was once, anyway. I have a feeling he's been a lot of things. In a lot of places."

The humid July evening was darkening the porch, which opened on three sides to our heavily treed front yard. I sat on the stone railing, facing Uncle Dan, who was half visible on the big oak glider. He was a thin, wiry man who looked younger than his sixty-two years, with a full head of neatly trimmed, graying auburn hair and a narrow unlined face highlighted by remote gray eyes. As usual he wore a light, neatly tailored suit with shiny black wing tips and a narrow black tie. His Panama hat sat on the glider next to him and a Camel cigarette smoldered between his fingers.

I was jumpy as hell, the Big Question sitting fat in my mouth. Uncle Dan knew that, and was enjoying the suspense. We both looked toward the driveway as Bill's '58 Fairlane Town Sedan backed along the side of the house and then took off up the street. "Where's he off to?" Uncle Dan asked idly. "His shift doesn't start till midnight."

"Probably gone to see Marybeth first," I mumbled.

"He's been at Ford's what, eight years now," Uncle Dan observed. "Think you'll be able to hang on that long, Ben?"

It took a moment for what he said to register. I stood, fists clenched, heart pounding. "Really, Uncle? When?"

"Monday week, afternoons, at the Rouge."

"Doing what?" Please, no sweeping floors.

"Hanging doors on Fairlanes and Galaxies."

I whooped. "Great! Beats sweeping floors."

My uncle inhaled on his cigarette. "Lot of good men sweep floors at the Rouge. I did it myself, for awhile."

"Hey, it don't matter! This is great! Now I can quit the freakin' grocery store and make some serious dough!"

"Sit down," he said softly. I complied. My uncle leaned forward. "You remember our deal. You're going to pass your courses next year and you're going to graduate high school. You're not a punk kid any more, you're a grown man, and you've got obligations."

"Yes sir, Uncle Dan," I said, toning down the excitement.

"I hear you're flunking anything, I'll get you fired out of Ford's. Hear?"

I wondered if he could really do that. Uncle Dan had seniority to burn, but was only a foreman. There was, on the other hand, a lot about him I did not know. That none of us, Daddy included, ever knew. "Yes, sir. And I'll pay you back for the car loan, right off the top."

"No hurry," he said, leaning back on the glider.

"Evening, Ben!" called a female voice from behind me.

I turned. "Oh, hi, Miz Wilder," I called back.

"Lovely evening," she said, smiling at us, strolling by alone in the gloom of the big trees.

"Sure is."

Uncle Dan was sitting up straight, peering past me. "Neighbor lady?" he asked softly.

"Lives up at the corner of Bentler."

"Mm. Nice. Miss or Missus?"

"Missus."

I caught him looking at me closely. After a moment he said, "Your mother was telling me about your new girlfriend, Debbie?"

I scowled. "Debbie Miller. She's not my girlfriend, just a sophomore chick who lives in the house back of us. Been hanging around here, and Mama's been egging her on, but there's nothing there. I'm playing the field," I ended bravely.

Uncle Dan's distant eyes were on me again, making me feel distinctly uncomfortable. I wished that I could smoke; it would have helped at moments like that. "Think I'll mosey along home," he said, as he stood and put on his Panama, "before Act Two starts."

That was fine with me. It was pushing eight o'clock; *Silent Service* was coming on. I walked with Uncle Dan down the brick steps and across the narrow lawn to the curb, where his brand-new Thunderbird convertible, the most expensive car Ford built, was parked behind my brand-new second-hand '51 Deluxe Tudor sedan. "What do you mean, Act Two?" I asked as we walked.

"Libby and her new, uh, beau," he said. He crushed out his cigarette, opened the door and got inside.

"Oh, I think Daddy done killed that thing dead," I grinned.

"I don't," my uncle answered, face bleak in the fading light. "I saw them together in there."

I had no idea what he meant. "Whatever happens, it won't affect me none," I said with bravado that was entirely felt.

"May you be so lucky, Ben." He started the T-Bird, waved, and pulled away up Bennett Street, motor purring, tires humming, taillights glowing red in the gathering darkness.

†††

Three mornings later, I hoofed barefoot into the kitchen, tugging my blue National Foods uniform shirt down over my head. "Mama, I threw my newer workpants down the chute the other day. You washed 'em yet?"

She glanced at me over her shoulder as she rinsed off a breakfast bowl in the sink. "I finished the wash yesterday, Benjy. Those pants weren't in there."

"I *know* I put 'em down the chute."

"They'll turn up. Wear your old ones for today." She shut off the water. "Miz Wilder called a minute ago. Her husband's gone away on business, and she wanted to know if you could stop by there this morning and move some boxes for her. I said you could."

Move some boxes, I repeated silently. "Sure," I said, "I'll stop by there before I go to work."

"Bring me a pig's head from the grocery." She took down a dishtowel and started drying her hands. "We're having Brunswick stew tomorrow."

"I'll bring you the dead pig," I grinned, "but I'll need some dough."

"Take a five out of Daddy's cash kitty."

"Daddy won't like that."

"You do like I tell you," she advised, "and let me worry about your daddy."

"Yes, ma'am." Easy for you to say, I thought. He doesn't ever hit *you*.

She finished drying and hung the towel back up. The house around us was Saturday silent. Bill was working overtime at Ford's; Daddy's schedule at Kerns Casket was four on and two off, causing his weekends to rotate around; Libby was out somewhere. My mother looked me over, and she seemed to decide. "Set down, Benjy. I got something important to talk to you about."

Nervous and uncomfortable, I sat. My mother took the chair across from me. Her squarish face was tired and her eyes lacked their usual fervor. Her blue housedress was already limp from early heat and humidity and work. She folded her hands, looked at them then at me. "You probably ain't aware of it," she began quietly. "You got your own life these days. But there's trouble in this house."

I was afraid even to breathe. "What kind of trouble?"

"Your sister," Ma said, "is still seeing that boy. That Jimmy Herndon."

Inside I sighed, and thanked my lucky stars that it was Libby's ass in a sling this time, and not mine. "How do you know, Ma?"

"Just a feelin'," she said. "Your momma ain't a total dern fool, you know. I know a lot about what goes on in this house." I wasn't about to touch that one. After a pause, Ma went on. "For example, I had a feeling that William knew more than he was lettin' on. So I asked him last night, and I was right."

"William" was my big brother Bill on the wrong side of Ma. "Right about what?"

Her lips drew back from her teeth for a minute and her eyes were steely. "Up till Wednesday, William was picking Libby up from summer school classes and driving her to meeting with that boy."

I couldn't believe it. "So Bill was helping her?"

Ma nodded grimly. "Your brother is weak. Libby asked him to, and he didn't have the gumption to say no. Last night he spilled everything. He told me that Libby didn't meet that boy Wednesday, like she said. They met two weeks ago. She brought him here Wednesday night because she was going to ask us to let him stay in the extra bedroom till he could find a job. Supposably he was quitting the carnival so he could stay in Detroit."

"Wow. Daddy ain't heard all this, has he?"

Ma held up a work-worn hand. "Your daddy must never know. He is very poorly. He don't need aggravation."

And God knows we don't need him aggravated, I thought. "What are you gonna do, Ma?"

"I thought about forbidding her to see Herndon. But Jane Lee says if you forbid a teenager to date someone, she'll turn right around and do it anyhow."

Jane Lee was a local advice columnist whose counsel Ma ranked just below that of the Gospels. "Jane Lee knows best," I said, echoing what Ma herself had said down through the years.

She ignored the sarcasm. "Bill swears he stopped helping Libby as of Wednesday. That's all the help I can expect out of him. For the rest, I'm looking to you."

I gaped. "Me?"

"You," Ma said in a cold voice. "I want you to find out for sure if they're still seeing each other. If they are—" She stopped abruptly and took a deep breath before going on. "If they are, then you will find a way to break it up, and get him out of Libby's life for good."

I sat there in our kitchen, listened to the silence, felt the pressure, impaled on a dilemma. On the one hand, I'd been brought up to obey my parents instantly and without question. On the other hand, I wanted no part of Libby's messes. And I was not, as Uncle Dan said, a punk kid any more. I was practically a grown man now, tired of taking orders. Plus, I only had a week before I went to work afternoons at the Rouge. My free time was running short, and I didn't want to waste any of it making like some kind of half-assed Richard Diamond, Private Eye.

Forget it, old lady, I said silently. Find yourself another patsy.

My mother said, "I'm not asking you for your daddy's sake, or for my sake. It's for Libby's sake." She pressed her lips. "That boy is trouble. I just know it. Libby's too young. She's strong-headed. Rash. Reckless."

Here goes, I thought. "Ma, I'm—I wouldn't know where to start." Good going, big man, I thought, disgusted. Good thing Fast Eddie and the Bubbas weren't there to hear me.

She smiled at me. "You'll find a way. You'll do it because you're my boy, and because I'm asking you to, hear?"

"Yes, ma'am."

"You do as I say, now."

"Yes, ma'am."

"Take care of your baby sister."

"Yes, ma'am."

†††

I locked up my Ford and joined Fast Eddie walking with a cluster of other customers up the long grassy meadow toward the carnival entrance. Thin-as-a-straw Eddie wore all black, as usual, and carried his Gibson acoustic slung by its black embroidered strap over his shoulder. He surveyed the sky with his dark eyes and held out his hands tentatively. "Think it might rain?"

"That's the chance you take, dummy, carrying that guitar around. What's it for, anyways?"

"Chicks," he said, his thin face wolflike.

"Well, you're on your own on that. I'm here to track down this Jimmy Herndon fella."

"I still don't get it, Benjy. What's talking to Herndon gonna get you?"

"I'm going to ask him if he's gonna hang around or leave town. If he's leaving town, our troubles are over. If he's hanging around, well—I'll have to figure out what to do then."

We got in line at the carnival admission booth. Fast Eddie studied me. "What's with you and the chicks department, Benjy? Having yourself a celibate summer?"

"I'm doing just fine, thanks," I growled, digging into my pocket for money.

Fast Eddie laughed. "You mean Debbie Miller? Your momma was telling me little Deb's got the hots for you. What a howl!"

"Forget it man. She's ugly, she's stupid, and she's only fifteen."

"So, what's the problem?"

As such operations go, the carnival wasn't very big. Its dozen rides included a rickety roller coaster, dodge 'em cars, a merry-go-round, a couple of pivoting saucer rides, and the inevitable Ferris wheel. Organ music shrilled from worn-out speakers, and the humid air was drenched with the scent of sawdust, beer, and animal dung.

We hit the midway, which stretched out colorfully the length of a football field, flanked with booths manned by loud, practiced carnies. There weren't many customers. Some of the booths had none at all. It was perfect, but I didn't feel all that good. I was hung over, for one thing; as usual, Fast Eddie, the Bubbas, and I had put away a case of tall boys the night before. On top of that I was nervous. I'd never done this kind of thing. I didn't know where to begin. Oh well, I thought, just dive in and fake it.

"Over here, Fast," I said, gesturing us toward one of the carny booths. This was a sort of ring toss game. You threw rubber rings at cases full of long necked bottles. If you got a ring to stick over a bottle top, you won a prize. The catch, of course, was that the rings were just barely big enough to fit over the necks, and the bottles were not seated solidly in the cases.

I ambled up to the counter. It was manned by a wizened, deeply tanned man in a baggy blue Truman shirt, ball cap, and loose pants. His face looked like it had collapsed on itself; it had no substance at all except for the wad of chew in his left cheek. As I approached, he sang, "Yes sir, yes sir, win a big prize. Two chances for a thin dime, five for a quarter. What'll it be, young fella?"

"Hi," I said, grinning at him. "I'm looking for Jimmy Herndon."

"This ain't the missing persons bureau. How many chances you want, now?"

"I don't want any. Look, I knew Herndon works here at the carnival. Where is he?"

The carny stepped back and glared at me, tiny points of light burning in his remote eyes. "You're blocking paying customers. Pay up and play, or move on, kid."

I glanced around. No one else was there. Not even Fast Eddie. Bored already, he'd wandered across the fairway to the Rifle Range and was chatting with the overweight blonde who ran it. She beamed at him in a way that women never beamed at me, and I felt the resentment that went back to when

Fast Eddie and I were six: *how in hell does he do it?*

I glared at the carny. "There's nobody else here, mister. Now I asked you a question. Help me out and I'll be on my way."

The sawed-off ball bat came up with blinding speed, swung down and smashed the counter top. I nearly jumped out of my shoes. The carny raised the bat again and waggled the business end like Rocky Colavito, staring hotly at me. "You heard me!" he screamed. "Get moving!"

I gulped. "Okay, okay. No offense." I backed away from the booth. Several other customers were staring at me. The other carnies paid no attention a all. Fast Eddie had vanished. So had the blonde lady.

I continued up the midway. Gradually my heartbeat got back under control. Big deal, I told myself. You ran into a hard nose first time out. Keep trying. Someone will come across.

Wrong. I worked the midway for better than an hour. I talked to carnies, concessions people, roughnecks, and drivers. Leaving out the ball bat part, they were as cooperative as the ring-toss man. Never heard of Jimmy Herndon. Get moving, kid. Mind your own business.

They were lying. I was sure of it. But, I thought as I retraced my route down the midway, there's no way to prove it. Dead end. I walked on, bound for the exit, wondering where Fast Eddie was, wondering what to do now—

"Hey, Benjy!"

I turned. Fast Eddie gave me the come-on wave. I trotted toward him. "What's up, Fast?"

He looked excited. "Come here. Quick, before she changes her mind." He led me between two of the carny booths. Behind the midway was a sprawling grassy area parked full of trucks. One of them, a big panel job, sat facing me with its tail doors swung open. Sitting on the bumper was the blonde woman I'd seen Fast talking with earlier. She was smoking a cigarette and looked nervous. "This is my friend Erma," Eddie said. "Erma, this is Benjy. Now tell him what you told me."

Erma's close-cropped hair hadn't always been blonde. She stretched a cowgirl outfit and big tall boots, and was ten years and fifty pounds ahead of Eddie, not that it made any difference to him. She scanned me indifferently, glanced around then said in a low voice, "Jimmy Herndon was a roughneck here at the carnival."

I glanced at Fast. He was beaming. "I know that," I told her. "Where is he?"

"I don't know."

"Tell him the story, Erma," Fast Eddie said.

She shut her eyes tightly for a minute. Then: "There was a big brawl last week in a bar up on U.S. 12 somewhere. A man got knifed. Throat cut, bled to death, Jimmy was there. Word is, he did it. He's hiding out. Cops are after him. He don't dare show his face around here."

"Nice guys your little sister hangs out with, Benjy," Fast noted.

"Shut up." I leaned close to Erma. She smelled of makeup and sweat. "You sure about this, Erma?"

"Swear to God." Her eyes flickered. "We're not supposda talk about him. Bad for business."

"I'll just bet." I stood. "Any idea where he went?"

She shook her head and inhaled on her cigarette jerkily. "I don't know, and I don't want to know. Jimmy Herndon is slick and tricky and pure trouble all the way through. You boys stay clear of him."

"We can't," I said, putting all the tough I could into my voice. "Him and me, we got business."

She smiled sadly. "Then be careful, boys. Be plenty damn careful."

†††

After thinking it over, I decided to park in the lot of the Michigan Bank, across from Redford High. I couldn't park too close or Libby would spot me. I couldn't park too far away or I'd miss her. This was perfect. Hopefully.

As I waited, the radio whispered the three o'clock news: Tshombe, Katanga, the Democratic Convention, and today's All Star Game. It was a warm and muggy Monday, had rained earlier and would again. I smoked a Camel cigarette and thought about what I was doing. I'd bombed out with Herndon. Now to go at it from the other end. Follow Libby and see where she went.

Gaggles of kids left the building as summer school classes let out. When I spotted Libby, she was walking east along the sidewalk on Grand River, about to cross Westbrook. Headed away from home.

When she stopped in front of Sock's Texaco amid a mixed group of whites and Negroes, I realized she was waiting for a bus. I put out my cigarette and started the car. Libby didn't seem anxious or furtive. She wore a generously cut pleated shirtdress in light blue, with a big wide belt and sandals, and carried her textbooks as if they weren't important.

A DSR bus came along and roared to a stop. I wheeled my car into one of the eastbound lanes of Grand River as the bus gobbled up its passengers and continued toward the distant skyline of downtown Detroit.

The radio began to croon Percy Faith's "Theme from 'A Summer Place.'" I'd heard it to death already. I twirled the knob to the next station: Elvis doing "Stuck on You." Much better. I kept the left lane of Grand River, and followed the bus at the thirty-five mph speed limit. The back ad panel advertised Channel 7, WXYZing, Detroit's Big Station.

I wondered where the hell my sister was going.

The bus stopped at every major cross street. Each time I hugged the curb, watching fruitlessly for Libby as people got on and off. We passed near the National Food store where I worked and I flipped it the finger as we went by, knowing I was out of there in less than a week. St. Mary's Catholic, Ward's and Penney's, the Bow Wow Coney Island, the Belshaw plant. Traffic was light, but the speed limit was thirty now and we crawled. Winkelman's, Sears, Charlie's Cadillac and Dawson Edsel; downtown was rising before my eyes and still no Libby—

I damn near blew it. The bus stopped across from the Riviera Theatre; I watched the disembarking passengers idly and then scanned the marquee: *A Tall Story* starring Tony Perkins and Jane Fonda. When the bus moved on, I did too, and belatedly spotted Libby half-jogging across Grand River for the front of the theatre.

Cursing myself, I U-turned in front of Kresge's and came back as several homebound commuters honked angrily. Libby was not in sight. One thing I knew for sure: she didn't need to come all the way down here for movies, not with the Redford Theatre right around the corner from our house.

I gingerly turned north on Riviera Street. Libby was half a block away, crossing the narrow street toward the front of a gaunt, gray, two-story apartment building. As I rolled slowly that way, she went inside. I pulled into the Riviera Theatre's parking lot across from the apartment building, drove down to the end, and parked by a tree.

Wesson Apartments was engraved in stone above the corner of Riviera and Yosemite streets, a modest looking neighborhood. I didn't know anybody down here. I wondered who in the hell Libby knew down here. I wondered what she was doing in there. Several times I opened my door, ready to go find out. Each time I shut the door and waited some more.

An endless, fidgety hour later, Jimmy Herndon came out of the Wesson Apartments with his arm around my sister. They kissed, he waved, and she walked away toward Grand River, stride bouncy, arms embracing her books.

I fired up the Ford and laid a hot streak of rubber as I swerved onto Riviera Street and rolled abreast of Libby. Her eyes widened when she saw me; then she looked resolutely ahead as she walked, "Go away, Benjy."

I kept my tone reasonable. "Need a ride, don't you?"

"I'm fine. Now go away."

I babied the Ford along, keeping even with Libby. "Come on, hop in," I said. "You really don't want to ride that sweaty old bus all the way home, do you?"

She looked at me suspiciously then tossed her head in what passed for acceptance. I stopped the Ford, she crossed in front and got in. I managed to keep the lid on till we'd turned the corner and were part of the westbound rush up Grand River.

"You're not seeing that son of a bitch no more, Libby Perkins, or I'll break both your arms for ya, I swear to God!"

"I'll see him all I want!" she shouted back. "And you got no right to spy on me."

I calmed myself with difficulty. "Listen. Herndon's trouble. He done got into a knife-fight, and somebody died, and the cops are after him."

I did not get the expected shocked silence. "He didn't kill anybody," Libby came back readily. "It was all a big mix-up. An accident. They're just picking on him."

"How come you know so much about it?" She didn't answer. "Don't tell me you were *with* him when it happened."

She shrugged and began to play with the window crank, mouth ugly. "What about you? You're not exactly Mister Simon Pure yourself. I've smelled beer on your breath, plentya times. And I know you're weedin' off every chance you get. And you prob'ly got some kind of trashy girlfriend stashed away somewhere."

"I'm seventeen," I said. "Makes all the difference."

"No," she shot back. "You're a boy and I'm a girl. *That's* the difference." She turned on the radio. It was playing "Itsy Bitsy Teeny Weeny Yellow Polka Dot Bikini." I shut it off on the third beat. Libby scowled and went on, "Mama put you up to this. She thinks just 'cause I'm a girl that I can't handle things. Well, I can. Every damn bit as well as you."

Silence prevailed till I made the turn onto Burgess, three blocks from home.

Libby said softly, "You just forget what you saw today. If you snitch to Mama and Daddy, I'll say you're a liar."

"Stay away from him, Libby."

"You can't stop me. Mama and Daddy can't stop me." She smiled. "Nobody can stop me. Nobody at all."

As we turned onto our street, I waved at Mrs. Wilder, and she waved back from her porch swing.

†††

"So," Fast Eddie said from the shotgun seat, "we gonna thump some rump this afternoon or what, men?"

I slowed the '51 to a stop in front of Sun Ya's on Grand River as the radio played "Cathy's Clown." "We're just gonna *reason* with Mr. Herndon.

That's all."

Fast grinned at me and jerked a thumb toward the back seat. "Is that why we're bringing along all this Bubba-beef? Because they're so articulate?"

I glanced in the rear view. The Bubbas filled the back seat with biceps, shoulders, football jerseys, and identical grins. "Reason with him," one of them said. "Damn straight," chimed in the other.

Their real names were Joe and Frank Szewczklieuski. But everybody had referred to them as Bubba, both singular and plural, almost as far back as I could remember. The handle was hung on them by my daddy. Being, like everybody else, unable to tell them apart, he was uncomfortable calling them Joe or Frank. And he never could learn how to pronounce their last name, no matter how patiently we tutored him. One day in frustration he called them Bubba, and it stuck.

It was a hot, sunny Tuesday noon. I'd worked the morning at the grocery and then collected the guys for our little visit to Jimmy Herndon. Libby was safely in summer school so I figured the coast was clear. My reasoning was, if I couldn't talk her out of him, maybe I could encourage him out of her.

The light changed to green, the song changed to "You're Gonna Miss Me," and the topic changed to the Detroit Tigers: sorry as hell, tied for fifth with the Washington Senators and going nowhere fast. I lighted a Camel and joined the bad-mouthing, which went from baseball to women, to beer to women, to Fast Eddie's new band to women, and from there, neatly, to beer.

"Hey, Ben," a Bubba said, "tall boys Saturday night."

"Your turn to buy," the other chimed in.

"Damn, that's right," I said. "Guess I'll be hitting the usual source. If I can catch Denny on duty. He still doesn't card, does he?"

"Nah," Fast Eddie said, "but I think he's on vacation."

"I'll figure it out," I vowed. "Don't worry, guys. It's only Tuesday. By Saturday, a case of tall boys will be ours."

We crossed Livernois; on the home stretch now. Fast Eddie rubbed his hands together. "I think we ought to take Herndon in an alley and lay waste to his face."

Eddie's zeal would have been disquieting if it were not so suspect. "Just let me do the talking, Fast," I said. "Y'all are along for moral support and that's all."

"You guys hold him," Fast said ominously, "and I'll hit him."

I rounded the corner and pulled into the half-full parking lot of the Riviera Theatre. We parked, got out, and crossed Riviera Street, making for the doorway of the Wesson Apartments. We'd just hit the sidewalk when Fast Eddie said blandly, "Hey, guys, I better stay out here and watch the car."

The Bubbas snickered. I glared at Eddie. "What do you mean, 'watch the car'? It ain't going nowhere."

He was already heading back. "I'll just sit on the hood and scare off the thieves. You guys have fun."

He waltzed away, whistling a cheerful tune. "Come on, guys," I muttered to the Bubbas.

The foyer of the Wesson was small, airless, and empty except for a row of metal mailboxes nailed to the cheap plaster wall. Each box had a name and not one of them was Herndon.

"What now?" I asked the Bubbas. Their only reply was a shared grin. I had a brainstorm. "Come on," I said, and led them to an apartment door. A brisk knock brought the face of a small busty woman with loose dentures, a small mustache, and a hairnet. "Yaaaassssss?" she asked, wobbling.

"Looking for Jimmy Herndon, ma'am," I said. "He lives in the building here. Big beefy guy? Blond? Works the carnival?"

"Upstairs," she said with a Smirnoff accent. "Try upstairs, the door with the Tigers decals." She slammed the door.

"Now we're cooking," I said. The Bubbas trailed me like a herd of steer, up a flight of narrow wood stairs to the second floor. I knocked on the door and it swung open obligingly.

I damn near swallowed my tongue.

It was a small one-room apartment with windows looking out over Yosemite Street. The Murphy bed was held down by the stark naked Jimmy Herndon, who gaped at us through the smoke of his cigarette, and a trim young dark-haired woman who, I realized as she gave a strangled "Eep!" and tried to cover herself, was not Libby.

"Excuse us," the Bubbas said in unison, having been raised to be polite.

"Want to talk to you, Herndon," I said sternly.

The big man's good-living face went sour for a second as he recognized me. "Oh, jeez. Okay. I'll see you in the hall there in a second, kid."

"Make it quick," I said threateningly, and pulled the door shut. "Hey, Bubba, trot on our there on Yosemite and make sure our little buddy doesn't slip out the window, okay?" One of them took off, clomping heavily down the stairs.

I lighted a Camel and smoked nervously. After a moment the apartment door opened and Jimmy Herndon came out, zipping up his pants. He grinned at me. "You're Benjy, right?"

"Ben. Ben Perkins. And you know why I'm here, so let's get on with it."

"Get on with what?" he asked pleasantly. His eyes clicked once to Bubba and then back to me, undisturbed.

"You and Libby. I want to hear you say that it's over."

"Well, okay. It's over. How's that, Benjy?"

His grin had not wavered. I dropped my cigarette to the floor and slowly crushed it out, feeling my heart pound and fists knot. "You smart-mouthin' me?"

He showed me palms. "No," he said deliberately. "Now don't get riled. I meant what I said. Libby and I are all through."

I loosened my hands marginally. "You give me your word on that?"

"Absolutely. Look, Ben—you don't mind if I call you Ben, do you?" He hooked a hand over my shoulder and led me slowly up the hall. "I like Libby. I really do. But she really is too young for me. I'm breaking it off. I'd already planned to, even before today."

"I see."

Herndon looked me straight in the eye. "As it happens, I'm leaving town for good. Tonight. So I'll be out of the picture. Fair enough?"

"Yeah. Okay." I gestured to Bubba. "Don't disappoint me, now," I warned Herndon.

"Don't worry, Benjy. I won't."

†††

The rain was dumping in buckets the next afternoon as I sloshed the Ford up Lahser on my way home from work. I'd put in ten hours at the grocery and I was whipped, grimy, and grumpy. My boss, whom I'd unwisely nicknamed Hitler, had been giving me the crappiest jobs in the place ever since I told him I was going to work at Ford's. Plus I was jumpy, wondering what kind of explosion waited for me at home. It had been twenty-four hours since my talk with Jimmy Herndon, more than enough time for Libby to find out that he was gone.

A familiar figure waved an umbrella to me from under the awning of Jim's Sweet Shop. I sloshed the Ford to the curb as my mother ran to the car, opened the door and piled in, dragging her umbrella behind her. "Lord have mercy, it's enough to strangle frogs! Thank you, Benjy."

"No problem, Ma." I wheeled the Ford away from the curb. "So how's things around the house?"

"Things?" she asked absently as she glanced inside her prescription bag. Then she arched a brow. "Oh. Things. Well, son, I reckon *things* are just fine."

"In the baby sister department?" I asked carefully. "What's she been up to?"

"Nothing special. Came straight home from school, like yesterday. Studied awhile. Then went out with her girlfriends. There's a new movie at the Redford over there, something with Dick Clark." She must have taken my silence for skepticism, because she added, "I know that's where Libby went. I walked up here with her and her friends, since it was right on the way to Kinsel's for your Daddy's prescription."

"Well, good," I said uneasily, swinging right onto Bennett.

"I don't know what you did, son, but whatever it was, it seems to've worked. I'm much obliged." She looked at me and wrinkled her nose. "Heavens mercy, what is that stench on you, Benjamin?"

"Hot sauce. Had to clean up a busted case of it."

She had her eagle eye on. "And those shoes! Why in the world did you wear those sorry old shoes to work?"

"Couldn't find my other ones. Looked everywhere."

She snorted. "You're too young to be going senile. First your pants, now your shoes."

"Sorry, Ma." I slowed down for our driveway. "I've had a lot on my mind."

She smiled at me. "I know. It was unfair of me, imposing on you the way I did. But I'm not sorry. You fixed it and it's over, and I'm grateful, Benjy. Right grateful."

I wished I could be as positive as she.

But everything stayed calm. At least as calm as it ever was around our house. Daddy came home mean as a snake from a run-in with his boss at the casket company, and had another tantrum when the news came over that Kennedy had, as expected, been nominated. Libby returned from her movie and ate dinner with the family. Then she spent the evening curled up on the living room couch, industriously studying her English. She was in a fine mood. I began to think that maybe Ma was right. Maybe the Herndon episode was over. Maybe Libby would pass her remedial courses and go on to tenth grade in the fall and life would return to whatever passed for normal around our place.

I wanted to believe it. I had my own life to live, and only a few days before hitting the line at Ford's. I wanted to cruise in my Deluxe Tudor, maybe turtle-race down Woodward Avenue, four cars abreast doing ten miles per hour; gobble Big Chief burgers at the Totem Pole, catch the Tigers playing the Yankees at Briggs Stadium this weekend, and, of course, have at least one more session guzzling Stroh's tall boys with Eddie and the Bubbas, assuming I could find a supplier.

But in the end I had to make sure.

†††

I stood before the apartment door and took a deep breath as the Wesson Apartments breathed silently around me.

For the dozenth time since getting up that Thursday morning, I wondered if I was being extra dumb, coming down here alone. But, I reminded myself, Herndon didn't seem all that tough. Big guy, for sure, with some experience on him, but mostly mouth. All lard and no hard, as my daddy would have said. I wouldn't need the Bubbas to handle him. If in fact he was still here.

I knocked on the door. After a moment it eased back, held cautiously by the dark-haired woman I'd seen Herndon with the last time. She wore a mint Grecian-sleeve dress with a polka dot sash around her slender waist. Her hair was pixie short and so was she: shapely but slight with the wiry build of a dancer. "You," she greeted me.

I wanted to tell her she looked better with clothes on, but caught myself in time. Not very nice, and untrue, besides. "Me," I answered, grinning. "Where's Herndon at?"

"Not here. Who cares where?" She smiled crookedly. "I sure as the dickens don't. I threw him out." She stepped into the hallway and pulled the door to. At my expression her face hardened and she pushed the door back open. "You want to search the place? Go ahead!"

"If I wanted to, babygal, I would." The line sounded better in my head that it did out loud. "What'd Herndon do, find somewhere else to live?"

"Somewhere else?" she mimicked sourly. "He never lived here. Hung around some, you know? But he never spent the night. We had some big laughs, okay? But nothing big-time."

"Seen him lately?"

"You deaf or something? I threw him out, I toldja." As she looked at me, I saw that her eyes, outlined in black, were the exact color of her dress. "The other day when you were here, I listened through the door. That's how I found out about him and your sister. That tore it. I never planned to marry the bum, but I wasn't going to be part of any harem, either."

"Any idea where he went?"

"If he was smart, he got out of Detroit. Cops are looking for him. You knew that, huh? I called 'em myself to let them know he'd been seen in the neighborhood here. Maybe they caught him, ever think of that?"

Nope. Not hardly. "Sure I did," I said importantly. "I'm stopping by the precinct right after this."

"Uh-huh." Her hips swayed slightly as she gave me the cool green once-over. "When you're done with all that, whyn't you come back and buy me a drink or something?"

"Wish I could," I said, taken by surprise. "But I'm, uh, more or less seeing somebody, you know?"

"At least you're honest," she said, which made me feel guilty. She walked with exaggerated grace back into her apartment and smiled and winked at me over her shoulder. "I hope she knows how lucky she is," she said before closing the door between us.

I idled the Ford at the Schoolcraft traffic light. On the opposite corner sat the C & H Party Store. I wondered if they'd card me if I strolled in and bought a case. I had no idea, and I had no time now. But I'd have to figure the beer thing out pretty soon. Saturday was only two days off.

But I had something bigger on my mind than the need for a case of tall boys. It was a feeling I'd never had before, not quite this way. The feeling that something was going on behind the scenes. That a great big fast one was being pulled.

That I was being had.

"He never spent the night here," his ex-girlfriend had told me. Then where the hell was he living, between the knife fight and now? Had I even thought to ask her? Nooooo.

"She was going to ask us to let him stay in the extra bedroom," Ma had told me. Of course, the negotiation had never gotten that far, thanks to my calm, cool, collected daddy.

And Libby had been acting awfully happy last night for a hotheaded girl whose first great love had ankled her.

The light greened and I geared the Ford up to high, half watching my driving. "There's trouble in this house," Ma had said. Yeah. Things hadn't been right. I'd been waking up a lot lately in the dead of the night. I'd attributed that to the jitters—starting work at Ford's would be no picnic, I knew—but what if. . . .

That morning I'd been unable to find my prized Redford High baseball jersey. And Bill had complained about missing a jacket. Either the laundry chute was eating our clothes, or Ma was going senile, or—

"Jesus Christ," I murmured. I sailed through the red light at Greenfield without even thinking about it. Could anybody be that brazen?

By the time I reached our neighborhood, I'd decided what to do. It was wild-assed crazy, but it just might work—if I could only talk Debbie Miller, my local admirer, into going along.

†††

She appeared, a ghostly, whitish-gray, faceless figure, behind the rippled glass of the porch door, and clicked the latch open. As I pulled the door, she put a finger to her lips and shook her head. I nodded. She turned and led me through the inner door into the house, through the kitchen, and up the carpeted back stairway.

The house had the sweet, foreign smell of strangers and was pitch black except for the faint tread of our feet echoing mutely on the old floorboards.

My heart was racing, and I was pumped and primed and as ready to go as if it were nine in the morning instead of just past midnight. God alone knew what the next hour or so would bring.

Debbie closed her bedroom door behind us and faced me. In the faint light of her bedside lamp, I saw that she wore white full-length cotton pajamas over pink bunny slippers. Atop that she wore a white satiny quilted robe that reached all the way up to a big button at her throat. She was about as physically inviting as a Barcalounger, which, I discerned in her opening comments, was no accident.

"Don't you lay a hand on me, Benjy Perkins!" she whispered sharply, gray eyes hard.

I sighed. So much for the big crush she supposedly had on me. Just as well. "That's not why I'm here," I whispered patiently. "I explained all that."

"Better not be. I'm not like that Beth Heinzeroth, sneaking boys into her house to do God knows what. I must be nuts to be doing this. I'm a good girl."

"I know. So listen, whyn't you keep yourself busy or something, while I do what I got to do? Go to sleep if you want. I don't know how long this'll take."

She rolled her eyes. "No, thank you. I'll just stay awake till your done with whatever strange business you're mixed up in. There's the window. Help yourself. And keep it quiet or you'll wake my folks—and you know what that means."

I went to the window, pulled back the drapes, and notched the blinds. Across the narrow adjoining back yards, I could see the backside of our house, half black and half silvery in the moonlight. Behind me, I heard bedsprings creak as Debbie arranged herself Indian-style against her headboard. I glanced back at her and she raised her chin and stared at me defiantly. I made what I hoped was an innocent, reassuring smile, turned back to the window, knelt and looked out and watched, waiting for something to happen.

An hour went by like that. Nothing happened outside. Inside was another story. Debbie just couldn't sit still. She flipped through magazines and paced, cleared her throat and smothered yawns, and gave me a clench-jawed, steely-eyed stare whenever I dared to look at her.

I was silently composing a speech in which I foreswore, for all time, any and all interest in her body, when I caught a motion outside at the northeast corner of our house.

It was Libby. She wore jeans and a sweater and nothing on her bare feet showing white against the grass. It was in the low fifties that night, cool for July, and she hugged herself as she walked purposefully in the moonlight to the double doors that covered the concrete stairs leading down into our cellar.

As I stared, I felt disbelief. I also felt something else, something new: pure cold joy. Got you, you bastard. I got you, got you, got you.

Libby bent and gave the cellar door three taps. After a moment it rose a couple of inches. She opened it the rest of the way, stepped over the threshold and followed the steps down, swallowed up in the deeper blackness as the cellar door dropped shut behind her.

Now! I thought fiercely. Now to settle some hash! I stood abruptly. Debbie jumped. "What is it?" she whispered.

"Christmas time. Got to go, sweetheart." I headed for the door. "You stay here. I know the way out. And thanks, kid. You done good."

She stood, nervously tugging the robe tightly around her. "I thought you'd be here longer."

"Long enough. Go on, get some sleep." I opened the bedroom door.

She licked her lips. "I enjoyed it," she ventured.

I waved and stepped out. As I pulled her door shut, I distinctly heard one whispered word: "Bastard."

†††

I closed the porch door silently behind me and moved at a fast trot across the Millers' back yard. In the weeds behind their trash barrel I found the Louisville Slugger I'd hidden there earlier. I hefted it and held it at my side as I crept around the copse of trees as quietly as I could. Too late. I heard the cellar doors creak shut and caught a glimpse of Libby rushing back the way she'd come. She'd been down there five minutes, tops.

Well, well. Now this would work even better. I crouched in the cool, damp grass, leaning on the bat, and counted to six hundred, plenty long enough for Libby to get inside, up the stairs, and into her room, out of harm's way. Then I stood and walked across our lawn, ducking under the clotheslines as I made for the cellar doors.

There I froze a moment. Not a sound from anywhere. I had to do this smart and quiet. I thought it through then bent and tapped on the cellar door three times, just as Libby had.

After a moment the door rose an inch or so. I stood facing out, with my back against the house, waiting and watching, as it closed. I bent and tapped on it again. Stepped back and hoisted the bat this time, cocked and ready.

The cellar door rose, opening wider and wider, revealing a male arm and then a blond head as Jimmy Herndon ventured up the stairs, back to me. He'd just uttered the first syllable of Libby's name when the fat of my Louisville ball bat thonked him squarely above the right ear.

He collapsed as if switched off, spluttering down onto the stairs. I dropped the bat, bent and took him under the damp armpits of his T-shirt and began to drag him out. He weighed a ton, but I didn't have far to haul him, and I was feeling too proud of myself to care. I'd done it. I'd taken out the villain, like Richard Diamond, Sundance, Roger and Smith, Peter Gunn—guys like that.

†††

Finally the gagging and retching stopped. I had both big windows of my '51 Ford open to the cool night air pouring in as I drove down the silent desertion of Grand River, but even that wasn't enough to dull the stench from the back seat.

"You had to do that, huh," I growled. "Ya had to puke in my brand-new secondhand car. Thanks a whole lot."

"You were the one who hit me, kid," Herndon said hoarsely. "You get slugged in the head, you puke."

All I knew was, it certainly wasn't something that happened to Richard Diamond, Sundance, Roger and Smith, Peter Gunn—guys like that. "Should of told me," I said. "I'd have stopped so you could do it on the street like everybody else."

"Sorry," he said, tone wholly sincere. "Mind if I come up there?"

"I don't care."

"You're not going to hit me anymore?"

"As long as you're peaceable I won't."

Jimmy Herndon stuffed himself over the seat into the front and arranged himself as far from me as he could get. I followed the night-blanketed street as it lanced toward the heart of Detroit, doing about sixty, catching the synchronized lights perfectly. After a moment, Herndon asked, "Where are you taking me?"

"The train station. You promised to leave town," I said sourly. "I'm holding you to it."

"That's fine, Ben. I really appreciate it—"

"Just shut the hell up!" I shouted. "Quit acting like you're anything but a crooked, devious, sleazy son of a bitch, okay?"

"I'm not all that bad."

"Aren't, huh? You been sneaking around with my sister. You been sleeping in the basement of my house every night. You had a whole bag of our clothes ready to take with you. And you're wanted for knifing that guy. If that ain't bad, what is it?"

"Survival." His smile was not kind. "Maybe when you're older, you'll understand what I mean."

I swung right on 14th Street. It was foggier down here, the street lights misty on the fronts of darkened houses and stores. "Well," I said, "this-here punk kid done took you out, pal. And I could make things even worse, as in turning you over to the cops. But I don't need the cops to fix you. It'd be too easy, somehow. There's a lot more satisfaction in running your ass out of town personally."

He absently rubbed his head where I'd hit him. "You're giving me a real break, kid. Thanks."

"No thanks needed. It ain't Christian charity. I just don't want my baby sister drug through the mud with you, hear?"

He was smiling at me. "You really are a pretty four-square guy, Ben. If there's something I can do for you before I leave, to make amends, just name it."

"Yeah. Right," I snorted. "At one thirty on a Friday morning." We were driving through a neighborhood of streets all named after trees. Nothing was open but the occasional bar. That gave me an idea. Yeah, right. Perfect!

As we reached Temple Street, I swerved the Ford over to the curb by a small building at the corner that said Temple Tavern. I put the brake on and dug in my pants pocket. "You want to make some kind of amends, go on inside there and buy me a case of Stroh's tall boys. Got it?"

I reached a five at him. He shook his head and came out of his pocket with a large wad of soft, open-folded currency. "Nope," he said firmly, "I'm covering it. Least I can do." He hopped out and strode into the tavern. Presently he appeared on the sidewalk again, embracing the case. I got out and opened the trunk; he put the clinking beer bottles inside.

Ten minutes later I delivered Jimmy Herndon to the Michigan Central Train Station, walked him inside, and watched him purchase a ticket to Chicago with several bills from his fat wad of soft currency.

When he completed the transaction, he turned to me, grinning. "Train leaves at six," he said. "Gonna wait around and wave a hankie as I depart?"

"Maybe I should. To make sure you go."

"Oh, I'll go. I promise." He looked around the cavernous train station lobby. "This town's too hot for me. I'm gone and I'll stay gone. You whipped me, Ben. I'm out of here."

I was exhausted. I was scheduled to do a twelve-hour shift at the grocery, starting at six A.M. I had to get home and rescue what sleep I could. "Okay. Just don't let me see your face in these parts ever again."

Back behind the wheel of my '51, beating gears headed northwest for home through the misty night, I felt pretty damned good. I'd won. Libby had been smack in the middle of big trouble, and I'd sorted it out. It hadn't been pretty.

I'd made mistakes. But I'd overcome every obstacle that appeared, and in the end I prevailed.

All for no reward—aside from the satisfaction of feeling like maybe I wasn't just a punk kid anymore. . . .

The siren made me swerve and I nearly took out a lamppost at the Outer Drive intersection. A cop car hung to my bumper, red bubble light and head-lights flashing angrily, punctuated by the whooping siren. Heart hammering, I hauled the Ford to a stop in front of the Christian Science church. Damn it to hell! I thought. Nailed. Speeding. My first ticket.

The officer sauntered up to my door and peered down. "Benjy Perkins?" he asked, in what had to be one of the last Irish accents left on the force.

"Yessir." How the hell did he know my name?

"Would you mind stepping out of the vehicle, young feller?" I did so, shaking. The cop took my upper arm and led me to the rear of the car. "Not anything special in the trunk, son?"

†††

My homecoming was not pretty.

Daddy, who didn't bother to bail me out of the 16th Precinct till eight thirty the next morning, nearly ripped my head off. Mama met me at the door to inform me that I was the first member of the Perkins family ever to go to jail. My brother Bill, just leaving for work, shook his head ominously when he saw me. And Libby, my sweet little sister Libby, all angelic in her summer school clothes, tossed her head at my appearance and greeted me with "Morning, jailbird!"

I could handle Daddy and Mama and Bill. Time would take care of my problems with them. But I had to settle accounts with Libby. When she got home, late that evening, I barged into her bedroom and slammed the door. "We got to talk, Libby," I growled.

She was sitting at her dressing table, brushing her short brown hair. "What do you want, jailbird?"

"First off, cut out the name-calling. This jam I'm in is all on account of you."

Brush, brush. "Really? Did I put the beer in your car?"

"No." I stepped closer, about to lower the boom and grimly enjoying it. "I caught Herndon last night. Dragged him to the train station and ran him out of town. He knew about the beer and he called the cops on me, to pay me back."

The smile went. The brush stopped. Libby looked at it, turning it over and over. Then tears sprang into her eyes and she tossed the thing hard onto the dressing table. "You hoodlum!" she shouted, eyes hurt and angry. "How could you do that to him?"

"*I'm* the hood? What about him? He's the one who knifed somebody. He's—"

She buried her face in her arms, knocking stuff off the dressing table as she writhed. "I loved him and he loved me," she wailed. "He would have taken me with him. But you butted in before he could make the arrangements. You ruined everything."

"He didn't love you. Look at me, Libby. He had another girlfriend at those apartments the whole time. Look at me, damn it! He wasn't going to take you with him. What would he do that for? He's ten years older than you. He was just using you, Libby! You were had, and I do mean had."

She kept crying. I went to her and put my hands on her shoulders. She whirled around with the hairbrush and nearly raked my eyes out with it. "Stay away from me," she hissed.

"All I ever wanted was to help," I shot back.

"I'm quits with you. You ruined my life. I will hate you as long as I live."

"You're breaking my heart!" I sneered.

She turned to the mirror. "We'll see how tough you are when Daddy finds out about the cash kitty."

"What the hell are you talking about?"

"I lent it to Jimmy," she said, resuming her brushing. "Two hundred and ten dollars. He was going to pay it back before he left town. But you fixed that, all right. He'll never pay it back now, and I wouldn't blame him."

I remembered the wad of soft currency from which Herndon had bought my tall boys. He must have laughed his ass off. "You expect me to take the rap for that? Get real. I'll tell Daddy what you did."

"Go ahead. Try. Who's Daddy going to believe? You're nothing but a jailbird. You can't compete against his baby girl Elizabeth, so don't even bother to try."

She stood, gave herself one final inspection in the mirror, and walked out of the room.

†††

And, for all practical purposes, out of my life.

Down through the years, we've mostly met up at funerals. Daddy in '63. Mama in '67. The Bubbas in '70. Uncle Dan in '84. All gone.

So are the Riviera and the train station, both boarded up. National Foods is now a hardware store. The Totem Pole is a Burger King. Fourteenth Street is a war zone, and the Washington Senators became the Texas Rangers—prime competitors of the Detroit Tigers, who in the interim have been better and worse, then better, and are now worse.

The Wesson is still there. So is Redford High. Annie Wilder got divorced and moved away, I never did learn where. Debbie Miller became an English professor at the University of Michigan. My brother Bill married Marybeth and still works at Ford's. You know all about Fast Eddie Anger if you're into pop music at all.

By a very circuitous route, I ended up a private detective. Like Richard Diamond, Sundance, Roger and Smith, Peter Gunn—guys like that, sort of. Fast Eddie was my client once. So, even, was Libby.

But it wasn't till tonight that I realized my very first client was my mother. Tonight, as I stood in the fairway of the Wayne County Fair, overrun with the memories triggered by the sight of the man running a ball-toss booth.

He stood behind the counter, twenty feet from me. He was too busy to notice as I stared at him, superimposing his image, etched clear in the bright lights of the County Fair midway, against the faded memories of three decades ago. Thirty pounds heavier. Hair grayish and wispy thin. Heavy lines had taken the face, and his bouncy swagger was gone. But it was definitely him.

I pictured myself going up to him. I had a lot of questions. Did he really knife someone? Did he ever get caught? How much jail time had he done in the intervening years? What was it like to be well past fifty and still roaming the country, working the shrinking carnival circuit for nickels and dimes? How many women had there been? How much money? How many promises? Did he ever think about the broken hearts and hurt feelings he left in his wake?

The ball-toss went momentarily vacant and Herndon, as if signaled by radio, turned, looked at me, away then back, locking his stare with mine. I grinned, remembering the sound of the bat as it hit his head. Now, all these years later, I wished I'd hit him harder—

"Ben! Hey, Ben?"

I turned. Will Somers, a muscular blond eight-year-old, galloped up to me, followed at a distance by my friend Carole Somers, great with child and looking tired. "Found the johns okay?" I asked.

"Finally," Carole said. "Who's that man over there?"

"Who?" I parried.

"That barker in the ball-toss booth. You were staring at him. Do you know him from somewhere?"

I glanced over at Herndon, whose eyes were still fixed on me. "Nobody important," I answered. I took Carole in one arm, Will in the other. "Come on, I'll buy you something to eat."

Afterword

Still my favorite story of the brood.

Though I am not a native of Detroit, I did live in the metro area for some 30 years and (as should be obvious from the stories) have come to love the place. While researching my novel *The Thousand Yard Stare*, which flashes back to this same period in Ben's life—his senior year in high school—I developed a pretty strong archive of historical data about Detroit during that period.

So when the time came to do "Tall Boys," I went to extreme lengths to make everything utterly factual. Every reference in the story—streets, ads, songs, radio stations, stores, etc.—all are absolutely accurate as of 1960-1961.

Even the reference to "Negroes." While there are more correct terms in use today, back in the upside-down year that was the approved term. The only exception to this absolute-accuracy rule is the reference to Kerns Casket, which did not exist as far as I know; I was stuck with it because I'd mentioned it as Ben's dad's employer in earlier works.

"Tall Boys" was the only time I was ever able to work Ben's parents into a story. Both are echoes of real people in my life, but certainly not my own parents. Nor is Libby in any way, shape, or form similar to my own sister. I have always depicted Ben's relationship with her as troubled, to say the least, but it was not till I wrote "Tall Boys" that I figured out the source of this.

As for Ben's adventures with Fast Eddie (who appears in other short stories and the novels) and the Bubbas, I can neither confirm nor deny that some parts may be drawn from my own rambunctious teenage days on the streets of Atlanta. . . .

Libby's Luck

As the coffin thumped into the bottom of the hole, my Aunt Rachel, assisted by one of her daughters, walked unsteadily up and dropped in a handful of red Georgia clay. I filed up behind other family members and did the same. Brushing my hands off, I stepped back from the grave, relieved that the ritual was over. Now for the rental car, the Atlanta airport, Detroit, and home.

I'd hoped to avoid meeting Libby, but she was waiting for me in the passenger seat of my rental car.

Without a word I opened the driver's side door, sat half in and half out of the car, and stared out across the cemetery as the black Cadillac hearse started to pull away. Distant relatives wandered slowly by my car, socializing in their north Georgia accents, and in the distance a backhoe fired up, getting ready to fill in the grave. I said, "You have a sudden attack of family feeling, or what?"

"He was *my* uncle, too," she retorted. Libby Perkins Gillespie was soberly dressed in a severe blue business suit and a floppy blue hat. Back when we had a family, it was said that Libby had gotten all the looks. Seeing her now for the first time in seven years—though we lived but twenty miles apart—it was evident to me that she'd peaked early and faded fast. She was just in her mid-thirties, a few years younger than me, but she was fleshier in the face, the neck, the waist. Our daddy would have said she looked like she'd been rode hard and put away wet.

I wrestled my keys out of my slacks pocket. "Nice talking to you, kid."

"Wait, Ben," she said in vintage Libby: demanding, imperious, owed things. "I need a ride to the airport."

"You can go back the same way you came up. Unless there's something else you want."

There it was, in her eyes, the Look: a slant of desperation, uncertainty, beaten-down hope. Transfigured from my sister to, by God, a potential client. She pursed her lips then said in a hard, uncaring voice, "I've got a job for you. You still do that . . . investigating work, don't you?"

Cars were moving past us on the gravel lane. In the distance, toward Uncle Andrew's grave, the backhoe bayed and roared. I eased back in my seat, pulling my legs in, staring straight ahead, wanting a smoke, a drink, and solitude. "I check up on stuff from time to time," I answered.

A pause. "Well," she asked abruptly, "will you take the job?"

"Could be, depends."

"Depends on *what?* I'm your sister."

"What the job is, and whether you can afford two fifty a day plus expenses."

"Oh, the money's no problem—"

"Maybe we can do business then." I put the key in the ignition.

"As for the job," she went on in her directorial tone, "I want you to find something for me. It's—"

"Just save it a while." I fired up the engine.

"I've lost my luck," she said softly as I put the car in gear and began rolling down the wooded north Georgia lane.

†††

Not even Libby could make the day worse. I'd taken the red-eye down from Detroit that morning, made the two-hour drive up to Rome, endured a lengthy funeral ritual, which included a joyfully macabre three-hour church service, a five-mile-per-hour drive to the cemetery (including a stop at Uncle Andrew's plain frame house—"taking him home for the last time," the locals called it), and an hour-long graveside service.

Even if my Uncle Dan hadn't asked me to represent him, I'd have come anyway. There weren't many of the old folks left. My daddy, supposedly the most robust, had died of emphysema back in '63. Now Uncle Andrew, a big, brawny, vigorous customer at seventy-nine, had been carried off when a tree he was felling twisted around and got him. Of the three old guys, that left just Uncle Dan: the oldest, supposedly the frailest, who'd survived air combat over France in World War I, and the murderous auto labor union wars of the thirties, and thirty-five years on the line at Rouge. He should have bought the farm long before his brothers, which proves that death makes about as much sense as everything else.

Libby and I made the I-75 in good time, and I pushed the whiny, thumping, capricious rental car to its top speed, which seemed to be seventy miles per hour downhill in a tailwind. Libby slumped in the passenger seat, taking belts from a silver flask, chain-smoking tawny brown cigarettes, making small talk to which I replied with grunts. The stink of liquor and tobacco smoke filled the car, and I kept my window cracked and concentrated on the road.

We'd passed Marietta, on the outskirts of Atlanta, when I asked reluctantly, "Okay, so what's this you've lost?"

I felt her gaze on me. She said, as if it was the most logical thing in the world, "My luck."

"G'wan. Jeez. I mean, get real for once."

She capped her flask and said stiffly, "Quit grinning. I'm totally serious. I've had it for years and now it's gone and I want it back."

"For this you don't need me, kid. Go out and buy yourself a rabbit's foot or a four-leaf clover or—"

"*Damn* it!" she exploded. "You going to sit there and smirk, or take a job for which I'm willing to pay you well?"

"Oh, I'll go for the money," I said lazily. "I don't do spec work. And, what the hell. We got half an hour before we get to the airport. So enlighten me with the facts, if any. In order, please, and from the beginning.

She lighted another tawny cigarette with her green Bic disposable lighter and said, "Very well. Back in high school—"

"Oh, jeez."

"*Back in high school*," she repeated in a hard voice, "in my freshman year, I, uh . . . goofed off in my last-quarter economics class and failed it. I had to have the credit to be promoted, and the school offered me the chance to take a special equivalency test. I took it on a Saturday morning after having been out the night before till five o'clock and coming home drunk. I blew the test, Ben, I've always known I blew it, figured the jig was up. But when the score came I had something like an eighty-six. I *passed* it. With a B, for God's sake."

"So," I shrugged, "maybe you're smarter when you're hung over."

She ignored me and went on stolidly. "I got into Michigan. Got involved in some of the usual student activities. Parties, boys—"

"Drugs," I suggested. I'd left home by then, but I remembered.

She stayed silent for a long moment. We were making the sharp bend onto the I-75/85 Connector in downtown Atlanta. Then she said, "None of this better get out."

"Not to worry," I said easily. "As eager as I am to make a buck, I suspect the publishing world isn't panting for juicy tidbits about the life and times of Elizabeth Perkins Gillespie."

She went on in a terse, clipped voice, "We were in a house on Fifth Street in Ann Arbor one night, it was '65, right around Thanksgiving. And we got busted, about ten or eleven of us. Taken to jail. But then the police released me. Just me. The others were tried and convicted."

Though concentrating on the heavy traffic, I shot her a quick glance. "Why'd they let you go?"

"I don't know, and I didn't ask. Just my luck, I guess. Then, while I was in college, I kept running low on money, you know how that goes, but money would just turn up. Cash. I'd find it on the sidewalks, in my textbooks. A ten here, a twenty there. My luck again."

I snorted, but my heart wasn't in it.

"After college," she went on after taking a deep drag on her cigarette, "I got a job with Agate Enterprises. A year later Retail Credit bought them out and pink-slipped everybody. I'll never forget it, I was totally devastated, didn't know what to do. Got home and a man from Nautilus called. You know, the computer company. They had a job for me. I started the next day. I'd never heard of them, never applied, but . . . it was my luck again, just in the nick of time."

I really had to pay attention to the driving now; Atlanta's Downtown Connector is an old, poorly constructed, chronically packed stretch of hair-raising highway. But Libby's story, which I had never heard, was starting to get to me. "What else?"

I felt her eyes on me, trying to decipher my vacant expression. She said defiantly, "I got—got involved with one of the executives. He was married. We tried to keep it quiet, but . . . people can tell. Rumors began going around. Word was, I was going to get the boot. Instead he was transferred overseas. The rumors died, and I never heard about it again."

I kept the little car twisting and turning through the traffic and, at the same time, fished a small cork-tipped cigar out of my shirt pocket. Libby lighted it for me with her Bic. Disbelieving, I said between puffs, "They . . . transferred *him* . . . and left . . . *you* alone?"

"Yes," she said rapidly, closing the sale, "and that's not all. I married Steve, and we decided to buy a house in Ann Arbor. I wanted something really grand, but the prices were just too high. Looked like we'd have to buy outside the city. Then our agent Chris Crandall, got a call about a place in the Georgetown subdivision. Perfect, and a great price. We saw it, made an offer, and it was accepted, just like that."

We passed the Capitol Interchange with its state government buildings and the stadium. It was cloudy, getting hotter, threatening rain. Libby suddenly uncorked her flask again, drained it, and shoved it clumsily into her handbag. "We wanted a big house for children," she said, her voice shakier, "but it turned out I was infertile. Detached fallopians, if it matters, congenital, irreversible. So we looked into adoption. The agencies poked and pried and asked embarrassing questions, then approved us with a big fat smile and put us on a three-year waiting list. Three years! We were . . . we were in despair, Ben. We wanted it so bad."

Considering the number of fast years Libby had spent trying not to get pregnant, I found this infertility thing ironic, but kept the observation to myself. "So what great miracle of circumstances happened this time?"

"A private adoption agency called me. Called themselves Outplacement Associates. They had a child, an infant, available. Did we want it? *Did* we!" Her laugh was almost crazy. "Little Stevie. It was my luck again, Ben, my luck came through for me."

I bent the car right on the I-85 highway, on the home stretch for the airport. Libby stayed silent for a long time, staring blankly straight ahead. I blew a stream of cigar smoke out the window and said, "Well, it's all very interesting, but don't give me this about luck. There's no such thing." She stayed stone silent. A sign ahead said HARTSFIELD ATLANTA INTERNATIONAL AIRPORT; I made the loop for the departing passenger area at the terminal. "So, what makes you think your . . . 'luck'. . . is gone?

Seeing the terminal coming up, Libby clumsily straightened herself, tugged at her suit, messed with her hair. She said in a scratchy, drained voice, "Oh . . . Steve's leaving me. Taking little Stevie with him. The work is—is going sour. Bad evaluations. Political problems. Want to know any more? I've got big tax problems, they're auditing me back to day one. I've been nailed and convicted three times in a month for moving traffic violations. That never happened before, they were always thrown out of court. . . . For months now I've been waiting for my luck to kick back in. Maybe it never will, maybe it's gone for good. But I have to know what happened."

I stopped the car at the curb by the terminal. A squad of skycaps moved toward the car, and I waved them back.

I turned to Libby. "I want three days' money up front."

Lips pressed, she nodded, went into her purse for her checkbook, and began writing.

"No guarantees," I said as she handed me the check.

"I understand." Having unburdened herself, she looked smaller now, less domineering.

Not that it made any difference. I folded the blue check, stuck it in my shirt pocket, and said, "I don't start till this has cleared, you follow?" A spark flashed in her eyes, but I held up my hand. "That's our policy for first-time customers. Now beat it. I've got to unload this crate."

She opened the car door, got out clumsily then bent down and, in a foolish and belated attempt at camaraderie, said, "We're probably on the same Delta. Meet me in the bar near the gate?"

"Don't count on it." I reached across and pulled the door shut. I didn't want to see her anymore; I had to get rid of the car. I had to think through Libby's problem. Weed out the "luck" mumbo-jumbo. Get a feel on how to find the fix. Because, I've learned, when you think the fix is in, it usually is.

†††

Seemed to me the smarted thing to do was to follow the path of least resistance, so I started with that strange Ann Arbor drug bust, one of the fishier elements in Libby's checkered past. First step: the records.

Getting into the records isn't too tough if you know what to ask for, whom to ask it of, and have leverage over the askee. The "what" was obvious; the "who" was Lud Danzig, an Ann Arbor assistant district attorney; and the leverage stemmed from my having alerted Danzig a few months back that a high-stakes poker game he was frequenting was about to be busted by the state police. This saved Danzig from a big, ugly, public mess. I could take his gratitude for granted. There was lots of mileage to be squeezed out of that little marker.

After doing some checking, Danzig informed me there was a record of Libby's arrest, but no indication of why she wasn't prosecuted. He suggested that I interview the arresting officer to get some insight. Only problem—a "slight" one, Danzig put it dryly—was that the officer, Darryl Rockecharlie, had been dismissed from the force in '80, having become, to use Danzig's delicate, lawyerlike phrase, "a procurer, extortionist, strong-arm, and broken-down drunken sleaze." There was a bench warrant out for his arrest, and though Rockecharlie was thought to be in Ann Arbor, Danzig indicated that the warrant was small potatoes and the lawmen weren't lying awake night worrying about it.

I put my friend Ron Narco on the problem. Ron's a fiftyish holdover from the drug culture of the sixties and looks the part: thin, gaunt, blue-jeaned, whiskered, longhaired. He's a smart, savvy street man, well acquainted with the dark corners and shadow people of Ann Arbor. It took him just a couple of days to turn up Rockecharlie for me, and we met him at the Christmas Café on Washington Street, a real good place to get knifed if you're interested in that sort of thing.

The bar was dark and packed and hot and noisy. Ron and I sat close together on one side of a wallet-sized table; Rockecharlie dominated the other side, hunched over, dressed in a dirty brown sports jacket and open necked wrinkled white shirt. He had big square cop hands, a big square cop face, short, dirty-blond cop hair, and dissolute ex-cop twitches, trembles, eyebags, and smell. Ron and I drank beer; Rockecharlie augmented his with repeated double shots of straight Heaven Hill, which I obligingly paid for.

Rockecharlie did a disappearing act with a shot of liquor, waved blearily for the tough barmaid, and turned to us, a spark of dim awareness and apprehension showing on his craggy, mottled face. "Yeah, I recollect that. Lot of years ago. Big bust." Rote words muttered through puffed lips, eyes dead.

I said, very distinctly, "There was a girl. Elizabeth Perkins. She was released on the same night without being charged. Nothing in the records says why. That's what I want to know."

Back by the bar a shoving match began, noticed by perhaps one percent of the noisy patrons. The jukebox started pounding out The Who's "Momma's Got a Squeeze Box." Rockecharlie's eyes went to slits. He hooked a fresh shot of Heaven Hill from the barmaid on the fly, got outside it with a gulp, and said, "She was took care of."

I leaned closer, perhaps pushing too hard. "So give over."

Rockecharlie's massive head trembled left and right. "Nooo, sir. Nooo way. You don't know what you're dealing with." The pushing match by the bar ripped outward when one of the contenders gave the other an elbow in the throat. I glanced around for bouncers and couldn't identify any; hell, aside from Ron, everybody in the joint looked like a bouncer.

Going for my wallet—which I'd tucked into my boot, as I usually do in such serene surroundings—I got out a fifty and held it up by the corner. "I pay my way, Darryl. Give me the name."

Someone splatted on the deck not far from us, scattering standing patrons. Rockecharlie eyes the General Grant and shook his head again, indifferently. I got out a hundred and held it up instead. "Doubt you ever paid your snitches this good, Darryl," I said in a normal voice, which probably wasn't audible more than twenty inches from us.

The sprawled patron crawled to his feet and leaped for someone at the bar. Rockecharlie shook his head again, bored. Sometimes money is enough leverage, sometimes you need more, perhaps a dramatic gesture. I took the hundred in both hands, tore it in half diagonally, stuffed one half in Rockecharlie's shirt pocket behind his crumpled pack of Winston's, and handed the other half to Ron.

"Call this a demonstration of sincerity," I said easily. "It's like I already spent the money, see? But you can't have it without giving me a name. Think about it. My friend, Ron, here, will hold the other half."

A sick grin flickered on Darryl Rockecharlie's face. He rose slowly, turned, and plowed his way to the door like a carrier cutting thirty knots in medium swells. Ron and I got to our feet just as another body, hurled out of everywhere, crashed into our table and knocked it to the floor, giving me a lapful of wet beer and Ron a case of bruised toes. We danced around the mess and headed for the door, for some reason laughing so hard it made my throat hurt.

I took Ron's arm as we stepped out onto the Washington Street sidewalk and whispered instructions in a low, urgent voice.

He grinned wickedly at me. "That's mean, Ben."

"Yeah, but pretty, ain't it?" I slapped him on the arm, turned, and headed for my car.

†††

It goes without saying that I looked pretty shabby and smelled even worse as I headed over to the office of Chris Crandall, agent for Wombwell Realty, on, and near the, Stadium. It was past dark when I got there, but the office was still open.

Crandall turned out to be female, a short, well-rounded looker in her late thirties, with longish straight chestnut hair, smoldering olive-skinned Mediterranean features, and that bright, hard-nosed demeanor your typical real estate agent gets in the presence of, to use their saying, "live meat." When she realized I wasn't buying, selling, or even remotely interested in real estate in Ann Arbor or anywhere else, she settled back behind her practically vacant mahogany desk and answered my questions sullenly, shooting glances at the phone that never rang the whole time I was there.

I wasn't surprised that she remembered Libby's Georgetown house deal. Any agent worth a damn who's worked a territory for any length of time can usually recite from memory the purchase-and-sale history, not to mention the features (pro and con), of practically any house in the area.

"It's a beautiful place on Brentwood Court," she told me. "The Gillespies got a hell of a deal. Too good to be true, actually."

Kind of a recurring theme. "Well, how come?"

"Luck," she answered with an elegant shrug. "They'd been looking for months. I did my best, but frankly, they just didn't have the bucks to buy what they wanted. Ann Arbor taste on an East Ypsilanti budget. Then this equity-owned deal came up."

"Equity-owned?"

She glanced at the silent phone again then reached into a desk drawer and came out with an Eve cigarette that I lighted for her. "FTO. The real estate subsidiary of Fantastico."

This wasn't much help. Fantastico's a multinational conglomerate, so immense that some almanacs quite seriously list it among the nations of the world.

Crandall took a long, practiced pull on her cigarette, her eyes sizing me up, and said, "It happened virtually overnight. FTO called me to say they were listing this house. I thought the asking price was some kind of mistake; fifteen, twenty bills easy under market value. No mistake. I showed it to the Gillespies right away—before it was even officially listed. Libby and Steve signed an offer on the spot. I presented it the next morning. It was accepted by noon. And we closed at the end of the week."

I eyed Crandall, wondering if this faint Fantastico trail could lead me anywhere, and doubting it.

Crandall went on, after an almost challenging look at the phone, "It's a crazy business I'm in. Equity-owned homes usually go for a tad below market value, but that's all, and then not until they've sat there a long time. And equity companies are notorious hagglers, especially FTO. Except in this case. They priced it way below market, going in. We offered a few bills less just on principle. And they accepted, no counter-offer, no nothing. I don't know about your work, Mr. Perkins, but sometimes things happen in real estate that make no sense."

Tell me about it.

†††

I spent most of the next day chasing my tail and getting more and more peeved.

Item: no one at FTO, Fantastico's real estate subsidiary, had anything constructive to tell me about Libby's house deal. No one there was involved in it—or would admit to it—and the records were, as they put it, "confidential."

Item: I hadn't heard from Ron all day about the Rockecharlie setup.

Item: Nautilus, the computer company that had mysteriously offered Libby a job just in the nick of time, and where she later had an illicit affair for which she suffered no consequences, no longer existed. At least it was in no phone or city directory for the Detroit metropolitan area.

Item: the people at Outplacement Associates, the private adoption agency that came across with a fresh kid for Libby in record time, were about as loquacious as G. Gordon Liddy. After a frustrating and fruitless half-hour morning meeting with some tight-lipped flunky, I went to the office of my friend Carole Somers, a lawyer specializing in women's issues, and enlisted her eager help in getting around Outplacement's defenses.

Having done all of that, and tired finally of beating my feet on the street and my head on the proverbial brick wall, I repaired to my Norwegian Wood apartment in Belleville. Carole arrived about a half hour after I did, dragging along her four-year-old son Will; they were staying at my place for a few days while the floors in their Berkley house were being refinished.

Shoes shucked, bare feet propped on the coffee table and some good Seger music playing in the background, I sat on the couch nursing a Stroh's and smoking a cigar and fuming.

"I did the best I could, Ben," Carole said in a resigned voice. She was at the other end of the couch, dressed elegantly in a white turtleneck top and slacks, her blonde Lady Diana haircut pristine in the late afternoon lamplight. Across the room, her boy Will, a stocky, big-boned blond kid, sat on the floor in front of the TV, half-watching *Scooby-Doo*.

"Tap city, huh?" I asked flatly.

"Turns out I know Annie Wyatt, Outplacement's director, pretty well," Carole said, "bit she's earnest as hell, straight as they come. No information available on the Gillespie adoption. None whatsoever.

"Aaah," I snarled, biting my cigar overly hard.

"Hey," Carole said in a consoling voice, "I know it's your sister involved, but lighten up."

"Sister, hell. It's frustrating for professional reasons only. That's it, pal." I puffed on my cigar for a minute. "You know what else sticks in my throat? This Nautilus business. Companies don't just up and disappear." I grabbed my phone, pulled it over to me, thought for a minute, and dialed. When the Com-Share operator answered, I asked for Jim Boddy, and was put on wait.

I turned to Carole and said distinctly, "I don't like Libby. Never have. There's no law says I have to, either." Jim Boddy came on the line. "Hey, old buddy," I greeted him, "Perkins here. You being such a computer maven and all, maybe you can help me out. . . ."

After I gave him the background on Nautilus, Jim talked for three or four minutes. Will wandered out of the room to use the bathroom and came back with his zipper down. Carole fixed him while I absently watched, listened to Jim, and smoked my cigar.

When Jim was done, I thanked him, arranged a bowling date for the following week (seventh frame winner buys the beer), and hung up.

Carole, ever the shrink-cum-social-worker, said to me as Will futzed with her shoes next to us, "But Libby's your family."

I drank my beer and said sharply, "That's just a biological accident!" Will went wide-eyed and headed into the kitchen. "My family isn't the Ozzie-and-Harriet, hey-Dad-where's-Mom, two point three kids routine, but this." I gestured at myself and at her. "Single man, divorced woman and her child who live under the same roof from time to time. The family of the eighties."

In the silence, Will came back into the room, somber-faced, and handed me a fresh, ice-cold bottle of Stroh's. I took it, laughing, grabbed the boy by the back of the head and gave him a clumsy squeeze.

"Carole smiled and changed the subject smoothly. "What'd your buddy tell you?"

"Oh, yeah. Nautilus was bought out by PBB. That's a subsidiary of none other than Fantastico."

Her eyes narrowed. "Oo."

"Yeah. What you might call a pattern is emerging, or something." We sat in the silence for long minutes; the boy went back to the TV and began doing some Muppets. I had one of those intuitive flashes. "What about this Outplacement Associates anyhow? Where does *their* money come from?"

"Damned if I know," Carole shrugged.

"Well," I said, handing her the telephone, "call your friend and find out."

"Ben," she said patiently, "Annie said she couldn't divulge—"

I fixed her with a stare and said inexorably, "It's very simple. Call her up and ask her if Fantastico's one of their funders."

She reflected, said "Ohhhkay," dialed, and talked. After a minute's conversation she hung up without changing expression. "Yup," she said to me.

I rubbed my hands together, thinking furiously about patterns and fixes and trying to decide on my next move. It was, however, made for me; the phone rang. I picked it up. "Perkins."

"Hey, Ben, this is Ron." Voice full of big news. "I'm over here at the jail. Rockecharlie got busted an hour ago. In Ypsi in River Town. Ypsi police rendered him over here."

"Where are you calling from?" I asked, reaching for my dead cigar and relighting it. Carole winced; even when my cigars are fresh she refers to them as Rolled Rat.

"Washtenaw County Jail, Ben," Ron answered helpfully.

"I gathered that. *Where* in the jail?" I asked.

"Oh, sorry. Bail and Bonds section, the waiting room. They won't let me in any farther and, frankly—"

"Listen to me. I want you to go over to the county building and find the office of Lud Danzig. He's an assistant D.A. Don't go in, just wait outside. I'll be in touch."

"Rog." He hung up.

I reached out, mashed the cradle button down, and held it. Carole said, smiling, "I don't think I care for that sly look on your face."

"Ohhh," I said lightly, "it's leverage, kid; just leverage." I punched out a number and raised Danzig, who squealed that he was just leaving for the day. "C'mon, Lud, this won't take but fifteen minutes," I said. "I heard tell my old friend Darryl Rockecharlie is now an unwilling guest in that mountain of rock you call a jail over there."

"I heard tell of that, too," Danzig said. "What a coincidence. I turned you on to this clown earlier in the week, and casually mentioned a half-assed bench warrant out for him, and the Ypsi police get an anonymous tip on his whereabouts and collar him. Wouldn't you call that a real odd coincidence, Ben?"

"Life is strange, I always said that. What's on his menu?"

Danzig cleared him throat. "In an amazing burst of administrative speed, his file just landed on my desk. Let me see. Oh boy, we've cracked a *big* one. Scofflaw. Couple dozen unpaid parking tickets. Plus damaging government property; seems he smashed up a Denver boot one of our officers affixed to the wheel of his car."

"A real enemy of the state, huh? Any problem losing the whole thing if he comes across with the information I need?"

In my mind's eye I could see Danzig biting his lips. He grunted, "I didn't want the damn case to begin with. Scofflaws aren't exactly high up on my list of law-enforcement priorities."

"'Kay," I replied. "How about spiriting Rockecharlie into your office right now? And there's an aging hippie-type lounging in your hall, friend of mine named Ron Narco, get him in there, too. And call me back when they're there."

"Anything to be of service, Mr. Perkins," Danzig said dryly, and hung up.

The rest was anticlimactic. Carole and I chatted tensely for ten minutes while the boy watched his Muppets, and then the phone rang again. I had Danzig put Rockecharlie on. The ex-cop was belligerent and half in the bag. I said gently, "You remember the question I asked you the other day? Now I want a name. You give it over, and you walk away from this in five minutes, guaranteed."

A long, long pause. Then, almost in a whisper. "Hooker. Al Hooker. One of *them* Hookers. I didn't ask why, I just took the money."

"You done good, Darryl. Put Danzig on." He did so. "Spring him. Squares our account, buddy." Danzig didn't answer, but I knew he'd come through for me as I'd come through for him. "Give me Ron . . . Ron? Give Darryl the other half of that C-note. And thanks, pal."

I hung up slowly, relighted my dead cigar, and stared off into space. On TV the old men were heckling Milton Berle and Fozzie Bear. Carole asked me, "So is it done?"

"I didn't know she even knew him," I said dreamily. "Hell, he and I were the same age, three years ahead of her in school." I got up, walked in a trance to my bookshelves, selected the 1961 yearbook, and brought it back to Carole. Leafed through to Seniors. Hooker, Alvin Marcus. Round, acne-farm moon-face, thick glasses, protruding lips, perfect teeth. Under his name, his activities: Library Club, Chorus, and Counseling Office Assistant.

"Do you *believe* this?" I asked of no one in particular, leaning back.

Carole flipped farther in the yearbook then stopped. "You know, you're ten times better looking now than you were then," she observed.

"Thanks, kid. Credit it to good clean living," I answered.

"So," she said, folding her hands together expectantly, "you going to tell me what you found out?"

"In a minute." I reached for the phone one last time, picked up the receiver and stared at it, wondering briefly if anyone in my line of work had ever broken a case by telephone before. Then I punched out Libby's number.

†††

You forget when you're in it that Elmwood Cemetery is totally surrounded by the city of Detroit. It's an enormous, rolling plot of heavily wooded land, studded with the elaborate graves of forgotten Detroit and Michigan *prominente*, and bisected by the last remaining segment of Bloody Run, the site of a decisive battle in the French and Indian War, which happened before my time.

Libby, wearing jeans, stylishly slim boots, and a snug brown leather jacket, was waiting beside her black Ford Econoline van at the site I'd specified, deep in the cemetery. I greeted her, said "Let's go," and hiked from the lane up through tall grass, threading my way among the old gravestones, mausoleums, and trees.

"*What* are we doing here?" Libby asked angrily, giving the area a distasteful look.

"I never knew you dated Al Hooker," I said.

"Al *Hooker?*" Libby said, startled. "Don't be silly. Well, we danced one time at a school dance. And he used to study with me in the library." She went silent. I didn't look at her as we walked. I felt the moisture in the long grass soaking my shoes and cuffs. Up ahead I saw the bank of Bloody Run, it wasn't far now. Libby went on in an indulgent, reminiscent voice, "Oh, he had some kind of weird crush on me for a while. He actually wrote poetry for me. Real sappy, embarrassing stuff. I finally sat him down and told him to back off. Poor little schnook."

We got to the bank. Bloody Run trickled by down below. Across the creek was more cemetery. Off to the left, sticking out of the back, was an enormous mausoleum of white granite, facing the creek. It was surrounded by a flagstone patio interspersed with ugly, pollution-pitted statues of insanely grinning gods in robes. There were also a couple of low stone benches, for the convenience of meditating mourners, I supposed. The mausoleum, a two- or three-generation-capacity job, had a dark, sober, stained glass window on each side and a heavily locked, greenish brass barred door on the front. Above the door was the legend, cut deep into the stone: HOOKER.

I looked at Libby, who was staring blankly at it. "Come on." We walked along the bank, angling down toward the mausoleum. "The fact that Hooker was out of a big bucks family didn't matter to you, huh?"

She said uncertainly, watching her footing, "Believe it or not, Ben, I'm not a complete mercenary." We got to the flagstone patio. Weeds leaped grotesquely from the cracks between the stones. The air was absolutely silent. Libby suddenly said sharply, "Ben?"

"Yeah, kid."

She looked pale. Her hands were balled into fists in the pockets of her leather jacket. "What does this have to do with my . . . luck?"

I tilted my head toward the mausoleum. "You asked me to find it for you. Well, it's in there. Help yourself."

She swallowed hard. "This is *crazy*."

"Al Hooker," I said distinctly, reciting the results of my morning's research while staring past her at the muddy creek. "His daddy founded Hooker Controls, pioneers in electronic relays back in the thirties. Made out like bandits in World War II. Gobbled up by Fantastico in 1963."

"So?" she asked in a shrill voice. "What does that—"

"He's in *there*, Libby. Has been nearly a year now. Eaten alive by liver cancer."

She stepped toward the mausoleum door then stopped, frozen in place.

I said, "Number one, your house deal. That property was owned by Fantastico. Number two, Outplacement Associates, your adoption agency. Funded by Fantastico. Number three, Nautilus, which hired you sigh unseen when you needed a job. Owned by Fantastico. I don't know about the cash you kept finding, and your fixed traffic tickets; you decide for yourself.

"Fact is that Mr. Al Hooker, thanks to his family name, was an executive with Fantastico. He had a fancy title and plenty of money. But like a lot of nepotism deals, he was a figurehead in the company, with no real work to do. So he apparently made it his business to watch out for you. A hard habit to break, since he'd worked in the counselor's office in high school and probably rigged your score on that economics equivalency test. And since he bribed an Ann Arbor police officer to spring you from that drug bust in '65."

She backed up very, very slowly and sat down on one of the granite mourner benches and stared at the mausoleum.

"It wasn't luck at all, Libby. It was just a poor little schnook with money and connections who must have liked you pretty good."

I turned and headed up the bank, moving as fast as I could in the slippery footing. I heard nothing behind me. When I reached the top of the bank, I stopped and looked back. Libby had her head down, fingers steepled over her forehead, not making a sound.

Then I started back toward her. I wasn't through with her after all. She owed me expense money.

Afterword

"Libby's Luck" was one of my earliest published stories, and it introduced a lot of elements that recur in subsequent work. These include Perkins's north Georgia derivation (kind of dovetailing with my own background in that part of the world) and his relationship, such as it was, with his sister Libby. (Question: Did I name her Libby so I'd have alliteration in the title? No idea.)

I'm startled now to see how cold toward, and angry with, Ben sounds toward his sister—and I never explained the background of their animosity till I wrote "Tall Boys" much later. Even now it's a bit puzzling. I know why Libby was mad at Ben—but why was Ben so mad at Libby?

I'm amused, on the other hand, to see that the hearse used at the funeral is a Cadillac—humorous, considering the Perkins family background in, and devotion to, the Ford Motor Company.

Darryl Rockecharlie, introduced here, has appeared since then, doing lift-and-carry, and has kind of smoothened out and rehabilitated since this inauspicious beginning. Al Hooker makes a cameo reappearance in a dream sequence in *The Thousand Yard Stare*. And Elmwood Cemetery, one of my favorite places and among the best cemeteries in Michigan, is also the setting for the climactic scene in The Quick and the Dead.

The story, of course, is about luck. But the message is that there is no such thing: dig deep enough in any situation, and what you'll always find is The Fix. That's a continuing theme in Ben's hardboiled world.

C Is for Cookie

"No" isn't a word I like to say to pretty women. But I'd said it to Charlotte Ambrose, in no uncertain terms, when she disappeared from the restaurant, leaving me stuck with her screaming two-year-old charge.

I hadn't wanted to meet her in the first place. Charlotte and I were an old deal, long dead and a bitter memory. But in that excited, rich-broad, enthusiastic way of hers, she'd persuaded me on the phone to meet her at Mr. Mike's in Westland to talk over an "assignment." There was money in it for me, she said. That tipped the scales in favor of going, if only barely.

It had been twelve years so she looked older, but she was still the white-blonde, creamy Nordic, limber, and sensual Charlotte that I remembered. And the money she offered was my usual rate—two fifty per day plus expenses. But the job was crap, a locate job on a boyfriend of hers who'd disappeared. I turned her down without a second thought, partly because I didn't like the sound of the job and partly for the satisfaction of saying no to her just once and, in that small, petty way, getting back at her for what she'd done to me years before. And then, without the slightest warning, she excused herself to go to the restroom and just plain dropped out of sight.

I didn't realize it at first, of course. I finished my beer and smoked a cigar and stared absently around the restaurant at the handful of people there. Then the kid, a chubby little blue-eyed boy named Will, commenced to screaming. I fidgeted, offering him crackers to eat and utensils to play with, but he sent up a howl to the ceiling, his plump face red like a balloon. Charlotte's pit stop stretched abnormally long, and I finally sent a waitress to check up on her. Gone, she said. Not in the parking lot, either. Leaving me alone with the brat.

†††

I know she's a bitch," Kate said, "but why would she abandon her kid? With you?"

We were in my apartment in Belleville and the kid was clinging to my leg, staring at Kate. He'd stopped hollering about halfway back from Mr. Mike's and was doing the shy wide-eyed bit, occasionally issuing a hiccup. Kate was staying with me for a few days because her ex-husband, whose name is, apparently, Asshole, was conducting his semi-annual harassment campaign against her and she needed a place to hide out. I said, "The kid's not hers. She told me she was babysitting him for a friend who was away for a few days."

Kate was short shaggy off-blonde, painfully thin and gaunt, and she wore her usual expression of half skepticism and half harried patience. "You know, in the six years we've been involved, I've seen you get people shot in my house, and I've seen you rough up deputy sheriffs, and I've seen you take some of the sleaziest characters in the world out for dinner. But I never imagined you'd bring home an abandoned toddler."

"That's why you should stick around, kid. Officially I may be just an apartment maintenance guy, but there's always more to Perkins than that." I disengaged Will from my leg and headed into the kitchen to build a drink and figure out what to do. Kate went over to the kid. "Are you hungry, Will?"

"Ha," he said seriously, his face still flushed.

To Kate's arched eyebrow I interpreted, having picked up a little of the kid's jargon: "Yes."

"See cookie," Will added.

"I'll check," she answered. As she pawed though the cupboards, I poured myself some straight Jack Daniel's. Groping among the boxes, wrappers, and debris, she said, "I take it you turned her down."

"I did."

She found a bag of stale Oreos and handed one to the boy, who practically inhaled it, looking hopefully and much more happily at Kate. "What was the job?"

"Some boyfriend of hers disappeared. She wanted him found. I wasn't up for it."

"Sure, Ben. But now you're stuck with the kid. What do you plan to do about that?"

Will had found the bathroom and I heard the toilet flush. Thank God—a good, disciplined, toilet-trained little kid. He came out of the bathroom sans jeans and trailing a long stream of toilet paper. As Kate and I both dived to gather it up, I said, "She's just peevish. Sooner or later she'll call me and tell me who the kid's mother is. Or, even better, I'll call her." I left Kate to pull the kid's pants back on, shoved the bundle of toilet paper into the wastebasket, and went to the phone where I found taped to it a slip with a telephone number.

"The Kroger's store in Belleville called," Kate said from behind me. "Apparently the check you passed there bounced."

"I didn't *pass* a check, I *gave* them one. And if it bounced, it's probably some screwup." At least I hoped so, since my checking account seemed to have a mind of its own. I reached for the phone and it rang as my hand touched the receiver.

"Enjoying the babysitting?" Charlotte asked sweetly.

I sighed. "Nice gag, Charlotte."

Kate leaned her blue-jeaned fanny against the edge of the counter, listening. The boy was studiously opening and closing cupboard doors but apparently was well brought up enough not to mess with anything inside. In my ear, Charlotte laughed and said, "I *do* rather fancy the idea of your taking care of a little baby boy, but I must confess that humor wasn't my only motive."

Charlotte never did anything that didn't redound to her advantage. "So fill me in," I said evenly.

"You take the job, Ben," she said. "Find Chuck Crane for me. And then I'll tell you where the kid belongs. Don't worry, nobody's looking for him right now. You've got enough time, if you're at all as talented at your work as I'm told you are. And I'll pay you as agreed."

The boy, having decided I was okay, I guess, was giving me a sunny, radiant look, which was about all I needed just then.

I said, "This is one sick, twisted game you're playing, Charlotte."

"But effective. And don't think about trying to track me down. I'm where you could never ever find me. You'll never find the boy's mother, either. When you have the answer, call my home number and leave word on my message box. Within four hours I'll call you back and we'll meet someplace. Do it fast, Ben." She hung up.

I slammed the phone down and banged my fist against the wall, which got me nothing but sore knuckles. Kate looked more gaunt than usual. I told her the story and she said immediately, "So turn the kid over to the cops. Simple enough."

I sat down on a chair and lighted a small cork-tipped cigar. After a long pause I said, "Nope. Not right now, anyway."

"Why, for God's sake?"

"Because," I said without looking at her, "I take care of things myself. I don't dump them off on someone else. You know that."

"So you're going to let that ruthless swine strong-arm you," she jibed.

The boy stood between us, eyes wide, not understanding the words but picking up on the tone, for sure. "I can't win every point, Kate."

"Yeah," she said grimly, pushing herself away from the counter and going to the sink. She made herself speciously busy with some dishes. "You just want to do it. This is just a convenient excuse to get involved with her again. You just don't learn, do you."

It was a dumb argument and one I'd run out of patience with. Getting to my feet, I said, "You got a choice. Come with me while I try to get a line on this Crane fella, or site here and sulk."

"I'll stay here, thanks," she said. "The boy's had enough moving around for one day. You go and help your girlfriend."

†††

Kate could sure turn on a person, I reflected as I headed out on I-94 in my '71 Mustang. It had been getting worse lately, worse than ever. After six years, it was finally going sour. I knew it and she knew it; what we hadn't got around to yet was what Bob Seger calls "the famous final scene."

She came close to starting one with that girlfriend crack, though—as if I wanted to do the job, as if Charlotte meant anything to me any more. Fact was, I was feeling nothing but cold burning fury at what she'd done, exploiting a helpless two-year-old and the boy's unknowing family. But it was like her.

We'd met in the mid-sixties under the most clichéd of circumstances: her mother and my mom fixed us up. The two women couldn't have been more different. Charlotte's mother was your typical Franklin Village matron, and my mom was a nursing home supervisor who boarded kids for rich folks to make a few extra bucks. (Sidelines, you see, are an old Perkins family tradition, though my mom's moonlighting was far more respectable than mine.)

One of my mom's boarders—and a real brat as I recall—was Charlotte's younger brother. My mom thought it would be good for me to find a "nice girl" from a "good family" and settle down. And forget the questionable job I had as aide to a union boss with a smudged reputation. What Charlotte's mother thought isn't on the record, although I suspect she welcomed the suit of a no-frills straight arrow like me after seeing a steady parade of giggle-headed rich kids march through Charlotte's life. Shy Charlotte wasn't.

It started for laughs and got heavy quick, quicker than either of us expect-ed. Unlike most of the women I'd known until then, Charlotte was dynamic. Her considerable physical attributes aside, she was bright, enthusiastic, chal-lenging, tough-minded, and exciting. Her bright light burned white hot, at-tracting people to her; and sometimes I'd sit and wonder what she saw in me, a straight, sober, hard-edged Detroit boy on the make.

We got ourselves a house in the Jefferson-Chalmers neighborhood. It was one of the older ones, a rambling yellow brick place on the Detroit River with its own boathouse. My job was increasingly intense and dangerous, and Charlotte was meteoric and unpredictable and not the easiest person in the world to live with, and yet, all these years later, I remember those days as being tranquil. I remember barbecue dinners out on the big airy porch; long walks along the river; card games and beer of an evening with one or two of the young couples who lived around us; evenings spent in debate;

sunrise strolls around the Belle Isle fountain; afternoons making love in the enormous second-story riverfront bedroom while the curtains floated in the air and freighters glided by outside in ghastly silence.

The riot in 1967 changed things for keeps. My mom's nursing home got torched and she died on the second day, trying to get an inmate out. The feds came after my boss and some other on tax and racketeering charges and they zeroed in on me, trying to make me Public Snitch Number One. I refused to talk, even though they gave me immunity; my name got in the papers; and one day, when it looked as if I was going to jail on contempt charges, I came home to find Charlotte gone. Not a word. Just empty closets and her car gone from the garage.

Things bottomed out then, thank God. The feds made their case via the net worth method, the defendants went off to Lewisburg, and I went off the hook. A lot of years passed and I never heard of Charlotte again—and thought of her as little as possible, which is to say once a day.

But I didn't rehash ancient history on my way to Southfield. Instead, I tried to piece together what I'd half-heard from Charlotte as she told me about her mysterious Chuck Crane. A thin, wiry, athletic man, she said, in his mid-thirties. She'd met him on St. Patrick's Day at one of the Irish bars on the west side. He lived in the Franklin Park Towers and drove a Corvette. He had lots of clothes, manners, style, money, and smarts, and he never seemed to work. He called himself an "investor." He and Charlotte made several long trips together, one to Switzerland, one to the Bahamas, and she introduced him to her daddy, whom I once sarcastically referred to as the "oil seal king." By Charlotte's standards the affair was serious.

Until he disappeared a month ago.

The Franklin Park Towers sprawls at the intersection where the Lodge Freeway dumps out onto I-696 heading west and Telegraph Road shoots north toward Pontiac. There's a lot of government land there, including a couple of military reserve outfits and an old Nike missile base; there are also shopping centers, synagogues, and endless miles of well-heeled subdivisions with names like Bingham Farms, Mayfair, and Beverly Hills. I've often thought of it as the place where Detroit busted open and gushed people north.

The apartments are huge and glum looking, the style known as Twentieth Century Insane Asylum. Pretty they aren't, but they happen to be one of the prestige addresses of the Detroit area. I found Crane's apartment and, with the timely help of a skeleton key I'd acquired at great cost some years before (the previous owner is now a guest of the state at Marquette), gained entry.

It was a single bedroom place, conspicuously neat and sterile; rented furniture, nothing personal on the walls, none of the little debris of personality in the place at all. I had the bizarre feeling that I'd broken by accident into the complex's model apartment—a place everyone looked at but no one lived in—not a place where a wealthy young man had lived for several years. Judging from the dry sink, the painstaking orderliness of the silverware and plates, the clean dry tub and the absence of dirty linen, it looked to me as if no one had lived there for a month or more, maybe. There was also a feeling of emptiness. Like a personality had been there once but had left for good.

The resident rental agent wasn't much help. He had, after all, a huge number of tenants to keep track of, and he didn't know any of them personally, let alone Chuck Crane. I also don't think he was overly impressed with my cover story that I was an investigator for Mass Mutual Insurance. He glumly went though his records anyway, giving me beady little hostile looks. Yes, Crane had rented the apartment. He'd paid his rent a year in advance (and the thought occurred to me: who in his right mind does *that?*). No, there were never any complaints about him. Where Crane worked was not an agent's business. The only concrete thing I could get out of him was Crane's license plate number. A thin, very frail thread, but the best I could do.

I headed south on Telegraph to the huge, cylindrical Holiday Inn, went inside to a bank of phones, and called a friend in Lansing. She's a financial analyst for the state of Michigan, and a damned good one, and she has that invaluable resource for a fellow in my line of work, direct and unlimited access to the state's computer records. She even carries a portable terminal home, which was where I found her. I think helping me is a kick for her, even though she fusses a lot about my occasional requests. I help her out with things from time to time, and buy her lunch in Detroit once a month, so it evens out. Sort of.

She put on hold and was gone quite a while firing up her terminal and going into the computer on her second telephone line. She came back to tell me that Crane's car was registered to a firm called Pan Peninsular Products— such a Michigan kind of name I was surprised they didn't throw a "Wolverine" in—based in the Penobscot Building in Detroit. I asked, in passing, for a run-down on the company and she said it would take some time and she'd get back to me on it later that night.

It was pushing late afternoon by then, but I headed straight down to the Penobscot. It was tired looking and half empty, like many downtown office buildings since the Renaissance Center went up a few years back. Pan Peninsular occupied a suite on the tenth floor. I stood in the echoing hallway and did my magic act with a skeleton key again. I found the suite stripped clean—nothing left but the stink of cigarettes, a couple of rickety, ready-for-junkyard desks, and severed coils of telephone cables. Pan Peninsular no longer existed, as far as I could tell, except for the name neatly stenciled on the rippled glass door.

†††

The TV flickered color into the otherwise dark living room of my apartment as I entered. In the strange strobe-like light, Kate's gaunt face looked stark and stony. She turned to me as I closed the door and said without greeting, "Garden City Medical Center called while you were gone. That check you sent them on your Uncle Dan's account bounced."

I went purposefully into the kitchen, poured myself a big shot of Jack Daniel's black, and rescued a bottle of Stroh's from the refrigerator. Back in the living room I saw that Kate wasn't drinking—a bad sign. I said, "Where's the boy?"

"Sleeping in your bed. He fell asleep about eight, after wiping out your Oreo supply, two hot dogs, and an entire can of pork and beans. God, if my kids had eaten like that. . . . What's with your checking account lately, anyway? You under-financed, or something?"

"Nah, that's not it," I said absently. I sat down at the other end of the couch from her and noted that she made no move to slide down and join me. In a feeble attempt to get past our awkwardness, I told her what I'd found out—which amounted to a big fat zero. I finished, "So Crane's a big phony. The only question is, what was his game and where did he go? Hopefully Lansing will get me some information tonight. Maybe I'll get it ironed out and get the kid back home tomorrow."

"And if not you can call the cops," she said flatly.

I got the telephone off the hi-fi cabinet, sat on the couch, shucked my shoes, and dialed Lansing. My friend picked the phone up before the second ring.

"Pan Peninsular's a shell, Ben," she told me.

"What do you mean?"

"It's hollow. Business license and incorporation papers only. No assets, no taxes, the officers are professional front guys. The outfit, as far as the State of Michigan is concerned, is a company in name only."

"Okay, kid, do me some blue-sky. In your experience, what does this mean?"

There was a brief hissing of long-distance silence and then she said, "All right, but this is off the record."

"Always. Always."

"It's one of two things," she said slowly. "Either it's an organization front, for laundering money or something or . . . just maybe . . . it's a government front, one of those 'sting' operations. I've seen it happen both ways. You get enough official paper to stand a cursory inspection, and go from there."

I got my last cigar out of my shirt pocket and lighted it from a wood match struck against my thumbnail. The smoke showed translucent gray, like a navy ship, in the light of the TV set. "Anything more you can tell me? Who do I talk to now?"

She laughed. "Either the organization or someone in Justice. You know the players better than I do."

"I hear you. Thanks, kid."

"Listen, for this you owe me London Chop House."

"And here I had a nice A&W Root Beer all picked out for you."

I heard her laugh as I hung up. Kate was watching *The Dukes of Hazzard,* and I pondered for a moment. Sure, I knew the players all right, but it had to be approached with great precision. Finally I picked up the phone, searched my memory, and dialed tentatively. My contact wasn't available, which was the routine; I hung up and a few minutes later the phone rang. I snatched it up. My contact was upset, highly upset. He spoke in that business-speak dialect that indicated he was worried about my phone's being tapped, despite the number of years he's known me.

I gave him a few pieces of information, but didn't muscle him, partly because I've never needed to, and partly because it wouldn't have worked. My strongest selling point was that Pan Peninsular had closed up shop and Crane had disappeared, so it was old business and there was no reason not to give me the story. My contact hemmed and hawed and then certified to me that Chuck Crane was not known among his colleagues, in either the Detroit or Pontiac operations, and that there had been no business involving such a person. I hung up, knowing that the next call would tell the tale.

The *Dukes* were on commercial. Kate stirred and said, "You know, it's a pity."

"What's that, kid?"

"We're alone in the room, and you're not even here."

Hell of a time for heavy mysteries. "Look, it's late and I've got a few more calls to make, okay?"

She shrugged. I picked up the phone again and called the highest police authority I knew, Detective Captain Elvin Dance of the Detroit Police Department.

I first got to know Elvin when he was a strikebreaker with one of the car companies in the early sixties. Fortunately, he went legit after that and joined the police department and did very well for himself. To no one's surprise. Elvin is a good, solid, practical cop, half politician and half lawman, a remarkable combination for a man who grew up in a slum and earned his Ph.D. at night at Wayne State. He was on duty, which wasn't unusual, and at his desk, which was.

"Run that by one more time, Ben."

"What I said was," I said distinctly, "you find whoever you have to and tell them I know about Crane and the sting operation he was running. I don't know what his game was and I don't care. All I want to know is where the man is." I felt my heart pounding. "Or I'll go to every media organ in town and turn them loose on it. Confidentiality guaranteed. This is information for a client of mine not involved in the business."

"You know, Ben," he said, his voice a coarse growl, "there's been some heavy federal action round here lately. Mucho sensitive. How much of that big nose of yours you want whacked off? I'm just asking, as a friend of yours."

I said, "You get the word out now. I want a call back from a top player tonight. That happens, and nothing further gets said to anybody."

He sighed, "I'll look into it, man."

The Duke boys were headed toward their showdown with the Boss, and I didn't feel welcome to interrupt. Instead I morosely smoked my cigar, thinking about the downside: red lights in the parking lot, handcuffs on the wrists, the fast hustle to the waiting car, the grim professional faces firing tough professional questions. I'd come close to it before, but usually for better reasons than helping a selfish, strong-willed, adrenalin junkie.

And the phone rang. I picked it up with a slippery hand. It was Bill Scozzafava, the bartender at my local watering hole, Under New Management.

"You ever heard of uttering and publishing, stupid?"

It was hit polite and legal was of informing me that one of my Detroit Bank drafts had gone rubber on him. I smoothed him over, promising him cash money the next day. I cut off the conversation as quickly as I could and hung up. I was getting tired and my mind was wandering and it seemed like only moments later when the phone rang again.

The voice was, as might be expected, unknown to me. Anonymous, masculine, bland, purposeful. It said, "You have made inquiries about a man named Crane. You have made certain guarantees. We accept the guarantees because we have the means to enforce them, as you probably recall from your encounter with us in the late sixties. What you need to know about the story is as follows. . . ."

When I hung up, Kate was gone. I found her sleeping with Will in my bed. It was a pretty picture. I went back to the living room and with thick fingers punched out Charlotte's number. Her answering machine gave a perky spiel and when the tone sounded I told her to meet me at the Belle Isle fountain at seven. Good a place as any.

I found a thin summer blanket in my linen closet and wrapped it around me like a shroud and fell into an awkward and restless sleep on the couch.

†††

She wore a white blouse open to the breasts and white deck pants over white sandals, and she sat on the rim of the defunct Belle Isle fountain. A short distance away on the curving drive was a knee-high, stainless steel DeLorean that I assumed was hers. I parked behind it and walked over to her. The sun was rising over Windsor to the south, bathing her white-blonde hair and casting ambivalent shadows of darkness and light over the pathetic grandeur of the dry fountain. I sat down a piece away from her and lighted a cigar, filling my rusted mouth and lungs with good coarse smoke.

"You owe me a name."

With an amused and triumphant look, she retorted, "*You* owe *me* the story."

"Know anybody in cocaine, Charlotte?"

She squinted into the sun and smiled at me, her impossibly white even teeth glinting in the new sun. "Of course. Doesn't everybody?"

"I'm talking traffic, not the trendy geeks into an occasional party snort."

"You know me," she said smugly. "I only deal with the top people in any field."

"Seen any of them around lately?" I asked wearily.

In the silence she slowly straightened and began, by God, to look a little uncertain. "No, it's gotten pretty quiet. What are you getting at, Ben?"

"Your friend Crane was DEA. That's Drug Enforcement Administration, the Justice arm that handles drugs since the FBI has never had jurisdiction in that particular area. Crane's part of a real small, elite group. They're called the Flying Squad. They're moles, Charlotte. They move into an area and live three, four, five years undercover. They work their way into the drug traffic, build the book on the top people in it, turn the case, and disappear. They never even stay around to testify, their work is that thorough. They don't have names. They don't have real identities or lives. The case is their whole life."

I hadn't noticed it before, but the sharp uncaring sunlight was showing a pattern of lines and creases in her face that weren't there twelve years ago. Apparently the years hadn't been any kinder to her than I was. It occurred to me how vital her flip, arrogant attitude was to her good looks. She said flatly, "So he busted them."

"He's in St. Louis now, burrowing his way in. You'll never see him again. It wasn't real to him, Charlotte, it was just a case and you were part of it."

She stood up angrily. "It was more than that to him. Believe me, I know." She thought of something. "After all, he protected me. He didn't turn me in with the rest."

She was asking for it and I didn't hesitate to give it to her. "You're a dilettante, Charlotte. A thrill-seeking groupie. He's a pro and he sized you up right away. He knew, with your social connections, he could ride you right into the mainstream. But once he had the case nailed down, you were nothing to him any more. He got the principals but didn't bother with you because you were nothing but small fry. And guys like him have no use for small fry."

She smiled, but it was forced, the bright light extinguished. "You know," she said, cocking her head to one side as she narrowed her eyes, "I had other reasons for wanting to see you. The assignment wasn't the only thing. I did care for you—"

"You didn't care for me. You loved my game. The union, the scandal, the investigation, the notoriety. I finally worked that out for myself, when I was trying to deal with the fact that you ran like a rat when my back was to the wall. You wanted to game, but you couldn't take the heat."

"No," she shouted, her face lean and ugly. "I left because you were just what you are now: nothing! Look at you! A maintenance man and . . . and a detective! All you've gotten is older. You haven't gotten anywhere, after all these years, haven't achieved a thing, just another flunky."

"As opposed to you, presumably."

After a long silence, she nodded abruptly and hooked her thumbs in the waistband of her pants. "Well, I got what I wanted." She took a step to go. "I wish I hadn't had to use the kid to muscle you, but the results speak for themselves. His mother will be out at your place this morning to pick Will up. She'll never speak to me again, of course, but that's not a big price to pay." She turned. "Goodbye, Ben."

"Just a minute," I said roughly, taking her arm. She turned, her blue eyes directed indifferently at me. "You're into this flunky for a day and some gas money. Call it two seventy-five and we're quits."

She smiled contemptuously, went into her purse, and counted out two C-notes and four twenties. I curled them into a stiff tube and stuck them into my shirt pocket, then fished out a crumpled five and gave it to her. Without another word or look, I headed back to my car. She called something that the rising wind muffled. It might have been thanks but, knowing Charlotte, it probably wasn't.

†††

The tension was electric in my kitchen. The boy was hunkered on his knees on one of my chairs at the small dinette, spooning Cheerios sloppily into his mouth. Kate was at the other end of the table, cupping a mug of coffee in her hands. And another woman sat between her and Will, a tall medium blonde with a long voluptuous figure and a Lady Diana haircut. She rose, a worried, uncertain smile on her face, and Kate said to me, "this is Will's mother, Ben. Carole Somers."

Mrs. Somers wore a one-piece denim dress that ended just below her knees, revealing elegant long legs beneath. Her eyes warmed up as she held out her hand and I shook it. "From what Kate's been telling me, Mr. Perkins, I owe you a ton of thanks—and a certain ex-friend a punch in the jaw." Despite the words, her dark brown eyes were merry, her smile as golden as her hair.

"Name's Ben, Carole. No thanks needed. Charlotte mentioned you were an old friend of hers?" I let her hand go, still feeling its warmth in my palm.

The boy was giving me that radiant, adoring look again, and this wasn't lost on Carole, who smiled. "Past tense, for sure. You too?"

"With seniority," I grinned. Kate sat straight-faced, watching me as I poured myself a cup of coffee and leaned back against the counter. "You leave the boy with her often?"

Carole shrugged. "Once in a while, when I have to travel. When I got in at Metro this morning there was a message from her telling me where to pick Will up. I was curious but not alarmed. Not until Kate told me the story." She gave the boy a smile. "You sure took good care of him."

"It was Kate," I admitted.

"No trouble," Kate shrugged.

"See cookie," Will announced.

"We're all out," Kate said. "This kid and cookies—"

"Oh, that's not what he means," Carole laughed. "He watches *Sesame Street,* and that's a song the Cookie Monster sings: 'C is for cookie, that's good enough for me.'"

Kate wasn't exactly mirthful that morning, but she laughed with us at that. Carole got up then, gathered up Will, and headed for the door. I followed her and found out as she thanked me effusively that she lived in Berkley and wanted to keep in touch with me. Well, that made two of us.

Back in the kitchen, Kate handed me the phone, which I hadn't heard ring. "Detroit Bank."

The lady was very upset with me. I bank by mail, mainly, and I'd sent in a couple of payroll checks and forgotten to endorse them. They promptly mailed them back for endorsement, but since I'm pretty lazy and don't open my mail more than once a week, I didn't know what had gone wrong until the bank, nervous, began bouncing my checks all over the place. I endured the lecture, promised to stop in and correct the problem, and hung up.

Kate was at the door, lugging her overnight bag. "What do you say?" she asked lightly.

Theoretically, after six years, plenty. But I inquired, "What about Asshole?"

"He's probably given up by now. If not I'll run him off. God knows I've done it before." She opened the door and turned to me, at the very edge of her composure. "Isn't it the damnedest thing. C is for cookie. Sometimes we forget." Then she hefted her bag and left quickly.

I shut the door and thought that, if she'd stayed, I'd probably have replied that C also stands for cocaine, checks, conspiracies. But I've found that you usually don't get to say everything you want to during the famous final scene.

I suppose you could say I netted out on the deal. Kate was gone, but there was Carole, whom I saw a lot of in the time that followed. And I made friends with a damned nice little kid, my first brush with domesticity.

Ironic, I guess.

Charlotte wanted something badly but didn't get it. I came into the situation not wanting or expecting anything, but got plenty. And got paid besides.

Afterword

This was my first published fiction. A signal event. I was always especially glad that it was a story featuring a little boy, who was about the same age as my oldest son John was then. As a matter of fact, it was John who unwittingly gave me the title.

The elegant and wise Cathleen Jordan, editor of "Alfred Hitchcock's Mystery Magazine" till she passed away in 2002, had turned down a previous story (which, revamped, became "The Long Slow Dive" and appeared in Hitchcock later) with my first-ever personal rejection. Encouraged by this, I sent her this story, and she bought it right out of the box.

It's not a bad little stage-setter. You get a sense of what Perkins is like, though still in somewhat an unformed state. There's his job and a bit of his history. There's a sense of the chaos that surrounds him in various aspects of his life.

Neither Kate nor Charlotte has ever reappeared. Elvin Dance has become a strong continuing character (though his past as a strikebreaker never gets mentioned). And Carole? She's still around.

The Rat Line

It sounded like a regular old adultery investigation, except for one thing.

"He's *how* old?" I asked, startled.

"D.P. Charlie? Oh, lots younger than me," my Uncle Dan replied, shifting his thin, withered frame under the sheets. "Late seventies."

"And his wife thinks he's having an affair," I prodded skeptically.

"That's what Peggy told me." Uncle Dan clasped his white skeletal hands together behind his baldhead, making his hospital gown tighten around his thin shoulders. "I told her my nephew was in the investigating business. I said you'd check it out for her."

Normally I don't like being volunteered for things, but this was Uncle Dan asking. I scratched my head and sat down clumsily in a cheap plastic chair next to his bed. I wanted a cigar, but the nice folks at Wayne County General Hospital would get *un*nice in a hurry if I lighted up. I asked, "You known these people long?"

Uncle Dan's crystal clear blue eyes glinted with humor. "At my age, I've known *everyone* long. D.P. Charlie and I worked together on the Rouge line. We were neighbors in Detroit, lived a block apart. They moved to east Dearborn back in nineteen sixty something." His offhand attitude toward the passing of years was understandable. Uncle Dan was my age in 1937.

"Charlie Steel," I muttered. "What's the 'D.P.' mean?"

"Oh, just a nickname. Stands for Displaced Person. He was a refugee from Poland or somewhere, immigrated here after the war."

I sighed. Not that I'm particularly picky about the jobs I take on, but this one sounded like a dead snore. I said to my uncle, "So she thinks he's sleeping out on her. Doesn't this strike you as a little, uh, eccentric?"

"No," Uncle Dan said from his hospital bed.

"I personally don't buy it."

"You personally are forever telling me how slow the investigating business is. You personally are forever telling me how broke you are. Peggy Steel has money and this problem, and I promised her you'd look into it."

I'd do anything for Uncle Dan, and he knew it. Plus he was bang-on right about my financial situation. I don't earn money, I rent it.

"Well," I snorted, "it'll be like shooting fish in a barrel, but sure, I'll check into it. What's their address?"

†††

They built lots and lots of these boxy little cookie-cutter homes in east Dearborn right after the war. The Steels' tiny two-bedroom had the looks of a place that had been inhabited by the same people for many years. Trim little patch of lawn, little shrubs carved into various geometric shapes, blankets of gaily colored flowers, a birdbath, a plastic ostrich, dwarf fruit trees. Every square inch of landscape had been attended to by people who obviously had plenty of time to do it.

Mrs. Steel answered the door, let me in, and wobbled away toward the bathroom after inviting me to sit. When she returned, her dentures were back in her mouth. Peggy Steel was a short, round woman who'd fought the fat fight for fifty years and then said to hell with it, I'm pushing eighty and I like to eat. Her smooth skin hadn't seen sun in a quarter century. She wore a tight reddish wig, lots of rings on her plump little hands, a pink-flowered house-dress and pink 29-cent thongs. Despite her age, she looked alert and moved well and probably still clogged up traffic on Michigan Avenue from behind the wheel of the sky-blue '65 Ford Fairlane that sat in the driveway outside.

She snapped off the game show on the gigantic color TV set, sat with a sigh in a big overstuffed swivel chair in the corner beneath a framed needlepoint hanging on the wall which declared that the occupants of this home wanted to live by the side of the road and be a friend to man, and smiled nervously. "So you're Benjy. Dan's told us so much about you."

I don't hear my childhood nickname that much anymore. I said courteously, "Ben Perkins, ma'am. Nice meeting you too."

She nodded, smile fixed, not knowing where to start.

The small house tocked with the sound of a dozen clocks. It has the old-house smell of old folks and old furniture and recently cooked food; and each piece of furniture, each picture, each knickknack was put precisely into place.

I said, "Listen, I know this isn't easy. Let me start. You told Uncle Dan that Mr. Steel has been acting strangely. You think he might be seeing another woman." I delivered the line straight and was quite proud of myself. "What is he doing that makes you believe that's the case?"

She sniffed, eyes fluttering, cleared her throat, and said, "It's—a lot of it is instinct, I suppose. When you've known a man for many many years, you develop an instinct."

"Uh-huh. Let's get to that in a minute. What specifically is he doing?"

She breathed deeply. "Charles is retired, as you probably know. He's not as active as he once was. He spends his days on the lawn and the garden or here, watching the TV. We don't get out much. Charles tires easily, his leg is bad, he's got the sciatica and has to walk with a cane, but he can still drive. But he doesn't leave home much except to go to the market with me. Until late last week."

In the pause, I studied her. She was staring down at her white knees half-covered by the pink housedress. I asked quietly, "What happened?"

She looked up suddenly. "He began going out. Walking. He's spent several afternoons away from home. He was late for supper last night. He's out right now, God knows where."

"You ask him where he's going?"

"I haven't asked," she answered with some pride. "He's told me he's going to the main library over on Michigan. That's ten blocks from here. He goes to read, he says." She leaned forward, staring intently at me through unaged eyes. "Benjy, my husband has never been a reader. His eyes are bad anyhow, it's all he can do to get through the sports pages."

"Mm-hm," I nodded judiciously. Suspicious as hell, all right. "What makes you think it's a woman?"

"Well, I'll tell you. He's gotten very quiet these past few days. But inside he's very excited. He moves around in his sleep at night and mutters nonsense words in a jolly voice. He stares off into space while we eat. God knows what he's thinking.

"*I* think it's a woman. After all these years, *that's* what I think. Why else walk? Why not take the car? He doesn't want the car spotted by somebody, that's why. Maybe she's married too. He just walks out of the house and up the street and vanishes for hours." She leaned back, burst of energy dissipated, facial skin sagging. "I just want to know," she said plaintively.

A long, long silence. I rubbed my forehead with my fingertips and said, finally, "Well, I look into these things on a pretty regular basis. I'll say to you what I say to everyone who wants to hire me to do this. That is: before you turn me loose, make sure you really want to know. Decide right now what you'll do if the answer I get for you is the worst one. Because I can get the answer, but then you're the one who's going to have to deal with it."

Her stare was on her lap again. "I'll just talk to him, that's all," she whispered. "But I have to know."

My feeling is, you get enough bad news on a regular basis, why go pay somebody to bring you more? But people pay me to do, not to think. I asked her a few more questions and didn't learn anything new. We settled the money part—I violated normal custom and didn't get an advance—and I left promising her a report in a couple of days.

D.P. Charlie didn't go for a stroll the next day, causing me to spend an incredibly boring afternoon in my '71 Mustang half a block down from his house, watching, wasting time. The next day, though, he set off alone on foot.

It wasn't exactly the chase scene out of *The French Connection*, though.

D.P. Charlie hobbled out of the house and headed up the sidewalk. He was a short stocky man, obviously powerfully built once, big-knuckled hand tight on the cane he used to help his right leg. He wore a white shirt, dark pants, heavy black work shoes. He still had a lot of hair and it was bristly, snow white, trimmed in a military cut. He didn't go fast. He couldn't have herded turtles. I felt silly in my Mustang with the hot 302 motor, three-quarter cam, four-barrel carb and Hurst shifter, getting ready to trail a man who'd have lost a one-on-one race with a tree.

I thought about dumping the car and following on foot, but I'm a Detroit boy; I like wheels under me. I let him get a full block's lead then fired up the motor and rolled up the street after him and past him and took up the watch in the following block. We played leapfrog like this for about half an hour till he got to Michigan Avenue. There he stood at the corner, cane gripped in both hands propping him up, till a SEMTA bus came, which he boarded.

Forget the library then. It was only three blocks away now, he could have walked it and maybe gotten there by the end of the month. I blew the stop sign at the corner, cut off the onrush of westbound traffic with a cheery wave, and followed the bus up Michigan, glad to be out of first gear. We passed the main part of downtown and went a couple of blocks with me snuggled up to the back end of the bus, inhaling diesel.

The bus stopped and D.P. Charlie got out. He hobbled north away from Michigan, past a row of old dirty brick buildings, then went into the Q Room. I parked at the curb a half block up and followed him inside.

Despite the name, the Q Room isn't a gay joint, not in Dearborn, Michigan, no sir. It's a pool hall and gin joint and a neighborhood hangout that was old when the first Model T parked there. It was jammed, even that early in the day. I cruised up to the bar and ordered a beer when I had a chance, eyes casually on old D.P. Charlie, who headed back to the tables.

There were four of them, all in use. Cues thwacked, balls clattered, men called their shots, talked and laughed and occasionally shouted. The noise from the patrons and the juke was deafening. D.P. watched the play, standing quietly against the wall. Then a table cleared and he got a cue. A thin, intense young man, wearing a dress shirt and slacks and no tie, got a cue also, and the two of them began playing and talking.

They played several games, badly, and talked all the while. I couldn't hear what they were talking about and didn't see any need to. D.P. Charlie didn't drink, didn't ogle the barmaids, didn't do anything but shoot pool badly and talk to the young fella and smile a lot and have a wonderful time. I was disgusted, not with him at all, but with the whole thing. I was wasting a tired old woman's money. I paid my bill and left.

†††

He doesn't play pool," Mrs. Steel said tersely on the phone.

"Not too well, anyhow," I allowed.

"I've known Charles better than thirty years," she insisted. "He's never played pool." She spaced the words out as if I was hard of hearing.

"Mrs. Steel," I said, "maybe not, but that's what he's doing. I followed him yesterday and today. He's getting out and having a little harmless fun. Nothing wrong with that. Fact, there's a lot right with it."

"What's *not* right," she said, voice rasping, "is that he's not being truthful with me about where he's going."

I said respectfully, "Well, ma'am, now you know. There's no more to it than that."

A pause then a sigh. "Very well. I'll mail you a check, Mister Perkins."

At least she'd quit calling me Benjy.

†††

I was more than mildly surprised when Dick Dennehy, an inspector with the Office of Special Investigations of the Michigan State Police, appeared on the barstool next to mine that night at Under New Management, my favorite dark dingy little drinking hangout.

He was a tall, half-out-of-shape, square-faced blond. His aviator glasses glinted as he grinned at me and ordered a beer from Bill. I said, "Long way from Lansing just to have a beer."

He grinned and lighted a Lucky straight-end, pulling the smoke knee-deep. "Came looking for you, buddy."

"Oh yeah?" Dick's okay but not exactly a pal, and he's usually only where trouble is. "Got a knotty investigative problem you need a hand on?"

"Yeah, right." He grinned sarcastically, picked up his beer, and swigged. "No actually, I'm a message boy this time."

"Ooh." My mind automatically flashed through my recent activities. No guilty conscience. No little nags and tugs and worries. Unless, of course, he was doing free-lance collecting for Master Card. "So what is it?"

Dennehy's beer was half gone. He inhaled on his cigarette and let the smoke wander out of his mouth as he talked. "I got this because I know you and I'm here to give you a friendly word."

This was starting to smell real bad. "Yeah?"

He looked at me square on. "Charles Steel," he said.

"Huh? Who?" I asked, startled.

"Lay off him," Dick said.

"Never met the man in my life," I said truthfully. Why in the hell would the Michigan State Police be interested in an old wheeze like D.P. Charlie?

Dick Dennehy squinted. "Don't argue with me, 'cause there's no point. I don't know what the story is, I really don't. This word comes from real top-siders, folks who get their way, period. Lay off Charles Steel. Roger?"

I answered evenly, "You can tell them, 'Message received.'"

The policeman loosened a little bit. "Take my word, Ben. Get the arch out of your back and I mean right now. Whatever's going on, back offa it."

"Message received," I answered, softer.

Dick Dennehy tossed some coins on the bar, slid off the stool and pushed his way out.

I'd received Peggy Steel's check that morning, and it was cashed and gone. But she was still my client and so, in a more fundamental way, was my Uncle Dan; and besides, once you let someone strong-arm you and get away with it, they get in the habit of doing it over and over and over again.

†††

The next day I got on D.P. Charlie's trail again.

Same deal. Walked up to Michigan Avenue, took the bus through town and went into the Q Room. Played pool and chatted with the same thin young man he's talked to before. I found this interesting. The man looked like a professional, neatly dressed and groomed and apparently friendly. I wondered who he was, and what he was doing in a place like the Q Room, and, most important, why he spent so much time talking to D.P. Charlie. I didn't get any answers, though, and couldn't without getting too close. And I didn't feel like doing that yet.

The next day was Friday. Hot and miserable, ninety-five plus temp, ninety-plus humidity, naked uncaring sun staring down baking everything. Some folks don't think we ever swelter in Michigan, but we do, we do. I followed D.P. Charlie's bus up Michigan again, parked, and strolled after him into the Q Room.

It was jammed. Friday: payday for the assembly line workers out of the Rouge, the Clark Street Cadillac plant, Wayne Assembly, Michigan Truck and Detroit Diesel Allison. Afternoon shift guys were loading up prior to going on shift; graveyard guys were hanging around soaking up brew and fun prior to their complaining wives and sweltering homes.

D.P. hobbled back to the pool area, as usual. I took up position at the bar, as usual. D.P. again began shooting pool with his friend. I noticed several other youngish men entertaining themselves at the tables—men dressed like D.P.'s friend, but paying no attention to anyone else.

This time, by God, I was going to eavesdrop a bit. I drifted over toward the pool tables and spotted a row of video arcade games against the wall. Wonderful. I don't like the dumb things—I prefer more athletic pursuits, like poker—but no one was dealing cards in the Q Room. I fished a handful of quarters out of my pocket and cruised up to a game called Mister Do and began "playing."

It took me a buck and a half to figure out the point of the game. From that point on I'd have been bored if I hadn't been doing something else—mainly listening to D.P. Charlie talk in his gravelly voice.

I could only get snatches of his words what with the noise of my game, the jukebox and the general commotion, but I gathered that they were reminiscing about the war. I heard reference to Germany and France, Belgium and the Russians. I could make no sense out of it.

After about an hour I heard D.P.'s friend say casually, "Hey, Charlie, how about it. I gotta go, okay?"

They stepped away from the table and other players swooped in to take over. I pretended to rattle the coin return on Mister Do and listened intently. D.P. said, sounding disappointed, "Okay, Paul, guess I'll head on home too."

"Listen, D.P.," the young man named Paul said, "How about I drop you off? You don't wanna walk all the way back there. My car's just outside. Okay?"

D.P. slapped his friend on the back with a hamlike hand. "That's kind of you. Very kind of you." He thumped his cane on the floor as they started toward the front door.

I pushed off from the game, walked as quickly as I could through the mob, and beat the pair to the door, mainly because D.P. Charlie was so slow. My car was about three spaces down at the curb and hotter than hell inside. I fired up the engine and waited for the men to emerge.

Before that happened, a black Buick Regal sedan pulled up to the entrance of the Q Room and stopped, engine running.

Then D.P. Charlie and Paul came out the door and down the steps, clumsily.

And three of the other young, well-dressed men came out after them, fanning out to herd D.P. Charlie toward the car.

As the back door of the Regal was opened from the inside, I threw the Mustang into gear and screeched out onto the street. D.P. looked angrily at the men and tried to push his way past them, but they wore frozen smiles and kept trying to nudge him into the car. I flung the Mustang in front of the Regal, punched the emergency brake, popped my .45 automatic out from the clip under my front seat, hurled the car door open, and stood, reaching the pistol over the roof of the car toward the men.

Everything freeze-framed, mouths and eyes wide.

Then I said, "Turn him loose."

Paul's mouth was ugly. "We had you warned. Buzz off."

D.P. took care of that problem by punching Paul in the face with the crook of his cane. The straight end he used at the throat of one of the other men, who went down gagging. D.P. hobbled around the front of the Regal toward me as I asked the other men, "Bullet holes, anybody?"

No one tested me. D.P., gasping, made it to the Mustang, opened the door, and tumbled in. I waited till he'd shut his door then lowered the automatic and with two very satisfying shots blew out the driver-side tires of the Regal. Dropping back into the car, I mashed her into gear, popped the clutch, and roared out of there, making a sliding rubber-burning turn onto westbound Michigan Avenue.

D.P. Charlie was pasty faced, sweating, and breathing hard. I concentrated on the traffic and building speed and distance between us and the trouble. It was a good thing I let D.P. speak first.

Because he said, "So you've been watching me after all." Voice tinny, gravelly, jagged.

Weird question. I grunted. "Yeah."

"I didn't think you men would forget about me. Thank God you didn't."

We blasted out of east Dearborn and were in the open stretch of Michigan Avenue in Ford country. I laid my automatic down on my lap and glanced at the old man. "Who were those guys?"

D.P. made an ugly, triumphant chuckle. "Well, they *said* they were one of you people. U.S. intelligence. Wanted to debrief me about my work for you after the war. But they weren't. I think they were . . . they were . . . some kind of hunters."

"Yeah," I said, bewildered.

D.P. Charlie's breathing was back under control. He said coldly, "After all these years, they're still after us. Thank God you men are around. You understand these matters. You remember what I did for you." I felt his flinty eyes on me. "You weren't in action in the war," he said.

"Came along after that."

We hit the fringe of west Dearborn and Michigan Avenue clogged up with traffic, slowing us down. D.P. Charlie was silent for a minute then said flatly, "You should have put those bullets into the men, not the tires."

"We have to be cautious these days," I said noncommittally.

The traffic started moving and we crossed west Dearborn slowly. "Ah," Charlie snorted, "not like the old days. By God, it was interesting talking about that again, when that *Paul*"—he spat the name—"asked me about the good old days in Bruges. We knew how to handle terrorists then. For every one of our men killed in terrorist attacks, we'd shoot ten civilian hostages. *That* was the way to handle those things. And the Communists, they're nothing but terrorist scum. But I helped you with the Communists after the war, didn't I? You men haven't forgotten how much I helped."

I became conscious of the .45 sitting on my lap, within the old man's reach. I casually slid it under the seat. We were advancing on the Telegraph Road interchange now, and I figured out how to handle it. I pulled into a side street and into the parking lot of Miller's Bar. "Listen," I said to Charlie as I shut down the engine. "I got to make some arrangements. You need a new place. We'll go in here where it's quiet and I'll make some phone calls."

"Very well," he answered crisply, an officer accepting the suggestion of a subordinate.

We walked into the bar slowly. It was quiet, air-conditioned, peopled with a few regulars. I parked D.P. at the bar. "Get yourself a drink. This'll take a few minutes." Then I went to the pay phone, dropped a quarter, and called Dick Dennehy.

Fifteen minutes later, as D.P. Charlie happily swilled beer and chatted with the friendly bartender, the place was overrun by feds.

†††

"Karl Stahlen," I said to Uncle Dan.

He sighed deeply and took a sip of his hospital Coke. "A German?"

"Yes. Second in command of the Gestapo office in Bruges, Belgium, from 1942 to 1944."

Uncle Dan's piercing blue eyes fixed on me. His expression was totally vacant. "A war criminal," he said flatly.

I nodded. "Not a big shot, but on the list. Convicted of murder in absentia in 1946. The Belgians never found him. Till last week, that is."

"How did he get here?" my uncle asked unwillingly.

I sat in the dumb uncomfortable plastic chair again, wanting a cigar badly. Thank God, in a few days my uncle would be back in his retirement community apartment where I could smoke when I visited him. "After the war he was recruited by U.S. intelligence. They used him to get information on communist sympathizers and activities in western Europe. They paid him in cigarettes, liquor, women, and lodging. He delivered the goods for them for several years, I guess. He was quite useful."

"And the intelligence people were grateful," Dan said bitterly.

"Yeah. Grateful as hell. Kept him out of sight of the Belgians. When his usefulness ran out, they smuggled him to Genoa, where he boarded a ship under an assumed name—Steel—and sailed to Bolivia. From there he made his was to the States. It was an escape route that our intelligence people used with several of the war criminals they became friendly with. The Rat Line, it was called."

"The Rat Line," Uncle Dan repeated softly.

"Came to Detroit," I said, feeling the need to finish the story, "married Peggy, went to work for Ford's, made friends with you, and all that."

"God," Uncle Dan said wearily. "Poor Peggy."

I had no answer for that.

Uncle Dan asked, "So what happened then?"

"You mean his little walks? I guess the Belgians got a tip as to his where-abouts somehow. Maybe tumbled to the Rat Line, after all these years. I don't know. Anyway, they approached the CIA and told them they knew about American complicity in hiding war criminals. Steel, in particular, by now number one on their list; the rest are dead or in jail. The CIA, in its wisdom, made a deal with the Belgians. They could put a snatch on Steel and smuggle him out and the Americans would look the other way. As long as the identification was absolutely positive, and as long as word about the Rat Line wasn't made public."

"Very accommodating."

"Sure." God, I wanted a smoke; I could smell a fresh cigar calling from my shirt pocket. "I don't know how the Belgians first made contact with Steel. But they did—this guy Paul—and he began meeting with Steel at the Q Room, a nice public place where you can talk about anything. Paul pretended to be an intelligence guy wanting to debrief Steel on his wartime intelligence activities. Actually, Paul is a Belgian intelligence operative, and he was questioning Steel to make sure he was actually Karl Stahlen, Gestapo, Bruges. Once he was sure, he tried to put the snatch on him, as agreed with CIA."

"But you were there," Uncle Dan commented.

"Yeah."

Dan finished his coke and set it on the tray table next to his bed. "Why did the feds confide all this to you?"

"Hell, they had to. I was there, I knew too much. They're scared to death the story of the Rat Line will get out. It would be embarrassing as hell, American intelligence agents recruiting Nazi war criminals and then helping them escape justice. I agreed to keep my mouth shut in return for the whole miserable story. I'm sure there's juicy parts they left out, but it's all essentially there."

"And D.P. Charlie? Where is he now?"

I shrugged. "Probably in Canada by now. Our people kept their deal with the Belgians. He'll surface again in a Brussels jail on war-crime charges in a few days, no doubt. And our people will never have heard of him."

We didn't say anything for a while. Footsteps went by in the corridor outside. My nicotine hunger grew. My uncle was staring blankly out the window at the dismal skyline of Inkster. I asked, "What are you thinking about, Uncle?"

"War crimes," he answered, not looking at me.

"Yeah. Well, you couldn't have guessed. He had everybody fooled, including his wife."

"I was thinking about myself." He looked at me and he was pale. "I had thirty-one confirmed victories in World War I. Thirty-one men died. That doesn't count at least that many victories unconfirmed. And the strafing missions." He groped for words. "There's blood on my hands too. But they haven't come to judge me, only D.P. Charlie."

I stood and said angrily, "Don't ever make that comparison again. The men you killed were combatants. Volunteers. Equally armed. You were better than them, that's all, and just doing your job. Stahlen's victims were innocent civilians." I calmed down. "Jesus, Uncle. What got you thinking like that?"

He sighed. "D.P. Charlie was my friend. I have to adjust, that's all." He looked up at me and I was glad to see that sardonic twinkle come back to his ancient eyes. "I was one of the good guys, huh?"

"One of the good guys," I grinned.

His grin faded and I knew he was thinking about D.P. Charlie again. "It's hard to tell who the good guys are anymore."

Afterword

I've been a student of history most of my life, especially World War II. So when the story broke about "the rat line," which really existed pretty much the way Perkins learns about it here, the story came together pretty well.

This was the first appearance of Ben's uncle, Dan Perkins. He kind of emerged out of my interest in World War I flying aces, and between appearances in several of the short stories, took off on his own. I've deliberately given him more victories than the real-life U.S. ace (Eddie Rickenbacker), because Dan flew for the Royal Flying Corps, and so technically his victories don't count as American. (And Rickenbacker was much cleaner cut, better connected, and had a better talent for publicity.) I have an enormous

back-story about Dan called "Glory Days;" maybe I'll live long enough to write it.

The general geography in "The Rat Line" is accurate. The Steel home and the Q Room do not exist, but Miller's Bar does. It was quite the drinking hole for me, back in the day.

Dynamite Park

The fairway of the number 5 hole at North Detroit Golf Club is wide and straight with a tricky right-hand dogleg to the green. We were halfway down, surveying the situation in the hot late summer sun. Borrello brought his hand down from his forehead and said, after a glance at his wife, "The three iron, I believe. Mister Perkins."

"Yes, sir." I slipped the club out of the crowded leather bag that was the diameter of a garbage can and handed it to him. Borrello assumed the position next to the ball, folded his big tan hands around the handle, and waggled the head a couple of times.

I thought he was concentrating on his shot, but he had enough excess mental capacity to say, "Joann Sturtevant recommended you quite highly to us, Mister Perkins."

"Nice of her." I wasn't playing, I was caddying, which kind of sums up my place in the scheme of things.

Now Borrello got serious about preparing for his shot. He was a big beefy gent, stacked high on bones and muscles and swathed all over with fat. He wore a red short-sleeved sport shirt open at the neck, white slacks and white patent-leather shoes. His gray hair was cropped relatively short and, like most execs hauling down three hundred plus a year, he had the kind of tan that made you wonder where he spent more time: Michigan or southern California.

He took his cut at the ball. The practiced, fluid swing produced a shot that soared straight and true down the fairway. Borrello stood with his back to us and stared, probably with rapture, at it. Barbie Borrello said, "Joann told us you recovered a huge sum of money that been stolen from her."

I don't blab about my cases, win or lose. I said noncommittally, "It was interesting."

Barbie Borrello stared at me expectantly. She was her husband's age, but looked much younger, thanks to a well-financed and, to date, successful conspiracy among hairdressers, physical therapists, clothing designers and oral and plastic surgeons. She wore purple track shoes, purple hot pants, a purple halter top, tiny purple earrings and, I was quite sure, absolutely nothing else.

Barbie Borrello smiled, but with her mouth only; her violet eyes reflected like a two-way mirror. Borrello finished enjoying his shot, handed me his club, and gave me a swat on the shoulder. "Well, if Joann says you're the man to straighten out my problem, then you're the man."

I slipped the club back into the bag, hoisted it onto my shoulder by the strap, and we began walking the gentle downslope. "Not that I object to getting fresh air," I said, "but I could have met you at your office, or at a bar, or somewhere."

"Not private enough," Barbie Borrello murmured.

Her husband boomed, "This is the electronic age, Perkins. Never know who's got a mike on you, you know?"

I knew, all right, but frankly, the kind of cases I get, James Bond-type electronic surveillance usually doesn't figure. I let it drop. "What do you want me to do?"

Borrello began, "There's this woman, see—"

His wife, who had drifted up very close to my left, interrupted, "It's harassment, Mister Perkins, and it has to be stopped!"

I shifted the bag on my shoulder, fished a short cork-tipped cigar out of my shirt pocket, lighted it with a quick blaze of match flame, and exhaled. I didn't like the feel of this thing. I didn't even know what the assignment was yet, and already I was having trouble finding out which one of them was really my client. I asked, "Let's take it from the top. Mister Borrello?"

The woman casually brushed an acre of bare, tan, smooth skin against my flank, but said nothing. Borrello didn't notice. His eyes were narrow and shrewd, thinking not about the job, but about finding his ball somewhere up ahead. "Rebecca Campanula. Becky. A clerical at the insurance company for a few months. I hardly knew her. Man in my position doesn't come into contact with clericals, as a rule. Ah, there we are. The nine iron, please, Mister Perkins."

"Ben," I said, handing him the club.

"Good, good," he beamed. "I'm Jake. This is terrific. We're all friends here, aren't we, Barbie?"

She didn't answer him, but, as her husband lined up his chip shot, she brushed against me casually again, which I suppose was answer enough. I shuffled casually away from her, dragging the golf bag along, cigar smoldering in my teeth. I'm no prude, but I have a funny habit of not fooling around with the client's wife, at least till the job's over.

Jake Borrello made his shot, a high-altitude number that sliced just right, then caught a good bounce that propelled it over a bunker and onto the green, ending up just five or six feet from the cup. Borrello turned and, raising both fists in the air in a victory salute, beamed. It was the same grin I'd seen him make in his campaign ads, which had just started that week.

Barbie Borrello said, without much enthusiasm, "Nice shot, Jake."

"Hey, I'm rolling now," he said exuberantly, handing me the iron. "Putter, Perkins."

I made a note to adopt that as a nickname if I decided to improve my station in life—not to mention my income—by becoming a pro caddy. "What about this Rebecca Campanella?"

"Campanula," he corrected, taking the putter. "Well, like Barbie says, Becky's gotten to be a real nuisance the past few weeks." We walked across the deep-pile green to the ball. Borrello began doing the Arnie Palmer routine, bending, sighting the lie of the putt, using his putter as a strange kind of plumb bob, apparently doing lots of fancy arithmetic in his head. I was impressed as hell. "She's pestering me all the time, calling me on the phone, sending me letters, running into me places."

"Why for?" I asked, letting the golf bag flop over with a clank.

Borrello finished his arcane calculations, rose, faced me, and said, "*I* don't know. But a man of my position, you know, with the campaign and everything, I don't need some strange chick making trouble, you know?"

I pulled at my cigar and exhaled slowly. Barbie Borrello stood, arms folded before her, staring off back up the fairway. "Any specific kind of trouble you can tell me about?"

Jake Borrello let his putter slip through his hands, caught it at the grip, and bent over the ball, lining up his putt. "Well, like, for example. I gave a speech at the Bloomfield Economics Club, Wednesday last week. Big crowd there, couple hundred. After my talk it was question-and-answer time. Way they work it there, you just don't holler out, you write your questions down and pass them up. I handled a couple of them then opened the next one. When I read it, I knew it was from her. I looked up, real quick, and saw her sitting out in the audience, grinning from ear to ear."

"What did it say?" I asked.

Borrello quit waggling his putter and positioned the business end behind the ball. "Don't make me tell you. It was embarrassing. I guess I'd say, uh, frank and suggestive and crude. *Real* crude."

I glanced at Barbie Borrello. She was still lost in her contemplation of the scenery. Well, I reflected, it wasn't *my* idea for her to be here. I asked her husband, "Did you ever have a romp with Ms. Campanula, Jake?"

"No," he said tonelessly. He gave the ball a tap. It tore across the green, missed the hole by at least three feet and dropped down the bluff back into the rough.

"Aw," Barbie said.

Jake Borrello straightened. His complexion was doughy, and from the look on his face and his grip on the putter I felt like he was deciding whether to break it over his knee or throw it at me. Instead, he exhibited remarkable self-control as he walked toward me and handed it out. "Nine iron," he said tightly.

I traded clubs with him gingerly and he skittered down the bluff to his ball. I backed out of the line of the shot and—hell of a coincidence—ran into Barbie Borrello, who made a giggling squeal and steadied me overly sensuously with one hand on my biceps and the other cradling my hip. I detached myself and stood rather primly to the side as Jake Borrello made an excellent chip that got his ball within two feet of the pin.

He made his beam at me as he traded clubs with me again. "I had nothing personal to do with Ms. Campanula," he said. "I think she's a very unstable young woman who's gotten fixated on me somehow and has started this little series of stunts. It's relatively common when you're in the public eye." He hoofed the bluff with me behind him and Barbie went to my left. "I could just ignore it, I suppose, but—"

Barbie interrupted, "But Jake is running for office and this woman is a potential threat. She must be stopped. That's what we're hiring you to do."

Borrello, ignoring us, bent over his ball and tapped it effortlessly into the cup. As he retrieved it and handed it to me, I said, "Has she made any demands upon you? Like 'Do X, and I'll stop pestering you'?"

"Nope. Not a thing." Borrello slid his putter into the golf bag and faced me, big tan hands on hips.

"Well," I said, taking a hit off my cigar, "then the only way to stop her is intimidation, and the only kind of intimidation that really works is physical. You follow?"

"We understand each other perfectly," Borrello grinned.

"Not really." I squinted, took a last puff on the cigar and dropped it on the turf. "I don't do strong-arm, at least haven't for years, not this kind."

"But such services can be purchased, I presume," Barbie Borrello said softly from very near me.

"I got a right to pursue my interests unmolested," Borrello said. "I've tried reasoning with her and have gotten nowhere. The woman is clearly irrational. I won't have her complicating my political campaign at this point. Have I made myself clear?"

I looked up into his flat, placid face and said quietly, "I suppose I can job it out."

"Perkins, I want to know what time it is, not how to build a watch. Barbie?"

She reached into the waistband of her hot pants and handed me a folded wad of paper something. I looked down into the smug face of Ben Franklin. The wad was crisp and thick, and warm and moist from Barbie Borrello's body.

"One thousand dollars now," Jake Borrello said, "and another thousand, payable in cash thirty days after my last contact with Becky Campanula. Fair enough?"

I'm pretty slow, so it took me nearly three seconds to decide that it was.

††††

I was trying to coax the defunct alternator out of my friend Carole Somers' car, a station wagon of foreign, mixed and highly questionable parentage, when my wireless telephone rang.

I wrapped a rag around my greasy hand, walked over and picked up the phone. It was Dickie Dukes, and even though the sound reproduction of these new phones is horrible, I had no trouble understanding him; his resonance would make Pavarotti envious. "Do me any good, Dickie?"

"No dice, man. Cocky bitch. Said to shove it. Laughed me outta the place."

I puffed, staring blankly over the wide grassy courtyard of Norwegian Wood. "Guess it's time for phase two, huh, Dickie?"

Dickie Dukes was brisk, as always. "What'll it be, fingers, or a knee or two, or what?"

"Let me think."

"How about the face? Can I have the face?"

"*Wait* a minute."

"You got no mind for plannin', man. Shoulda figured I might run into this. I *ast* you if I had the remodeling option open to me before going in there. 'Oh *no*,' you says. 'Just try to scare her first.' Had to drive all the way over here to Dynamite Park 'fore I could find a phone. Christ!"

Everybody's a critic. "She got stairs in that joint?"

A pause. "Yeah, she do."

"Well, show her those."

"Ain't no flair to *that*, man."

"Results matter more to me than style. Get rolling, Dickie, and report back to me."

"Oooohkay, boss. Be—"

Glass exploding. A booming in the distance. A scream, Dickie's scream, and then silence, except for the TONK TONK TONK of the phone receiver tapping on the glass window of the phone booth somewhere in Dynamite Park.

††††

The meat wagon was pulling away—no siren or light—by the time I found the place. It was one of those big pull-offs by the river practically in the center of Dynamite Park and, like it is most bright summer days, it was jammed with teenage kids and their vans, motorcycles, tape players and marijuana clouds. Aside from myself, the only strangers were the five or six uniformed and plainclothes police officers milling around the phone booth at the foot of the dead-end.

From my Mustang I could see that the phone booth, probably the last glass-enclosed booth left in the state of Michigan, had been blown apart, from the looks of it by a shotgun. Blood-soaked glass lay in shards on the concrete and reflected wetly from the grass in the afternoon sun. Forensics people were poking with intent faces through the debris; investigators had cornered a handful of scroungy teenagers over against the side of a city of Detroit black-and-white, and none other than Elvin Dance, chief of homicide, Detroit police detective bureau, was directing the madness from his perch on the front fender of his plain Chrysler LeBaron.

When I saw Dance, I mashed my Mustang into reverse, but he spotted me and shouted, "Perkins! Park it and walk your ass over here, boy."

I parked, disembarked, and strolled over there. Elvin slid down onto the pavement, straightened his coat and glowered at me. He's a short, heavily muscled bull of a man, skin a rich black, hair shaved so short his skull gleams, suit green and natty, eyes mean as a snake, or maybe that's only when he sees me.

"What you doing, cruisin' for poon, Perkins?"

"Nah, I'm not in the market for herpes, Elvin."

He let the silence drag. Cops know that people with something to hide tend to yak on and on, explaining themselves when there's really no reason. So I waited him out.

"So what you doing here, boy?"

I shrugged. "Was taking a short cut down Haynes Drive over there. Saw the black-and-whites and the meat wagon. You know me, Elvin; nosy."

"Yeah, I know you, Perkins, shuckin' and jivin'."

I spread my hands. "I'm a world-class rubbernecker, that's all. Some crime in that?"

He wasn't buying. "What's this all about here?"

I squinted toward the wrecked phone booth. "I'll take a wild stab at it. Looks like maybe a shotgun got somebody over there, judging from the glass and the blood and stuff."

"The somebody," Elvin Dance said deliberately, "was one Dickie Dukes. Know him?"

"Sure I know him. Strong-arm, isn't he?"

"*Wasn't* he. Unless Wayne County General got real good at head reattachment, Dickie ain't gone be strong-armin' or hypin' or much of anything else any more."

"I didn't know he was a hype," I said.

Elvin Dance leaned back against the fender. Stone-sober cop weariness appeared on his face. "A real pro job, looks like. Dickie was on the phone; kids saw a man with a duffel bag walk right up to the booth. They didn't see no gun, must of been sawed-off, hid in the bag. Two shots, gut and face, right through the phone booth windows. Hit man kept right on walking up the hill, through them woods. Must've had a car waiting there on Joy Road."

"Slick," I agreed.

Elvin Dance pulled a pack of Kools out of his coat pocket and shook one into his lips. I lighted it with a wood match, which I also used to light a cigar for myself. Elvin said softly, "I hate this goddam park. Sucker runs on for miles along the river here, couple thousand acres of woods and trails. Become a kids' party joint this year. You know, ex-partner of mine was up at the Soo last weekend, three- four-hundred miles away, saw a bumper sticker on a car there says, 'I Party at Dynamite Park.' Families don't come no more, it's become a place where bad things can happen, and usually do."

He jerked a thumb toward the phone booth. "Like *this*." He glared darkly at me. "You sure you don't know nothing about it?"

"Nope."

He grunted. "Well, in that case, it's a goner. This type of deal, either we break it right away or forget it. You make tracks away from here, Ben, while I go put this thing in the someday maybe file."

†††

That Dickie Dukes was hit right after visiting Rebecca Campanula was troublesome enough—gunplay always troubles me unless I'm the one doing it—but what troubled me even more was the nature of the hit. In the parlance, it was an "open-air" job, solid pro all the way from location to weapon to getaway. Dickie Dukes was no Florence Nightingale, but his action was nowhere near heavy enough to bring him to the attention of the guys best equipped to carry out this kind of quick, clean execution.

And I found it an incredible coincidence that the hit happened right after he tried to strong-arm Campanula. Which meant that if he wasn't involved with the professionals, maybe Campanula was. Question was, why was she involved. And what, if anything, did it have to do with Borrello?

I had to get to the bottom of those questions before moving on Campanula again, so I did some asking around. My kind, generous, public-spirited paid informant Kenny Slingluff, a middle-management grunt at Michigan Bell, pulled the file on Campanula and gave me the name of her employer: Ritchie Enterprises, Box 36682, Detroit. Meant nothing.

I also put out an inquiry through contacts in Detroit's underground intelligence network—yeah, buddy, there is one, and it's faster and more accurate than the Eyewitness News Team—for anyone with information on one Campanula, Rebecca.

A couple days later I got a call from Amos Walker, a private detective over in Hamtramck. He told me he didn't know Campanula, but a client of his had worked with her at Borrello's insurance company, and might have something helpful to say. We agreed on the fee—which wasn't money, simply my promise to lend him a hand sometime, legal tender in this line of work—and Walker set up a meeting for me with his informant at the Donut Hole shop on Fort Street in Lincoln Park.

I'd run into a dead-end trying to track down Ritchie Enterprises, Campanula's employer of record. Not in the phone book, not in the crisscross, not in the Chamber of Commerce or BBB registrations. So this thin, slender, secondhand lead of Walker's was going to have to help me, or else I'd have to go straight at Campanula and maybe end up at the wrong end of a shotgun like the unlamented, and very late, Dickie Dukes.

†††

She was a big, chubby, vivid redhead whose face showed evidence of a long-standing friendship with the grape. She was in her mid-forties, wore lots of rings and had her hair poufed back in one of those old-fashioned beehive styles. She wore jeans and an old Teamsters Local 299 windbreaker, and she huddled over the small table, a steaming cup of black cupped in one large hand and a fistful of half-eaten donuts in the other.

She started by telling me that Amos Walker was a nice man who'd helped her out once, and she was glad to do anything he asked—which was, apparently, to spill her guts to me.

"What's your name?" I began as I got a cigar going.

"Gayle," she said in a husky voice.

"Last name?"

She smiled, showing miles of red lips. "Unspecified."

"Unspecified!" I grinned. "What nationality is that?"

"Survivor."

"Good breeding." I drank some coffee. "What's the book on Campanula?"

"Sweet Becky Campanula," she laughed richly.

"Meaning what."

"Oleo legs," she answered through a mouthful of doughnut. "Smooth and easily spread."

"Like for who?"

"You look like a busy man, so I'll save you some time by saying that the mail boy at the insurance company was the only one *not* getting it."

My coffee was gone and I waved for the waitress. "I take it, then, that Jake Borrello was on the hit parade?"

"Very definitely. Among other transgressions."

"Such as?"

The waitress dropped off a fresh jug of coffee, took Gayle Unspecified's order for a half-dozen cherry-filled, and scooted away. Gayle leaned toward me, bringing me within the effective range of her dime-store scent. I covered it up by puffing extra hard on my cigar. The woman said, "You ever hear the carrot story?"

"This a dirty joke?"

"Sort of," she giggled. "Mister Borrello was always dieting. Weird diets—carbohydrates, starch-free, Cuppa Soup—stuff like *that*, you know? Once he went on carrots. Yeah! Carrots! Skipped his meals, munched carrots all the time. Gnawed on 'em so much his hands turned orangeish, sorta. 'Bugs' Borrello, the staff started calling him."

I wanted to follow up on the comment about transgressions. "This leading somewhere, Gayle?"

"Hold your horses, bud." Her doughnuts came. She grabbed two, squeezed them together and bit, smearing her mouth with jelly. When she'd swallowed enough to breathe, she went on furrily, "He started walking around the office with a carrot stub hanging out of his mouth, like a cigar. One day in the middle of a staff meeting, Ms. Becky Campanula went up to him and bit the carrot right off. And chewed it. And swallowed it. You shoulda seen the look on his face. After we *knew* something was going on."

No doubt, but who cared? "Transgressions, Gayle."

The half-dozen doughnuts were gone. Gayle inhaled her coffee, set the mug down, wiped her smeared mouth primly, and said, "Aside from Sweet Becky, plenty. Like, fudging his expense reports. Unauthorized trips at company expense. Ladies other than Becky; he wasn't even faithful to *her*. Stuff like that. The guy was in business for himself."

My mug was almost empty, the coffee about as cold as this lead. "Any involvement with the gentlemen in suits? Either Borrello or Campanula?"

She tossed the wad of napkin down suddenly. "I wouldn't know about that. I was only a typist, Mister Perkins."

I stared wearily at her then fished out a five and tossed it on the table. "Get yourself another half-dozen, for the road." I rose.

"Thanks, Mister Perkins!" she said cheerfully. "I sure hope Mister Borrello isn't in any kind of trouble. He's such a nice man. I'm going to vote for him. Aren't you?"

†††

So Borrello was no angel. I didn't care about that. My job was to get Becky Campanula off his back. I wasn't going to try another Dickie Dukes routine till I knew for sure who was backing her. The only lead I had left was Ritchie Enterprises, whoever *they* were.

The next morning I strolled into the Grand River Avenue post office promptly at eight A.M. and took up watch within sight of Post Office Box Number 682. Mission: intercept whoever retrieved the mail and follow him to Ritchie Enterprises.

Just after ten o'clock, a guy opened the box and took out the mail. My excitement died when I saw him take the mail from a dozen other boxes as well. A paid courier service, I realized; hired to pick up the mail and deliver it to his customers. I didn't even follow him. I had no way of knowing which of his stops was Ritchie Enterprises, unless I got real lucky.

So I found a stationery store on McNichols, bought a bright red nine-by-twelve envelope, addressed it to the President of Ritchie Enterprises, and mailed it at the Grand River post office.

The next morning, the courier showed up at ten sharp and retrieved the mail, which included my empty red envelope. I got on his trail. There followed a boring four-hour tour of Detroit. I watched him with binoculars at each stop, looking for the red envelope as he sorted and delivered the mail.

Finally, he delivered my envelope, along with a wad of other stuff, to a mansion on Jefferson Avenue in Saint Clair Shores. I sat there in my Mustang, stupefied, as he drove away. I knew that house.

†††

Art Drinkard stared at me as I slid two C-notes along the bar and left them before his fat little hands. "Who do I have to kill?" he asked in his scratchy, shrill voice.

"Nobody," I said easily. "Just take some pictures for me."

"Oo," he said. He adjusted his thick tortoise shell glasses and licked his prominent lips. "Pictures is what I do, Perkins." He glanced at me warily. "This isn't another one of your kick-in-the-door, 'Get your pants on now' jobs, is it?"

"We call 'em domestic matters. No, it isn't one of those."

"'Kay." Art Drinkard signaled to Bill, Under New Management's evening bartender, and Bill supplied us with another round of Stroh's. "Gimme the poopy."

"You know Dynamite Park?"

"Yeah." Drinkard downed half his beer, throat bobbing.

"There's that dead-end just south of the Newburg cutoff. Late night make-out site. East of that, off Joy, there's a bluff that looks down on the dead-end."

Art Drinkard finished his beer, which was a good thing because, the way he was sweating, he had a lot of liquid to replace. Only guy I know who can put away a six-pack and never hit the head. "I been by there."

"Tomorrow afternoon you set up with a tripod and telephoto lens on that bluff. When I pull into the dead-end with my car, you get a couple miles of shots of me and whoever's sitting in the passenger seat." I gave him some additional instructions.

Drinkard bit his lip and studied his thumbnail. "You're driving what, '71 Mustang convertible, blue?"

"Yeah. And I want nice clear, crisp shots of me and the other party, then you do just like I told you."

Art Drinkard's fat hands closed around the bills, compressed them into a spit wad, and made them disappear. "You're too generous," he wheezed.

"Top pay for top work, Art," I answered.

†††

Becky Campanula's Dodge Aries broke down half a mile from her apartment, on Inkster Road just north of the Jeffries. I pulled up behind her as she got out and strode up to her as she fought her way through a cloud of steam to her hood. "Looks like you got a problem, ma'am."

"Overheated!" she hollered over the noise of the rush-hour traffic darting around us.

I popped the hood and winced as superheated steam charged from the radiator into my face. I coughed and said, "Something screwed up in the radiator," I said.

"Oh Christ!" she snapped. "Can you give me a ride somewhere?"

Better and better. "I'd be delighted." We got into my Mustang and rolled away.

Rebecca Campanula was maybe 35, a tall, limby lady with a sharp nose, pale blue eyes, and knowing, ruthless mouth. Her rich chestnut hair was probably quite long when it wasn't done up like it was now, braided in a rope and wound around her head, with odds and ends sticking out and bangs arcing over her patrician forehead. She wore a pale green sleeveless one-piece dress that went down just to her well-shaped knees. Her body was a sexually definitive statement, reclining languidly there in the bucket seat of my Mustang as we drove.

I'd bet myself that she wouldn't talk till we got to Haynes Drive, and I nearly won. We were just north of there when she said, "Hey, friend, you just passed a gas station. Turn around."

"I don't think so, Becky."

I felt those cold blue eyes on me. "Who are you?" she asked coldly.

"Your kidnaper, bitch. Now shut up and be quiet." I wheeled onto Haynes Drive and kicked into fourth, heading for the entrance to Dynamite Park.

She sounded amused. "My kidnaper?"

"Yeah. You don't think your car just up and broke down by magic back there, do you?"

"Didn't it?" she retorted.

"Hell no. Put a pound of plaster of Paris in the radiator and say goodbye to the water pump. Old gag, works every time."

We wheeled into Dynamite Park. The narrow blacktop road was lined with pickups and vans and cars, the picnic areas cluttered with Frisbee throwers, picnickers, gangs of kids. I reached to my dash and hit a button, killing the soft Springsteen that had been playing from the big speakers on the rear deck.

Becky Campanula shifted in her seat, crossing one well-made leg over the other, which, quite consciously I'm sure, hiked her dressed up her thighs a couple of inches. "Men always *have* gone to extreme lengths to get dates with me."

"Yeah?" I asked. "Sorry, I'm spoken for. This little meeting is designed for me to find out about you and Jake Borrello, and what gives with all that."

The traffic lightened up past the midpoint of Dynamite Park, and in a minute I pulled into the dead-end by the Newburg cutoff and parked at the end. I shut off the motor, leaving the key in the accessory position.

Becky said coldly, "You know who Steve Ritchie is?"

"Vaguely," I lied.

"If you *really* knew, you wouldn't toy with me."

"Why?"

"A man messed with me a couple days ago, and I made one call to Mister Ritchie and the man got blown away in this very park, bud. That answer your question?"

"I want to know about Borrello," I said stolidly, staring straight through the windshield at the bluff.

I felt her leaning very close to me. "Mister Ritchie and his friends—and if you don't know who *they* are, you may find out very soon—support Borrello's opponent in the election. They're paying me to harass Borrello. Keep him edgy and worried so he makes mistakes. Simple job, but important. Important enough to Mister Ritchie that, if I make one phone call about you, you'll find out what the bottom of Lake St. Clair is like. Permanently. You read me, buster?"

I looked at her then dropped my eyes. "I didn't know it was anything like that," I said. "Listen, um—I'll drop you off at the cabstand, and we'll forget about the whole thing, okay?"

"You'll drive me back to my car," she said icily, "and get it running again, and *then* maybe I'll consider not sending Mister Ritchie's boys after you. But only maybe. Now drive."

I obeyed her orders precisely. When her car was running and she'd driven away, I popped the cassette out of my dash, slid it into a pre-addressed container, and dropped it into the mail chute at the Redford post office. Only then, as I headed for home, did I light a cigar and relax, just a little.

†††

I was picking up my mail, two mornings later in Marge's office at Norwegian Wood when a pair of Mister Ritchie's hired guns showed up.

It was a Mutt and Jeff team: the tall guy was older and thin, the short guy was younger and stocky. They wore dark suits, had dark hair and five o'clock shadows, and the senior man wore a gap-toothed smile. "Mister Perkins? Why don't you come with us."

Marge, Norwegian Wood's sales manager, glanced nervously at me. I said, "Maybe I don't feel like it."

The young turk kicked Marge's office door shut with the back of his heel. The tall, older one produced an S&W .38 Centennial, pointed it at me, and said, "Don't make us get ugly."

Marge squeaked, covered her mouth, and looked at me with frozen eyes. I said with a resigned voice, "Sure, fellas. But I got to take some stuff with me for this meeting. Okay?"

They stared at me silently. I turned to Marge and said, "You still got that overhead projector and cassette player?"

She uncovered her mouth, revealing white lips, and pointed shakily at the credenza behind her. I walked to it as Mutt, the one with the gun, moved forward toward me. I said, "I'll go quietly, but I've got to be prepared." I rescued the heavy, bulky overhead projector from the credenza, along with the cassette player, then retrieved a couple of packages from my mail and said cheerfully, "Ready?"

The gunsels gave me doubtful looks as they shooed me out of Marge's office. We stepped out of the building onto Norwegian Wood's parking lot. I said to the senior man, "My suggestion is that you get someone with real authority to meet with me."

The young turk said, "Hey, Gangemi, we got a wiseass on our hands."

"Unless, of course, " I said casually, "Mister Ritchie wants to see some real ugly material about him appear in the papers this week."

The black Chevy Caprice at the curb was theirs. Gangemi, the older man, said sympathetically, "Listen, Perkins, we got our orders, just go along quiet and don't complicate it, okay? We're just a couple of working guys trying to get through the day, you know?"

The young turk opened the back door of the Caprice and said, "In there, wiseass."

"Okay," I said helplessly, tossing the overhead projector and the cassette player in ahead of me. "I feel sorry for you fellas. What I've got in these envelopes is also in a safe deposit box, and the keys to that box are in the hands of my attorney and an inspector with the Michigan State Police, with instructions to open the box and provide the contents to the newspapers should I, shall we say, turn up missing."

The men stared placidly at me. I sighed. "Sure, I'll be dead, but when the stuff hits the fan about Mister Ritchie, so will you. So do yourselves a favor. Take charge of your lives. Make a decision for yourselves. Show some executive judgment, why don'tcha."

Gangemi said to his partner, after a silence, "Watch him." He trotted back into the building. The young turk, who had the kind of upwardly mobile enthusiasm that's highly sought after in the corporate world, told me with great relish what plans were in store for me. I nodded a lot and ignored him, watching the doorway of Norwegian Wood's main building.

When Gangemi came back out, I knew what he was going to say. "Slight change of plans," he grunted to his disappointed partner. "Temporary," he growled at me over the seat. We roared away from there, with the young turk at the wheel, Gangemi riding shotgun, and me in the back with the projector, the tape player, a couple of envelopes, and a world-class case of nerves.

††††

They escorted me to the plush conference room of a large law firm in the Titanium Towers complex in Southfield. The room contained nothing but an oval-shaped mahogany table surrounded by plush chairs, a portable podium in the corner, and a retractable screen hanging against the far wall. Lights filtered indirectly from recessed fixtures in the ceiling. The place was empty and silent.

Gangemi said, "Drop the stuff and sit tight. I'll be right back." He left me and his partner to breathe air conditioning for a few minutes; then the door opened again and Gangemi came in behind a tall, hawk-faced, dark-haired man with fighter-pilot good looks. He held out his hand and grinned as we shook. "Rick Savastano, Mister Perkins, how are you?"

I matched his easy coolness as best I could. "I'm Ben, Rick. Real good, real good."

"Glad to hear it, Ben." Rick Savastano wore a gray vest, matching trousers and a white-on-white shirt with a burgundy tie whose knot was held forward by a gold collar pin. He had more bucks on his body than I have in my entire closet. He put a solicitous hand on my shoulder and asked, "You have everything you require for this meeting?"

"Brought my equipment and stuff with me. I'm all set."

"Can we get you any refreshment? Coffee? Soda? Maybe something stronger?"

"Thanks, no. We ready to talk?"

"Sure, Ben. Be right with you." He turned to the young turk. "Frank, would you excuse us? Tell my girl to hold my calls. Mister Gangemi and Mister Perkins and I will be busy for, oh, fifteen minutes or so."

Frank Whoosis nodded and backed out, shutting the door behind him quietly. I set up the overhead projector and the cassette player, plugged them in and turned them on, then opened the envelopes. One contained an unlabeled Phillips cassette, the other a wad of heavy plastic transparencies. While I made the arrangements, Gangemi took a chair between me and the door, and Rick Savastano took another halfway down on the other side of the table, propped one leg casually over the other, and cupped his hands at the back of his head.

When I was set, I said to Savastano, "I kind of hoped I'd be meeting Mister Ricci," intentionally using the pre-Anglicized pronunciation of his name.

"Steve couldn't make it," Savastano said apologetically. "He's been fully briefed, of course. Now, why don't you show us what you came to show us."

It didn't take long. The transparencies, which Art Drinkard had made from his black-and-whites, were just beautiful, showing me and Becky Campanula in the front seat of the Mustang, while our voices came with startlingly vivid fidelity from the speaker of the cassette player.

Me: "This little meeting is designed for me to find out about you and Jake Borrello, and what gives with all that."

Becky: "You know who Steve Ritchie is?"

Becky again: "A man messed with me a couple days ago, and I made one call to Mister Ritchie and the man got blown away in this very park, bud."

Becky yet again, her voice so real I could feel her sitting next to me: "They're paying me to harass Borrello. . . . Simple job, but important. Important enough to Mister Ritchie that, if I make one phone call about you, you'll find out what the bottom of Lake St. Clair is like."

At the end of the tape, I shut the overhead projector off and commented, "From what Mister Gangemi's friend Frank told me, my appointment today was with Lake Erie, not Lake St. Clair, but otherwise Ms. Campanula's comments were reasonably accurate, wouldn't you say?"

Rick Savastano shrugged. "I wouldn't know; I don't get involved in operations." He brought his hands down and cupped them before him on the table, leaning forward on his forearms, hawklike gaze on me. "The pix, I can see how that was done. How'd you tape her without her knowing?"

"My in-dash cassette system is a recorder, too. Uses the speakers as mikes. Comes in handy, sometimes."

"I should say."

To have something to do, I hit the rewind button on the cassette player and said, "I assume, Rick, that my appointment with Lake Erie is cancelled now."

Savastano sniffed and stared past my shoulder at the wall behind me, considering. "On what basis, Ben? You're here, and so are the transparencies and the tape. I anticipate retaining these and sending you on your way with Frank and Mister Gangemi, as planned."

I felt Gangemi's cold eyes on me as I laughed shortly. "What do you think I am, right off the boat? This stuff here, it's all copies. Like I told Gangemi, the originals are in a safe deposit box at this very moment. The keys to the box are in the custody of my attorney and an inspector with the Michigan State Police."

"Who?" Savastano asked sharply.

"Dick Dennehy. Special Investigations."

Savastano arched an eyebrow at Gangemi, who shook his head slightly.

I went on more soberly, "It's the old bit. Anything happens to me, anything at all, and the box gets opened and the contents go to the newspapers. There will follow lots of nice stories about Mister Ricci being involved in manipulating an election, not to mention the murder of Dickie Dukes."

"Such things can be managed, Mister Perkins."

"But why bother?" I leaned toward Savastano. "Is keeping Jake Borrello from being elected so important to Mister Ricci that he'd go through so much publicity and the hassle, on the account of a flaky dumb broad like Campanula? I know you guys; you operate on a risk versus return basis. While you had her doing your bidding with minimal risk, it was a paying proposition, but the equation has shifted, and you know it."

A long, long silence. If they heard my heart thumping, they gave no sign. Finally, Rick Savastano sat up straighter in his chair and said, "Okay, but what about you?"

"What *about* me?"

He smiled, showing no teeth. "What's to stop you from getting this information publicized anyway, just for sport?"

"I'm not into sport. I'm just a working lug trying to do my job. You stay offa me, I stay offa you. Fair enough?"

Savastano's face elongated, his eyes turning to slits. "Your *job?* Just how *did* you get involved in this, Ben?"

No reason not to tell him. "Jake Borrello hired me to get Becky Campanula off his case. No big deal."

Savastano smiled, showing teeth this time. "But you haven't *done* your job, Ben. Nothing about the arrangement we've agreed on gets Ms. Campanula off Borrello's case."

"Hm. Forgive my oversight. I'm assuming you'll take care of that little loose end for me."

†††

Jake Borrello's voice at the other end of the phone was hushed and respectful. "You couldn't have missed it. It's in this afternoon's *News.*"

"Haven't seen the papers," I answered. "My girlfriend's starter motor is shot and I've been—"

"Dynamite Park!" he interrupted. "They found Becky there. Strangled. Her body was bloated practically beyond recognition. She'd been in the river for days."

"Guess she won't be bothering you no more, huh, Jake?"

"I didn't hire you to kill her, Perkins!"

"And I *didn't* kill her," I answered impatiently.

"My God, this is just awful," he muttered.

I lost my temper. "Let me spell it out for you, Borrello. You hired me to get Campanula off your back, and as it turned out the only way I could do that was to use her as a patsy to get leverage on the people behind her. What happened to her is their way of dealing with patsies, that's all."

"No specifics, for God's sake! I don't want to know!"

"No reason for you to. Just stay in your squeaky-clean corporate world and write this whole thing off as your first close brush with the street, where bad things can happen and usually do."

"I didn't want her dead," he said sullenly.

"But say hey, she got dead anyhow. Tell you what. I won't lose any sleep over it if you won't, okay, Jake, old son?"

The scandalized silence stretched on for a full minute. Then Jake Borrello said, "In view of this development, I think I can see my way clear to waive the thirty-day waiting period we'd agreed to. You'll have your money this afternoon."

I did, too. Hand-delivered by an anonymous courier. In cash.

Jake Borrello won the election the following November. No one was more delighted than me. Sure, he's a crook, but at least he's *my* crook.

Afterword

Well, then: "Dynamite Park." So hardboiled I almost did not include it in this anthology. But hardboiledness aside, it's always had a certain resonance for readers, so here it is. I kind of like it; my only wish is that it had a bit more humor.

Dynamite Park itself is the euphemism I use for Hines Park, a metro Detroit greenbelt that spans the River Rouge its length from western Wayne County into the city of Detroit (where it becomes Rouge Park). Name change aside, it's depicted with reasonable accuracy, up to and including the types of people that once populated it. Since establishment of permanent sheriff department presence, Hines Park has become much more tame.

Borrello seems to have been a one-shot (Perkins's concluding comment notwithstanding) and leads a series of amazingly corrupt politicians peopling my stories. His carrot diet is based in fact; the man who tried it actually did have his skin turn orange as a result and, as it happens, he was pursued by a woman remarkably similar to poor Becky Campanula in every respect but her fate.

As for Barbie Borrello, she has not turned up again, though she should have. The mob scene is part of a thread that winds through the stories as well as the novels; I enjoy having Perkins push them to the point where you think he's blown it. Finally, Art Drinkard, a sort of human Smurf, is one of my favorite sidekicks, a handy guy to have around.

If anything, this story displays an unfortunate tendency of Perkins, at least in his younger years, to take on a job for money even when he's clearly not on the side of the angels. I think in cases like this he figures there *is* no angels' side, so what the hell. I'm pretty certain he would not calculate it quite that way today.

My Brother's Wife

Don't blame me for not spotting Marybeth sooner. The bar was crowded, I was on a case, and most people, private detectives included, don't notice people in places where they don't expect to see them.

The case was one of those generally dreary prospective-employee background things. I was with a woman named Angie in a bar called Rushing the Growler, a rompin' stompin' burger and beer joint in the city of Frederick, Michigan. Angie was an ex-squeeze of the investigatee. They'd broken up bad, she was eager to talk, and she was a lady who liked her drinks, so I asked her what she'd have.

"Three Hole Punch," she said to the bartender.

I lighted up a cigar and stared into Angie's dark eyes. "What in heaven's name is that?"

She smiled. "The latest thing, Ben. A shot of 151 Bacardi, a shot of dry gin, and a splash of Golden Grain, shaken with pineapple-grapefruit juice over rocks in a tall glass with a maraschino cherry on top."

The bartender set it before her. I swear I saw the cubes smoking. No problem loosening *her* tongue, I thought. I ordered a beer, turned to Angie to begin the casual questioning, and in the far corner of the bar, just visible around the edge of the high back of a booth, I saw Marybeth.

She sat across from a broad-shouldered young man with short, smooth black hair. They were alone, and they were talking, and they didn't see me.

I watched them as I absentmindedly probed Angie for information about my subject, information which, under the terrifying momentum of Three Hole Punch, she seemed glad to provide.

As we talked, I considered how perfect Rushing the Growler was for illicit meetings. Loud, crowded, smoky, big booths, lots of little alcoves. I was, after all, here on a somewhat illicit mission myself. The fact that it led to something more personal with Angie—albeit brief—is not important. I could do that. I wasn't married. Marybeth was. To my brother.

†††

Since I got the information I needed from Angie that night, turned in my report the next day and (not incidentally) got paid, there was no reason for me to go all the way back out to Frederick the next night. But I did anyhow.

Marybeth showed up about seven, with her young man in tow. They sat at a secluded corner booth and talked and drank for nearly two hours. She didn't notice me. I wondered what she'd have done if she had.

And I wondered what I was going to do about it. For the next couple of days, I made a brave, determined attempt to do exactly nothing. None of your business, Ben. Don't you have enough trouble of your own to handle, Ben? That routine.

But one thing I've never been able to do for very long is kid myself. I know my own cons too well. I'm a nosy bastard, is the point. Which is, probably, why I'm a detective. I wondered how other detectives dealt with this kind of situation. Have to bring it up at the next meeting of the Greater Detroit Nosy Bastard Club, private detective division.

A few nights later, I rolled over to the Ford assembly plant in Wayne. A big lazy moon hung high in the hot, black summer sky as I parked three spaces down from a gleaming, sky blue Ford Econoline van. I nervously smoked a cigar as I waited, leaning against the hood of my Mustang. A bell shrieked from the distant plant, signaling shift-end, and men and women poured out, fired up their cars, and got the hell out of there. After a couple of minutes my brother Bill Perkins came strolling down the lane toward his van. I raised a hand and he nodded and continued toward me, black lunchbox hanging from one hand.

Bill's eight years older than me. We don't look much alike. He's short, stocky, almost totally bald now, with a narrow face and big nose and squinting eyes. He's placid of face, calm of voice, a man of slow, totally predictable movements. He wore a green short-sleeved dress shirt, snug slacks, highly polished black loafers. "Hey, Ben," he said as he reached me.

"Bill," I nodded. "Buy you a beer?"

"Why sure." I pulled a cold six of Stroh's off the front seat, snapped two loose, handed him one, and popped mine. Bill set his lunchbox on the hood of the Mustang and opened his beer as I leaned an elbow on the ragtop and took a gulp. "What brings you out this way?" Bill asked.

Impossible to answer truthfully because I didn't know myself. I mean, I knew, but I wasn't going to blab about having seen Marybeth twice in a saloon with a stranger. I was, so to speak, sounding him out. I didn't know what I expected to get done here, which is a dangerous way to do business. Carole Somers, a trial lawyer acquaintance of mine, says that the cardinal rule of examination is: Don't ask a question unless you already know the answer.

"Haven't seen you in a while," was my lame answer.

"Ee-yeah. Couple-three months. We doing Stapfer on the Fourth again, right?"

"Sure." This was about the only tradition my family had left. When we were boys, our daddy and Uncle Dan always took us fishing on Stapfer Lake on the Fourth of July, which was a couple days off now. Bill and I continued the tradition even though Daddy died back in '63, and Uncle Dan was permanently disabled and living in a rest home (I mean, retirement community). "Uncle Dan coming along?" I asked.

"Talked to him yesterday," Bill answered. "Said he'd try." Uncle Dan hadn't come with us—had been physically unable to—for fifteen years. But we always invited him, and he always said he'd try.

I dropped my cigar on the dirty pavement and crushed it out with my boot. Over the rim of my beer can, I eyed my brother as I tipped beer into my mouth. His face was shrouded in shadow; his baldhead gleamed in the moonlight. He leaned silent, placid, solid as a bridge abutment. I groped for words, for the angle that, in my investigating work, usually came easily, and could think of nothing. Bill was my brother, but as adults we were strangers. The few conversations we had over the course of a year fell into well-worn, predictable patterns. Cars and tools and baseball and the old neighborhood, none of which could help me find out what I wanted (not necessarily needed) to know.

The parking lot was silent now, afternoon shift on their fast ride home through the dark, the graveyard gang starting their turn on the thumping, screaming, hot assembly line inside. Bill broke the silence. "Saw baby sister the other day."

He let the unasked question hang in the air. I hadn't seen Libby in two years, not since our Uncle Andrew died.

With just the slightest shrug, Bill sipped his beer and went on.

"Took off a lot of weight. Looking damn good now. She got her a job counseling in one of those weight-loss places. Doin' good."

I set my empty beer can on the ragtop, fetched myself a fresh one and, as I popped it, asked casually, "How's Marybeth?"

"Fine, thanks."

"Still working that job out there?"

"City of Frederick police. Right. Just a typist, but the pay's good. You know them civil service jobs."

"Pretty long drive, though."

"Oh well, I-94 straight out, not too bad." Bill drained his beer. "She's staying out at her sister's in Jackson for a few days. Having a little visit, drive to work's a lot shorter from there."

Bill absently drummed his empty beer can with his thick fingers. I asked, "'Nother one?"

"Naw, better roll, Ben. Thanks." He handed me his empty, picked up his lunchbox, and headed toward the Econoline with that slow, rolling walk that reminded me so much of Daddy. Over his shoulder he called, "The landing at Stapfer. The Fourth, six A.M. sharp. Got it?"

"Yeah, bro." I gathered up the empties, tossed them into the back of the Mustang, and got out of there.

Driving through the hot night, I thought about Marybeth staying at her sister's in Jackson. A visit? Or had she left Bill? Or had he thrown her out? And what about the guy she was meeting at Rushing the Growler? What the hell gives there, anyhow?

It was none of my business, but it didn't feel right. I'd have to look into it, keep an eye out, and if something needed fixing, I'd sure God have to fix it.

†††

It wasn't like I was between jobs and had nothing better to do. My big corporate client had six more job applicants who needed checking out, at five hundred per, cash money. Carole Somers had called that morning about a client in Wayne County jail, charged with murder, thought maybe I could help. The outdoor maintenance work at Norwegian Wood was getting pretty intense, this being the height of the summer, lot of work to schedule and ass to kick. But I did as little as I could get away with the next day, drove like hell to Frederick during the supper hour, and by dusk, about the time Marybeth arrived with her Mister Wonderful, I was ready.

My battered old Canon, loaded with a fresh roll of twelve-hundred-speed print, worked great. I shot up all ten frames, getting virtually every angle except from directly overhead, as Marybeth and the man leaned close together over the table, talking, laughing, drinking drinks, absorbed in each other. Then I strolled out of there, unobserved by both.

†††

I was back the next night, cameraless. I grabbed a stool at one corner of the bar and watched Marybeth and her swain as they went through the routine. The guy must have had a bladder of prodigious capacity, because it seemed like hours before he finally excused himself and went to the john. I followed him.

It was empty except for us. While the guy did his business at the far end, I busied myself combing my hair at the mirror, gambling that he was fastidious enough to wash up after. He was. I let him get his hands full of soapy lather before I said, "Think we can do some business, pal?"

He hardly glanced at me as he scrubbed. "Buzz off."

I shook my head regretfully. "Not good." I reached into my hip pocket, pulled out the nice, crisp, three-by-five color glossy, and dropped it on the aluminum shelf below the mirror in front of him. "That's what I'm selling," I said softly. "You interested?"

The picture was a tight shot of him and Marybeth, noses inches apart over the rough-hewn booth table in Rushing the Growler. I was quite proud of it. Good focus and composition, sharp and clear, with only available light yet.

He stopped scrubbing and studied the picture as the water rinsed his hands clean. He was a young fellow, younger than Marybeth—dark-haired with deep eyes and a thickly muscled, symmetrical, almost handsome face, the skin of which showed five o'clock shadow. He wore a light gray jacket, open-necked white shirt, and dark slacks. His tan could have come from the sun or a lamp, you just can't tell any more. He shut off the water and flicked the wet off his hands and straightened up to face me. He did not look happy.

I said: "For shame. See that ring on your finger? No, not the pinky ring, the one of the *next* finger there. That means you're married, remember? And so's she."

"What's your interest?" His voice was a toneless, husky whisper.

"Not financial, for once. It's just this. Get off her and stay off, and this goes no further."

He nodded, lips pressed tight over his white teeth. Then he said, "Now I'd like to show *you* something, friend. I'm going into my inside jacket pocket, real slowly, fingers only. All right?"

I was unarmed and had made no threats of violence, but I nodded. He reached inside his jacket, came out with a small black wallet, and opened it. The badge gleamed, an embossed picture-ID next to it. Donald Boltz, special agent, Michigan Bureau of Investigation. I said, with more assurance than I felt right then, "That supposed to mean something important?"

"You know," he said, "there's a thing called obstruction of justice. There's another called interfering with an official investigation. I could mangle you lots of ways, ways you haven't even heard of yet. You follow?"

"I'm scared to death here. Really I am. So humor me."

"I'm on police business," he answered, closing the wallet and putting it away. "There's no funny stuff between her and me. Now, if you don't mind my asking, who in the hell are you?"

For some deep instinctive reason, probably because he would have died laughing, I did not show him my private detective license. "Ben Perkins. I'm her brother-in-law."

Boltz stared at me. Then he dumped his head back and laughed at the ceiling, even white teeth gleaming in the fluorescent light. I stood impassively, hands folded in front of me, wanting badly for some reason to hit him very hard. When he recovered, he mused, "Isn't that a riot? Out of the way place like this . . . no suspicious eyes . . . her brother-in-law!"

"Yeah. Real thigh-slapper. What I'd like to know is, why is the MBI interested in Marybeth?"

He still smiled, but the humor had fled his eyes. "I don't have to waste my time explaining anything to you. She's your brother's wife, so fine; I've explained there's nothing personal going on, and that's all you need to know." Boltz's jaw tightened. "Don't cross my path again. I get upset really easily."

He walked past me, brushing intentionally close, to the door and then out without looking back. I stared at the space he'd left, remembering his casual yet high-quality and expensively tailored suit, his six-hundred dollar lizard-skin shoes, the gold pinky ring with diamond chips. For a policeman, Special Agent Donald Boltz seemed to pull down an abundance of disposable income.

†††

Dick Dennehy studied the picture through his aviator glasses. He snorted. "So. One of the glamor boys."

"How's that?"

Dennehy stared at me bleakly. He's a big, somewhat out of shape, grayish blond, wound tight with the cheerful malevolence of the career cop. He wore a gray suit—I believe he buys them by the gross at Kmart—and the inevitable Lucky straight-end smoldered from the fingers of the hand in which he held the picture. We sat in a booth at Pringle's, the Novi saloon in which we met once a week to straighten out the world.

Dennehy, eyes still on me, dropped the picture. "Glamor boys," he repeated. "I'm with the state police, remember? We're the ones who get called in on cases *after* these glamor-boy clowns with the 'Michigan Bureau of Investigation'"—he snarled the name—"screw them up."

"I get the picture." The barmaid expertly dropped another Signature and rum-and-coke on our table. "Thanks, Cindy," I said absently. "So," I said to Dick as he took a pull from his drink, "since apparently you state police boys don't get along with the MBI, can I assume there's no way you can find out what—or if—Boltz is investigating that involves Marybeth?"

Dick made a gleeful, crooked smile. "O ye of little faith! Sure I can, my spies are everywhere. Be glad to." He slipped the picture into his jacket pocket, fired up another weed, leaned forward on his elbows, and asked quietly, "You think he's doing the dirty deed to her?"

"Hell, I don't know, Dick."

"What'll you do if it turns out he is?"

"Don't know that, either."

"Huh. Now that we're clear on what you don't know, tell me: what *do* you know, Ben?"

"I know what I feel. I feel like Boltz is a bad act. I got a real bad smell from him. I don't trust him—I don't trust much of anything, anymore—but I trust that feeling." I stared over his shoulder at the window that fronted the place. "I feel like I have to watch out for Marybeth, at this point."

"You don't mind my saying so, I didn't think you and your family were particularly close."

"We're not." I met his eyes. "But I still watch out for them."

††††

The next morning I waited at the curb in front of the City of Frederick police department. At ten sharp, Marybeth Perkins came out the big revolving glass door, stopped on the steps, and scanned the street looking for me. She didn't spot me right away because I was right there in plain sight. Then she grinned, waved, and walked toward me. She passed a tall, gray-haired hump-shouldered uniformed man headed into the building and said cheerfully, "Good morning, Chief Harran." He nodded. I got a good look at him before he disappeared into the building. It isn't every day you get a good look at a chief of police, even of a small burg like Frederick. I was impressed.

It was a brilliantly clear hot day, and I had the Mustang's top down. Marybeth swung into the passenger seat with the agility of a dancer, slammed the door, and said, "I'm on break. I've got ten minutes. Drive." I fired up the motor and rolled away slowly.

Marybeth lighted an Eve cigarette from the dashboard lighter, hung her right elbow out the gunwale of the car, and looked at me. She was tan and freckled, thin and supple, whiplike, energized, and just Bill's height, which explains why she wore shoes like the flat brown dress sandals she had on today. Above that she wore pink snug slacks, and a ruffly white-on-white blouse with a gold pin inserted over her left breast. Her brown hair was a series of waves that ended neatly just above her shoulders. She had a keen mind and, sometimes, a sharp mouth, and I braced myself a little, wondering why she'd asked me to meet her here.

As I swung right on the Milan road, she said, "Don Boltz told me about your conversation with him."

"Look, it was strictly by accident I saw you two there—"

She interrupted with an edge in her voice. "You thought I was stepping out on Bill."

"The thought crosses my mind. But—"

She waved her hand. "Never mind. I'm going to tell you what Don told me not to tell anybody." She breathed deeply. "I'm helping the MBI investigate our department. On deep background."

I glanced at her. "Funny stuff going on?"

She drew on her cigarette and said quietly, "Worse than that, Ben. It's the chief. He's dirty. Dirty as can be. I've been there eight years, I've seen a lot, and it starts right at the top. Kickbacks, protection, grease, you name it. I looked the other way for a long, long time. Finally it got to be too much. So I contacted the MBI."

"Does Bill know?"

She stared at me, composing her thoughts, and said, "No. Don said not to tell *anybody*. Besides . . . well, you know Bill."

"Sure I do. But go on."

She took a last offhand hit from her half-smoked cigarette and flicked it away from the car, as I made a right into an old residential neighborhood and circled a big block, headed back toward the police station. "Bill's very . . . traditional. He's a quiet man. He absolutely detests confrontations. He avoids trouble. He's very dutiful, a good husband, Ben, but underneath he's scared. He worries and frets. He doesn't understand trouble, and he doesn't understand people who get into it. You know what I mean?"

It rang true. It explained part of the narrowness of my relationship with my own brother, the tight groove of conversation limited to cars and tools and baseball and the old neighborhood. Bill had really liked Charlotte, my first serious girlfriend, and never understood why I didn't marry her, had never married anybody. He'd never understood why I left my assembly line job to be a gofer for a union boss. During the endless federal investigation of my boss's racketeering and tax-evasion activities, in which I was a notorious and uncooperative material witness, Bill had refused to speak to me. He found my private detective work incomprehensible and never asked about it. For two guys who'd slept in the same room for better than ten years, we'd grown about as far apart as two people can get.

I right-turned on red onto a major street. The police station loomed ahead on the right, and I threaded through traffic toward it. Marybeth said pensively, "I don't make a habit of keeping secrets from Bill. But this time I have to, at least till it's over. And I'm asking you not to tell him, either, ever; you let me do it when the time is right. He's your brother, but I'm his wife, and I'm calling the shots. You've got to help me."

I stopped in front of the station and turned to her. "Of course I'll help you. Anytime, anywhere, anyhow."

She had her door half-open when she froze, turned, leaned over and kissed me. I gave her a squeeze and patted her back. She was warm and smelled good, but it was brother-sister stuff, no more. I eased her away and said, "Just one thing: I know the street, I know this work. Something doesn't feel right about this thing, this Boltz fellow. You take real good care, Marybeth. Stay in touch." I grinned. "*I* don't mind trouble. It's what I do."

She smiled, nodded, got out, and walked across the sidewalk toward the door. "I'll be watching out for you," I called.

†††

I held the tester up and examined the colors. The pH was right on, the chlorine a tad down. I threw three concentrated chlorine eggs into the skimmer, screwed down the lid, and headed back to Building One of Norwegian Wood as a battalion of kids carrying towels and flotation devices screamed out the side door toward the pool. The phone in the maintenance office was ringing when I got there. It was Dick Dennehy.

"You hollered?" he asked.

"I got the story already. MBI's investigating the Frederick P.D. It's dirty, top to bottom, the chief included. Right?"

"Wrong," he answered equably.

"No, I'm not. Marybeth told me all about it." I drew up short as Dick's meaning sunk in. "No word of it out there?"

"Nope. Nothing like that. Boltz is a soldier, nothing more. His thing is chop shops, bad-check artists, stuff like that. Listen, Ben, Boltz isn't senior enough to be doing something like a background inquiry into a police department. Even if he was, he wouldn't be doing it alone. There'd be a task force. And the state police would probably be doing it, not the MBI." Static whirred in the line for a second. "This smells like leftover fish, pal."

The phone receiver felt very warm and damp in my hand. I struggled to sound certain, and failed. "Maybe your contacts are uninformed."

"Don't underestimate me. My contacts are topsiders. They'd know, no matter how quiet it was. Whatever Boltz is up to, he's in business for himself."

"I don't like the sound of it."

"You'll like *this* even less. Boltz is thought of as an operator. A little fast, a little flashy, they think he's been off the reservation more than once, if you catch my drift, only they've never gotten the goods on him. No idea what his game is right now, but if I was you, it being the sister-in-law involved, I'd be extra careful."

"I'll do that, Dick. Thanks."

"Chalk up one to that instinct of yours."

"I'll take a bow later, if it's all right with you. You, uh, you want a piece of this, maybe?"

"Thought you'd never ask. Hell, I'd like nothing better than to find dirty hands on an MBI guy. Tell you what. In this deal, the Michigan State Police is at your service. You just let me know, and we'll, like, charge over the hill to the sound of bugles, flags streaming."

†††

Fortunately, it was a weekend. Everything was under control at Norwegian Wood, and my corporate client didn't expect progress on his applicants till Monday. So I had plenty of time for real excitement: following Donald Boltz around.

He worked at the MBI substation in Adrian. He lived in a swanky lakefront condo near there. He drove thirty-plus G's worth of loaded Audi 5000. I literally took up residence in my Mustang. I lived on drive-through Wendy's and Macs, washed up in gas station johns, slept stiff and cramped across the bucket seats, and tailed Boltz real smooth, real careful.

Problem was, he didn't go anywhere, or do anything, suspicious.

By Sunday evening I was a wrinkle-clothed, sore-muscled, aromatic, exhausted mess. And for it I had to show exactly nothing. And though he'd gotten in his car in the late afternoon and set off northeast, in the general direction of Detroit, my initially rising excitement dimmed considerably when he ended up at the Kmart in Westland. Kmart, for God's sake.

He knew what I looked like, so I hung way back from him in the crowded store as he strolled back to the men's clothes area and began browsing. I kept several rows of clothes between us, engaged with him in a long-distance, surreptitious dance of surveillance, while he leafed in a casual, almost bored fashion though racks of trousers and shirts and jackets. Suddenly—a little *too* suddenly, considering how lackadaisical he'd been operating till then—he selected a snappy green blazer and a pair of green-checked slacks and walked swiftly to a pair of freestanding dressing closets. The one on the left was closed and occupied; the other one was open, and he locked himself inside.

Crowds swirled around me. Muzak blared from loudspeakers, interrupted by an announcer pitching blue-light specials. Moms herded gaggles of kids. Teenage girls in cutoffs and tank tops floated along in a daze of nubile youth. I watched the closets for what seemed like a long time. Then the door on the left opened and a man stepped out. Tall, gray-haired, hump-shouldered, dressed casually in civilian clothes. Carl Harran, chief of police, City of Frederick.

He looked around quickly then walked away into the crowd while I stared at him, frozen.

After a minute, the right-hand door opened and Donald Boltz came out. His hands were empty except for a business-sized envelope that he tucked into his inside jacket pocket as he strutted toward the front of the store and away.

The single pay phone at the entrance to the store was being used by a skinny teenage kid in a whacked-off T-shirt and jogging shorts, grinning and whispering into the receiver as he leaned against the glass wall. I took the receiver away from him with one hand, handed him a quarter with the other, growled, "Call her back in a minute," then broke the connection and began to dial as he stared incredulously at me. The phone rang in my ear as the kid started to say something, but one look from me stifled him. Finally the ringing stopped and Marybeth said, "Hello?"

Thank God.

†††

We slogged ankle-deep up the steep incline of an enormous sand mountain. Beyond us sprawled the dunes and rubble piles and the cratered landscape of the abandoned sand and gravel quarry. The rusted snout of a huge crane reached high into the black sky. A couple of tin buildings, roofs sagging, stood sentry at opposite ends of the flat, sandy yard far, far below us. There was no one there. We stopped at the bluff and stepped back, panting from the exertion, Dick Dennehy most of all.

Jerry Mooney, Dennehy's squat, short, bull-shouldered partner (the term "brick outhouse" was coined with him in mind), adjusted the strap of his walkie-talkie, checked his watch, and said in a hoarse whisper, "Ten minutes to three. Ten minutes to three A.M., on the Fourth of July. Jesus Christ." He looked at me in the darkness. "Your theory better hold up, Perkins."

I retorted, "All I know is, Marybeth told me that Boltz told her to meet him here tonight. Something real fishy's going on, believe me. Anyhow, if I'm right, for you state police guys it'll be a dream come true. You'll catch an MBI guy engaged in a criminal act."

"He's right, Jerry," Dennehy said.

"Don't worry," I added. "If this works out, I don't want any credit for it, hear? It's your collar."

"*Our* collar?" Dennehy snorted. "Hear that, Jer?"

"I heard that. Hee-hee. *Our* collar. Right."

Dennehy checked the time. "Everybody in place?"

"Oughta be," Mooney answered. He slogged through the sand to the bluff, peered over, and said tensely, "Whoa. Here she comes."

Dennehy and I crawled to the bluff, flanking Mooney, and looked down. Marybeth's light-blue Escort sedan, lights off, rolled down the narrow, weedy, sandy lane from our right and parked next to one of the tin buildings.

Jerry Mooney whispered into his walkie-talkie. Dennehy kept his eyes on the woman, who wore a light poplin raincoat, as she got out of the Escort and stood alongside it, and got out his gleaming Colt Python. My heart was thumping as I pulled my .45 automatic from the waistband against my spine and cocked it. There was no need to work the action; I carried a live round under the hammer.

The woman leaned against the door of the Escort, face indistinct in the half-moonlight, layered brown hair flowing down to her shoulders. An engine hummed from our right, and a black Mercury sedan approached the tin building and stopped near the Escort. Its engine kept running as the driver's door opened and a man got out.

The moonlight caught the man's features and I said, "That's not Boltz! It's Harran!"

Chief Carl Harran wheeled, raised a .38 revolver over the roof of the Mercury, and shot the woman five times. The flares from the snout of the revolver flashed well in advance of the boom of the shots. The woman went down.

"Let's do it!" Mooney shouted into the walkie-talkie. As the three of us charged over the bluff and down the sandy slope, a siren wailed to our right, and two state police cars roared up the lane toward the chief, headlights illuminating him as he jerked his head around wildly. From our left, another police car swerved on the sandy lane toward him, cutting off that escape route. He hurled his empty revolver away and ran diagonally to our right. I skidded to a halt, dropped to a crouch, and fired three times. Even in the hands of a marksman, which I am not, the .45 auto is ineffective at that range, but the plumes of sand from the heavy slugs bursting around him were convincing, and he skidded to a halt and sprawled into the weedy sand. The cars stopped, the doors flung open, and the policemen converged on him, weapons extended warily.

Breathing hard, I dropped my gun hand to my side and walked over to the Escort. Up this close, the woman looked little like Marybeth. She was on her feet, the bullet-riddled raincoat open, showing the heavy pleated armored vest. I grinned at her and she grinned back and gave me the thumb's up. Behind me, a woman's voice called, "Ben?" I turned and Marybeth Perkins, who'd been in the back of one of the state police cars, waved and ran into my arms so hard she nearly knocked me down. I held her, she held me, and we said nothing; but when she finally stepped back, my cheeks were wet from her tears.

Dick Dennehy came up to us as Jerry Mooney directed the loading of the chief into one of the cars by the other officers. "Harran's singing like a bird," he told us grimly. "Boltz sold Marybeth out to Harran as an informant in return for ten big ones. Jerry 'n' I are going to pick Boltz up now. Fun, *fun!* Wanna come along?"

"I do," Marybeth said.

I checked my watch. "Not me, thanks. I got a date."

"At four in the morning?" Dick demanded.

"Fishing," I grinned. "See y'all!"

†††

It was five after six and the sky was brightening fast when I arrived at the landing of Stapfer Lake. Bill's green seventeen-footer with its Chrysler outboard bobbed in the water at the end of the landing. His blue Ford Econoline van dragged the empty trailer that was parked in a V on the gravel lot. Bill Perkins himself sat patiently on the rear bumper of the van, wearing a narrow-brimmed canvas hat, chambray shirt, dark blue slacks and knee-length rubber boots. He looked at me calmly as I walked up to him. "You're late," he said.

"Sorry."

He rose and we walked down to his boat. It was fully equipped with two sets of tackle, a full bait buckle, nets and anchors and extra gas and oil and all the rest. Good old thorough Bill. As he made ready to cast off the boat, I said, "Reckon Uncle Dan's not coming, huh?"

"Reckon not."

I climbed clumsily into the boat. "One of these days, Bill."

He gripped the transom, dug his boots into the wet sand, shoved the boat out into the water, and climbed nimbly in. "Yeah, bro. One of these fine days."

We fished all day, didn't catch much, and talked about cars, tools, baseball, and the old neighborhood. Back at his house, we devoured Marybeth's terrific steak dinner, and I got home early. I don't know if she ever told Bill the Harran/Boltz story or not. I've never asked. It's none of my business.

Afterword

This one once again presents Ben with a mix of family dynamics and crime. He's again not hired by anyone, but is confronted with a situation that imperils someone he cares about. True to form, he deals with it on his own; the help he gets from the state police is motivated by their own self-interest, not because Ben's state cop friend goes out on a limb for him.

Frederick, Michigan, is fictional. I suppose I invented it because at story's end its police chief is a crook, and one wouldn't want to imply that about a real town, no sir. Marybeth Perkins is introduced here and enjoyed a solid run in Ben's life. I always thought he was just a little too devoted to her for his own sake, but one thing's for sure: she's a better sibling to Ben than either of his own.

Jerry Mooney, Dick Dennehy's state police partner, makes his sole appearance in a Perkins story here. He also appears with Dick in a non-Perkins short story.

For the most part, as I review these stories, it seems to me they aren't terribly dated. There are, of course, exceptions. In this one, Ben has to use a pay phone.

How quaint.

Perfect Pitch

The kiddie cop sucked in his gut, thrust out his chest, and imitated an adult male voice. "Okay, bud, that's far enough. Turn around and take a walk."

I gestured at the pizza boxes stacked at my right. "Domino's, partner. 'We deliver,' and all that."

The kid squared his bony shoulders under his wrinkled blue uniform shirt. "Nobody goes in without authorization."

I eyed him, from the gold braid on his Kmart cop cap and the intimidating private-security insignia on his shoulders to the Sam Browne belt (a Sam Browne belt, in Detroit yet, for God's sake) and the holster that housed cuffs, walkie-talkie, and a very official looking .38 Police Positive. Stifling the impulse to ask if he had a permit to carry that thing, I fished a yellow flimsy out of my shirt pocket and scanned it. "Delivery for Jerry Mattson, Commando Studios, Seven Mile at Evergreen. Two deluxes loaded, with anchovies. Gah! This the place?"

The kid's expression changed from ersatz Eastwood to honest, innocent relief. "Oh. Well, okay. Take that door there, go down the hall. Studio's on the left. Mattson's the drummer." He turned and swaggered past me, creaking from all the leather and jingling so loud I was tempted to check him for spurs.

Inside the door was a long, windowless, dim, tiled hall. A trash barrel being handy, I dropped the empty pizza boxes into it without a glance and walked jauntily to the end, where an unlocked door gave me entrance to the studios.

There were a lot of people in there to notice me, but no one did. On the wall to my right was a broad glass window, behind which sat a bearded, skinny fellow with headphones holding down his short, curly hair. He was virtually surrounded by the blinking lights and turning tapes of electronic equipment. The room in which I stood was a crowded, layered maze of wires, microphones, conduits, musical instruments, and people, most of whom I knew at least by sight. You couldn't have been a rock and roll fan from the early sixties on without knowing the faces of the Sidewalk Commandos.

The hulking, bearded Jerry Mattson lounged behind a Ludwig drum set to my left. Bill Cuffaro and Gil Gould, the Mutt and Jeff of guitarists, stood in front, instruments at the ready. Lon Maretsky, pony tailed bass player, leaned against the back wall. In the corner near the glass window, facing me, was a Steinway grand piano with the tall, outdoorsy Ellen Long standing in the curve, a baritone saxophone draped in front of her. Facing Long, sitting at the keyboard, was the short, round-faced, impassioned singer, group leader, and principal composer: Lisa Goodnight.

I leaned against the wall and, with my right hand, fished my .45 automatic from my waistband and held it out of sight behind my back.

A voice issued from an intercom, and the lips of the man behind the glass moved: "Rolling tape."

Lisa Goodnight said, "Okay, let's call that B, and from here it's a bounce-down to A-seven, people, with a nice tasty break from Jerry, then we back into the basic with vocal rolling on top. Three, four."

The instruments commenced on cue, filling the smallish room, guitars and piano and bass underneath; then after a fluttering break from Mattson, Lisa Goodnight began to sing. I honestly don't remember the words. I was gripped in place, the only realities in the room the music of her voice and the warm steel of the .45 in my hand.

After sixteen bars the guitars trailed off, but the piano continued, and Lisa Goodnight, leaning close to the bulbous microphone, delivered four more lines then quit, sagged back, panted. The other group members stared at her.

"Rolling tape," the engineer said metallically.

Goodnight snapped, "I *know* we're rolling tape. You don't have to keep reminding me."

Ellen Long leaned toward Goodnight. "Where'd *those* lyrics come from? I mean, the sheets don't—"

"Who knows?" Goodnight answered. "Hope we caught 'em. We rolling tape?"

"Rolling tape," came the voice.

Good a time as any. I stood forward from the wall, raised my .45 and pointed it two-handed at Goodnight, sighting down the long steel length of the weapon at the half-inch section between her upper lip and nose.

Cuffaro and Gould, who'd been talking quietly, stopped and stared at me.

"You're dead, bitch," I said, and fired.

†††

Jeannie Riley, my current "interest," as the gossip columns would say, loves word games. One favorite is making words out of the three-letter segments of license plates. Another is coming up with one word that describes something completely.

Her word for Arthur Brooks, whom she met once, is "dour."

I thought of that as I sat across from his area-code-size mahogany desk a couple of days before my visit to Commando Studios. Arthur Brooks is pushing sixty, thin and short with a square, grim face fronted with rimless glasses and topped with white, crewcut hair. He owns fifty three-piece suits, all of them first-rate navy blue, and six hundred shirts, all of them white-on-white and built of a material invulnerable to the ravages of wear. His eyes have the cold, accepting look of a man who had dealt with much in his years of representing people with things to hide, including members of the union for which I once worked way back in them bad old days.

The spines of hundreds of law books stared at us as we exchanged banalities. Then he said, "The Sidewalk Commandos."

I looked long at him. "Decent band, least while J.D. Fredericks was alive. Haven't recorded since then."

"Lisa Goodnight."

I shrugged. "Good singer. I hear Fredericks and her were tight. She's supposedly running the show now. You want to know more, check the latest *Rolling Stone*."

"They're working here in Detroit now, you know."

"Sure. Goodnight's from here, Dearborn Heights as I recall. So after Fredericks died she moved the group from New York to here."

I was starting to get impatient, and Brooks picked up on it. "Your assignment," he said coldly, "is Lisa Goodnight. I want to know what gives."

I got out a short cork-tipped cigar and took my time lighting it with a kitchen match struck on my thumbnail. I certainly could use the work—between my jobs as an apartment maintenance supervisor and private detective, I just barely keep financially afloat—and I knew Brooks was good for the tariff, but I'm funny; I like to work toward more specific objectives than simply finding out what gives.

But lawyers in general, and Arthur Brooks in particular, are not an especially forthcoming breed. To give myself time to think I asked, "Got any aspirin?"

He blinked. "Certainly. Got a headache, Ben?"

"Nope. Had two wisdom teeth removed yesterday."

He opened his drawer. "Little old for that, aren't you?"

"I put off pain as long as I can, and now I'm glad I did." I *was* hurting. My lower jaw felt like it had two craters in it in which helmeted men worked industriously with picks.

Brooks tossed a tin of Anacin onto his desk. "Didn't they prescribe anything for pain?"

"Sure. Tried one. Made me exhibit symptoms of senility."

"You mean people could tell the difference?"

I looked sharply at Brooks and saw that the dourness had given way to a big, toothy, delighted smile that radiated from his entire being. I grinned, took a big pull on my cigar, and said, "You're a riot, Art, I always said that. Now. What's the deal on Goodnight? Come on, pal, give over."

The aura of humor was gone in a flash. He leaned forward, forearms on the edge of his desk, and slowly rubbed ten fingertips together. "I'm her personal attorney. It's low-volume business, the kind of g.p. work I don't normally handle and certainly don't need; but I was her father's lawyer so I've kept the account. Call me sentimental."

Like hell. "Okay."

A light on his phone began to blink soundlessly. Brooks ignored it. "She brought the band here last summer, about three months after J.D. Fredericks died in New York. I've seen her two or three times. Frankly, Ben, I've become more troubled each time. Certainly she's in mourning—she was close to Fredericks, as you know—but she doesn't seem to be pulling out of it. To be blunt, as her attorney and a friend of her father, I've become concerned that she's not competent to take care of herself. My sources of information are, for all practical purposes, nil. I need to have someone I can trust, someone with impeccable judgment, to get close to her, assess her and her situation and, to the greatest extent possible, soive whatever problems she has."

"You got money to burn, huh, Art?"

"Whatever it takes." The finger rubbing stopped. "I have the sick feeling something is terribly wrong with her, Ben."

I looked sharply at him, surprised at the tension and depth of feeling in his courtroom-trained voice. I shrugged. "Well, okay, okay. Couple-three days, I can size the thing up and get back to you." I watched him give me a curt, stiff nod. "But," I added, "what's my pitch? How do I get in there? You got any thoughts on that?"

Brooks's flat face relaxed, and craftiness came into his eyes. "Matter of fact, yes. A security angle. They get a lot of attention, as you know. I understand they've hired rent-a-cops to protect them. I don't think this is adequate. I suggest that you get inside the group by demonstrating just how poor their security is—the idea being that you have been hired by me to arrange better security. . . ."

†††

Jerry Mattson said, "You picked a hell of a way to show how bad our security is, Perkins." He picked up my .45 from the desk and hefted it with his massive hand. "Pretty cheap stunt. Blanks and everything. Lisa's walking a precarious edge now, this kinda thing on top of what happened to J.D., it's just bad *taste*, you know? It just won't *do!*"

"Well, maybe I let my taste for street theater get away from me," I said. "But the point remains. Those kiddie cops, you know they're worthless if a lug like me can walk right past 'em with a couple of empty pizza boxes, a line of improvised malarkey, and a .45 automatic." I reached into my pocket for a clip of .45 ammunition and waved it at the drummer. "Some guy could just sashay in here with *these* in the butt instead, and then you'd be scraping Goodnight's brains off the walls."

"Don't remind me."

"So what I've got for you is solid security. Guys who carry and know how to use, and know the moves, and know how the street creeps operate. Plus me on Goodnight personal, guaranteed."

"We heard your pitch already. Ellen's checking it out with Leese. So till then we wait, and you're not going nowhere."

So we waited, and I smoked, and Mattson fidgeted, and the guitarists standing behind him chattered mindlessly; till finally, as the daylight dimmed in the window above Mattson's head, there came a tap on the door, and the rangy, elegant Ellen Long came in. "Lisa says okay, Jerry."

Mattson said, "Okay."

Ellen Long faced me.

"Lisa's gone on home," she said. "She wants you over there later." She gave me a Dearborn Heights address and handed me a small flat box. "Give her this when you get there." I looked down and saw that it was an eight-inch reel-to-reel tape.

"Yes, ma'am," I said, feeling foolish. I turned to Mattson. "Piece." He tossed my .45, which I caught one-handed. I booted the clip of blanks, worked the action once to eject the blank under the hammer, jacked in the clip of live rounds, and worked the action once again to put one in the chamber. "Real thing, this time," I told him, securing the automatic in my waistband against my spine.

He rose to full massive height behind the desk and walked around it. "Far out," he winked at me then herded the guitarists out, still chattering.

I breathed deeply, suddenly wanting a fistful of beers and the opportunity to tell the story to my cronies at Under New Management. But I had work to do. I sat down at Mattson's desk, picked up the phone, and began punching numbers. I don't know about other cities, but in Detroit there are guns for hire—good guns toted by good men who work for their buck—and inside twenty minutes I'd lined up a squad of them, guys like Johnston, Rader, Rockecharlie, Scozzafava, and the rest.

As Commando Studios emptied into the noisy evening, I fired the kiddie cop service, welcomed the new men, gave them one-on-one duty on the band members, and then, finally, tape in hand, headed out into the suddenly magical evening toward the Dearborn Heights home of my personal assignment: Lisa Goodnight.

†††

It sat square in the middle of a small, lower-middle class neighborhood south of Joy Road and east of Telegraph on the frontier of Dearborn Heights, where it butts up against Dynamite Park at the Detroit line. There the houses are small, two- and three-bedroom bungalows on oversized wooded lots, none of them, if I'm any judge, running more than forty or forty-five bills. It occurred to me, as I parked my Mustang at the curb in front of Lisa Goodnight's place, that a person with her bucks could afford a lot better neighborhood than this.

The door swung back at my knock and Lisa Goodnight, in shadow from the lights of the living room behind her, said, "Ah. My assassin. Come in."

She led me into the small living room, where the house's outward impression of modesty was instantly erased. The furnishings and decorations were first-rate, brand-new, and perfectly balanced: the smoke-gray sectional sofa, the twin matching easy chairs, the deep, luxurious, white shag carpet, the chrome and glass shelving units bearing books, and the massive entertainment center on the far wall holding a forty-inch Sony Trinitron, a video deck, and an audio system worth more than everything I own put together. A white brick fireplace attended by big pillows scattered before the hearth and illuminated by track lighting stared out from the far wall. It was a cozy, comfortable room, rich without being ostentatious.

Lisa Goodnight faced me. She was shorter than I'd thought, barefoot, dressed in snug embroidered jeans and a loose white shirt whose tails were knotted above her navel, showing a tan, flat stomach. Her face was smooth, youthful, vulnerable, one of those faces composed of parts that were individually all wrong but collectively made a thing of beauty—those dark eyes, trim nose, wide cheekbones, direct, assertive chin. Like the rest of her, her loose, wavy, short brunette hair was unadorned yet perfect. Though her name suggested British descent, I sensed in her dark eyes, unassuming posture, and general air of melancholy the influence of Eastern Europe. The woman with me now was quite different from the sharp-tongued shrew I'd taken a shot at in Commando Studios.

She asked in her resonant voice, "Got something for me?"

I'd forgotten I held the tape box. "Yes, ma'am."

She grinned. "For God's sake, call me Lisa. I'm younger than you."

"Not by much." I handed her the tape.

"Thanks." She looked me up and down. "So 'Babbling' Brooks sent you to guard me."

I snorted an honest laugh. "'Babbling'?"

"He's so sweet. He frets and fusses about me as if I'm still two years old. Well, if Babs thinks I need you, who am I to argue? C'mon, we'll tour the place and you decide if I'm secure or not."

She wasn't. Plus points: the front was well lighted, the back was fenced, neighboring houses sat a distance away, thanks to the big lots with no clumps of trees to hide intruders. Minus points: the locks were a joke, particularly on the windows. I made mental notes as we walked through the house, which included a well-equipped kitchen, luxurious master bedroom, and fully equipped tape editing studio in the second one. I mean, she had enough electronic gear in the place to keep an army of junkies financed for a year.

Back in the living room, I ran it down for her: the next morning I'd send some guys in to install an electronic alarm system and new locks top and bottom. She paced the room aimlessly as I talked, feet shuffling the shag, bare arms dangling, and when I was done she looked at me. "What about you?"

"I'll be around. I'll cover you from a distance, you'll hardly know I'm there. Like tonight, I'll keep watch from my car at the curb."

Her lassitude turned abruptly to animation. "Oh, but that's awful for you, sitting in your car for hours and hours!"

"Comes with the job."

She skipped over to the stereo system and flicked a couple of buttons. From the massive speakers softly sounded the intro of an old Commandos album, *Eclectic Guitars*. She faced me again and the lassitude was back. "This is a nice neighborhood. You don't have to turn my house into Fort Knox."

"This is Dearborn Heights," I retorted.

"This is my home. I grew up on this street, two doors up." She smiled sadly. "They didn't want to sell, so I bought this one."

Well, that explained why she hadn't bought into Bloomfield, Farmington, or Birmingham like the other Commandos. As the music gently filled the room, I looked into Goodnight's eyes, remembering Brooks's comment: "I have the sick feeling something is terribly wrong with her, Ben." Certainly her demeanor was erratic, energized one moment, sluggish the next. Certainly she acted like no one I'd ever met. But in addition to being a singing star and composer and leader of the near-legendary Sidewalk Commandos, she was also a pure creative; and creatives are known to have toys in the attic, it's almost a prerequisite. And I realized even that early that I was losing my hard-edged street objectivity. This was Lisa Goodnight, not some . . . um . . . client.

I cleared my throat. "Well, I've done about all I can for now. I'll go take up my position. See you tomorrow."

"But you haven't had your drink yet! Come on, let me be hospitable." She smiled. "You can protect me just as well from in here, can't you?"

"Why sure. Um, how about a beer?"

"Is that all? I've got anything you want here. Anything."

"Well, maybe a shot of black Jack to pave the way."

"Ah," she beamed. "*Dee*troit. It's good to be with a real *Dee*troit man again. No daqueeries for you, huh, Mr. Detective. Please, make yourself at home."

She skipped out of the living room into the kitchen. I ambled to the front door, peered out, saw nothing, secured the lock then sank into the sectional sofa at the end nearest the door. Lisa returned with a full shot glass and bottle of Stroh's for me, and a pint of red pop for herself. As she reclined on the sofa halfway down from me and pulled one tightly blue-jeaned leg under her, I raised the shot to her and dumped it down my throat with one smooth swallow, then cooled the sudden conflagration with a couple of slugs of beer. The voice of experience, which I can take or leave, said: Steady on, old son, this is a job, remember?

I gestured at her red pop. "Goin' easy, huh?"

"Oh," she said lightly, " I can't drink. In fact, I have to be real careful about drugs of any kind. The least little thing can mess me up."

"Oh."

She sipped at her pop. "Surprised?"

"Well, I've read stuff."

"Bet you expected to walk in here and see a pile of coke on the table there, with spoons and straws and everything."

"I don't go anywhere expecting anything. I wait and see for myself." I pulled a short cork-tipped cigar out of my shirt pocket. "Mind?"

"Please." She put a bare foot out and slid an ashtray on the coffee table toward me as I fired up the cigar. She watched me keenly as I exhaled a cone of smoke into the music-filled air then said, "Are you a fan, Ben?

"Casually. I like Springsteen, Clapton, Seger, Pink Floyd, Lennon, Eddie Anger, at least his old stuff."

"How about the Commandos?" she asked slyly.

"Oh sure, some of it. Y'all haven't put out anything new since Fredericks died, though. That a new album you were working on today?"

She laughed strangely. "Just something for the can. We've got enough in there for three or four LPs, but I'm not ready to put out a new package yet. Did you enjoy the session today?"

"I only heard a minute or two of it. But yeah, live performance, that's what makes it for me."

She bounced herself up abruptly to tuck her other leg under her. "Oh hey, then you'd enjoy one of those bar band gigs we do every now and then."

"I'd like that a lot. But you don't publicize 'em. Obviously."

"Don't tell Rocket this, but we'll be doing one before too long. I'll let you know when and where. Just as soon as I get the special project done."

I busied myself with drinking some beer, trying to figure out which question to ask. "Who's Rocket?"

"Oh yeah," she laughed, "how would you know? Jack Rocket's our business manager. Mr. Numbers. Hates the bar band gigs like poison, he's always pushing for the big dates, stadiums and stuff, where the bucks are. Well, hell!" she said with fervor, "we're filthy rich already, each record makes us more so, we don't need the big dates—"

"I'm Perkins, not Rocket," I interrupted.

She charged right on. "—the audience is one big faceless mob. In the little bars, fifty or a hundred people, you get close, you feel them, you can try things out, get instant feedback. But Rocket, well, he was with J.D. from the beginning, and . . . J.D. could handle him, but I don't know—"

Such volatility in that face, from assertive leader to angry fighter to little lost lady, all in the space of a sentence or two. As she went suddenly silent, so did the music, then auto-reverse kicked the tape over to the second side. I tapped a long gray hunk off the end of my cigar and asked, "What's the special project?"

She looked at me sharply, as if I'd read her mind, then said offhand, "J.D.'s last album. Hey, Ben, your beer's gone. Fresh one?"

"Sure. Just that, please."

She set her red pop down on the coffee table, sprang agilely to her feet, and headed for the kitchen. "How about a fire? The stuff's all there."

"Gotcha." She disappeared, I shut away my unwholesome thoughts, and grabbed her bottle of red pop. It was less than half gone. I sniffed it then took a tentative sip. It seemed to be nothing but soda, with no special ingredients that I could detect.

A teepee of wadded newspapers, kindling, and logs was already built in the fireplace, so I fired it up from my cigar, sat on the upraised hearth, and studied it as the blaze went up, almost at once. Lisa returned, handed me a cold Stroh's then dropped and sat cross-legged below and very near me, leaning on a cushion against the hearth. The flickering glow from the fireplace played off her face, revealed flecks of gold in her dark, wavy hair, and made her look even younger than she did already. Twisting her strong fingers together in her lap, she said without looking at me, "You know, it was twenty years ago I joined J.D."

"Just a barefoot teenager, huh?"

"I was eighteen." She half-smiled. "Behind the stadium after the last De-troit concert on the Commandos' first big tour. Two A.M., for God's sake. I was back there with a mob of kids waiting to see the band leave. All hell broke loose when they came out, everyone pushing and shoving, and some-thing propelled me right up to J.D. We talked, and he asked me to come along, and—"

I said nothing, and she looked me in the eyes, face hard. "There was noth-ing personal, not then, anyway. It took me a long time to figure out why he took me with him, why he knew I'd be good in the band. You know why?"

"Well, uh—"

"I have perfect pitch."

"What's that?"

"The ability to identify the pitch—A, B, C, and so on—of any sound you hear. Or the ability to make any of those sounds without hearing anything first. It's very rare."

"Oh." Nice piece of trivia to drop on the guys in the saloon sometime.

"I'd been a pianist since I was four, but I didn't know I had perfect pitch. J.D. knew, though. Somehow. And something else, something that's never been published. Everybody in the Commandos has perfect pitch. Even Jerry, the drummer."

The blazing fire was beginning to cook my back. I set my beer on the hearth, slid down to the floor, and leaned against the cool slate.

Her warm hand touched my forearm. I glanced at her quickly. She said, "You remind me of him."

Wait a minute.

She studied my arm, squeezing it gently with both hands. "So strong. You're a working man, like J.D. was. Oversized hands, like his, too."

I took her slim wrists with my left hand and held them gently. "Lisa—"

She freed herself, took my two hands in hers, smiled warmly, and kissed me.

I pulled back after a moment, mouth dry. The cold, unemotional voice inside me said, this is Lisa Goodnight, and a client, and a woman you just met—three strikes, fool, you *know* better, this is trouble stamped from the oldest mold in the world. But there's another voice in me, not a voice ex-actly, but a presence, whose whispers of "what the hell?" I hear via charged adrenaline and a pounding heart. One of my failings is that I seldom prevail against that "what the hell?" voice.

She asked softly, "Do you have perfect pitch, Ben?"

"Well, I've completed a pass or two in my time."

She laughed, leaned to me, whispered, "It's been so long," and we kissed again, hard.

†††

I swam up from deep, almost unconscious, sleep. The only light was indirect, from the lamp Lisa had set on the floor on the far side of the bed. The digital clock on the nightstand said four A.M. I was alone in the small bedroom, and my jaw throbbed like hell from my missing wisdom teeth.

I thought dully, first aspirin then Lisa.

I pulled on my pants. Ambled into the bathroom. Turned on the light. Winced. Opened the medicine chest above the sink. Usual supplies, including aspirin. Took on the childproof cap, finally busted the bastard, and popped three. Put the bottle back then spotted the squat prescription pill bottle.

The house was silent. I read the label. "*Patient: Lisa Goodnight. Doctor S. Rimm. Directions: One capsule twice per day. Medication: Doxepin HCI.*" I opened the bottle and saw that it was nearly full of big lime green capsules.

I was wide awake now in the shining bathroom, which was redolent of the bright clean scents of her. I capped the bottle again and went to look for her.

I found her in the second bedroom, the one that had been transformed into a tape editing studio. She wore an enormous red flannel shirt and jeans and perched high on a stool at the broad, gleaming console. Lights blinked, several tape units wound slowly, and she hunched there with big headphones clamped down over her ears, her back to me, hands expertly working switches. She jumped when I touched her.

"Oh, hi," she said absently. She stopped whatever she was doing and shoved the headphones back onto her neck.

I showed her the bottle. "Found these in the medicine chest while I was getting some aspirin."

"Yes?"

"What are they?"

"A mild antidepressant." She straightened on the stool and looked at me earnestly. "When J.D. died I . . . I began having some very hard times, you can understand that. I went to Dr. Rimm in New York for help. He knows my history, knows I can't tolerate much in the way of drugs, but he prescribed these and they work well. They're extremely mild, Ben. They take the edge off, that's all."

"Oh. Just nosy, forget it." I surveyed the massive and virtually incomprehensible console. "What are you doing?"

"The special project. J.D.'s last album." She hurried on. "It's called *Trapped Behind My Eyes*. It's an idea he had for years and years, worked on it, but never got it done."

"So you're finishing it."

"He taped bits and pieces of it, usually by himself. We've got hundreds of tapes in the archives, rehearsals, jams, ideas, miscellaneous conversation; Ellen takes care of those and gives them to me one by one." She gestured at an open tape box lying on the floor at her feet. "Like the tape you brought me tonight. I'm going through them and pulling out the bits that belong on the album."

I squinted at her. "How can you tell?"

She smiled. "Oh, I just know. It's like a mystery story, finding the clues. I sit here and listen, and then there'll be silence, and then there's a piece of it. Sometimes I even hear J.D.'s voice say, 'Okay, Leese, here's one for the record,' or something like that."

Sounded like a weird ego trip to me, but I said nothing.

"It's a way for me to be close to him for just a little while longer," she added.

I said briskly, "Listen, I'm going to grab a few more z's. You coming?"

"Not now. I'm really rolling here. You don't mind?"

"No." I went to the door, pill bottle in my hand, as she put the headphones back on and flicked switches. If I hadn't stopped at the door and turned for one more look at her, I would not have heard what she said next, it was that soft.

"J.D. is alive."

Back in the bathroom, I put the prescription bottle back in the cabinet then stared at it, opened it, shook out three pills, put them in my pocket, and replaced the bottle. Then I went back to bed, but try as I might I could not sleep.

†††

Despite her lack of sleep, Lisa Goodnight literally danced into the studio when we got there at nine o'clock. I trailed along behind her and leaned casually against the wall as the other band members milled around, talking. Behind the engineer's window the thin, curly-haired man messed expertly with his switches and pulled on his headphones. Lisa took her position at the piano, called imperiously, "Okay, kids, let's saddle it up, okay?" and, as the band members got themselves organized for the day's work, Darryl Rockecharlie, whom I'd assigned to protect Jerry Mattson, tapped my shoulder and motioned me outside into the hall.

"Message for you, boss," he grunted, handing me a pink slip.

I unfolded it. "See Jack Rocket, 1250 Book Bldg., ASAP."

"Hm. The promoter."

"I don't know who he is," Darryl growled, "but he come on like Mr. King Cowflop on the phone. Like he wants to see you yesterday and won't take no for an answer."

"Well," I shrugged, putting the message away, "Ms. Goodnight's pretty well set here for a while. I might as well run down there and see what this hotshot has on his mind."

Rockecharlie, a cashiered cop long on muscle and short on brains, propped his blocklike hands on his hips under the tails of his cheap coat, revealing the massive butt of a revolver sticking out of his waistband in front. "Listen, Bill and Norris and the rest of the boys are staked out around the joint. They got everything under control. Want me to ride shotgun with you?"

"Nah, thanks, Darryl. You hang tight and keep everybody honest."

I smacked him on his marble-hard upper arm, walked out the back into the bright sunlight, waved at Bill Scozzafava, who covered the back door, and got into my Mustang for the ride downtown.

†††

The door of the 1250 Book Building said:

ROCKET INTERNATIONAL
Exclusive Managers of the
Sidewalk Commandos
New York

Somebody's a little fuzzy on the geography, I thought, as I entered the waiting room.

The receptionist, who had Upwardly Mobile Temp written over every blonde, busty inch of her, took my name, muttered conspiratorial things into an intercom, then told me to make myself comfortable; Mr. Rocket would be right with me.

Neither thing happened. The couch on which I sat felt as if it were stuffed with old studded tires, and Mr. Rocket took a full fifty minutes to clear his schedule and make a moment or two to confer with little old me.

When I was finally invited into the sanctum sanctorum, I found it to be much more luxuriously appointed than the waiting room where the mere riffraff had to cool their heels. It was about twenty feet square, with paneled walls dense with dozens of expensively framed, inscribed photographs. Along the far wall was a broad, sun-drenched window from which I could see the Sheraton-Cadillac Hotel, the Pick-Fort-Shelby Hotel, Cobo Hall, and even Canada, lending legitimacy, I supposed, to the use of the word "International" in the name of Rocket's company. Just this side of the window was a large mahogany desk with nothing on it but a sheet of paper and a twenty-line telephone set, bulbs unlighted. Behind the desk, reading the paper, sat Jack Rocket.

"Sit down," he said without looking up.

I remained standing, sick of taking orders and in no mood to be patient. Rocket spent a few more minutes on his paper then stood, hands flat on the shining desktop, and stared at me. He was past middle age, about five eight, and on the slight side, with long wavy black hair, heavy black-framed glasses, a mustache shaped like a frown, and large, knuckly, veined hands. He wore a noisy plaid coat over an open-necked lime green shirt and orange corduroy pants. He seemed to be all teeth, hair, and gold chains, and he wasted no time on amenities.

"I want you away from my group, Perkins."

"You didn't hire me. You can't fire me."

"*I'm* the manager, and *I'm* telling you to get lost."

"You're a dim little plaid-clad hustler in a sublet office with pictures of has-beens on the walls. Pardon me for not being impressed."

"I'm from New *York*, New *York*, and soon as I can talk some sense into Miss Twist Goodnight, we're getting out of these woods back to where we belong. I don't need janitors posing as private detectives messing with my talent."

"I'm from Detroit, Michigan, which is where you are right now, and in case you haven't figured it out by now, bro, here in Detroit we do what we're hired to do; and though I looked real hard, I didn't see your signature on the bottom of the check I got."

"If money talks, Perkins, maybe we can do business."

"No sale."

Rocket's face softened into something like a smile. "I talked to Arthur Brooks this morning. He thinks maybe hiring you was hasty. He thinks I ought to wave you off."

"Well, fine, absolutely, if Brooks says so."

"Then we understand each other."

"Just get him on the phone and let me hear it from him."

Rocket's smile winked off. "Brooks ain't the only one who has muscle for hire, if you get my drift."

"Then bring 'em on, Rocket." I turned for the door.

"Perkins." I turned back. Rocket looked serious and worried. "It's the Commandos I'm concerned about. J.D. Fredericks has been dead over a year, and they haven't toured, haven't put together a package, haven't done nothing but cost money. I want them screwed together and running in one direction again, that's all, and they don't need outside distractions. Particularly Lisa. You understand?"

"Don't talk policy with me, Rocket," I told him. "You're wasting your time. I'm just a janitor posing as a private detective from out here in the woods. Remember?"

I slammed the door to his office and walked past the receptionist toward the door. At my appearance a man in a dark suit, seated on the couch, threw down his magazine and looked up expectantly. I was entering the elevator before I realized that I'd seen the man before. I was in my Mustang headed back to Commando Studios before I got a handle on where and when I'd seen him. And I was lounging against the wall of the studio, watching the band do a new song, before I remembered who he was.

†††

There was only one relatively private phone in the studio—it was in the office where Jerry Mattson had interviewed me the day before—and it took me a few calls to get hold of Carlo Infante and set up a meet. I hung up the phone and left the office in time to see the engineer—"Rolling Tape," as I thought of him—sauntering around the corner of the hallway away from me. I beetled after him but was interrupted by Lisa Goodnight, Ellen Long on one side and Jerry Mattson on the other.

Lisa hugged me fiercely, stepped back to the smiles of her comrades, and said, "A great session, a *great* session! God, it's good being back in Detroit. I feel like I'm breathing and rolling again. Ben, we're sending out for a couple of kegs of Stroh's and a truckload of Domino's pizza. Let's stuff our faces and get goofy, okay?"

"Nothing sounds better," I said, meaning every word, "but I've got business. Be back for you later, okay?"

"Okay!" She bounced away with Ellen, but Jerry Mattson fell in beside me. He asked, "What's up?"

"Not sure. Don't know." And I truly didn't, then.

†††

The place is called Tattoos, Boots & Motorcycle Parts, but it's really a saloon. It's on Ford Boulevard in Willow Run area of south Ypsilanti, walled in on one side by World War II defense housing, on another by I-94, on the third by the old Liberator bomber plant, and on the fourth by the four-lane no-man's-land of U.S. 12. It's not my regular drinking hangout (Under New Management has that dubious honor), but being a part-time rider of an old customized Harley Sportster, I know the joint and its reputation as a place where you're left alone and absolutely ignored as long as you keep exchanging currency for drinks.

That's why I arranged to meet Carlo Infante there, and true to form he was early. Nobody else knows I know this, but Carlo Infante is one of the top financial wizards of the Detroit organization. He used to work for the rival operation in Pontiac, but a couple of years ago he got on the wrong side of Pontiac boss Ezra Goforth (could be, though I've never confirmed this, due to Carlo's extended affair with Goforth's wife), and the order went out for Carlo to be erased. This information came my way in the course of a completely unrelated matter, but being an unwavering believer in the sanctity of human life, I tipped Carlo off, he gave Goforth's boys the slip, signed on with the Detroit operation (with, as part of his compensation, twenty-four-hour protection) and became, out of gratitude for my tipping him, my chief informant on the mob.

Carlo's grateful to me, but he's not stupid. He won't give anyone, even me, information about organization activity that could endanger him or jeopardize the organization's interests. But otherwise he's a good, willing, and dependable source, and that's why I thought of him when I identified the man in Rocket's waiting room.

"Didn't know you knew Gangemi," Carlo said after I'd ordered a beer.

"There's a lot you don't know about me, old son, which is just as well. Actually, it was through him that I met your boss, Rick Savastano, on a rather unpleasant matter last year. But who cares? Tell me, is Mr. Gangemi still employed as a collector for the organization?"

Infante fidgeted with his cigarette. "Yeah, major accounts work, mainly."

"So, can I assume that, if I saw him in an office this morning, the boss of that office is a delinquent account receivable?"

"Stands to reason."

"Well, then, let's play word association." I paused. "Jack Rocket."

Carlo Infante smiled into my eyes and said, "Transfer business out of NYC."

"Respectable weight?"

"Couple units average balance. I haven't checked the printout this week, but he's been running a few points above that since we took over the business."

"Well, *well*. He been covering the vigorish?"

"Not so you'd notice." Infante gestured at the barmaid for another round, as I fired up a cigar, then faced me. "Story from his end is the old flimsy weak cash flow bit. He manages the Sidewalk Commandos, which you undoubtedly know, and they've been dormant in new product development since coming here, poor revenue enhancement for Jackie boy. He's got big talk about new acts, but each one seems to die in Pittsburgh or Grand Island or someplace. His stories, they break everybody's heart all to hell around the office, believe me."

"I can imagine." The drinks arrived and I schlooked down half of mine then set the plastic mug down with finality. "So I can safely assume that your friends are displeased with Mr. Rocket?"

Infante's eyes went distant. "We're patient. The word on him from New York is favorable. Rocket's aware of his obligations and isn't hesitant about taking steps to honor them. So we're working with him."

"Uh-huh."

"For the moment."

"Gotcha." I stuck my cigar in my teeth, dropped a sawbuck on the table, and rose. "Nice talking to you, Carlo. Stay well." I threaded through the tables of hulking, tattooed, denim-clad grunts down the narrow hallway by the bathrooms and out the back into the misty gravel parking lot, and crunched to my Mustang at the rear.

I slid the key into the ignition and sat for a moment. I'd picked up something, the end of a thread, by God, and now I'd have to pull on it. Rocket was into mob shylocks on a serious basis and had no means of covering his bills except by making the Sidewalk Commandos produce on stage and in the studio—but the Commandos, under Lisa Goodnight's direction, were disinclined to do this for the moment. Nobody knew better than I how much pressure the mob could put on a debtor. The question was, how far would Rocket, reacting, go to make the Commandos do his bidding?

I reached for the key and had started to turn it when a bullet blew my rear view mirror into a million pieces.

Fortunately, my instinctive reaction was to lunge to my left, so the second and third shots did nothing but blow out the windshield ahead of me. I let out a loud moan and fell to my right onto the passenger seat as the rest of the windshield exploded in shining, noisy fragments around me. Then, silence. The skin of my left temple felt torn, and warm wetness ran tickling through the whisker-stubble under my chin, but otherwise I was unhurt. I squirmed my .45 out from under my belt and held it in a slick hand against the floor, and lay in the silence for several long moments, waiting for the face to appear, as I knew it must.

When it didn't, I thought, could he be this stupid? Or, could I be this lucky?

More silence. I flipped open my glove compartment, took out a fistful of ketchup packets from Burger Barn and, one by one, ripped them open and smeared ketchup on my shirt and up my neck and down my arms. I expected curious people to converge on my car, but no one did. Well, it was that kind of neighborhood. Still prone, I wrestled the receiver of my car phone to me, hailed the mobile operator and, after a moment, raised Elvin Dance, captain of Homicide, Detroit Police Department. It took some convincing, but when he heard me out he chuckled and promised action immediately. I hung up the phone and lay back and practiced being a corpse.

Moments later I heard heavy boots crunching toward my car on the gravel outside. The crunching stopped, replaced by a new sound, a continuous, metallic, liquid *whooooooong* on my right rear hubcap. Great, I thought sourly. Bad enough my car's been shot up; now I have to put up with *this?* But I stayed put as the sound stopped and the footsteps crunched over to the right side of the car. I had my eyes open in a passable imitation of death, and in my peripheral vision I saw, upside down, a heavy, bearded face staring in at me.

"Oh bummer," the man grunted. "Wow. I mean, what happened to you, man?"

After I moment I answered, "I've been *shot*, and I'm lying here *dead*, fool. What the hell does it look like?"

"Looks like maybe a ketchup bottle exploded all over you or somethin'."

So much for special effects. "Listen, partner, someone just tried to do me, and I want to run a game on him, and I need your help."

"Hey, I can really appreciate your situation. What do you want me to do."

"Wayne County EMS is on the way here now, we got to dress this thing up. Think you can organize a crowd to stand around, stare with sick curiosity, mutter speculation, stuff like that?"

"No problem, leave it to me, man."

Sure enough, inside two minutes half the patrons of Tattoos, Boots & Motorcycle Parts were thronged around the Mustang, talking excitedly, peering in at me one by one. Then events moved quickly. A siren-whooping EMS meat wagon shrieked dramatically in, a pair of brisk, muscular, white-clad paramedics lifted me out of the Mustang onto a stretcher and from there into the back of the wagon, and we peeled away, siren screaming, one of the EMT's clamping an oxygen mask overly hard on my face as the other one played Andy Granatelli at eighty miles per hour on Michigan Avenue headed toward Detroit.

When we were well clear of the saloon, the paramedic took the oxygen mask off my face, and I raised myself on the stretcher feeling a little light-headed. He grinned. "I've been on some weird calls, but this one takes the cake, Jake. Don't it take the cake for you, Stu?"

The driver said, "Takes cake for me, Lee. But we don't mind, we sure don't."

"No, sir," Lee answered, swaying as the wagon changed lanes repeatedly at high speed. "If the cops ask us for a favor, why, we're only glad to oblige. Hoo-boy, fella, you stink of ketchup, you know that?"

Eight minutes later we arrived at the emergency room entrance of Wayne County General Hospital. The paramedics carried me briskly inside to an examining room and left me alone in there with Captain Elvin Dance.

†††

He sat on a stool, as dapper as always in a bronze pinstriped three-piece suit and maroon tie over a white silk shirt. Gold rings gleamed on his cocoa-colored fingers, which he tapped pensively in front of his grin. "Well, sonny," he sighed, "what you got me into this time?"

I told him the whole story except for Carlo Infante's name. When I was done, Dance thought for a long time then asked, "So now you're dead. That's the word they'll put out from the hospital here—Ben Perkins, D.O.A—east till I tell 'em to issue a correction. Okay?" I nodded. Dance pressed, "So what's that gotten you?"

"Well, whoever tried to kill me thinks I'm dead and out of the way, and they'll proceed to do whatever they were going to do before I got into the picture, only now I'll be watching."

"Uh-*huh*. And, pray tell, what's all this trouble I've gone to gotten *me?*"

"Oh, I don't know, Elvin," I grinned. "Except maybe something real ugly seems about to happen to the Sidewalk Commandos, and anything involving them'll get big publicity for the cop on the spot."

"What makes you think I'm interested in publicity?" Dance asked indignantly. After a long silence, he went on. "You make sure I'm put on top of it when it goes down?"

"Guaranteed. I owe you. I'll trade your name in the papers in return for keeping my name out. Oh, one more thing."

Elvin Dance sighed. "Yeah?"

I fished from my pocket the three pills I'd swiped from Lisa's medicine chest and handed them to him. "Mind having an analysis run on these?"

"Hell, why not? I done stuck my neck out into the next county already. This whole thing better pay off big, Ben."

I nodded. "That's one thing I don't think you have to worry about."

†††

The next morning I sat parked on a side street kitty-corner from the Commando Studios, where I had a good view of the side and back entrances.

I was thick-tongued and scratchy-eyed from lack of sleep. After Dance left the hospital the night before, I took a cab over to the Shine In, a carwash on Telegraph in Redford, where I keep stashed a couple of old but serviceable cars that I use for tailing people from time to time. The beast I collected there was a tired '74 Ford Granada that I'd picked up for peanuts at a police auction. It was ugly but anonymous, faded and half-rusted and in appearance like about nine million other cars on the streets of Detroit, and I drove it to Lisa Goodnight's house, parked up the street, and kept watch.

From the lights, I could tell she was there, and she was there alone. Nobody else was watching her, far as I could tell. No security, no nothing. Dozing unwillingly at ten-minute intervals, I stood watch the rest of the night and then followed her to the studio in the morning, where she was joined by other band members.

My boys were gone, and the kiddie cops were back, lounging around outside the studio, looking vigilant as hell. Mr. Rocket had gotten his wish.

After I'd been there a while, a plain black Chrysler LeBaron made a right onto my street from Evergreen and rolled slowly toward me in the sunlight. I knew before it had come ten feet that it was a cop, and before it had gotten ten feet more that it was Elvin Dance. I held a hand out my window and Elvin U-turned, parked at the curb ahead of me, sauntered back, and slid into the passenger seat.

"This crate hot, Perkins?"

"Certainly not. You wanna see title and registration, ossifer?"

"Nah, just don't let it happen again. Against all *kinda* laws for dead men to be operating a motor vehicle on the public streets."

"Plan was to *pretend* I'm dead, as I recall."

"Hey, you're *dead*, bro. *Free Press* says so." Chuckling, he handed me a clipping. It was a two-inch column with a piece of Garfield on the back. The small headline said BELLEVILLE MAN GUNNED DOWN AT YPSI BAR. Details were scant but included my name, the information that I'd been D.O.A. at Wayne General, that no suspects were in custody, and that the investigation was continuing.

Elvin went on, "Tellya, the city's reeling with shock at this tragedy. Haven't seen such an outpouring of grief since Melon Grungo was found half-decomposed under the D.T.&I. overpass with a quart of Ripple in his hand."

"I'll just bet," I said sourly, stowing the clipping in my pocket to save for my children, of whom I have none.

"Well," Elvin said casually, "your sister Libby read that. Called me this morning after talking to the hospital."

"Wonder why. She inherits no part of my estate and she knows it."

"This ain't funny, man. She was in a state of shock."

"Yeah, bet she dropped her fingernail file and everything."

Elvin let it go. "Listen, on them pills."

I yawned. "Yeah?"

"Well, you gimme three. Two of 'em's the same, a mild antidepressant, kiddie stuff—"

"Doxepin or something."

"Right. But the other one's stronger. Ethchlorvynol."

"You practice that word all the way over here, Elvin?"

The policeman ignored me. "Also known as Placidyl. A potent hypnotic. Definitely high-horsepower stuff. You don't take that unless you know what you're doing."

He opened the car door and put one polished shoe on the curb. "I'll leave it with you for right now. Don't you forget. Next name in the paper better be *mine*, not yours, so you keep me clued in."

I thought about Doxepin and Placidyl and wished that I were a pharmacologist. I wished I had a change of clothes, ketchup-free if not clean. I thought of gunshots blowing the windows out of my prized '71 Mustang and wished the job was done and I was in bed, not necessarily mine and not necessarily alone.

I said, "Sure thing, Elvin. Hey, one thing you can do. Call into the studio for me and send Jerry Mattson, the drummer, walking this way alone, okay? Don't give him my name, we don't want to panic the lad."

†††

Mattson strolled in my direction about fifteen minutes later. He wore faded old denim from neck to boots and walked with that deceptive grace some very big men have. He looked puzzled and tentative till he got close to my car, then he stopped and stared at me, walked quickly to the passenger window, leaned down, and glared.

"Perkins," he said in his shifting-gravel voice.

"'The reports of my death,' et cetera. Why don't you hop in for a minute."

"What I'm thinking about doing is dragging you out and playing pogo-stick with you up and down this-here street."

"Something on your mind?"

He jerked a kielbasa-sized thumb toward the studio. "That poor lady is inside there burning herself out on accounts you. Now it turns out you've pulled some cheap rotten little stunt!"

"Get in. Tell me about it."

He opened the door and seated himself, causing the car to lean perceptively his way. "We got the word late last night. Lisa went home and was up the whole night. Came in this morning with a new piece, 'Kiss of Death.' You get the idea? J.D.'s dead, you're dead. She thinks it's on account of her."

"That's nutty, Jerry."

He leaned toward me. "You better have a damn good reason for this. Because seeing Lisa mashed up gets me real peeved. Hell, gets *all* of us real peeved. And what about your own friends and family? Don't you care what they'll think when they hear this?"

"My sister Libby knows already. Heard she dropped her fingernail file and everything."

"That's about as funny as a cramp, Perkins."

"Seems to be the consensus. Now hear me out." I gave him my thoughts on Lisa's erratic conduct, the evidence of the doctored pills, and the strategy behind posing as dead. I ended with, "Somebody wants to do her real dirty, Jerry. I got ideas on why, and even a glimmer of who; but there's big holes in the piece yet, and I need some insight if I'm to protect her."

Jerry Mattson had retreated from belligerence to thoughtfulness. He leaned back heavily in the seat and said quietly, "Well, 'course we know she hasn't been right since J.D. died. Can't blame her. We just been waiting for her to get past it the best I can tell you. I'd seen some of the stuff you're talking about, but it didn't hang together for me like it does when you tell it. Maybe I've just been too close. And the pills. I didn't know she was on anything, let alone that somebody was cooking them."

"You know about this 'last album' of J.D.'s?"

"Sure. I figured it was fifty-fifty it would never happen. But that's up to Lisa."

"She gets the tapes from Ellen Long?"

Mattson rubbed his nose. "Not exactly. Ellen pulls them from the archives and gives them to Kenny Durga to run through first to make sure J.D.'s on them. No sense Lisa wasting her time."

"Who's Durga?"

"Our engineer."

"Oh. 'Rolling Tape.'" Well, well, I thought, how interesting. "Tell me about him."

"Kenny?" Mattson smiled for the first time. "He's okay. Good engineer, not exactly brilliant but then he doesn't have to be. Lisa produces us and does most of the mixing and mastering herself. What's good about Kenny is he'll stand there at the controls for hours and hours and do what he's told. And he's a good gofer, goes out for ciggies and sodas and stuff."

"That's what's good about him. What's bad about him, Jerry?"

"There's nothing *bad* about him. He plays four-chord guitar—you know, monotonous stuff over and over and over—and tries to write songs and plays them for us, and they're the Godawful-est stuff you've ever heard in your life. It's become kind of a running joke. He's a good sport, he doesn't take it personal."

"What about Rocket? He get along with her?"

Mattson's smile was ugly. "He's a pain in the ass, like a broken record. Wants us to release 'best of' albums. And solo albums by each of us individually. And big stadium dates. Exploitative stuff, unfair to the fans. If he hadn't been so close to J.D., Lisa'd have canned him long ago."

Better and better. "One more thing, and this'll sound weird."

"Shoot."

"Lisa said everyone in the group has perfect pitch."

"She told you that, huh? Well, strange, but true."

"That include Kenny Durga?"

"*Kenny?* Oh *hell*, no. No way."

†††

Ten, eleven, then midnight passed, and I opened my car windows and took off my jacket hoping the early autumn chill would keep me awake.

It was a struggle.

The Sidewalk Commandos had worked nonstop in the studio till past eight o'clock. Then they dispersed to their homes. Lisa left, driven by one of the kiddie cops in his Toyota; I followed at a discreet distance in my feeble Granada. At her house in Dearborn Heights, he dropped her off, gave her a wave, and left her to go into the house alone. Great security.

I took up position half a block away from the house, and watched as the darkness deepened and the chill intensified. It was a quiet street with Lisa Goodnight's house the quietest of all. No change in the lights. No noises. Nothing to watch.

I didn't know what to watch for, but on the other hand, knowing wouldn't have made the wait any less boring.

Finally I decided I had to get out and stretch, move some blood around. I clambered out of the Granada and eyed Lisa's property. It occurred to me that, during my check of her house a couple of nights before, I'd neglected to take a close look outside. Why not now? I thought. Real thorough detective-like work, with the benefit of exercise besides. I headed off.

She had about a half acre. The backyards of the adjacent homes were fenced in; Lisa's was open except at the back, where an old chain-link fence divided her property from a dense section of woods that stretched away deep and black.

I walked along the fence on Lisa's side across the back, keeping an ear cocked for suspicious noises. Nothing.

There were a couple of sizable trees in her neatly trimmed lawn, nothing more. An unused concrete patio extended twenty feet from the back window-wall of the house. A light shone from one of the windows: the tape editing studio, I decided after mentally reviewing the internal floor plan.

I'd reached the corner of the yard and made the turn to head streetward when a light suddenly shone in my eyes and a firm male voice said, "Hey. You."

I froze, blinded. The voice came from the yard on the other side of the fence from me. It was middle-aged and not at all hesitant. I said, "Yes?"

"Who're you?" The light stayed steady in my squinting eyes.

I said, "Just checking things out back here."

"Casin' the joint, huh? That's how you guys put it."

"No. I'm a private detective on an assignment." As I talked I heard a noise from Lisa's house, like a door slamming. I glanced that way then back to the light. "Nice talking to you. I gotta go."

"Oh no! You stay put! You're a private detective, huh? You work for Miss Goodnight?"

"Yeah." Which wasn't strictly true. Besides, how do you describe your relationship with a woman who thinks you're dead?

"Well, we'll have to be sure of that," the man said. "Us neighbors look out for each other. Hand your ID over here. By the way, Mr. Detective, what I'm holding in my other hand pointed at your belly button is a **Ruger Security Six, three five seven maggie."

That's all I needed right now, a hopped-up neighborhood security junkie with a hand-cannon pointed at me. I was in the middle of getting my wallet out very slowly when I heard a car horn honk from Lisa's house. I glanced that way again and saw just the tail end of a car, parked at the curb by the driveway, motor running. What I could see of the car was yellow.

A cab. At damn near one o'clock, on the wrong side of midnight.

I flipped my ID toward the man and said, "Hurry up, I got to run."

"Sure, sure," he answered easily, bending to the ground and then back up. "You know, I never met a private eye before, but I read about you guys all the time. You know: Nameless, Spade, Spenser, McGee. Let's see if you're any of those guys."

"Come *on*, sir." The "sir" was a desperate afterthought, brought on by the sound of the taxi's horn honking again.

"Perkins," the man read. "Nope. You ain't any of those guys. But this looks legit enough, all right. Okay," he ended in an officious tone, "you can carry on." He tossed the ID back to me and headed toward his house. I sightlessly pawed the grass, found my ID, stuffed it into my pocket, and ran around the side of Lisa's house.

To see the cab pause at the stop sign a block up, make a left, and disappear.

Grimly, I went to the front door in the wan hope that the cab had picked up someone else. The door stood ajar, I walked in. The living room was empty, there wasn't a sound in the place. I called her name twice, got only my echo back.

It seemed as if every light in the house was on as I stomped through it, searching. Everything appeared to be in place except in her bedroom, where the closet door stood open and a couple of bureau drawers jutted out with clothes draped down their fronts. In the editing studio, next door, all the equipment was turned on and humming, waiting.

I stood there, staring at it, trying to think hard and cold and clearly. Where would she go, at this miserable hour?

As I thought, I drifted over to the console. A tape was mounted on the primary hubs, and the earphone lay as if tossed across the control panel. For the hell of it, I put the headphones on, rewound the tape for a couple of seconds, and then turned the lever to PLAY.

Silence, then the snap-crackle-pop of old tape and a light hiss in the background. A male cough, the flick of a guitar pick on unchorded strings, abruptly choked off. Then chords, just the guitar, slow and easy in six-eight meter, and the voice of J.D. Fredericks—as immediately recognizable by as many people as Sinatra's—singing:

On our anniversary, I will come again
Be there,
Be there,
Just like when we began.

He sang it just once. Then, with jarring abruptness, the tape switched to a full jam session, a screaming, raunchy cover of "Sweet Hitchhiker." I rewound the tape and played the three lines again, listening carefully. *On our anniversary, I will come again.* "Our" anniversary. J.D.'s and Lisa's. *Just like when we began.*

Lisa had told me, "It was twenty years ago I joined J.D.," which took care of when, maybe. As for "where," all she'd said was "behind the stadium."

And, later that night, she'd also said, "J.D. is alive."

It hit me then, blinding me like the neighbor's flashlight. The tapes, the drugs, Kenny Durga and his four-chord songs that brought comic relief to the Commandos; Gangemi and his collection activities for the mob, Jack Rocket and no big concerts or packages for a year. Oh, Jesus Christ.

I shut the thought away. Nineteen sixty-four, the Sidewalk Commandos' first national tour. Where did they play in Detroit? Which "stadium"? I had no idea, I wasn't a fan back then. But I knew someone who was.

I trotted to the living room, picked up the princess phone, thought for a minute, and dialed an Ann Arbor number. It answered after twenty rings. "Yes." Sleepy female voice.

"Libby. Ben. Sidewalk Commandos, 1964. Where'd they do their Detroit concert?"

It occurred to me then that I could have started the conversation better because, after a long shocked pause, she—no other word for it—screamed: "You're DEAD! It was in the PAPER! I READ it!"

I broke in roughly. "Little misunderstanding. Come on, the Commandos' concert, what about it? I'm short on time here."

Libby ignored me. "That policeman, Captain Dance, he confirmed it. Oh, Ben, I was so upset!"

I overcame the temptation to use the fingernail file line again. When material doesn't work, you drop it from the act. "See if you can get your marbles together and answer my question, please, Libby?"

"What time is it?" she muttered. "Oh Jesus. You call me at one in the morning to ask a dumb question about a concert twenty years ago."

"Believe me, if I had any choice, you'd be the last person I'd call. Now come on. You were a Commandos' fan back then, before you flunked out of U of M. And I remember you went to their concert. Where was it?"

"I didn't flunk out. I dropped out in the midst of a life-goals crisis."

"What *ever*."

She made an exasperated sigh. "It was at Olympia."

"You sure?"

"If I wasn't sure, I'd surely say, 'I'm not sure, Ben.'"

"For sure," I said sarcastically. "Thanks. Go back to bed now and sleep well, secure in the knowledge that your brother is alive and well and on the job in Detroit." I slammed down the phone, ran out of the house without locking it, and jumped into the Granada, hoping and praying that the feeble old beast would get me there in time.

Two A.M., Lisa had said.

†††

Olympia Stadium, the big red barn on Grand River, is a pitiful reminder of Detroit's glory days. Back before anyone conceived of Joe Louis Arena and Pontiac Silverdome and Pine Knob Amphitheatre, Olympia was a place that jumped. The Red Wings hockey team played their championship seasons there. Big bands and top acts of all kinds played their Detroit dates there.

Now, victimized by corporate money's flight to Oakland County on one hand and the riverfront on the other, Olympia is, far as I know, completely unused. It stands there on Grand River, glaring with soot-stained red brick pride over the Jeffries Freeway—the Red Wings' logo still etched defiantly in its façade—looking like a lady who's lost her husband to a younger woman but who refuses to quit wearing her wedding ring. The wrecker's ball will catch up with her one of these days, soon as it gets done finishing off the rest of downtown.

It was just past two when I eased the wheezing Granada to the curb up from the stadium. I checked my .45 in the glare of bright streetlights then scanned the six-lane avenue. There were few cars and no people at all; even winos get a day off, it's in their contract. I got out of the car and walked toward the deserted stadium.

There was a big chain-link gate hanging open at the southwest corner along Grand River, and an alley ran back from there along the stadium into utter blackness. I remembered Lisa's saying that she met Fredericks behind the stadium after the concert. Glancing both ways for observers—there were none—I walked through the gate and down the alley.

It was clammy and rancid, real rat country. Twenty paces in, the glare of the streetlights died, cut off by the corner of the building. I got out my .45 and held it alongside me, not that I cold see anything to shoot. I passed a row of overflowing dumpsters set at erratic angles along Olympia's walls. I tripped over a bottle and stepped in something soft. A mufflerless car roared by behind me on Grand River, and a transport plane on a low approach to Detroit City Airport screamed by overhead, momentarily killing the sound of crunching glass under my boots.

Olympia finally ended. I stopped, tucked myself against the wall at the corner, and scanned the broad open asphalt area behind the stadium. I think it was once a parking lot, but it was empty of cars now, dead weeds poking up through heaves and cracks in the litter-strewn pavement. Cold dark bulbs peered down from the arms of rusting iron stanchions. The only illumination came from a row of streetlights that ran along the back of the property, off in the distance.

I didn't see anybody.

Automatic held against my right thigh, I edged my face around the corner and looked along the backside of the stadium. It was broken up by a series of concrete docks that jutted out from the building, rimmed by waist-high steel guardrails, with steps running to ground level. It was almost totally lightless there, and I used all the old tricks for seeing in the dark—looked through the corners of my eyes and all that garbage—but didn't see anything and wouldn't have, if Lisa Goodnight hadn't moved.

She stood on the second dock down, about sixty feet from me, at the guardrail. I recognized her profile, nothing more; it was too dark. Some kind of overnight bag stood on the cement at her feet. She had her hands on the rail, but her posture was not relaxed; she was erect. Waiting.

I unconsciously made a dry swallow. For a moment there I think I was tuned into the world of her thoughts, and I saw crowds—crowds of noisy, excited teenagers, a sea of them, drunk on love, intermingled with uniformed, tense Detroit policemen—waiting to give a climactic scream as the Sidewalk Commandos trotted out between rows of cops to their limousine. And, mixed in with the noise but loud and clear, I heard J.D. Fredericks' voice: *I will come again. Be there.*

I started for her then stopped after just a step as the sound of a car motor issued from the alley behind me. It did not fade away down Grand River, it simply idled, echoing off the wall of Olympia Stadium.

Crouching, I swung around the corner. Headlights lit the alley. I was shadowed by the dumpsters. I slid along the wall and into the gap between it and the first dumpster. The car's motor dropped from idle into gear, and the car started to roll very slowly up the alley toward me.

I was behind the third dumpster when the car passed by, still rolling at idle speed, as if the driver wasn't sure where he was going. In the split-second available before the car passed, I saw a familiar profile behind the wheel, illuminated in bluish green by the dashboard lights. I waited between dumpsters till the car was twenty feet past me then walked out into the alley and hoofed along in the car's wake, .45 held at a forty-five degree angle in my right hand.

As the car neared the corner of Olympia, I veered to my right, pointed my automatic, and shouted, "Hey!"

Brake lights winked twice. I saw the driver, in silhouette from the bright lights at the back of the lot, look over his right shoulder toward me. The brake lights went on and stayed on, and the driver's arm came over the top of the seat with a pistol at the end. But he did not fire. I was, intentionally, at a bad angle for him, and he didn't want to shoot through the back window of his car, even if he hadn't minded shooting through the back window of mine.

I set into position—.45 pointed straight ahead in my right hand, left hand bracing my wrist, arms extended but not locked—and shot to kill.

The boom of the heavy automatic was deafening. The slug went straight and true through the back window and exploded the side vent and driving mirror on its way out. The driver disappeared. I corrected my aim and fired again. I think I got the driver's headrest that time, which slowed down the big slug so much that, tumbling, it took out a garbage-can-sized piece of the windshield safety glass. I still couldn't see the driver. I lowered my aim for dead-center on the back of the front seat, but the brake lights went off. The car, still in gear, started to roll slowly, and the gunman's pistol flew out the side window and arced high into the darkness of the parking lot, followed by muffled screams.

Automatic still extended, I trotted after the car as we passed the corner of the building. I caught up with the driver's door as the panicky screams continued from inside. Still trotting, I popped open the door and aimed, but it didn't look as though a final shot was necessary. Track-shoed feet below blue-jeaned legs dangled out the door; above them, the rest of the man sprawled across the front seat, decorated like a Christmas tree with shards of winking glass.

I grabbed him by the handiest ankle and jerked him like a slot machine handle out onto the pavement. The car rolled on as I turned him over roughly, straightened, planted a foot on his chest, and stared panting into the twisted bearded face of Kenny Durga, composer of four-chord songs, engineer for the Sidewalk Commandos, Mr. "Rolling Tape."

I pointed my revolver at his right eye and slid my boot up so the heel was centered on his sternum and the toe poked into the soft area under his chin. It is a most painfully effective way to control a struggling man without using your hands. "Well, this is your lucky day, you son of a bitch! Two shots and I missed you!"

"Don't hurt me. Please don't hurt me."

I put more weight on my shoe and held the automatic so close to his eye that he could look up it like a telescope. "May have gathered, I don't like people trying to kill Lisa. I also don't like people trying to kill *me*. But you know what *really* hacks me about you?"

I heard Lisa's voice, soft and uncertain, behind me. "Ben?"

I ignored her. "You hurt my car!" I roared at Durga. "Gonna cost me a bundle! *New* rearview mirror. *New* windshield. *New* ragtop—"

Lisa, closer, repeated, "Ben?"

I kept my foot clamped down hard on Durga and turned. Lisa Goodnight stood erect and still ten feet from me, denims blackish blue in the unnatural light, leather overnight bag held in both hands against her knees. Her eyes were glassy, her face pasty and drawn. Somewhere behind me, Durga's car hit a stanchion with a solid metallic *chunk* and the motor ground and died.

Neither of us noticed. I looked at her for what seemed like a long time then said, "What I want to do is walk over there and hug you hard. But if I let go of this son of a bitch, he might run."

She said, "I'm glad you're back."

I looked back down into Durga's eyes. "On the other hand, if I let him go and he takes off, then I'll get to run him down and stomp him into the pavement."

A siren gained on us from the distance. Durga began to gag, and I lightened up a little on my foot then released him entirely and walked to Lisa. I took her into my arms and hugged her then glanced back at Durga. He hadn't moved.

"Easy, Leese," I told her as the siren got closer.

Her body seemed to have no substance in my arms. She disengaged herself from me, brushed some hair back from her forehead, looked around, and said, "Where's J.D.? He should have been here by now."

†††

Arthur Brooks said, "So all along you figured it was Durga."

"Oh, hell no. I'm not psychic. But I figured he was involved in the attempt on me at the Ypsi bar. He was outside the office at the studio when I called to arrange the meet. He was the only one who knew where I'd be."

"He *was* the shooter, though."

"Yep. Ballistics established that. Plus, he sang. Hell, he's still singing. He's doing a solo version of *Aida* down there in the Wayne County jail."

Arthur Brooks sat there, square-faced and solemn, dressed as always in an immaculate navy blue suit and white-on-white shirt. The office was silent, the phone buttons dim. "Durga must have wanted you out of the way bad."

I poked a cigar into my face and fired it up. "Yeah, him and Rocket both. My appearance threatened an act they'd had wired for months. That night behind Olympia, that was the twentieth anniversary of when Lisa met J.D., down to the minute. They primed her. Durga cooked the tapes over a period of months with 'messages' from Fredericks—really outtakes from other sessions. Durga arranged for the Placidyl substitutes in Lisa's prescriptions—he was the band's gofer, brought her her refills all the time. Kept her off-balance and flaky, led her around by the nose."

"The point of all this being?"

"To get Lisa away somewhere, alone and late at night and helpless, where they could kill her."

Brooks shifted. "Why do it so elaborately? Why not simply kill her at home?"

"Rocket and Durga absolutely could not allow suspicion to come their way. Lisa's getting killed on her own turf would have led to the cops asking everyone associated with the group a lot of embarrassing questions. On the other hand, if she got killed behind Olympia Stadium—where, far as anyone knew, she had no business being—at two A.M., for God's sake, it would have looked like just a random street-crazy shooting. With Lisa's eccentric behavior the past year, cops'd have figured she just wandered off where she didn't belong and got nailed. Typical drug-head rock star behavior."

"I'd like to think the police would be a little more persistent than that," Brooks said.

"Hey, so would I. But let's face it."

"Yes." Brooks pressed his palms together so tightly his knuckles whitened. "Does seem to me that killing Lisa would be killing the golden goose for Rocket, though."

I drew hard on my cigar and blew a stream. "That's not the way he saw it at all. Lisa was an impediment to what he wanted—cash, and lots of it. Rocket wanted the group to put out solo and best-of albums. Wanted them to do big stadium dates. Lisa said no. She only wants to do original material no matter how long it takes. And she hates the big stadium dates."

"So Rocket's motive essentially was business control," Brooks agreed. "What about Durga?"

"Rocket promised Durga a performing and leadership role with the band—he's not qualified for that and never will be."

"And Durga *bought* that?"

"Sure. Rocket's essentially a salesman. He gave Durga a perfect pitch."

The lawyer leaned back in his chair, maintaining the steeple in front of his chest. "Well, I have to admit that when I hired you I had no idea something like this was going on. All things considered, I'm pleased at the outcome. You saved Lisa's life. You showed courage and resource. You did your job, Ben. Thank you."

"Appreciate the kind words," I said shortly, rising.

Arthur Brooks handed me an envelope. It was thick with, I found later, one hundred dollar bills, which I'll take in lieu of kind words any time.

"Have you been out to see Lisa yet?"

"Yeah, yesterday."

After waiting for elaboration, he said, "Stay in touch."

"Sure." I left.

†††

Forty minutes later, as early autumn darkness closed in, I walked into Under New Management, my habitual drinking hangout on Ecorse Road near the I-275 interchange. The guys were all there, as arranged, and they jumped to their feet and whooped and shook my hand and pounded my back as I entered. We took the big table in the center of the saloon, Eddie brought us pitchers and shots, and we got going on the evening's mission: to get roaring drunk.

But try as I might, the booze and good times didn't bring on enough oblivion to erase the memory of my visit to Lisa Goodnight the night before.

She was staying at a small, unpublicized, extremely expensive sanitarium in the pastoral setting of South Lyon, Michigan. Her doctor had determined that she'd become dependent on Placidyl, and you don't back off that without a lot of help; so she committed herself to the sanitarium to take care of that and to restore her precarious biochemical balance. In addition, I was told the headshrinkers there wanted to help her recover from her state of mourning over the death of J.D. Fredericks. I didn't doubt they could unscramble her chemistry, but I had serious doubts about their ability to help her recover from Fredericks. I'm uneducated, but I know that you don't ever get over the death of someone close to you. Rather, you change your thinking and closet the pain away somewhere, where it waits to jump out at you in an unguarded moment.

We spoke briefly in the sanitarium's library. She wasn't unfriendly, but she was quiet, grim, distant. She thanked me for helping her and promised to let me know about the band's next unpublicized bar gig (she never did), and to send me a copy of her latest single, "Kiss of Death." She never did that either, but that's okay, it's been on the radio a lot lately.

I left there reasonably confident that she'd come through okay. Lisa Goodnight is keeping a delicate balance between sanity and insanity, dragged hard on the one hand by the cloudy, limitless world of creativity and, on the other hand, by the real world, a world of cruelty and greed. Freed of drugs and master of her grief, she has a shot at maintaining that delicate balance, preserving her sanity, bringing the beauty of great music to the world and, just possibly, getting some happiness for herself.

The only insoluble problem was not hers, it was mine. She did not love me any more.

As the boys and I drank and sang obscene lyrics to the C & W pounding out of the juke, I thought, hell! I've been in this business a long time. I've learned that clients are a lot like your family. You love them, you go to the mat for them, but smart money says they'll turn right around and break your heart.

I looked around at the faces of the guys—Rockecharlie, Moscone, Johnston, Scozzafava, Rader, Putnam, and one more silent face, staring up at us from the center of the table: Ben Franklin. I thought, well, like Daddy always said, you can't pick your family, but you can pick your friends. And these were good ones. I knew they'd stay with me. Hell, I was buying.

Afterword

This story happened during a very difficult point of my life, personally and professionally. I remember it being an escape for me, a hiding place; I remember feeling sad when it was done. Considering that, it surprises me now the amount of humor (albeit hardboiled) I was able to work into it.

Most of the characters were one-shots. Lisa Goodnight I always liked and would like to work into a project again. Ditto her lawyer, "dour" Arthur Brooks. Jeannie Riley was a major presence in *The Harder They Hit*, the second novel, and never appeared again. The mob figures are part of an organized crime thread that sprawled out through the books and novels and even beyond the Perkins' projects somewhat. And then there's Libby, continuing to work her will!

In this one the strong sense of place of metro Detroit really comes through. It's something I've always developed with great care. Tattoos, Boots, & Motorcycle Parts never existed (but should have), and recurs; Olympia Stadium is now completely gone, and the Shine In, one of the better continuing bits, occurs here for what I believe is the first time.

The penultimate scene, in which Ben "explains it all to you," is a trite plot construction that I make every effort to avoid. Obviously I didn't feel as strongly about that then.

And finally, the title: one of the better ones, I think. Even if it's technically incorrect. As my mother, a brilliant classical vocalist and musician, reminds me, the trait shared by the band members is not perfect pitch, but absolute pitch.

Absolutely, Mom.

The Forever Trip

1. DRINKING TOM AND JERRY

Uncle Dan stared down the length of his sheet-covered body. "So, Benjy, they're gonna take another piece of me."

I knew what he meant. At the end of him, under the crisp white hospital sheet, his right foot showed and his left foot didn't. Diabetes, controlled for years, had gradually gained on him and caused the circulation in his left foot to fail, resulting in gangrene. Twice in the past year they'd had to amputate, removing the foot first and the leg below the knee second.

"Just your gall bladder this time, Uncle," I answered, seating myself in the chair next to his bed.

"Just." Uncle Dan stared at me coldly with his crisp blue eyes. His face was lined, pale, and wasted, marked indelibly with the gall bladder pain that had kept him in a near-fetal position for the past week in his retirement community bed. He looked every one of his eighty-seven years.

"Listen," I said cheerfully, holding up some envelopes, "I picked up your mail. Want to go through it?"

"You go ahead," Dan said dourly. "Let me know if there's any movie role offers in there or anything."

"Sure," I grinned. I inventoried the mail. Mostly ads, which I tossed. The last item was a six-by-nine manila envelope. I ripped it open. A small note fell out, clipped to a Baggie that had another envelope inside it. I opened the note and read it to my uncle. "'Dan: This just came today. Thought it might be important. Do you believe that crummy post office? Love, Millie.'"

Uncle Dan looked at the Baggie and then at me, eyes narrow. "Millie! My old landlady. What'd she send?"

The Baggie had one of those printed messages from the post office on it, apologizing for the delay in delivery. I ripped the plastic and took out the note-sized envelope. It was faded, wrinkled, addressed in a scrawl to Uncle Dan at his old apartment in Schaefer. I held it up to him. "Looks really old. Want me to open it?"

"Sure, why not."

I opened the envelope and shook out the note. It was small, written on cheap paper, and short. "'Tuesday morning,'" I read. "'Dear Dan, I'm in desperate trouble. If you meant what you said, meet me at the bar tonight. I need you. XXX-OOO. Lila.'"

I looked at my uncle. He'd raised himself slightly on his thin elbows, staring hard at me, eyes burning, face pale. He whispered hoarsely, "Ben. The date. What's the date on the envelope?"

I checked the cancellation and my heart nearly stopped. "1939," I said. "August 16, 1939, afternoon. Postmarked Detroit."

"Forty-five years," Uncle Dan muttered, lips dry.

"Wow." I stood and read over the note and the envelope again. "This is really something, Uncle. Who's Lila?"

The back of his baldhead faced me as he stared out the bright window of the Detroit Metro Hospital at the Jeffries Freeway/Farmington Road interchange far below. After a long silence he said without looking at me, "She was special."

I walked around the bed to where I could get a look at his face. "What happened to her?"

"I don't know. She disappeared. I never heard."

My amusement evaporated as the tone of anguish in his voice sank in. I said, "She really *was* special, huh?" He didn't answer. I asked, "What bar was she talking about?"

"Burly Curly's," he answered. "We met there practically every day for weeks . . . months."

I wanted to press him further, but decided not to. He was going under the knife in the morning to have his gall bladder removed, and he was weak and drained from the pain and in shock from the letter. I went to a grocery sack that sat on the floor next to my chair and took out a red thermos. "Hey. Uncle. I brought some Tom and Jerry."

"Hot?" he asked hopefully, turning to face me.

"Of course." I opened the thermos and poured some into a plastic glass that sat on his tray table. "Egg, milk, sugar, brandy, a tad of salt, just the way you like it."

"Well," Dan said with a wan smile, "just a taste." He took the glass in his thin, veined hand and gulped. I refilled the glass and he gulped again and set the glass down jerkily. Sighing, he lay back on the bed. "Guess I blew it, Ben. She needed me and I didn't show up."

"Well hell," I said, pacing to the window, "how could you know? You didn't get the note."

"Wonder what happened to her?" Uncle Dan whispered. "Wonder where she is?"

"We can find out."

His smile was distant. "You've got cash-paying clients to take care of, Ben, you don't have to do detective work for me. Besides, it's been too many years. I'll never know what happened to her now."

I stepped toward him and fixed him with a stare. "Come on," I said harshly. "You done survived three years in the air over France, and then the union troubles in the thirties; and you're gonna get out of here, too, and by the time you do I'll have the answer about Lila. Believe it."

His smile did not change. "Of course." He looked at me sharply. "You still flying?"

"Sure, every chance I get, Uncle."

"Be careful. I've read some articles. Those ultralight airplanes are dangerous."

"No worse than the bamboo and wire crates you flew. And I don't have people shooting at me up there."

He waved a wasted hand at me. "Go, take off. I gotta rest up. And take that crap with you."

I picked up the mail. "I'll be back tomorrow to look in on you after they're done." He waved without looking at me, and as I walked out of the hospital room I saw him drink the last of his Tom and Jerry.

†††

I called the hospital the next morning. The operation, scheduled for eight, had been delayed till ten. They told me I could come by and see him in the afternoon. So, with time to kill, I located an old picture of Uncle Dan and drove through the late fall rain to the Detroit Library main branch on Woodward.

The Detroit telephone directory for 1939 showed a listing for Burly Curly's in the three hundred block of Cass. I drove over there, not expecting much, and wasn't surprised: the block was a devastated shell of burned-out buildings. On the way back to the hospital I stopped at Bullet Realty in Wayne where Owney Busbee, the owner/broker, was hunched over his cluttered desk; he agreed to run a title search on the Burly Curly's property to try to get a line on the owners.

Back at Greater Detroit Metro Hospital, I found Uncle Dan unconscious in his bed, looking white and shrunken. He sprouted tubes, one conveying, I could tell, oxygen. I sat by the bed watching him for what seemed like the longest time and he did not move. A doctor, who introduced himself as Ahmed Senatkor, stopped by briefly. He told me that the gall bladder operation has gone as expected, but that the post-operation X-rays had revealed a bowel obstruction. He said that they had Uncle Dan on oxygen and fluids and had inserted an abdominal tube to drain the bile that was collecting in his abdominal cavity.

I found a pay phone in the hall and dialed my sister Libby's number. No answer. I dialed my brother Bill and got him. He said he'd be over to the hospital right away. Instead, about fifteen minutes later, his wife Marybeth arrived.

She gave me a hug and a kiss on the cheek, sat down in a chair facing Uncle Dan's bed, and got out her knitting. Bill, she told me, hadn't felt up to coming. She said she'd stay with me till visiting hours ended. And so we stayed and watched Dan, who did not regain consciousness. Marybeth knitted and occasionally moistened Uncle Dan's mouth with a damp washcloth, and talked to me. I stared at my uncle and took a few trips down to the smoking room and thought about the forty-five-year-old letter and Lila and the long-gone Burly Curly's bar, till visiting hours ended.

2. THE BALLOON BUSTER

The morning sunlight drenched Uncle Dan's bed. I stood over him, holding his thin hand. He stared up at me through blue eyes that were crystal-clear no more. "Got two of 'em today, huh, Frank?"

"I sure did, Dan," I answered.

Uncle Dan chuckled. "You got *guts*, Frank. Them balloons are *crawling* with D-7's to protect 'em. And you get past 'em and blow the balloons all to hell anyhow."

I said through a dry mouth, "Those observation balloons are just too fat and pretty a target to ignore, Dan. And they're valuable to the Jerries. They keep tabs on movements in the trenches from the balloons."

"C'mon, Frank," Dan said, mouth twisted with sarcasm, "you don't go after the balloons because of their military value. Don't kid me. You go after 'em for the glory. 'Frank Luke, The Balloon Buster,' they're starting to call you. And you love it."

I grinned without feeling. "Got me there, Dan."

"Yeah. Hee-hee. I got you there." His face went pensive and he looked away from me. "I heard something about you the other day, Frank. They tell me you carry a .38 with you to knock yourself off if your plane catches fire."

I squeezed his hand. "Dan."

His thin-lipped mouth went into rictus. "Not gonna catch me doin' that, Frank. I don't think burning up'd be so bad—"

"Dan—"

"'Dan'? 'Dan'?" He stared into my face, eyes fierce and blue. "I'm *Uncle* Dan to you, youngster!"

"Yes, sir."

"Listen, Ben," he said softly after a long pause. "That'd have been a man's way to die. Burnt into ashes in the skies over France. *That'd* have been a right fine way to go out."

I struggled to keep my voice steady. "Take it easy, Uncle. You're not going to die. Just take it easy."

Back home in my apartment there was a message from Owney Busbee. The owner of Burly Curly's in 1939 was named Earl Eidson. There was no listing of that name in the phonebook, but a check with a contact at the credit bureau gave me an address in Franklin. As I left for my car I remembered the devastated block of Cass where Burly Curly's had stood so long ago and thought that, judging from the address, Earl Eidson had gotten out in one financial piece, indeed.

†††

Earl Eidson offered me a cigar. Margrit Eidson offered me tea. I turned down both offers with thanks. We sat on their patio deck that offered a splendid view of Smithfield Lake beyond a long, smooth, freshly mowed zoysia lawn. It was warm and humid and muggy, the kind of weather that signals the end of Indian summer.

Earl was short, burly, bald, and tan, dressed for golf. Margrit was tall and lanky in short-shorts and a roomy printed blouse, at the tail end of her years of real beauty. They were childless, wealthy and, from the welcome they'd given me, anxious for company.

I said to them, "I'm a private detective, trying to track down a woman who used to frequent your bar on Cass back in the late thirties."

"Burly Curly's," Margrit Eidson said affectionately. "I miss those days."

Earl Eidson's voice was booming, domineering. "We had lotsa regulars in those days, Perkins. Folks from when my dad ran the place. I inherited it from him, you know."

I didn't know, and didn't particularly care. "Woman's name was Lila." I paused. "That ring any bells?"

They looked at each other, shook their heads, and looked back at me expectantly.

I got my old picture of Uncle Dan out and laid it on the glass table in front of them. "She used to meet this man at your bar. Several times a week for months, I'm told."

They squinted at the picture then reared back and reacted in unison, Margrit with an "Eep!" Earl with a grunt. Margrit looked at me and said in a strained voice, "I *knew* him! Dan! I knew him!"

"You bet she did," Earl said, voice low, glance averted.

"Where is he?" she asked me. "What's he doing?"

"Pushing up daisies, I hope," Earl grunted.

"He's my uncle." They studied me silently. "He's quite ill."

Margrit clasped long-fingered hands in front of her. "I'm sorry to hear that." She looked anxiously at her husband and said, "Please, Earl. It was so long ago." She smiled sweetly. "I don't bring up Lucy, now do I?"

Eidson gave her a dark look then said with a flat, stiff-lipped voice, "Sorry, Perkins."

Part of me was embarrassed, another part was amused. I'd always known Uncle Dan was a lady killer in his day. "Do you remember the woman my uncle met there? Anything at all?"

Margrit Eidson straightened her spine, gave her husband a hesitant look then said to me, "I remember her. I was . . . I was interested in Dan. It was over by the time he began meeting her there. I was jealous, I watched them." She put her hand on her husband's and squeezed it tightly. "Earl," she said urgently, "it was *her!* The mystery woman!"

His face brightened as he looked intently at his wife. "The shooting? The Joe Verdi thing?"

"What shooting? What the hell does old Joe Verdi have to do with this?" I asked faintly.

They looked at me like I'd just arrived from Mars. Earl Eidson barked, "You don't remember the Joe *Verdi* case?"

I raised both hands in a back-off gesture. "Joe Verdi I've heard of. But hell, in '39 I wasn't even *born* yet."

Margrit Eidson fairly bounced with excitement. "Quick, Earl! Get the scrapbook!" Earl scraped his chair back and trotted into the house. Animation made Margrit's face look twenty years younger. "We never knew her name! The police asked us and *asked* us. And the reporters. Oh, we were in the news for *days* after that."

Earl Eidson returned with a string-bound scrapbook as thick as a lengthwise brick and laid it on the table in front of me. He sat back down next to his wife and, as I opened it, they leaned toward me, expecting me to be fascinated.

And I was.

††††

Carlo Infante arrived at the I-75 rest stop near Trenton just after I did. The place was a mid-afternoon madhouse of truckers and tourists who stared anxiously at the threatening sky and ran ducking against the cool wind into the little buildings to answer the call of nature. As Infante dropped gracefully into the passenger seat of the Mustang and greeted me, I had to make an effort to divorce myself from the scrapbook and its vivid depiction of the Detroit organized mob scene of the late thirties. Carlo Infante, a top finance guy in today's Detroit organization, fit today's image well. Young, cool, smooth, colorless, a businessman.

"Had hell breaking away on such short notice, Perkins," he said as he got a cigarette and a lighter out of his snappy suit jacket. I don't know why he carries smoking equipment around with him; I've never in my life seen him actually light up.

I stared past the restroom buildings at the flat horizon, angry gray clouds roiling above it. "Joe Verdi still alive, Carlo?"

He stared at me, obviously caught off guard. "Well, sure he is, Ben. Retired, though, been for years. Why?"

"I want to see him."

Infante's surprise faded and he became guarded.

"Why?"

"There's an old bit I want to ask him about. Fellow named Henry Porch, gunned down back in '39 at a bar called Burly Curly's on Cass. Word is Verdi knows something about it."

Infante smirked. "You've got me at a disadvantage. I wasn't around then."

"Neither was I." I stared into his thin face. "Porch was an organization finance man. Department of Justice turned him, used him to get an indictment against Verdi for you-name-it. Pre-trial, smuggled him to Detroit, kept him in hiding till testimony time. But the Justice boys ran into a slight snag."

Infante sighed. "Since you mentioned a shooting, and since Verdi's never been convicted, do I have to guess what the snag was?"

"Porch was gunned down late in August. Government lost its witness, Verdi walked. Strutted, more like."

"They prove anything on Verdi?" Infante asked.

"Nope. 'Course not. Had a pretty decent alibi, like about thirty-six thousand people at Briggs Stadium with him watching the Tigers."

"So what's your interest?"

I fired up a short cork-tipped cigar. "I'm not after Verdi," I said firmly. "I should give a damn, after all these years? But there was a woman in the bar. When Porch went down, she ran to him and hugged him and screamed. Then she took off, before the cops got there. Nobody ever got a line on her. 'The mystery woman,' the papers called her. I want her."

Infante toyed with his cigarette and his lighter for a long time, staring distantly out the windshield. "What makes you think Joe knows something about her?"

"Just hoping." I looked at him again through the upward stream of cigar smoke. "This is," I said distinctly, "historical research for an old, extremely important client. Nothing kicks back on nobody, guaranteed."

Infante smiled faintly. "I believe you, Ben. Question is, can I deliver a piece like this for you." He thought. "I'll get the word to Savastano. He's next step up. Best you can hope for is a meet with him. I'll let you know."

As he opened the Mustang door, I put my hand on his shoulder. He looked at me. I said, "It's personal, Carlo. Extremely important to me personally. I got no other angles."

"What you gotta hope," Carlo said as he got out, "is that Savastano believes that as much as I do."

I was just approaching the I-94 interchange on the Southfield Freeway when my car phone rang. It was Marybeth. "Trouble at the hospital," she said.

"You there now?"

"Yes. Hurry, Ben."

"Ten minutes."

I swerved into the left lane of the Southfield and floored the accelerator. The big secondary carburetor ports opened to suck air and the Mustang leaped forward, turning the center lane stripes into a white blur.

†††

Marybeth, dressed office-style in brown skirt and sleeveless white top, stood at Uncle Dan's hospital room and clapped her hands together when she saw me approach. "Ben—"

"Where is he?" I pushed past her into his room. It was a disaster area: furniture askew, paper wrappers strewn around the floor, closet door ajar. My uncle lay on the bed, atop the covers, strips of cloth binding his wrists and ankle to the chrome railings of the bed. His face was frozen solid, lips pursed, and every wasted inch of his body bucked against the bindings as he gasped air convulsively through his mouth.

I felt Marybeth behind me. "What happened?" I asked.

"Cardiac episode," she whispered, taking my hand. "His respiration became irregular. All of a sudden the place was overrun with doctors and nurses, working on him. They shoved me out into the hall. I just got back in here a few minutes ago." She pressed her face against my shoulder. "It's the bowel obstruction. They're taking him into surgery soon. They say they—"

I cut her off with a gesture and approached my uncle. He bucked and wheezed, gasped and panted, eyes glued shut. I touched his forehead. It was burning up. I looked at Marybeth. "You call Bill?"

"Yes." She bit her lip. "He won't come, Ben. He can't stand this kind of thing. You know that."

"Libby?"

"No answer."

A nurse, an orderly, and an older man in a white jacket came into the room, wheeling a gurney. I stepped back around the bed to Marybeth as the nurse and orderly untied my uncle and transferred him to the gurney. The doctor said to me, "We're taking him into surgery now."

He didn't look familiar. "You're Dr.—"

"Levin. Mr. Perkins' attending physician."

"Where's Dr. Senatkor?" I asked.

We stepped back to allow the gurney through the door. Dr. Levin repeated, "I'm the attending physician."

I found strength in my voice. "What *happened* to my uncle, doctor?"

Levin, a moonfaced, kindly looking man, said, "It's the bowel obstruction. He's collecting too many fluids. Infection could result. And he's weakened, especially his heart. We were hoping to build his strength first, but we have no choice. We have to correct the bowel obstruction now." He looked at Marybeth and back at me. "He's almost in a coma now," he said in a tone he assumed was comforting. "It's distressing to see, but he feels nothing, I assure you." He turned and left.

Marybeth walked aimlessly past Uncle Dan's empty bed to the window. "What are we supposed to do now?"

"Wait, I guess," I answered.

I'd just seated myself when a nurse's aide walked importantly into the room. "Oh, hey," she piped, "you've got to get these things out of here, folks."

"My uncle's in surgery," I said tonelessly.

"Well sure, but after that he'll be in ICU. Intensive care unit. Sixth floor. We need this bed for someone else." She began collecting Uncle Dan's things—suitcase, pillow, shaving kit, and other items—out of the closet. "You can take these to your car if you want," she said hopefully. "He won't need them up in ICU. Okay, folks? Thanks!"

I hijacked a wheelchair and used it to dolly Uncle Dan's things downstairs and out to my car. Back upstairs, on the sixth floor, I met Marybeth in the waiting room of the intensive care unit. We sat and waited, and looked at each other and at the TV, and watched other pinch-faced people waiting for word, throughout the afternoon, into the evening, well past nightfall.

Finally a young curly-haired man in a surgical gown came in the door and said, "Mr. Perkins?"

I bounded to my feet, followed by Marybeth. "That's me."

The doctor was twenty-eight, twenty-nine, tops. Where's Robert Young when you need him? He said, "I'm Dr. Sims. Bowel thing's squared away. Your uncle's in the ICU now. He handled it 'bout as well as we could expect."

Marybeth said, "What are his chances for survival?"

Dr. Sims seemed to suppress an urge to shrug. "A lot better than they'd of been if we hadn't gone in again."

Take it at face value, Perkins, I said to myself. Don't press. But I had to ask, "What happened to Dr. Levin?"

Sims did shrug this time. "I'm the attending physician now, Mr. Perkins. You can see your uncle in the morning. Check the ICU visiting hours schedule on the bulletin board." He turned and left.

†††

The United Airlines 747 had been at the gate for five minutes when the door from the jetway opened. Carlo Infante said to me, "Rick always flies first class. He'll be one of the first off."

"Fine." I watched the passengers start to stream toward us through the door. It was mid-morning, but for these passengers on the Los Angeles red-eye, it wasn't even sunrise yet, and they looked it.

I recognized Rick Savastano as he strode into the gate from the jetway. He was tall, well-built, with fighter-pilot good looks, dressed in a pale gray suit and maroon tie and carrying a wallet-thin leather briefcase. He nodded at Infante and his eyes flickered coldly with recognition when he saw me. We fell into step walking up the concourse toward the terminal.

Savastano said, "Carlo filled me in by phone, Perkins. Make your case."

I did so, as briefly as I could, adding information about Lila and her relationship to Uncle Dan, and the note that had taken forty-five years to reach him. Savastano said, "This kind of soppy syrupy sentimentality, I didn't expect that of you, Perkins."

"It's important."

Savastano's mouth twisted distastefully. "You're aware, of course, that Mr. Verdi has been retired from the business for years now. Steve Ritchie is running things."

"I know that. I don't want to step on anybody's toes. I want to go through the channels."

We entered the terminal and threaded through crowds between the Delta and New York Air desks toward the big glass doors. Savastano looked at me and said, "First it's up to Steve. I don't smell any rats, but he might, and he's the boss. Then, if he goes along, it's up to the old man. That's where it ends, Perkins. We'll be in touch if it's a go."

We went through the automatic swinging doors. The sky was lead-gray and the wind crisp and chilly as we headed toward the curb where a cream-colored Cadillac stretch purred. "I appreciate it," I answered, feeling bitter at being at this man's mercy. "Let me know either way, okay?"

The chauffeur trotted around the front of the limo and had the back door open just as Savastano reached it. Savastano looked down his long nose at me and said coldly, "We'll be in touch if it's a go, I said."

I thought about Uncle Dan strapped down convulsing in his hospital bed, and as I looked into Savastano's eyes I thought about how much I'd welcome a chance to take a real damaging poke at these bastards. It was a struggle to keep these feelings off my face, but I succeeded. I thanked them, waved, and trotted off for my car as Infante and Savastano boarded the Cadillac stretch and sighed away into traffic.

†††

Visiting hours in the intensive care unit were strange and rigidly enforced: odd hours only, ten minutes' duration. I showed up for the first, eleven A.M., directly from the airport.

Uncle Dan's room was half again the size of his former one. Much of his extra space was taken up with equipment: an electronic monitor on the wall showed changes in his heartbeat in digits and reflected the same in a scrolling, jagged series of lines; trees of IV bottles stood on each side of the bed, their tubes snaking down and under his sheet; a ventilator loomed on the left side of his bed, its big plastic accordion-like plunger going up and down with pneumatic sighs, echoed by the rising and falling of my uncle's thin chest.

He lay stiffly on his back, the oxygen tube affixed to his nose, ventilator tube inserted in his mouth, his arms tied down to the rails of the bed. His eyes were closed.

I leaned down to his ear and said, "Uncle?"

His eyes opened. Though cloudy, they showed recognition. He raised a clawlike hand and waved to me. I said, "I know you can't talk. Don't try."

His mouth formed a grisly smile around the mouthpiece of the ventilator. His wasted face, so unfamiliar, made me feel sick inside. I said heartily, "Thirty-one victories, remember, Uncle? Thirty-one of them Jerries."

He nodded jerkily and his right hand contorted into a thumbs-up. Poor guy. I was trying to hearten him, and all he wanted to do was hearten me.

I said, "You done got through that, and you done made it through this operation, too. You're gonna walk out of here, Uncle. Take a lot more'n this place to kill you, you tough old son of a bitch. Be sure to kiss the nurses as you go. Maybe even pat 'em on the ass, too. They won't mind."

He kept smiling.

"I'll be back here later on today, Uncle. Marybeth's coming for the afternoon visits. Libby'll be by later, too. You'll see."

I looked around the room. Hard to talk when nothing gets said back. I looked back at him. "On Lila. I'm making some progress. I know part of the story. I ought to know the rest soon. I'll keep on it, Uncle. You and me'll whip up some Tom and Jerry, and I'll fill you in later. Okay?"

He nodded again, eyes fixed on me, filled with spirit and defiance. The ten minutes were over and I said goodbye and went back to my apartment to wait for Savastano's call.

†††

But Marybeth called first, about three-thirty. She was crying. "He looks so awful, Ben."

"Hey, he's been through two operations—"

"But he was *crying!*" she wailed. "Both times, when I saw him. I tried to cheer him up—told him about the family and old times, and—"

"Steady on, kid," I said, not so steady myself.

"He keeps pointing to his mouth. It's so dry and—his lips are cracked and—he wants something to drink and—I can't give it to him and—I can't *help* him!"

"Once he's off that damn ventilator, we'll be able to help him, Marybeth."

"Ben," she said, getting control of herself, "do you think he's going to die?"

"Hey," I said loudly, "Dan's been through it all. He survived the fight on the overpass in '36, remember that? When three union-busting goons tried to put him away? He survived that, and he'll survive this."

"Okay. Okay." We stayed silent for a while, then she said, "You coming back later?"

"Yeah, I'll make the seven for sure. And Libby'll probably be out today, too."

"No, she won't," Marybeth said. "She says she'll come but she never does and she never will and you know it."

"I'll be out later," I said, and hung up.

Five minutes later, Rick Savastano called.

†††

Our Lady of Perpetual Mercy Hospital is a small, exclusive, private facility on the lakefront foot of Edgemont in Grosse Pointe Park. A pair of anonymous, suited goons met me at the doors and walked me to another pair, who rode up with me in the elevator and turned me over to yet a third pair on the sixth floor landing. These gentlemen escorted me into a suite that was more like a luxurious hotel than a hospital. Lying in the center of the large bed facing the picture window which looked out over Lake St. Clair was the wizened, yet vigorous looking, Joe "Gunboats" Verdi.

Flanked by his goons, I stopped at bedside. Verdi, a jowly man with a full head of solid gray hair and dressed in loud red pajamas, smiled at me sardonically. His voice was, totally unexpectedly, weak, wispy, forced. "Ben Perkins?"

"Right, Mr. Verdi."

"The boys said you wanted to talk to me about the old days," Verdi wheezed. I realized that by "boys" Verdi meant Steve Ritchie and Rick Savastano, each of whom was pushing fifty if not past it.

"That's right. I'm wondering about the shooting in Burly Curly's bar back in '39. I told Savastano this is research only, nothing you tell me'll kick back now or ever."

"I should worry about kickbacks?" Verdi squeaked. He patted his bull-like chest. "I've got the Big C, liver. I got maybe a month or two. Nothing that happens now could ever hurt me worse'n I'm about to be hurt." His eyes turned crafty. "But if you're asking me if I ordered the hit on that rat-faced little snitch Porch, I'll be forced with all honesty to say, 'No comment.'"

The last thing I expected to do there was laugh. This was, after all, Gunboats Verdi, Detroit organization boss for fifty years with maybe four times that many murders on his sheet. And though he was dying, he was dying in a place with ten times the luxury of the little room in which Uncle Dan was fighting for his life. But I laughed anyway.

Verdi laughed too, ending in a sick, rasping cough that turned his lined face purplish-red. He took an empty cup and spit into it then set the cup down. When he looked back at me, his eyes were cold and dark, the eyes of a dying old man looking at a vigorous younger one. "What do you want to know?" he whispered.

"My uncle was meeting a woman there at the bar," I said. "He was deeply involved with her, but he didn't know much about her. She disappeared right after the shooting. Witnesses have told me that the woman he was meeting seemed to know Porch very well." I paused. "Her first name was Lila. I'm trying to find her. Do you know anything that might help me?"

"Quicksilver," Verdi rasped. He coughed again and repeated the name. "Lila Quicksilver. Porch's fiancée. He brought her to Detroit with him while he waited to testify against me."

Oh boy. I felt my heart pound as I said, "Where'd she go, Mr. Verdi?"

"Chicago," he answered readily. "Still there, in fact." He squinted at my expression and smiled. "How do I know? I kept tabs. I didn't know if she might decide to turn state's evidence the way Porch tried to. And she was an interesting chick. . . . Your uncle has good taste. A lot like me."

I thought, Uncle Dan's like you only in that he's dying, too. It was the first time I'd consciously thought that Uncle Dan was going to die.

Verdi said in what for him was a kindly way, "You're trying to find Lila for your uncle, is that it?"

"That's right."

He waved an imperious hand at one of the goons. "Larry, call Savastano for me. Tell him, the notebook in the safe, under the name Lila Quicksilver. Have him call her, give her Mr. Perkins' name and say he's trying to reach her. Ask her to call him."

"Sure, Mr. Verdi," one of the faceless goons stirred.

Verdi smiled at me. "There. That help you, son?"

One last exercise of power of a dying man. But he could have refused to see me, could have refused to help. I smiled and nodded. "Thanks, Mr. Verdi."

"Maybe," Verdi said with a narrow look, "you'll remember that I did you this service."

"I *will* remember it, Mr. Verdi. Thanks."

Not that he'd be around long enough for it to do him any good.

†††

I met Marybeth in the ICU waiting room just before one the next day. She looked pale and exhausted and though she held her knitting in her lap, it didn't look as if she'd made any progress since the previous day.

As I sat beside her, she took my hand and said, "He wasn't so good at eleven o'clock. He refused to look at me. Didn't wave, didn't wink, didn't smile."

I breathed deeply. "What'd the doctor say? How's Dan doing?"

"Dr. Bates talked to me. Said Uncle's got serious infections. They're fighting to stabilize him, changing medications."

"Bates? Who's Bates? Didn't you talk to Sims?"

"Sims? But Dr. Bates said he's the attending surgeon now."

I gritted my teeth and said in a low voice loud enough to attract the attention of the other visitors, "Can't a man have a *doctor* of his *own* anymore?"

Marybeth shrugged helplessly.

"What about the ventilator?" I asked in a lower tone.

She shook her head. "Doctor said Uncle Dan'll need it at least another week, till he's under control and they've turned the infections around." She gnawed her lip, reached out and put her hand on mine. "Brace yourself. He's accumulated fluids. He's gained twenty-five pounds in fluids just since yesterday, Ben. He looks just . . . awful."

One o'clock came and we went into Uncle Dan's room. Nothing had changed. Same equipment, same bottles, same tubes, same monitor with its blinking numbers and jagged line, same ventilator hissing a wheezing, breathing life into Uncle Dan.

The fluid retention was obvious. Uncle Dan looked swollen and shiny, like a newborn baby, skin stretched so tight it looked as if it was about to split. His eyes opened when I spoke to him. "How's things, big fella?"

He stared at me and did not move.

"I'm back again, Uncle Dan," Marybeth smiled as she leaned and kissed him on the cheek.

He looked at us and then raised a hand as far as the cloth restraint would let him and pointed toward the ceiling.

I looked where he pointed. "What is it, Uncle? What do you need?"

He lowered his hand then raised it, pointed his index finger to his temple and dropped his thumb.

I looked away quickly, eyes burning. Marybeth looked at me with frightened eyes and said as cheerfully as she could, "The doctor says you're getting along fine, Uncle Dan. No time at all you'll be out of here. And we'll have a big party for you. Right, Ben?"

We talked like that for the full ten minutes, more to each other than to my uncle, and all the while he pointed to the ceiling again and again and again.

†††

I'd just arrived at my apartment to shower and change clothes when the telephone rang.

"Ben Perkins?" asked the long-distance female voice.

"You got him."

"I'm Lila." Silence. "Lila Quicksilver."

"Oh. Hi." I sat down on the couch, pressing the receiver to my ear. "Glad you called, I—"

"Actually my last name is Brockmann now, I'm married."

"Uh-huh. Okay." Silence. "The, uh—you get told why I wanted to talk to you?"

Her voice was guarded. "Something about the shooting?"

"Really I'm calling about Dan. Dan Perkins. He's my uncle."

This time the silence went on so long I thought she'd hung up. But she said, "Dan? How nice. How's he doing?"

"Not so good. But Lila—Ms. Quicksilver—Mrs. Brockmann—let me ask you, you were close to my uncle, right?"

"That was many years ago."

"Forget that! You were real close, I know that. How'd you meet him? What was your connection with Henry Porch?"

"I don't want to talk about that. It's nobody's business. It's past and buried."

Unwillingly, I said, "Fine, tell me or don't tell me, that's not important now. What is important is something that you never knew." I paused. "Dan never got your note. Not till just a few days ago."

A long pause. "*No.*"

"It's true. He never got it. He never knew what happened to you. You disappeared and he wondered about you for all these years, and *he never knew* and he never forgot about you."

"No," she said definitely. "Even life isn't that cruel."

"Oh yeah? Well, try this. Right now my uncle is in intensive care at Greater Detroit Metro Hospital. He's strapped down and on a respirator and . . . and he's eighty-seven and alone and drugged and fighting for his life. *Tell* me about cruel, Lila."

"Well, what am I supposed to do about it? All that was my whole life ago. I cared for Dan, but he wasn't there when I needed him, and there's nothing I can do for him now!"

"You just do what you want," I said, standing. "But you should know that you were special to him. And he never got your note. And if he had, he'd have been there at Burly Curly's for you. And he never married, Lila, and he never forgot you. Just do what you want, though. You just do what you damn well please."

I slammed the phone down and stomped in several aimless circuits of my living room. Withholding information from a private detective *just isn't done*, I thought.

Then I went into my kitchen in search of a Stroh's tall boy and the half bottle of black Jack I'd been saving.

3. THE FOREVER TRIP

The ringing phone brought my eyes open. I focused on the orange numerals of the bedside clock. One thirty five A.M. I wrestled the receiver to my ear with numb hands. "Perkins."

"This is Detroit Metro Hospital," came the brisk female voice. "The doctor has asked me to contact the family of Dan Perkins. We think you should get here right away."

"What's wrong?" I mumbled, raising myself.

She said carefully, "There's been some cardiac disturbances. The doctor thought it best that family representatives be present."

"Okay, all right, I'll be there." I hung up the phone, switched on the nightstand light, picked up the receiver again, and dialed my brother Bill's number. He answered with a grunt. I said, "Wake up, bro, there's trouble at the hospital."

"Oh no." He paused. "You going, Ben?"

"I'm rolling. You?"

Marybeth came on. "I'll be dressed and on my way in five minutes, Ben."

"I'll pick you up."

"No, it's quicker, I'll meet you there." She hung up.

†††

The intensive care unit never closes. The waiting room was thronged with exhausted people, waiting for word on traffic victims and shooting victims and disease victims; they bore identical signs of strain mixed with equal measures of hope, fear, and resignation.

Marybeth, dressed in jeans and a white top, met me at the big double doors, and we silently pushed through them and went to the desk. I gave my name to the nurse. "Oh, yes, the Perkins family," she said. "Just step into the office there, the doctor will be right with you."

We went into the closetlike, booklined office. Marybeth took the single chair, I leaned against the door. We said nothing. After a few minutes a short black woman in a white coat that blinked with stethoscope and other hardware came in. "I'm Dr. Johnson," she announced to us generally. "You're the Perkins family?"

"Where's Dr. Bates?" I asked then repeated with her: "You're the attending physician."

She smiled at us and stepped past Marybeth to seat herself behind the tiny desk. Marybeth asked, "What happened to Uncle Dan?"

She was smooth, practiced, professional. "He had an episode of cardiac arrest. But, happily, we were able to resuscitate him and restore his blood pressure."

For the first time since Uncle Dan had gone into the hospital, my sister-in-law Marybeth let go. Not angrily, but with ultimate despair. "Oh, no. *Why* did you bring him back?"

Dr. Johnson blinked, her composure broken for a moment. "Well, we had to, in order to—"

"He's *dying!*" Marybeth pressed. He's been dying since he came here. Why, oh *why* didn't you just let him *go?*"

Dr. Johnson sat back and drew herself up. "There are no instructions on file as to the family's wishes in the event of a life-threatening crisis," she said formally.

"You want instructions?" The woman looked at me. "*I'll* give you instructions. I don't want my uncle strapped down like a piece of meat anymore. I don't want him hooked up to miracle machines and pumped full of drugs and fed through tubes any more. I don't want my uncle reduced to the level of an experiment for the ego-tripping doctors. I don't—"

Dr. Johnson cut in sharply, "If we remove medical support, your uncle will die."

"Then so be it." I looked at Marybeth for approval and saw it. "If he can't live without the machines, then he ain't living; and if he understood that, he'd agree with me."

"Very well," Dr. Johnson said, briskly rising. "We'll call you when we're ready."

It took ten minutes, and then we were ushered into Uncle Dan's room and left alone with him there.

Marybeth sat on his left, I sat on his right. She took one of his hands, I sat there and watched him. His eyes were open and dull, his body shrunken, his chest rising and falling in accord with the puffing of the ventilator. I became fixated by the numerals on the monitor that registered his heartbeat. When we came in it was reading in the one hundred thirties.

Long moments went by. A nurse looked in on us. One hundred twelve. I looked at Marybeth. Her face was narrow and pinched and she tried to smile at me and looked back into Uncle Dan's face.

The rate dropped below one hundred.

I stood up and walked around the bed, looking at my uncle from each angle. He was silent, vacant. The machine said sixty-five.

I sat back down. Marybeth looked up at the monitor then bent and kissed Uncle Dan and whispered something in his ear. Down to forty now.

I tried to say something, thought better of it then said it anyhow: "I won't forget your stories, Uncle."

"No," Marybeth chimed in. "None of us will." The monitor read into the thirties and, as I watched, dipped to twenty-five. The graph register below showed its jagged peaks much less frequently now, and they weren't as sharp-edged.

Twenty, fifteen, ten, seven, two, zero.

Zero. Zero. Zero.

The graph register made waves like the long swells of a gentle ocean and then went flat.

The ventilator pumped mindlessly on.

Marybeth looked up at me, tears streaming silently, heavily down her thin cheeks. I sighed and wiped my eyes and pressed Uncle Dan's hand one last time. The door to the room opened and Dr. Johnson came in. "Please accept my condolences on the passing of your uncle," she said.

We stood. I said huskily, "Thank you, doctor."

She said, "If you would, I need some information about the arrangements, Mr. Perkins."

I looked at Marybeth. "Would you?"

She nodded, throat bobbing. She walked around the bed and pressed the entire length of her body against me, dampening my shoulder. Then she turned and followed the doctor out of the room.

I looked down at my uncle for a long, long time. Then I stepped out of the room, closed the door, and stood with my back to it in the empty hall.

I thought: No one can touch him any more. I won't let them. I'm the detective and he's my client, and I fix things and help people and protect them, and I won't let anyone hurt him any more.

†††

Libby said harshly, "I demand an explanation as to *why* my uncle was cremated so quickly."

We sat, the remains of Uncle Dan's family, in the cool, well-furnished silence of the funeral home's parlor: my sister Libby, slimmer than when I'd seen her last a couple of years before, dressed in a white blouse and expensive blue suit; my brother Bill, short, bald, big-shouldered, wearing a tan blazer and tie and dark slacks; and his wife Marybeth, tall, whip-thin, and elegant in a midnight blue dress with a thin string of pearls around her neck.

Mr. Roski, the baby-faced, pudgy funeral director, adjusted his thick glasses and looked at me. "Those were the instructions we had from Mr. Ben Perkins, Mrs. Gillespie."

Libby shot me a dirty look. I said, "It's what he wanted, Libby."

"Like hell!" she spat. "You had no *right* to make that kind of decision without clearing it with the family, you insensitive ghoul!"

Bill and Marybeth looked uncomfortable, their eyes meeting no one. I said as evenly as I could, "I most certainly knew what he wanted, Libby. I took care of his finances for him for years. I visited him every week. Where the hell were *you* on his birthday and Christmas? Where the hell were *you* when he was dying in the hospital? Who the hell are *you* to swoop in here and start calling people names?"

"I'm his *niece*," she shot back shrilly, "and I *won't* stand by and allow my uncle to—to be *discarded*, like some kind of *refuse*, without a proper funeral!"

Mr. Roski cleared his throat and said carefully, "Of course, our facility stands ready to assist the Perkins family with whatever arrangements you mutually decide to make." He had his eyes on Libby all the while.

She said, ticking fingers as she talked, "We want a *coffin* and a proper visitation period, and a service in the Baptist church and burial in a nice cemetery. The way it's supposed to be." She looked imperiously at my brother. "What do you say, Bill?"

He sighed, flicked me a look, and nodded to Libby.

"Marybeth?"

Her look my way was regretful, but she had to go along with her husband.

Mr. Roski clapped his hands and stood. "Then it's decided! Very well. Mrs. Gillespie," he said, taking Libby's arm, "we have a fine selection of coffins and vaults to choose from in the next room. Let me show you. . . ."

They left the room, Bill and Marybeth trailing them. I walked out, turned, went through the lobby, and left the building.

As I crossed the parking lot to my car, I looked at the rolling stone-dotted hills of the cemetery and thought, there's no way I'm leaving my uncle in this place.

†††

The visitation at the funeral home the next evening was, thanks to Libby's calls to the newspapers, well-attended. Libby herself held forth in one corner, flanked by Bill and Marybeth and surrounded by old people who knew Dan somewhere or another. I sat alone in the opposite corner, my eyes on the closed bronze coffin, which sat on the altar-like stand amid an array of floral arrangements.

Toward the end of the visitation, as the crowd started to thin, I became aware of a woman standing near me. Late sixties, wisp-thin, heavy gray-streaked dark hair cropped close. "Mr. Perkins?" she asked.

She wasn't familiar. "Yes."

Her blue eyes were large in her thin face. She stepped closer to me, looking at me intently. "Mr. *Ben* Perkins?"

"Yes," I said with some impatience. Probably some mortuary ghoul or professional mourner or something.

Her smile made her look younger. "You do look a little like him. He was just about your age when I knew him." She caught my look and added, flustered, "Oh! Excuse me! I'm Lila. Lila Quicksilver."

"Well, jeez." I stood clumsily and shook her thin, firm hand. "You made it, huh? Well, that's something."

"I thought about it," she answered, looking away from me. "It must have been a lot of trouble for you to track me down. And Dan and I were—we were very close." She looked back at me. "And you said he never got my note."

"Never did."

She shook her head. "Such a shame. How different our lives would have been, if. If, if, if."

"Yeah." She took the chair next to me and we sat and looked at the coffin. "So, tell me. How did it happen? How did you get to know Uncle Dan?"

She sighed. "Henry and I were engaged. Living in Chicago. He decided to turn state's evidence in an investigation of Joe Verdi. The FBI brought us to Detroit incognito to wait for Henry to testify. We thought the trial would start quickly. But it didn't. We waited and waited. Days. Weeks. Months. Hiding."

"How'd you meet Dan?"

"I'm getting to that." She paused. "I was afraid. Afraid and bored. I hadn't known the depth of Henry's involvement with the mob till then. I was afraid of what those men would do to him if they caught him. And I was bored, cooped up in that grimy little motel room day after day. So I began to go out, alone."

"To Burly Curly's."

"Yes. I met Dan there." Her voice softened and I felt her eyes on me. "He was a fine man. Much older than me, of course. But so handsome and dashing, a real wicked twinkle in his eye, yet decent and gentle, too. I became infatuated with him, Mr. Perkins."

"Did you tell him about Porch and the investigation?"

"Of course not! I never even told Dan my last name. I was afraid. And ashamed. I began to think about Dan, about leaving Henry and going to Dan, where I'd be safe."

I closed my eyes and sighed. "So what happened?"

"One day Henry got a phone call. I don't know what was said, but it terrified him. I was convinced that Verdi's people had tracked Henry down and were going to kill him. I dashed off a note to Dan and mailed it, asking him to meet me that evening at Burly Curly's. I was going to tell him the whole story and ask him to take me away. I went to the bar and waited, but Dan never came. Instead, Henry showed up. He'd gotten word of where I went, somehow. As he came in the door, two men with shotguns followed him and shot him."

She touched my arm and I felt her tremble. After a moment she went on, "I . . . I went a little hysterical, I think. But I got out of there and made it to the bus station and grabbed the first bus west. All the way back to Chicago. And I've been there ever since and lived a quiet life and thought all that trouble was behind me." Her voice deepened. "Till the other day, when that horrible man from Verdi's organization called."

"I'm glad you came," I said.

"Just wish I'd come in time to see him."

We stared silently at the coffin a long time. It was late, everyone else had gone, leaving us alone in the room. She said suddenly, "One thing I know for sure. Dan wouldn't have wanted—"she gestured around the room—"all *this*."

"You're right." I roused myself and stretched and looked at her. "I got some thoughts on that. Want to help?"

"How?"

I told her.

She looked back at the coffin and then at me, eyes misty. "I'm with you," she whispered. "But I want to be in it all the way, Ben."

I snorted. "Come on! It's gonna be dangerous."

She smiled wickedly. "I may look sixty-eight, but I'm as young as you, maybe younger. And I want to do this for Dan."

I shrugged. "Okay." I glanced around, the room was still empty. "Now's as good a time as any. Ready?"

She stood, went to the door of the visitation room, peered out then nodded to me.

I walked up to the coffin, hoping it was unlocked.

It was.

†††

People drifted across the grass away from the gravesite, hunched in their jackets against the cool, sun-drenched breeze. Lila and I were halfway to my car when Libby caught up with us. She certainly was dressed for the role of chief mourner in a black dress, black stockings, black shoes, and a black hat equipped with a veil, for heaven's sake. Ignoring Lila, Libby took my arm.

"I'm sure glad that's all over," she sighed. "These things are *so* hard on a person, don't you think?"

"True enough."

She swept the veil back from her face. "But don't you agree with me now, Ben? This is the right way, the *proper* way to see to things."

"Anyway, you got it done."

"Listen," she said eagerly, "I'm having everyone over to the house for an early supper. It's important that the *family*—"she gave Lila a meaningful look—"hang together in times like this, don't you think?"

I felt sick. "Thanks anyhow. We've got business." Taking Lila's arm, I turned my back on Libby and made for my car.

†††

The second seat—which I generally use for cargo, never for a passenger—of my modified Maxair Hummer sits directly behind the pilot's seat. I helped Lila into it and strapped her in. She sat nervously, looking tiny in slacks and a warm wool jacket, but she nodded at me with a defiant smile.

I completed the pre-flight inspection of the aircraft by checking the translucent plastic gas tank one last time. Full. Dropping into the bucket seat, I tucked my leather jacket tight around me—despite the full sunlight, it was a chilly day—positioned my feet on the rudder bar, primed the engine with a couple of squeezes of the pressure bulb, set the choke, cracked the throttle, and after yelling "clear!" (even though there was nobody but Lila in sight), I gave the T-handle a good jerk. The 250cc Zenoah engine engaged, barfed, blatted, and caught into a good healthy purr from its mounting ten feet behind us. Killing the choke, I set the throttle at about two thousand rpm and sat back to let her warm up.

It was midday, mid-week. There were no golfers using the Norwegian Wood course. Wind was steady at twelve knots out of the southwest—a bit stronger than I'd have preferred, but this wasn't exactly a pleasure flight we were embarking on.

Everything was set. "Here we go!" I hollered over my shoulder. I goosed the throttle and the Hummer began to roll. I swung her around toward the southwest, edged the throttle up a little more, and pressed the stick forward to raise the tail. We passed high taxi. I gave her more gas, the aircraft rolled faster and swayed, the wind began to sing in the flying wires, and just as we reached the eighth green, we left the ground. I did the pattern, tested the wind, checked the trim of the ship then made a sweeping turn and, gaining altitude all the while, headed almost due west toward Stapfer Lake.

"This is wonderful!" came Lila's ready voice amid the rush of the wind. Your first time in an ultralight does that to you. You're sitting out in the open, no cockpit, nothing above you but wings and nothing below you but a couple of aluminum frame members and, way, way down, the ground.

We were at a thousand feet by the time we got to the lake. It wandered around jerkily in a wide blue howl, marred here and there by whitecaps, circled by dense woods. I circled the lake and then, applying maximum stick and throttle, took her up close to five thousand.

The wind was calmer there. The lake looked smaller. Roughly in the center was the small wooded island that Uncle Dan owned. I could see, amid the scrub and trees, the charred ruins of his old cabin, torched a few years ago by a maniac who was trying to kill me and got someone else instead. I put the aircraft on a steady trimmed course traversing the lake, gripped the stick between my knees, reached to the down tube, and unstrapped the medium-sized aluminum canister from it.

The screw-top was hard to get loose but I finally spun it off and tossed it. I reached around the seat and put the canister in Lila's waiting hands. I side-slipped for a moment to correct my course and then, when dead center over the lake, I said, "All right."

Lila leaned down, tipped the canister, and let the ashes stream out.

They fell in a solid gray funnel. Caught by the windstream, they fanned out wider and wider in a descending ever-lightening V. When the canister was empty, Lila tossed it over the starboard side. I poured power to the Hummer engine, climbed steeply then leveled, and we looked down silently.

Caught by the lower wind currents and illuminated by the sun, the ashes fell toward the blue water in a just visible, glinting veil then disappeared.

I sat up in the bucket seat. Couldn't do France for you, Uncle, but this is the next best thing.

I kicked the wings over, set the throttle a notch higher to maintain lift in the tail wind, and headed for home.

Afterword

I was 32 when I first watched someone die. It was my aunt Lila, and her final days mirrored Dan's in every technical sense. The story was my way to react to the experience, and to deal with what in retrospect was in fact a very significant turning point in my life—with long-range consequences no one concerned could ever have foreseen. Ain't that just like life?

Though this story is the first in this anthology to utilize Ben's ultralight, he's had one from the first novel (*The Back-Door Man*). I put an inordinate amount of time and effort into researching ultralight planes and various aspects of flying them. Clearly I take a bit of creative license here. Ben's home is practically on a straight line between metro Detroit's two major airports and, in the real world (whatever that is), I think it's unlikely he'd be allowed to drive the thing around the sky the way he does.

But it sure comes in handy, doesn't it?

Fly Away Home

The pigeons descend in twos and threes, lighting on the short ledge of the roof. They flutter and strut among the debris and droppings, warbling deep in their throats. Occasionally two or three collide, and there is a squawking, flap-winged argument, with the loser taking wing in a shallow dive off the ledge.

I watch them intently, a cigarette smoldering in one hand, a coffee cup steaming black in the other. It is early summer and early in the morning in Detroit. The city comes awake with increasing sounds of traffic from fourteen floors below. To the south the heavily industrialized Zug Island sends smoke into the air to war with the haze. To the east freighters bay on the Detroit River. Up here I am alone with my coffee and my cigarette, dressed as always in white shirt, neatly clipped tie, dark pants, and black wing-tipped shoes. I look like a clerk, which I am; and I look like I'm about to begin another routine workday, which I am not.

The pigeons descend in twos and threes, lighting on the ledge at the edge of the roof. The turnover is constant, new birds descending to the ledge, others dropping away. Where do they go? A phrase comes to mind from nowhere: fly away home. Fly away home. I think it's a nursery rhyme. Probably recited to me by my grandmother many years ago. I cannot remember the rest of the poem. I do remember my grandmother, and I see her fresh in my mind's eye, kneeling at her flower bed, short spade in hand, straightening and smiling and rising as she watches me approach.

Footsteps sound from behind me, ascending the seldom-used stairwell that rises from the guts of the building to the roof. I turn impatiently, waiting to see who is coming. It was the sound of footsteps like these that started the mess, just a week ago. . . .

††††

I turned as the footsteps reached the top of the stairs and crushed out my cigarette as Connie came through the door. She was a big, beefy bull of a woman, dressed in an immense purple balloon of a dress, with dark brown hair permed high on her head. She had a happy, goofy, angelic face, except when she was forced to talk to me. "Someone to see you," she said flatly, standing at the door to the stairway as if afraid to come out on the roof toward me.

I glanced at my watch. "Well, *who*, Connie? The work day doesn't start for fifteen minutes."

"Maurie's lawyer," she said through a pinched mouth. "And she's brought some kind of detective with her. You'd better get down there. They're going to interview everybody today, in alphabetical order."

That put me first on the list. Bad luck. I huffed a sigh and followed Connie down the dark stairwell. As we approached the heavy fire door leading into our company's suite of offices, she turned to me, face softer and somewhat scared, and said, "You don't think Maurie did it, do you?"

"I'm sure of it," I said sincerely.

Connie's meaty, clownish face looked somber. "Mo was such a nice girl. Maurie is, too. I just can't believe Maurie would kill her. Think there's a chance the lawyer can get her off?"

"There's always a chance, Connie," I said heavily. We entered the suite, air-conditioning gushing coolly against my hot, moist skin. "Where are they waiting?"

Before my eyes, as if she realized who she was talking to, Connie's face changed back to that look, that look that women always had for me: suspicion, contempt, loathing. "Conference B," she answered through pinched lips, and swept away from me.

I headed over there.

†††

I entered the room, closed the door behind me, and stood still, feet apart, hands clasped at my waist in front of me, a polite smile on my face. To my left, at the head of the conference table, sat a tall blonde woman in her mid-thirties, dressed in a navy-blue skirt, matching jacket, and white blouse with spaghetti-thin ties down the front. She had dark eyes, a creamy complexion, and a snub nose, plus a look of competent self-importance. A thin hand-tooled leather briefcase sat open on the table in front of her.

To her right sat a broad-shouldered, very tan, very fit-looking man in his early forties. His full head of thick black hair swept back along the sides and down to the collar. His dark blue eyes shown brightly from the deep tan of his face, and he had a variety of laugh and squint lines to go with the broken nose, broad forehead, and squarish jaw; but mostly he looked sleepy, cynical, contemptuous, inimical. His short-sleeved chambray shirt revealed hard, tanned, heavily muscled arms matted thickly with black hair; intermittently, whitish scars showed against the tan. Below, he wore jeans. In appearance and dress he looked better suited to mowing lawns or digging graves than to presenting himself for discussions in a professional place of business.

Taking the bit in my teeth, I introduced myself and went on. "The lawyer and the detective. Which, may I ask, is which?"

The man looked bored, the woman amused. "I'm Carole Somers, Maureen Frye's attorney." She tipped her head toward the man. "This is the private detective I've retained to assist me in the case. Ben Perkins."

The detective's eyes locked on mine, and instantly I knew him. I knew those men, all of them. Muscled and tanned, with full heads of hair, big white smiles, hearty laughs, and slaps on the rump, jokes and repartee that turned English into a foreign language. Oh, yes, I knew those men. The high school jocks who stared through their intellectual superiors as if they were bugs, who drove fast cars, joked easily with big-busted girls, and were handy with tools. I knew those men, all right. The slow-moving, lazy hunks who cluttered dark after-hours bars, who bought lottery tickets and cheap beer in dozen lots, who wolfed down ground rounds and watched big-TV sports with packs of their fellows in bowling alley cocktail lounges.

If Perkins read anything in my face—something I worked hard to avoid— he didn't show it. He nodded at me, extracted a short cork-tipped cigar from his shirt pocket and, with the snap of a wood match in his thumbnail, began filling the conference room with an evil stench.

Carole Somers said briskly, "Please be seated. We'll try not to take up too much of your time."

I took a chair and composed myself neatly, watching the two as Somers took a yellow legal pad out of her briefcase and Perkins smoked his cigar. I wondered if they had gone to bed together, and then I was sure they had, probably many times.

Somers looked at me, face expectant, professional. "Maureen Stevens: 'Mo.' Maureen Frye: 'Maurie.'" She paused. "Tell me about them, please."

I shrugged. Under the stares of the lawyer and the detective, my palms became moist; to dry them off, I placed them on the padded arms of the chair. "I don't know much. They worked here together. They shared an apartment. They were close friends and well enough liked by everyone who knew them. This past Monday, Mo was found bludgeoned to death here in the office. The police have arrested Maurie and charged her with murder." I smiled indulgently. "Maurie has retained you to help her. You have retained this man to help you." I raised my now-dry hands palms up. "Not much help, I'm afraid."

"You're doing fine," Somers said without raising her eyes from her notes. "Do you personally believe that Maurie killed Mo?"

"No." Palms dry now, heart pounding steadily, mind icily calm, I felt gutsy, daring, brave. "I am convinced she did not."

Somers' eyes met mine. "The police have what they believe is a strong case. During nonworking hours, only authorized personnel are permitted access to the offices. They must sign in at the security guard's desk downstairs. Mo was here very early in the morning, as was her habit; and during the time she was here, only Maurie signed in downstairs. Further, the police theorize, there was some competition between the two—competition for men, leading possibly to a motive of jealousy."

"Certainly Maurie denies that," I said stoutly.

"Of course." Far as Somers was concerned, the detective, Perkins, was not in the room, which would have been fine with me. She was cute. "Maurie says she stopped at the office to pick up some proofs that had to be at the printer first thing in the morning. She swears that Mo was alive when she got there, that she talked with her, that Mo was alive and well when she left. She says no one else in the office or elsewhere in the building except for the security guard. Further, while both women were single and, ah, fairly active in their involvement with men, there was total openness and communication between the two, and no jealousy between them as far as Maurie was concerned."

I ignored the vacant stare of the beefy detective and kept my eyes candid and friendly on the luscious Carole Somers. "That is consistent with my observations," I said. As usual, particularly when talking to a woman, I felt I sounded stilted and pompous, but Carole did not seem to notice.

She leaned back in her chair and studied me. "In your observation, would you characterize Mo and Maurie as, shall we say, fast women?"

"Nice girls, both of them," I retorted.

She smiled. "Please. There is already evidence on record attesting to a certain level of what some would characterize as promiscuity. It speaks well for you that you defend your friends, but what I think of you personally is irrelevant. I remind you that Maurie is charged with first-degree murder, and if I'm to defend her adequately, I must have the truth."

"Well." I adjusted myself in my chair, studied the backs of my hands, found the detective's flat, vacant stare, and turned my eyes to the lawyer. "You're interviewing everyone in the office today, so I might as well be the one to tell you. Mo and Maurie were—how shall I phrase this?—cheerfully voracious where men were concerned. One heard . . . jokes about them. Some referred to them as 'The Maureens.' As in, 'The Maureens are looking for a few good men.'" I smiled sadly. "I felt that such jokes were in the worst possible taste. Not at all what I consider appropriate in a professional setting." I felt perfectly composed now, strong, confident, secure.

Ben Perkins began to stub out his filthy-smelling cigar in an ashtray and spoke for the first time. "You get any of that?"

"I'm sorry?" I asked politely.

His eyes stayed on his cigar as he crushed it. "Either one of them. Or both."

I played dumb. "I'm afraid I don't follow you."

Perkins finished snuffing his cigar and rubbed his jaw with the back of a heavily knuckled hand as he fixed his blue eyes on me. "What I'm asking you is, was one of those 'few good men' you?"

Irrelevantly, I detected a trace of a southern accent in his heavy, husky voice. I brought myself up straight in my chair and looked at Carole Somers. Rather than giving Perkins an annoyed look, she was watching me expectantly. So.

"I'm a married man," I said, allowing some heat to enter my voice.

"So?" Perkins responded, the syllable a Neanderthal grunt.

I gnawed my lip impatiently. "Certainly not."

Perkins did not change expression. He leaned forward, elbows on knees, eyes on me. "Worked here long?"

"Many years."

"Associate with either Maureen away from the office?"

"I believe it imprudent to develop personal relationships with co-workers. That is my rule."

Paper ripped as Carole Somers tore a blank sheet of paper off her pad. She slid it over to me, along with a pen. "Write something."

Smooth team. Smooth team. But so stupid. They watched me as I selected a pen from the plastic carrier in my pocket and, without a word of protest, wrote the standard "quick brown fox" sentence on the paper. "Satisfied?"

"Right-handed," Perkins told Carole Somers.

"Brilliant deduction, Ben," she answered sarcastically.

That would have angered me, but Perkins only grinned. To me he said with infuriating jauntiness, "Medical examiner says whoever beat Mo to death was left-handed. How they figure that kind of thing I'll never know."

"And you suspect *me*," I said stiffly.

Carole Somers said evenly, "I have an obligation to my client to conduct a full investigation."

"Seems to me that's a job for the police."

Perkins snorted. "Police already figure they got their perp. Maurie's left-handed. She can be placed at the scene at the approximate time of the murder. Motive can be presumed. Detroit's finest are overworked, understaffed; they'll grab the path of least resistance and go for it."

I consciously steadied myself down, forced myself to relax in the chair. Somers and Perkins watched me blandly. I made a smile and said, "Certainly no one would be more happy to see Maurie cleared than myself. I do not doubt that she is innocent." I scratched the bare skin of the side of my head. "But, Mister Perkins, what make *you* think she's innocent?"

Perkins leaned back in his chair and crossed an ankle over his knee. Eyes empty, he answered quite lazily, "Yeah, well, number one, I'm being paid to think so. Plus, I've talked to her, and I really do believe it."

Carole Somers had her elegant hands folded over her pad. Obviously she was finished questioning me, and I wanted to be gone, but Perkins kept talking. "Anyway, these things generally get sorted out if someone who gives a damn goes to work on 'em. Guys like me, who make a living asking around and checking up, get a feel for this stuff, get experience; whereas guys who do murder tend not to do it but once, so they don't get experience, and they leave tracks. See? I'll mess with it awhile and get it sorted out."

The big, hard-muscled man sounded so matter-of-fact, so confident, so strong, that I felt loathing rise in me like a gorge. I consciously willed it from showing on my face. Of Somers I asked, "Is there any other way I can be of service?"

"No. You're excused. And many thanks for your help." She gave me a sincere, radiant smile, but it was too late; anybody who'd go to bed with a man like Perkins could be of no use to me.

"Thank *you*." I went to the conference room door and, before leaving, turned back toward Perkins. "Any theories as to the actual murderer?"

Perkins was lighting another filthy cigar. "Nary a one." He puffed. "I don't work that way; I start out clean. One thing, though." He pulled the cigar from his mouth and looked at me. "Judging from the pics of the stuff, whoever did her must have had one hell of a reason."

†††

He was certainly right about that. But where did it begin?

Perhaps at home, with Pam. Married eleven years; friends for, perhaps, the first seven. It did not change overnight. As our jobs got worse, and the money tighter, the economy sank its teeth into us. We got older and heavier, less vigorous and more bored. Friends and colleagues moved up in their careers and away to the coasts, leaving us behind; or they bought houses in the suburbs, began to rear fat babies, and preferred to associate with others like them rather than us.

And the guerrilla warfare began. The ambushes. From in the kitchen, or over the phone, or in bed at night. "Why don't you get a better job? Why don't you fight for a promotion? When are you going to stand up for yourself? That piece-of-junk car of mine is going; what are you going to do about *that*? I need *money*. We'll *never* be able to buy a house, *never*. Everybody has nice houses. Everybody has nice cars. Everybody goes on nice vacations. Everybody else but *us*. And all *you* do is sit here with your nose stuck in a book. When are you going to *do* something? When? When? *When?*"

I was a good husband and provider. I changed jobs and worked desperately hard to improve my position and advance myself. I did it all for her and it was never enough. And the time came when I realized that if there was to be a reward, I would have to get it for myself. I had earned it, and I was going to get it.

That was when I decided on Mo Stevens. Everyone else enjoyed her. Why not me?

As the two-day computer seminar in Cleveland drew near, I made it a point to stop by her desk frequently. I was clumsy and shy, as always, but she, unlike the other women at the company, was offhand and friendly, with lots of secretive smiles and casual, seemingly accidental brushings.

On the first day of the seminar, we sat at opposite sides of the classroom. Among the forty other attendees and the droning instructor, in the hot, stuffy August heat, our glances met many times. I felt alone with her. I felt eager and energized for the first time in years.

That night I asked her to dinner. She pleaded a headache and said she'd stay in her room, but she smiled regretfully and, before retiring, gave my arm a warm squeeze that lasted the rest of the night.

The second evening—our last in Cleveland—we had drinks and then dinner. We talked about everything but the real subject. I strolled back to her room with her. She got out her key. I reached for the key and took her hand instead, awkwardly. She faced me, a searching, speculative look on her face. Then she leaned forward and kissed me. I moved against her and kissed her hard. Her arms went around me, the key clinking against my back. She pulled back, a secretive, knowing smile on her face, and said, "B plus." Then she unlocked her door, swung it open, and beckoned me in.

†††

Back home in Detroit, I spent the next two days—Saturday and Sunday—waiting for Monday, waiting to see Mo at the office. It was terribly hot, and Pam was at her vicious best, but for once she didn't get to me. Because now I had Mo. I wanted to call her right away but didn't dare; I respected the fact that she'd want our relationship to be kept a deadly secret. So I waited, strung out with happy, excited anticipation.

On Monday morning I found her at her desk. She smiled at me but kept her manner cool and professional. Good lass, I thought, good lass. Casually I invited her to lunch. She declined, pleading a doctor's appointment.

On Tuesday I went out during lunch hour and rented a room at the Sheraton Cadillac. I called home and informed Pam that a business emergency required me to go to Toledo that night. Back at the office I wrote a brief note, sealed it in an envelope, and left it on Mo's desk. At quitting time I fairly flew to the Sheraton, ate a quick dinner then went to the room and waited. I waited till past eleven o'clock, and Mo never arrived.

Mo wasn't at her desk much on Wednesday. I finally encountered her emerging from the conference room. Placing myself between her and the others, I clumsily asked her what had gone wrong the night before. Her face froze, she stared through me, then she made an icy smile, shook her head, and walked away.

She didn't come to work on Thursday. I did my work in a state of nervous, preoccupied dread. At lunchtime I called Mo's apartment. When she heard my voice, she hung up.

The next day I felt none of the usual end-of-the-week relief. I stayed in my cubicle, sorting and shuffling my papers and typing my forms, feeling strangely immobile and detached, dreading going home, dreading staying in the office. Just before lunchtime, I heard voices in the passageway outside my cubicle, and Mo glanced in at me. She turned to her companion, excused herself then entered, set a file down on the table before me, opened it, and bent down as if to discuss something in the file with me.

But what she said, in a voice light and airy enough to have caused no interest in anyone who couldn't understand the words, was: "Listen, you warped little creep, maybe Cleveland gave you the wrong idea. That was a one-shot, you understand? A whim. The fact is, you make my skin crawl. There is no way it will ever happen again, because even standing this close to you makes me want to puke. Is that clear? Have I made myself very, very clear now?" She closed the file, gave me a casual wave for public consumption, and left. I sat there, a noise like a waterfall roaring in my head.

The noise roared in my head throughout the weekend and was still there the following Monday, very, very early in the morning, as I stood with my back to the wall around the corner from Mo and Maurie as they chatted lightly in the deserted office. When Maurie left, I walked around the corner and toward Mo's desk. She jumped when she saw me, her eyes flashed briefly, then her face paled as I brought the short length of pipe from behind me and tapped its end lightly in my palm.

I asked, "Am I too close now, Mo? You feel like puking, maybe?"

She slowly rolled on her chair back from her desk. Her eyes grew and grew, and she started to say something, but her mouth was too dry.

I kept approaching her, tapping the pipe. "How about your skin? Is it crawling now, Mo?"

She lunged clumsily up from her chair. I took a final step, gripped the pipe with both hands, and swung in a flat, arm's-length arc. I didn't feel the impact, but she flew back as if jerked off her feet by a rope around her neck and sprawled with a blaze of tan legs and white underwear over her chair. The roaring in my head built suddenly to full gain as I kicked her chair aside, straddled her like a runner in the starting blocks, and dealt her the two-handed swing again, again, again, again. Over the roaring I heard my own voice: "Made myself clear now, Mo? How about it, Pam? Have I made myself clear? How about it, Mo?" And then it was just the two names, Mo, Pam, Mo, Pam, as if I didn't know who it was.

†††

In the days that followed my interview with Carole Somers and Ben Perkins, I saw the detective around a few times.

I saw him one afternoon in the pub on the ground floor of our building, drinking beer (naturally) and chatting with a handful of people from our company. He gave me a sober-faced wave and nod, nothing more.

I saw him in one of the back halls of our office suite as I was sweeping up the shards of a coffee carafe that one of our clumsy secretaries had dropped on the way to the conference room. As he passed me, Perkins gave me a crooked grin and a nod, nothing more.

I saw him at the curb of Congress Street, leaning out the window of his souped-up blue Mustang (naturally), chatting with Bernie, an elderly, hump-backed man who from time immemorial had been a private message runner and one-man delivery service for downtown companies. Perkins didn't see me that time.

Otherwise I knew nothing about Perkins' "investigation." And I didn't think about it. My plan had been sound, the execution flawless. No sub-educated, inarticulate grunt was going to make a case on me. Besides, my thoughts centered on my other problem. The one with Pam's name on it.

†††

I stare impatiently at the stairwell as Ben Perkins emerges onto the sun-drenched roof. He squints from the light but seems unsurprised to see me. He says, "Told you I'd sort it out."

Does he really think I'm such a fool? "I don't want to hear about it." I flick away my half-smoked cigarette.

"Sure you do." Perkins grins. "They all do." Today he's as well-dressed as he probably ever gets, in a blue blazer, matching slacks, open-collar white dress shirt. The warm morning breeze whips his thick black hair as the pigeons wheel in the air above us, light on the ledge to my left, and drop into space to fly away home.

Perkins glances around the roof, probably looking for a place to sit. There is none, except the ledge, so instead he leans against the wall and with a big, knuckly hand fetches one of his short cigars out of his blazer pocket. "I found that other way into the building, the one you used to get past the security guard."

I stare at him. The front of my face feels numb. "You think *I* killed Mo?"

He flares a wood match on his thumbnail, applies the flame to the end of his cigar, and nods as he puffs. "Oh yeah," he answers casually, waving the match out and tossing it. "See, I talked to old Bernie, the delivery fella. He's been working these buildings for years, knows 'em better than the rats. This building wasn't always secure; used to be a passageway on the sixth floor between the Olivetti firm's offices and this building. Hardly anybody remembers it now. But you used to work for Olivetti, right?"

I deny him the satisfaction of changing expression. He shrugs easily. "Show me how you bat," he says casually.

Defiantly I start into the stance then freeze and straighten again. Perkins' eyes are cold and assured. "Lefty," he murmurs. "You write right-handed, sure. But I saw you swinging a broom the other day. You're sort of ambidextrous. For some reason, lefty's the way you swing a bat, a broom, an ax—and a club. Right?"

I hear the pigeons flapping off the ledge. Traffic noise builds from fourteen floors below as the morning rush hour begins. I sneer at Perkins. "Not precisely what I'd call hanging evidence, Perkins."

"Hey, man's got to try." He puffs on his cigar, studying me. "That Mo, she liked action, right? What'd she do? Turn you down? Or tumble and then dump you? It's an old story, man. A real old story."

As if Perkins cares. I notice he has positioned himself near the door, as if to intercept me should I try to escape. Fool.

Perkins folds his arms across his chest with his cigar jutting from two fingers and yawns. "Anyway, I talked it over with the detectives. They got a search warrant last night for your house. They're there right now. Checking your clothes and stuff. For evidence and that. Routine."

My eyes close for just an instant, and in that instant I see what the police will find. Mo, Pam! Mo, Pam!

I turn and stroll casually to the ledge. Pigeons glare and scatter with fluttering squawks as I sit on the ledge with my forearms on my knees, facing the detective. He's stood and taken a couple of steps toward me, eyes narrow. I smile at him. The narrow, tense expression wipes away, and he says, "Well, that about covers it. Come on, let's go downstairs. It's getting right hot up here."

I feel the empty air behind me. Now I can hear the traffic much clearer from the street fourteen floors down. Perkins stands fifteen, twenty feet away from me, waiting for an answer that does not come. Through my mind runs the litany: fly away, fly away, fly away home. Then I remember: it's about a ladybug. Figures. Helpless insect, eaten alive by stronger ones.

Perkins says in a low, calm voice, "You know, once some wise men got together to come up with an absolutely universal truth, and what they came up with was, 'This, too, shall pass.'"

"So?"

He smiles in what I imagine to be a friendly fashion, but I know better; he's no friend. Men like him never are. He says, "You can get past this, pal."

I'm too tired to argue. I simply say, "No."

"You don't want to die. No matter how bad things are, you don't really want to die. Nobody does. You know why? Because there's nothing then. No rushing wind, no blinding light, no incredible feeling of peace, no welcoming faces of the previously departed. There's absolute, stone-cold nothing."

Fresh in my mind's eye I see my grandmother, kneeling at her flowerbed, short spade in hand, straightening and smiling and rising as she watches me approach. I snarl at Perkins, "Spare me your supermarket-tabloid shrink shtick, Perkins."

His voice was still gentle. "Come on, walk back over here."

"No."

His face changes, goes dark and angry, the tendons showing against the tan skin as his jaw tightens. "Okay, so what the hell do I care? Go ahead, jump. World could sure use one less sniveling, twisted, four-eyes puke-bag. Only thing, I hope you don't land on some innocent citizen down there. Be a real shame if a normal person got hurt by a sick piece of worthless garbage like you. Go ahead, jump! Have a nice trip!"

I grin with contempt at this futile stratagem. He wants to anger me, make me attack him so he can drag me away from the ledge. Even if I hadn't seen *Dirty Harry* and known how the con is supposed to work, it wouldn't have, because all my rage is gone. I am harmless now and know what I am going to do, and no one can stop me, most particularly this son of a bitch.

In the long pause, the traffic noise builds from the amphitheater far, far below. Perkins knots his fists. "What are ya, chicken? Need a hand? Well, buddy, happy to oblige. Call me a public-spirited citizen." He starts for me.

I tease him and play with him and tempt him, sitting still, letting him think I'm so stupid I'll let him grab me and pull me away from the ledge. Just as he lunges for me, I tumble over backward and leave the ledge.

And get just a glimpse of Perkins' reaction, which fills me with joy. His face is a mask of shock, horror, fear, despair.

The wind tears at my clothes and blinds my eyes as I laugh soundlessly. I've beaten him! I've won! I've—Grandmother?

GRANDMOTHER?

Afterword

I have always enjoyed experimenting with point of view. First person, which is the usual Perkins mode, is limiting in a way, but also gets you under the character's skin. And I enjoy the challenge of it.

In "Fly Away Home" we see Perkins, for the first and only time, from the point of view of someone else. I had a lot of fun with this. With stories from Perkins's point of view, it's tough to get a thorough description of him in without glaring contrivance (i.e. "The man I saw in the mirror had dark blue eyes. . . ."). In this story I was able to describe him fairly objectively for the first time.

Of course the person doing the describing cannot be fully relied upon. He sees Perkins through the prism of his own sickness and prejudices. But this point of view also, I think, allows Perkins's humanity to come through more powerfully than it does in other stories. Ultimately, the protagonist is a sad and somewhat tragic figure—not so much evil (though he certainly does evil things) but a man who, in the end, is unable to resist the drive of his appetites and emotions.

The Man Who Called from Tomorrow

Now, Mr. Perkins," Mrs. Weingarten said ponderously, "I must impress upon you how distressing this latest incident of non-sufficient funds is."

I glared at the phone receiver then put it back to my ear. "Now, Mrs. Weingarten. I've been with your bank damn near fifteen years, and this is only about the third time I've overdrawn. So lighten up. It isn't like Guatemala has just defaulted on its loans or anything."

"This is no laughing matter, Mr. Perkins."

"It wasn't even my fault, really. A client paid me by check, and it did the old bounce-a-roo. Kinda had a trickle-down effect on my own checks. Domino theory, sort of."

"A *client?*" she asked, disbelief oozing from the word.

"Yeah, I'm a private detective."

"Is that a fact? Then I suggest that you go and detect yourself two hundred eighty-three dollars and ninety-two cents, sometime in the immediate future. At *least* bring your balance up to zero, Mr. Perkins, won't you?"

"No problem." I hung up the phone with a slam of plastic and stomped down the silent hall of my apartment to the bedroom. As I changed clothes, my irrational hatred of banks changed into a very rational hatred for Freddie Flynn. The little weasel-face had hung a big fat hunk of bad paper on me and probably was even now giggling into his whisky rocks in one of the scummy east side bars he frequents. Well, I'd find him, and I'd get my five bills from him, and I'd teach him a lesson. Take *that* to the bank, Mrs. Weingarten.

I was, figuratively speaking, dressed to kill and headed for the door when the phone rang. I grabbed it on the fly. "Detectives!"

No voice, just the sssssss of long distance for ten seconds. Then a male voice: "Gail there?"

"Wrong number, pal."

"Who is this?" came the faint voice.

"What matters is I'm not Gail. 'Bye."

"Wait a minute!"

Though in a rush, I did.

"Is this—" he read off a number.

"Was the last time I checked."

"Five-one-three area code?"

"Nope. This is *three*-one-three, *Dee*-troit, Michigan, go Tigers! and all that. What you want is Cincinnati, which is down in Ohio where it belongs."

"Oh. Okay. Sorry I bothered you."

"No problem, we all get butterfingered every now and then." I hung up and blew out of there, plotting a trajectory with Freddie Flynn as ground zero.

†††

By eight thirty I was back home, mission accomplished. Flynn, whom I located as predicted holding forth in a dive on Kercheval, had used all of the oily stratagems of the practiced deadbeat in his attempts to deter me. Maybe I didn't owe you the money anyway, Perkins. Then, my bank screwed up, I'll straighten it out and call you next week. Then, gee whiz, Ben, I'm tapped out, just today I dropped two large on a half lame filly at DRC. Then, have a heart, bro, my little girl's in Wayne Hospital, costing me seven fifty a day. I reasoned with him without having to get too strenuous about it, and returned home with my money, every nickel of it, in mostly small bills that looked like they'd seen duty as cow cud. But it was good United States legal tender and would spend just fine, thank you. Persuasive Perkins, they call me.

I'd just finished sorting, counting, and flattening out the bills when the phone rang. I snatched it up. "Perkins."

The male voice, fuzzy with the distance, sounded familiar. "Are you the man I talked to before?"

"Yeah, but this still isn't Cincinnati, sorry."

"You said you're a detective."

"Huh?"

"When I called before. You said 'detectives' when you answered the phone."

I leaned back and lighted a short cork-tipped cigar. "I get in these puckish moods. Sometimes I answer with 'Joe's Mule Barn' or 'Your dime, start talking' or stuff like that."

"Are you a policeman?"

"Private detective," I answered, puffing smoke, wondering what the hell was going on here.

"Well, uh, I want to hire you."

"Is that so."

As his words rushed on in a torrent, a mental image of him burned in my mind. Male, obviously. American, accentless, possibly Midwestern but lacking the nasal sounds common to upper Midwesterners. Educated, professional. Anxious, under stress, very far away.

He said, "That number I was calling in Cincinnati, it's my wife Gail. When I called with the right area code, I found out the number belongs to someone else now, who'd never heard of Gail. I don't know where she is, and I've got to find her."

"Wait a minute, hold it," I said. I reached behind into the writing-table drawer and pulled out a pad and a pen. "There're some essential facts missing here."

"Like what?"

"Like your name, for starters."

"Murray. Paul Murray."

"'Kay." I wrote it down. "Where are ya?"

A pause. "Apra Harbor, Guam."

"Say what?" He repeated it. "Guam?" I echoed. "Isn't that in the Pacific Ocean somewhere?"

"Close enough."

Hell of a good connection, I thought; I've had worse connections calling my sister Libby in Ann Arbor, which makes sense when you think about it. "Wow," I said. "Like what time is it there?"

"Ten thirty A.M., if it matters."

"Yeah?" I checked my watch. "It's eight-thirty P.M. here."

"It's, uh, Tuesday there, too, right? Tuesday night. Here it's Wednesday morning."

"That's tomorrow," I observed.

"Uh huh. Listen, I'm serious, I want to hire you. I want you to go to Cincinnati and find my wife."

I doodled with my pen. "Well, I mean, how come? Why don't you know where she is?"

A long pause. "Okay, I'll level with you," he said, which, I couldn't help thinking, is the way a client usually prefaces a pack of lies. "I left. I ran out on her eight years ago. I can't help it, I'm a wandering kind of guy, I keep hitting the road—"

"Long road to Guam."

"Tell me about it," he said soberly. "But—I—I want her back. I miss her." Pause. "I love her. I'll beg for her forgiveness. I'll do anything—"

"So catch a plane and come back here and do it."

"No. I don't want to make the trip till I talk to her. So I want you to find her and tell her about me and bring her to your place. Say, uh, seventy-two hours from now, on the nose, I'll call you again. You have Gail there and I'll talk to her, and we'll see what happens."

I rolled my eyes, took a last hot toke off my cigar and mashed it out in the ashtray on my kitchen table. What the hell, it was irregular but, I told myself, every case doesn't have to be a dead boring snore. "Where should I start looking?"

He gave me an address in Montgomery, a Cincinnati suburb. I wrote it down. "One more thing," he said. "She might be, uh, skeptical. So to prove it's really me I want you to give her this exact phrase: 'Let's boogie tonight.'"

I snorted and grinned and wrote that down, too. "Okay," I said finally, "but first there are certain financial arrangements. I get two fifty a day plus expenses. *American*," I added.

"Chicken feed," Murray said. "Given the distance, it probably would make you happier if you got paid in advance. Give me your bank account information, I'll wire the cash into there."

While I found the whole situation unlikely as hell, I didn't see any risk in giving him the poopy. I dug out my checkbook and read off the essentials.

"Okay," he said, "it'll be there in twelve hours, max."

"I'll be waiting," I answered.

"Get it done for me," he said, and hung up.

†††

Next morning, nine-oh-three sharp, the phone rang. It was Mrs. Weingarten at the bank. Her voice had a respectful tone in it that I'd never heard before. "I wish to confirm the receipt of the inter-bank funds transfer," she said.

I wasn't fast on the uptake. "Huh?"

"The wire transfer," she said patiently. "We've credited it to your account."

I remembered now. Though stupefied, I managed to put the right superior tone in my voice. "About time."

"Your balance," she went on hastily, "excluding any unpresented debts, is now two thousand two hundred sixteen dollars and eight cents."

Two point two gee, I thought. Less the negative balance, that meant Mr. Paul Murray had sent me two and a half large. Ten days' pay for two days' work.

"Very well," I said.

"We appreciate your patronage, Mr. Perkins," Mrs. Weingarten said, and hung up.

I hung up the phone and sat down slowly at the kitchen table. I sat there for what seemed like a very long time, thinking about Guam and a wandering husband and a misdialed number. It was all very real now, and I had cold hard cash in my account to prove it. Time to go to work.

I fetched the book and picked up the phone and called Delta Airlines to arrange an immediate flight to Cincinnati.

†††

The engraving on the brass doorknocker said BELTZMANN. I rapped it. After a moment the door swung back and a short, voluptuous, permed redhead dressed in jeans and a blue open-necked shirt smiled expectantly at me. "Gail Beltzmann?" I asked.

"Yes?"

"Gail *Murray* Beltzmann?"

"I was married before, but—" Her smile vanished. "Who are you? What do you want?"

"Ben Perkins from Detroit. I represent Mr. Paul Murray, who hired me to locate you."

"Paul."

"Yes, ma'am. We need to talk. Can I come in?"

She backed up a half-step. "Not here," she said, voice low, bright blue eyes intent on me. "Not now." She gripped the door harder. "Paul!" she whispered.

"So where and when? I'm not from around here, I'm on a tight schedule—"

"One hour, all right?" Voice soft and deadly intent. "Um, the Ground Round on Beechmont, in the bar."

"Beechmont, the main drag just south—"

"One hour," she repeated, and swung the door shut.

I wheeled the rented Ford LTD up Denallen Drive and reflected with some smugness that locating Gail Murray hadn't been so tough. I'd gone to the address in Montgomery that Paul Murray had given me, to be informed that the current owners had purchased the place five years before. I went to the realtors, laid a first-class charm job on the agent who handled the transaction, and elicited the information that the previous owner, Gail Murray, had sold the house on a land contract, the monthly payments for which were sent to an address on Denallen Drive in Anderson Township, some ten miles south of Montgomery near the Ohio River. Went down there, knocked on the door, and found the woman, just like that. Now all I had to do was meet her at the Ground Round and pass on the message and try to convince her to come to Detroit with me to receive the expected phone call from her errant ex-husband.

A hitch-free investigation, I thought.

If you didn't count the tail I'd picked up.

The guy, whoever he was, wasn't all that smooth. Vaguely groping my way toward Beechmont Avenue, I took Denallen to Holiday Hills Drive to Eight

Mile Road, and accidentally took a right instead of a left. A charcoal gray Buick Riviera did the same. A quarter mile later, at the Clough Pike intersection, I realized my mistake and U-turned on a Convenient Food Store parking lot to go the other way on Eight Mile toward Beechmont. The Riviera did exactly likewise, which tends to make guys in my line of work uneasy.

I drove on, maintaining the speed limit, keeping an eye on the Riviera in the rearview. The solo occupant breezed along five car-lengths behind me. I reached Beechmont on yellow and punched the gas to beat the light, interested to observe the Riviera do the same, roaring up almost to my bumper to do so. He fell back some as we proceeded out of the built-up area and into an undeveloped district of steep hills, thick forests, and tight curves. I increased speed as we crossed the I-275 overpass, and the Riviera laid on additional gas to match me.

I felt peevish. Things had gone so well here in Cincinnati, I didn't want them screwed up by some half-assed tail. I continued at the best speed I could manage as the terrain became increasingly rugged and then, as I headed up the steepest hill yet, I found my chance.

I floored the accelerator, crested the hill at top speed, then geared down and mashed the brakes and went into a shrieking, smoking, controlled spin on the coarse blacktop. Who cares, the car was rented. I ended up at a shuddering standstill with a queasy stomach, facing back the way I'd come, straddling the center line. The Riviera charged over the hill toward me, jinked to my left but not quite enough, and whacked my front fender and slid sideways into a weedy ditch.

Now I was crossways in the road. I opened the door and got out. The Riviera was wedged driver's-side doormost against the mud and its driver—a big beefy short-haired guy—restarted the engine, put the car into gear, and started to pull out. He'd made two feet in the damp berm when I reached his car and tipped the door open. "Not so fast, fella."

He had short bristly hair, tiny eyes set deep in a face composed of jowls and a snout, and wore an ill-fitting business suit. He glared at me, eyes two pinpricks of dark light. "Back away from me. I'm in a hurry."

Lunging, I gave him an open-palmed punch in the side of his face that knocked him longwise on the bench seat. I switched off the Riviera ignition and stepped back, tossing the keys in my hand. The man, shaking his head and panting, groped back to a sitting position behind the wheel. "You'll wish you hadn't done that," he muttered.

I grinned and leaned on the open door. "Why're you following me?"

As he glared up at me, I saw the sheen of blood on his lower lip. Must have bitten himself when I hit him. "I wasn't following you."

"Sure you were, let's not get silly about this. The question is *why*."

He rubbed his cheek where I hit him, eyes reflective. "It's none of your business."

I sighed and gestured with my fingers. "Okay, come on. Let's have some ID."

His face went tired. He nodded, reached a hand under the lapel of his suit jacket, and came out with one of those little baby automatics, probably a Smith & Wesson Model 61, barely four inches by three inches and employing a .22 long rifle slug that can kill you very dead. His small eyes had a satisfied sparkle. "This good enough ID for you?"

I stepped back from the door, very slowly. "Oh yeah, perfectly fine."

He gestured with his lethal peashooter. "Gimme the keys."

I cleared my throat. "Here's how we'll work this. I'll back up in my car and drop your keys on the road when I get there."

He stared levelly at me for a long moment, then murmured, "Let's do it."

He kept his weapon trained on me as I backed up on the rough macadam. When I reached the open door of my LTD, I carefully lowered myself into the seat, my left hand with his keys in it in plain sight. With my right hand I fired up the LTD and banged the column shift down. As I floored the gas, I gave the keys a hard, high lob over his car, going probably thirty feet into the dense overgrown thicket. The door almost slammed on my arm as I crested the hill and was gone.

As I crossed back over I-275, I exhaled the breath that I felt like I'd been holding all week. Nice move, Perkins. Decent mix of violence, daring, and cunning. Except for one problem. Aside from the definite pro smell I sensed in him, I still had no idea who he was or why he was tailing me.

†††

I slid into the far corner booth in the bar of the Ground Round, across from Gail Beltzmann. She still wore her jeans and open-necked blue shirt, and the afternoon light from the window illuminated her tightly permed red hair, a pleasant contrast to her bright blue eyes. I sensed congenital playfulness in her, suppressed by an attack of almost terminal suspicion. "So what's this about Paul?" she greeted, fingers playing idly with the wide-mouthed glass that seemed filled principally with fruit.

"Hey wait, lady, let's get some essentials took care of first." I flagged down the waitress, who organized me a beer, and I took a slug of that and lighted a cigar before beginning my story. I delivered it flatly and noncommittally, aware of Gail's narrow-eyed disbelief. "What he told me was," I concluded, "he feels guilty about his wandering ways, and he wants you back. But he doesn't want to come back here from Guam till he knows where you stand."

She nodded slightly, eyes dead. "So I'm supposed to go to Detroit with you and wait for him to call."

"Tomorrow," I agreed, and took a belt of beer.

She took just the teeniest pull of her drink through the plastic straw and set the glass down. "Wanderlust," she said. "Oh yeah, that's Paul, all right. All those years we were married I could never count on him. That bastard. All those excuses. Days and weeks away with no explanation. Oh, he was a real *fine* husband. Now eight whole years later, without a single word, he wants me back. That's just *precious*."

I exhaled smoke and said, "Hey, listen. I'm no marriage counselor; I'm just a paid messenger boy here. Your choice is either come back to Detroit with me and talk to him when he calls, or tell me to tell him to pound sand crossway where the sun don't shine. Makes not a whit of difference to me, kid."

Her eyes narrowed and her soft, inviting mouth hardened. "I've *remarried*. I had Paul declared *dead* over a year ago. Strikes me he ought to just stay that way." Her eyes bore in on me. "Matter of fact, how do *I* know you're on the level? I've never met you before. How do I know you really talked to Paul?"

I coughed, whacked excess ash off my cigar, and said, "Well, he gave me a phrase to give you. Said you'd understand. Phrase is: 'Let's boogie tonight.'"

Her bright blue eyes faded, became teary. "That's him. That's Paul," she sniffed. "Oh, Lord." Her throat bobbed and she used the back of her wrist to wipe her eyes.

I looked away respectfully and said, "So you want to come back with me?"

She dropped her hand from her eyes. "For *that* bastard? After all he's put me through? Hell, no." She picked up her drink and took a vicious pull from it.

"Okay, fine," I said, thinking what do I care.

She glared at me across the rim of her glass. "Not that Paul's all that unique. Sometimes I wonder if men are bastards in general, or did I just have a bad run of luck. My husband Ronnie's not good at much except growing beer wings. Can't even keep a job. If I hadn't gotten the Montgomery place from Paul's estate, we'd be living somewhere like Lower Price Hill now." She pursed her lips then gnaws on her lower one, eyes going far away. "That's one thing I have to admit about Paul. He worked hard. Knew how to bring home the big money." Her voice coarsened at the end, and she looked away from me, pressing her knuckles hard against her cheekbone.

After a long moment I ventured, "So do I book you a seat, or—"

"In a pig's eye!" she shot back. She leaned forward, eyes hot, nearly spilling her fruit. "Look, Perkins, quit trying to *sell* me, will ya? I wouldn't cross the sidewalk to put out that bastard if he was on *fire*."

"Lady," I said, my voice a rattle, "I'm not trying to sell you the teeniest, weeniest little thing, believe thee me!" I looked around for the waitress, anxious to get the bill and pay it and get the hell out of there.

She was nowhere to be seen.

We sat in hard-eyed silence for several minutes. Gail speared several pieces of fruit with her cocktail straw and ate them. I mashed out my old cigar and lighted up a new one. Then she asked quietly, "Did Paul give you *any* idea what he's been doing all these years?"

"Nary a word." The waitress hove into sight. I made scribbling motions in the air and she nodded and headed toward us.

"Mm," Gail said. She was chasing a piece of grapefruit without much success. "Could have been something awful. Maybe he was kidnapped . . . or got amnesia . . . or was badly injured. Something like that." She pouted and her eyes went shiny and a wet trail ran brightly down a freckled cheek. "What if something awful like that happened to him? Poor guy!"

I licked my lips and took two deep breaths, considering my reply carefully, then plunged. "There's one way to find out."

"*Oh, it's probably the same old garbage!*" Gail snarled, small fists clenched on the table. "Booze and broads—and parties—and—"

The waitress arrived then and not a minute too soon. I didn't even look at the bill, just shoved a ten into her hands, told her to keep the change, and got to my feet. "I'm outta here," I said to Gail, and headed for the door.

She caught up with me on the sidewalk. "You may be a pretty decent detective, Perkins, but God *damn* you're dense."

I spun to her and flung my hands in the air. "Gail, lemme clue ya. Sometimes in this work no amount of pay is enough. You follow?" She winced and suddenly looked very small and lost. I took a deep breath and cast my eyes upward and said, "All right, listen. I'm heading for the airport now, flying back tonight. You change your mind, you call me first for directions." I gave her the number.

"Don't hold your breath," she said.

†††

The crash woke me. I lurched upward in the unfamiliar bed as male voices boomed outside and something crashed against the door again. I scanned the early morning darkness with panicky eyes, then realized I wasn't at home at all but at the Best Western motel near the Cincinnati airport—because all the Detroit flights had been booked up the evening before.

The door crashed again and flung around so hard that the inner knob buried itself in the drywall. Four guys barreled into my room, guys in suits, armed with heavy revolvers, led by my beady-eyed friend from the Buick Riviera. He stopped halfway to the bed as his cohorts fanned out in the room and pointed a very impressive Colt Python at me. "Where is she?" he asked.

"Who?" I asked stupidly, pulling the sheet up around me.

Somebody hollered from the bathroom. "Not here, boss."

"Gail *Murray*," Beady Eyes said to me, gesturing with his gun. "Where is she? Where'd she go?"

"Damn if I know," I said through sleep-numbed lips. "*Home*, I reckon."

The other guys finished their intent tour of the room. "No sign she's been here, boss," one of them said to Beady-Eyes.

He made a puff-cheeked sigh and holstered his weapon under his coat. "No, she's not at home," he muttered. He turned to one of his guys and said, "Airport, blanket it," and the man ran out.

When he looked back at me, I was ready. "You guys some kind of law?"

"What's it to you?"

"Yeah, you're law all right, that clumsy tail of yours yesterday confirms it." He didn't answer. "So," I went on, "you come busting in here and cause me great emotional distress, and if you got no warrant and there's no probable cause or something, I can go to the papers and ACLU and folks like that, and end up taking a big piece of change off you guys, not to mention the embarrassment and career problems y'all'd experience personally."

"We were impulsive. We slipped up. Many apologies."

"Not good enough. And you know it."

"National security," Beady-Eyes said, spacing out the syllables.

"So come on. Buy me. I'm easy. Tell old Uncle Ben all."

Beady-Eyes glared at me then jerked his head at his cohorts. "See you in the car in five minutes."

As they left, I asked, "Can I get into my clothes first?"

†††

It was only by the merest chance that I was in my apartment when the phone rang at four thirty Friday. "Detectives," I answered.

"Just want to thank you," came Paul Murray's very long-distance voice. "You did perfect."

I lowered myself to a chair at the kitchen table. "So," I said, "you still at large?"

"Oh, for sure."

"Gail's with you, I presume."

Murray chuckled. "See for yourself." Silence, a snatch of female giggling, then Gail herself said, "Hi, Ben."

"Huh. Coulda swore you wanted nothing to do with him."

"I know," she drawled, "and what I said about Paul is true, he can be *such* a bastard—but I can't help it. I love him." She squealed and laughed as if she'd been touched somewhere sensitive.

Very deliberately I asked, "You knew all along he was selling defense secrets to the Soviets?"

"Of course," she answered airily. "We're married. We keep no secrets from each other." I heard some muffled whispering, then Paul Murray came back on, voice casual. "So you know the whole story."

"Not all of it, no, sir. Where you been all these years?"

"Here and there," Murray replied. "See, it started when I was on a West Coast trip, and I got a tip that my cover had been blown, the company was suspicious of me, and the FBI was closing in. Fortunately, it wasn't any big problem to fly from Seattle to—to the Far East. And I got lost there."

"Close call."

"Ah, risk of the trade. Anyway, I fully intended to send for Gail, but one thing led to another, I kept putting it off . . . I can't help it, I like to get around, have fun, see what's going on . . . I had plenty of money, no responsibilities. *You* know how it is, Ben."

"Not exactly, no. I've lived right here most of my life."

"Well, trust me. Anyway, what I said about Gail before was true. I finally got fed up. I had to find her and get her back. I *do* love her, Perkins." A pause, some muffled giggling from that end. "But I couldn't come back for her myself. I knew my name and face were on every **ho list there is. So I called for her—and lo and behold, our phone number belonged to someone else."

"Specifically," I said, "the government guys. They took over your number. Spent all these years hoping you'd call, hoping to get a line on you."

Murray snorted. "So *that* was it! Sneaky bastards!"

I sighed and rubbed my forehead. "Not as sneaky as you. That special phrase you gave me to tell Gail—I thought that was some personal lovey-dovey bit at the time. But it wasn't, was it? It was a code message, right?"

"You're doing fine."

"So she'd know it was you."

"We set it up years ago, when I began my—my freelance work. Just in case things went sour and I had to get word to her."

"That phrase," I went on, "it verifies it's you, right? Probably also tells her where exactly to meet you."

"Right on, Perkins. The middle word's the location. 'Party' means Madrid. 'Get it on' means Rio. 'Disco' means Cairo. 'Boogie' means—well . . . God-*damn*, you're smart. Gail wasn't all that impressed with you, but you're okay, you know?"

"Only thing I can't figure is how Gail slipped past the Feds. They had the airport covered."

"*Cincinnati* airport, yeah. But she drove up to Dayton, caught a flight to Chicago. From there, it was a direct flight to. . . ."

"To where?"

Murray laughed. "Hey, I better run, this call is starting to cost me serious dough. Besides, this woman here is having trouble keeping her hands off me." Silence, then he muttered, "Cut it out, babe!"

I breathed deeply. "So you don't want to tell me where you are. Just give me one hint. Is it tomorrow there?"

"Yeah, it's tomorrow."

"So, uh, how *is* tomorrow?"

"Fantastic."

"Tomorrow tends to be like that."

Silence broken only by a low surflike hiss. "You sound bitter, Ben."

"Hey, I was a patsy. I helped a confessed spy. Forgive me for not feeling too ticked just now."

When he answered, his tone was indignant. "Even confessed spies deserve help every now and then, and where else can we turn but to a private detective? Personally I feel real lucky I stumbled onto you. Don't be such a bigot."

"Plus which," I pressed on harshly, "I nearly got *myself* mangled up by the Feds on an accessory rap. Thanks loads."

"I notice," Murray said deliberately, "that you're at home, so they must not have been able to make it stick all that well."

"Be that as it may."

"*And* you got paid, and pretty handsomely at that."

I retorted doggedly, "Maybe I don't want any part of that kind of money. Maybe I'll just give it away to a worthy cause."

"Fat chance." Silence, muffled giggles. "Hey, gotta go, pal. Seriously, thanks again. And so long from tomorrow."

†††

On reflection, I realized that I didn't really help a confessed spy. What I did was help reunite two estranged lovebirds. Gave me a nice warm fuzzy feeling.

Even if Murray hadn't earned the money honestly, I had.

And money has no conscience.

So I spent it.

Afterword

I lived in Cincinnati for a couple of years. As a matter of fact, I was living there at the time I sold my first fiction. I love the place and always have. So Cincinnati recurs in the stories from time to time.

As a matter of fact, most of the Cincinnati locations depicted in this story—the suburbs, the streets, even the Ground Round—really exist pretty much where I place them.

This case may be the only time Perkins ever worked without meeting the client face to face. It also puts him once again (unwittingly, this time) working not quite on the side of the angels. I prefer for my protagonist not to be omniscient—no one in real life is, and I have little patience with people (fictional or otherwise) who claim to be. I suppose in a perfect world Perkins would not only have figured out what was going on, but would also have been instrumental in arranging the arrest of the admitted spy. But alas! Things don't always work out, not even in fiction.

That said, this story carries forward some ongoing Perkins' themes: financial difficulty and utter failure to understand women being two of them.

The Eye Went By

"You're a private detective, right?" Carole said.

"Sixteen hundred dollars!" Pat Sajak said. "What do you want to do now?"

"I'll spin," said the contestant.

"Okay," Sajak said doubtfully as the contestant bent to the wheel.

I pried my eyes away from the TV and looked at Carole. "You know I'm a private detective. So what?"

She flattened her paperback on her stomach and slid into a half-upright position on the sofa. "Detectives are supposed to be *exciting*," she said.

"Says who?"

The contestant asked for an M. Sajak gave his regrets. The next contestant spun the wheel to the claps and cheers of the audience. I looked back at Carole, who was giving me a dark stare. "Says all the books and the movies," she answered.

"Oh, them."

"Yeah, *them!* I've been reading a lot of these books lately, and—"

"Maybe you'll pass along some pointers sometime." I looked back at the screen just in time to see the wheel hit BANKRUPT.

"*And*," she went on, "*these* detectives *are always* doing exciting things. Solving mysteries, apprehending criminals, righting wrongs. Then I look at you, lying there on the La-Z-Boy, cigar in one hand, beer can in the other, feet up in the air with a big toe poking through—"

"You making some point here?"

She turned and sat straight on the sofa and crossed one mile of tanned leg over the other. "I don't know. I invite you over for the evening, and what do we do? Sit around, *that's* what we do."

"Hey, I'm not particular. Find me a tasty little crime and we'll fool around with it, kid," I grinned. "Beggars can't be choosers."

"I'm no beggar!"

I snorted. "I didn't mean you. I meant—"

"Beggars can't be choosers!" the contestant squealed.

"You got it!" Sajak trilled as the orchestra played and the audience applauded.

"I got it before *she* did," I muttered.

Carole did her sarcastic one-hand clap. Will Somers, Carole's stocky, blond six-year-old, trotted into the living room. "Ben, can you help me, ole buddy?"

I should mention here that Will isn't my kid, he's Carole's. And Carole, who'd been a steady squeeze for a while, wasn't any more. We had a platonic relationship based on mutual need. She lawyered for me, I did fixing for her. Service for service, no cash changing hands; just two more cogs in the great underground economy.

"What do you need, Will?" I asked him.

"Can you read me this book?" Will asked, advancing on me shyly.

"Sure, kid." I hadn't seen Will much that evening; besides, the contestant was choosing her prizes, and I just knew she'd end up with the life-size porcelain dog.

Will handed me the book. I knew the blue cover well. *The Fly Went By* by Dr. Seuss. I knew the story even better, having read it to Will about six zillion times. A kid gets involved in a chase, with a whole sequence of connecting episodes. About as much like real life as the detective thrillers Carole reads. Will could never seem to get enough of it. He'd sit there and listen to me read, nodding, mouthing the words, eyes bright and face happy, innocently secure in the predictable. The essence of entertainment.

"Gentlemen," Carole said. We looked at her. "First, if you don't mind, an errand. We need milk."

"Ohhhh," Will said.

"No problem," I answered, aware that I was almost done with the last beer in inventory. "Take care of it right quick. Have to pick up some gas, too. I'm running on fumes."

"Can I go with you?" Will asked.

"I don't care. You care?" I asked Carole.

"I don't care. But, Ben?"

I squinted at her as I rose.

"Just a *small* candy bar. And don't do any lollygagging out there."

I held out my hand to Will, who took it. "Just going for milk," I said to Carole. "Routine. Like you say: boring, boring, boring."

†††

"Can I have a treat at the store?" Will asked.

"We'll see." I answered absently, because I'd become interested in the gold Toyota Corona ahead of us. There was a couple in the front seat, and in the early evening light I could see that they were having an argument. The man drove, the woman rode shotgun, and they looked at each other more than straight ahead, tossing silent shouts back and forth. I kept my '71 Mustang front bumper hard up on the Toyota, watching the occupants intently.

"Maybe some bubblegum," Will said.

"Sure, fella." The woman in the Toyota lunged at the driver, smacking him in the side of the head. The driver grabbed her permed hair with his right hand, pulled her toward him then jammed her head hard against the passenger side window. I gripped the Mustang wheel harder. "Jesus Christ!"

"What, Ben?" Will asked.

Red reflected blip-blip-blip in my rearview mirror. I tossed a glance over my shoulder. Cycle cop. I pulled over, slowing, praying for him to zip past me. He did not oblige, just followed me down as we slowed to the curb. I shut off the engine, popped open the glove compartment, and dug for the paperwork as the cop propped his bike on its kickstand and swaggered toward my Mustang. "We got trouble, Will."

"Oh no," the boy answered.

The young, fresh-faced, helmeted policeman leaned against my Mustang. "Okay, let's see it," he said.

I handed over license and registration and proof of insurance. He squinted at it then looked at me. "You know I gotcha doing fifty in a thirty-five."

The Toyota was long gone. I frowned up at the cop. "So, like, guilty as charged. I can take the weight. Write me up and let's be done with it."

"'Preciate your cooperation. Lemme go pester the computer, I'll be right with you." He started back toward his cycle, but had made only ten feet when an old rusted station wagon blasted past us, sideswiping a VW bug parked innocently across the street from the cop. The next thing I heard was the cop's cycle fire up. He cruised up to my car, hollered, "Drive more careful next time," tossed my paperwork at me, and shot past like a bullet after the station wagon.

"What happened?" Will asked.

"There is a God, my boy," I answered, as I put the Mustang in gear and gunned up the street.

Will sat on his knees in the bucket seat, peering over the dashboard. "What's the policeman doing?"

"He's going to catch that bad guy there. Watch." I was doing nearly fifty on the side street, trying to keep up with the cop, who in turn gained fast on the rusted station wagon, flasher blinking. The station wagon did not slow down. The cop, who drove the bike with the flamboyance of a rookie, swerved left and pulled up alongside the wagon. They rode side by side like that for a second. Then the wagon, without slowing, pulled left, crowding the bike, forcing it closer, closer, closer to the lefthand berm till the cop—who didn't have the sense to slow down or speed up—shot off the street onto the shoulder and down into the grassy ditch. Even so, he probably wouldn't have lost it if he hadn't stood on his brakes. The bike slewed sideways and then down in the shaggy weeds, the cop flying the other way head over heels like a cowboy who'd been shot off his horse.

I slowed slightly as we reached him. The cop was crawling shakily to his feet, apparently uninjured except maybe for his pride. I hollered out the window, "I'll get him for ya," slammed my shifter into second, and popped the clutch. The Mustang catapulted forward with a long scream of rubber and hurtled forward, pressing us back into our bucket seats.

"We gonna catch him, Ben?" Will asked excitedly.

"Yes, sir. Friend to law enforcement everywhere," I muttered.

The station wagon hung a right. I did the same, faster, thanks to my racing suspension, and changed up, gaining on him. We entered an older residential area, the street parked sporadically with cars on both sides. The wagon heedlessly slalomed back and forth, dodging cars. I stayed with him grimly, sure that he couldn't keep it up for long, and he didn't. He tried to shoot a four-way stop ahead of a pickup truck, just barely missed being broadsided, and had just recovered from that when he suddenly had to jink right to avoid being hit by a car backing out of a driveway. His outboard tires slammed the sharp stone curb on the right and then jumped it and mowed down three mailboxes in rapid sequence, gaining fast on a Hertz rental truck parked peacefully at the curb by a vacant lot. His right front tire, apparently damaged by the curb, chose that moment to let go, and the station wagon lost control completely, going into a smoky sideways spin, which ended when he plowed into the rental truck.

I geared down, squealed to a stop at the curb fifty feet back of the collision, shut off the motor, retrieved my .45 automatic from its clip beneath the bucket seat, and threw open the door. The wagon's driver side door was open and a young skinny permhead was racing like a track star into the vacant lot, which was empty except for weeds and a forest of Detroit Edison electrical towers. "Stay put," I hollered to Will, and jumped out of the Mustang and took off running after the perp. A hundred yards into the race I knew it was no good. The perp was twenty years younger, was in better shape, and had adrenaline to fuel him. Arms and legs pumping, he gained steadily then took a ten-foot chain-link fence with a scrambling climb and effortless drop like he'd been doing it all his life. I skidded to a stop in the weeds as the perp ran on and was engulfed by a thick stand of trees. My .45 hung heavy and useless in my hand. No matter how tempting it is, I don't whack a man just because he drives like a maniac.

Panting, I hoofed heavily back toward the Mustang. Will had disobeyed my orders and was walking hesitantly toward the station wagon, which sat on two flats, steaming, married to the back of the rental truck. "Get back in the car, kiddo," I hollered.

Will looked at me, and I thought he said, "Baby crying."

"Back in the *car*, damn it!"

"Baby crying!" Will shouted back.

I trotted to him, and from somewhere in the wagon heard a thin wailing. Holding Will back with one hand, I opened the back door. The evening light was rapidly fading, but I had trouble seeing the securely belted child seat, the little booties waving in the air, and the tiny toothless teary-eyed baby face wailing plaintively at me.

†††

"Is it a boy or a girl?" Will asked from the backseat as we drove.

"Boy, I guess. Wearing a blue shirt. Haven't researched it further." Though, judging from the smell, I'd have to pretty soon.

The baby's crying had tailed off to an occasional breathy wail. I heard Will say, "Nice baby." Then: "What're we gonna do, Ben?"

"Find a phone," I said, hanging a right on a four-lane commercial street. "There's a name and phone number stenciled on the baby seat there. Must be the mother."

"Why'd that man run away from him?"

"No idea." A self-service gas station hove into sight on the left. "We'll drop on in here, top off the tank, and make our call from here, okay, Will?"

"I have to go to the bathroom."

"We'll take care of that, too." I wheeled the Mustang in and stopped at the pump island next to hi-test. As I got out, a young dark-skinned man in denims strolled out of the building toward me. "Fill it up for you, sir?"

"Thought this was self-serve."

"Happy to oblige," he grinned.

Miracles never cease. Nobody'd pumped my gas since Nixon was in. "Suit yourself. Got a phone here?"

"Busted. Sorry." He pulled the nozzle from the pump, hit the switch, opened my gas cap, stuck the nozzle in, and started to fill. "Try up the street."

"Okay." Will climbed out of the Mustang behind me. "Round the side, I guess," I told him. He nodded and walked away. I leaned against the fender and glanced through the back window at the baby. He lay there in his car seat, mouth agape, staring around, mostly quiet now. Tough kid.

"Where's your boy going?" the attendant asked me.

"The head," I answered offhand.

The pump shut off. The attendant withdrew the nozzle and snapped it back into the pump. I hauled out my wallet and was picking through the bills in search of a sawbuck when I saw that the attendant was walking away. "Gas free, too?" I called.

He didn't look back or respond, just walked purposefully to a newish Chevy Nova parked in front of the station office and got in.

"Hey. Hey, Jack. Where are you going?"

He fired up the motor, squealed back then shot forward and swerved out of the lot onto the crowded street.

I held my wallet, staring dumbly after him then swiveled and stared at the station office. Empty. What the hell, guy fills up my tank and then splits. I had no time to puzzle over it further, because just then Will appeared around the corner of the station, walking stiff-legged, eyes saucerlike, mouth moving soundlessly. I instinctively started for him and found my voice. "What's up, Will?'

The boy raised a big fist and jabbed his finger back the way he'd come. "A man! In there, by the pee-pot!" he managed.

I moved faster. "What man?"

"In there, Ben! You gotta help!"

I reached the boy, almost ordered him to stay put, then changed my mind and took him with me to the half-open men's room door, from which issued a black work shoe topped by a white sock.

†††

For having been robbed, pistol-whipped, drop-kicked, gagged, and left hog-tied around the men's room commode, the gas station attendant was pretty damn arrogant. When I'd released him, he refused to let me use the station phone. He refused my offer to wait around to give the cops my story. He shrugged off my solicitous comments with a sneer. This was the eighth time he'd been robbed and relieved of the smallest take yet, only twenty-two bucks. It was routine for him, probably rating a casual mention on his job description. He didn't even call the police, just reported the event to his corporate office and then lighted a cigarette and stood fidgety and obnoxious, plainly desiring my immediate departure, behaving as though I was the one who committed the crime instead of the one who freed him from his wire and adhesive tape bond on the soiled stinking men's room floor.

I loaded Will into the Mustang and motored up the street, bound for a grocery store. Will sat in the back, excitedly telling the gurgling baby the whole story. I sat in the front, planning my strategy. Call the phone number from the baby's car seat, get an address. Pick up the milk and beer I'd started out for. Go to the address and drop off the baby and then head the hell back to

Carole's house, where we'd be safe.

The light was about gone when we reached the grocery store. I parked in the crowded lot, hoisted the baby out of his car seat, and carried him with one arm while holding Will's hand with my free one as we headed for the entrance. The baby felt toothpick light, soft and warm, totally trusting as he cooed and whispered nonsense to the side of my face. Will looked up at me and smiled confidently. Six-year-olds trust you, too.

The entranceway to the store was deserted except for a trio of young men, the oldest maybe seventeen, dressed uniformly in dark tight pants, tight white shirts open to the solar plexus, gold chains shining against their brown skins. One of them, the biggest, sauntered toward me as we reached the sidewalk. "Hey, man, do me a favor," he said snottily, half blocking my way.

I stopped and dropped Will's hand. "Not tonight, pal. Go screw."

"Now ain't *that* some way to talk," he sneered, jamming his hands meaningfully into his pockets. "Want you should fetch us out here a six of PBR longnecks, that's all."

"You're not old enough, wise guy."

He drew himself up straight and nudged me hard with his shoulder, eyes narrowing. "Old enough," he answered. His partners spread out, circling us. "Old enough, you read me? Whaddya say?"

I smiled. "Oh, sure, you seem like a reasonable enough sort to me. Excuse me just a second." I held the baby down and out to Will, who extended his arms. "Can you handle this, Will?"

"Sure, Ben," Will said. He took the baby, jaw set, eyes fearful on the others.

I grinned. "Knew I could count on you, guy." Then I turned to the leader. "I suppose you got something lethal in that pocket, huh, bro?"

"Lethal enough."

"Mind if I see for myself?" I grabbed the kid's floppy white shirt collar and gave it a hundred-eighty degree twist, pulling him toward me roughly. At the same time I thrust my other hand middle-knuckle deep into his pants pocket, gripped it hard, and tore it off.

The clasped switchblade clattered out onto the sidewalk, accompanied by a rain of change. I said, "Oh no, a deadly weapon," tightened my grip on his shirt collar, and gave him my best short-armed left jab, square on the nose.

He screamed though a spray of blood. I threw him back against the grocery store wall and faced the others just as one darted toward Will. He stopped in freeze-frame. I fixed him with a stare. "You move one step closer to that child, and I'll run you down and stomp you. I swear I will."

The leader wheezed and moaned on the sidewalk behind me. The punk ahead of me raised his hands and shrugged. I held my hands out to Will who handed me the baby. I cuddled him against me and took Will's hand. "I better not see you later, gentlemen," I said, and led Will into the grocery.

†††

The milk was no problem. Neither was the beer. The problem was my phone call, which I attempted from a public phone at the front of the store. The number kept ringing busy. I must have tried twenty times in ten minutes, with no success. Finally I got smart and looked up the woman's last name—Evans—in the book. There was an Evans with the correct number at an address just a few blocks away. I'd just finished writing it down when I noticed a disturbance by the checkout counter.

A tall, clean-cut young blond guy was passing the checkouts, carrying a case of cigarette cartons toward the automatic doors. One of the bagboys straightened from his work, stared at him then yelled, "Hey, stop! You haven't paid for that!"

The blond crouched into a trot, headed at maximum speed for the exit. The bagboy knocked aside a couple of old ladies and gave the blond a clumsy, full-body tackle. They went to the floor and the case of cigarettes hopped away, landing against a freestanding display of canned corn. The blond, stronger, more agile, more motivated, regained his leverage first and braced the slighter bagboy and throat-punched him. The bagboy gagged but did not relinquish his half-Nelson on the blond.

The crowd of customers and grocery employees stood frozen, shell-shocked, gape-mouthed. One of the cashiers found her voice. "Somebody help him."

I was already handing the baby to Will, who had the presence of mind to hang on tight. I threw myself at the grappling pair and slammed into the blond, managing to get a good grip on his longish hair. He kneed the bagboy back from him, slipped me easily, and came up with an uppercut to my chin that rang my gong with an almost audible sound. I went back and down, ass colliding hard with the unforgiving tile floor. The blond turned clumsily to make good his escape, but I managed to trip him, and he skidded down, sliding toward the door. He skittered up immediately, with all the advantage. I was headed up from all fours, firing up the rockets again, when the blond, unaccountably, came hurtling back past me into the vegetable display, sending it over with a crash of canned corn. He lay there, eyes open but unfocused, as I lurched to my feet and looked toward the entrance while the onlookers exhaled all at once.

There, grimacing with pain, rubbing his fist, stood the white-shirted kid from outside. His right-hand pants pocket flapped free where I'd ripped it.

His nose was bent, his upper lip was black with drying blood, his eyes were pinched, but he grinned at me snottily. "Not bad, huh, bro?"

"Why?" I managed.

"My brother," he said, staring down at the moaning shoplifter. "I've told him and *told* him not to commit no crimes."

Customers were moving all at once, most of them intent on escape. I went to Will and took the baby back as Will picked up the grocery bag. We met the punk at the door and, at my instructions, Will gave him the six-pack of beer we'd bought.

†††

The baby's address was on a narrow, curbless street about six blocks from the store. I drove at a fast crawl, squinting at the house numbers in the near darkness. I wanted to be done with this. The baby had been pretty good so far, but he was starting to fuss and whine. Probably needed feeding or changing or something, damned if I could tell; I don't know nothing about babies, birthin' 'em or anything else.

Will perched on his knees on the bucket seat next to me, leaning forward, eyes intent. "We almost there, Ben?"

"Gotta be one of these on the right." I slowed. "Yep, that's it, praise be . . . oh, hell's bells!"

A boxy, silver Ford Escort wagon had backed out of the driveway and was tearing up the street away from me. I scanned the flat-roofed, single-story brick house it had left. The correct address, all right. No lights on. Place was deserted, and whoever lived there was taking off up the street in the Escort, nearly out of sight now.

"Buckle up, Will," I said grimly, popped the clutch, and gunned the engine.

The Escort was long out of sight, having rounded a corner. I followed as fast as I could, ignoring the 25-mph speed limit. I caught sight of it again as it made a right on a larger artery. By the time I made that corner, I had gained quite a bit. There were no cars between us. I began flashing my brights and honking my horn as I closed on the Escort, trying to catch its attention. Half a block ahead was a railroad crossing, and as we approached, the warning lights began to flash, the bell began to clang, and the blinking gates started down.

"Okay, Will, we got 'em cornered," I said.

The Escort slowed to a halt then lurched left and started around the gate. Off to the right a dissonant train whistle blared. Some distance yet, but could be coming fast. As the Escort rolled onto the rails it twisted right to go around the other gate, but it never made it.

It stopped there, dead on the tracks, as I screeched to a halt at the crossing.

Over the rumbling of the Mustang motor I could hear the whine of the Escort's starter motor. The driver, apparently alone, hunched over the wheel. The train whistle issued again. I ripped open my door and jumped out. "Stay put, Will," I hollered, then trotted toward the Escort as the driver climbed out clumsily.

She was a short young butterball with long black hair rubber-banded back into a ponytail. In the bleaching light of the Mustang's headlights her eyes were enormous, her face corpse-pale. "It needs a tune-up!" she wailed. "I've been meaning to get around to it!"

The train horn sounded again. I could smell gas. "Flooded. Get yourself off these tracks, Mrs. Evans."

She started toward me, blinking. "You know me?"

"No, but I've got your kid back there in the car." I went to the Escort and opened the driver's side door. "*Other* side of the tracks!" I snapped. "I can't push your car back the way you came."

She froze. "My baby! My little Charlie! How'd you—"

"Never mind." I reached into the Escort, fiddled the stick into neutral and, leaning on the doorframe, began to push.

"I want him!" she screamed. "Get him for me! My ex snatched him right out of the nursery—I'd left him alone for just a second—"

I released the car, having moved it about one foot. "Okay. You get yourself to the other side there, well back." I dodged the flashing gate and ran back to the Mustang. Will had the passenger seat pulled forward, enabling me to squeeze the baby carrier out of the back. I ran back over the tracks to where Mrs. Evans waited. Tears as big as marbles ran down her round face as I handed her the baby. "Oh thank you, thank you," she sniffed, looking down at him. I was halfway back to the Escort when I heard her say, "Didn't you even *change* him?"

The train horn screamed and the engine's headlight caught me as it rounded a curve, churning hard. I resumed my position at the driver's side of the car and leaned against the doorframe, rocking the car. Back and forth, back and forth, the train horn screamed again, and the Escort broke loose and rolled off the tracks. I gave it one last vindictive push then, as it rolled slowly to a stop on the other side, I dived headlong back over the tracks and under the gate, sliding hard on the coarse gravelly asphalt as the train, with one last vicious scream, reached the crossing.

I climbed clumsily to my feet, limped to the Mustang and fell in the driver's side. I was sore and scraped and revved up with adrenaline. Will for once paid no attention to the freight cars chugging by; he was beaming with admiration at me. "You beat the train!"

"Reckon so." I leaned back in the bucket seat and lighted a short cork-tipped cigar and smoked it silently as we waited, and waited, and waited. Finally the caboose came and went and the gates lifted. The young butterball, and her baby, and her Escort, were gone. Naturally.

†††

We'd almost reached Carole's house when, lo and behold, the gold Toyota appeared ahead of us.

Almost immediately I saw the driver backhand his companion across the face. She got hold of his free arm and bent to it and seemed to bite it. The Toyota swerved and nearly jumped the curb. I fell back from it, just to play it safe, and felt Will's eyes on me.

"Aren't you going to do something?" he asked hesitantly.

"Nope."

Will looked ahead at the Toyota then back at me. "But they're fighting."

"Let 'em." I glanced at him. "We done took care of our share of problems, Will. For one night, anyhow."

The Toyota made a sudden left turn from the right-hand lane and disappeared. A few seconds later Will broke the silence.

"I was scared."

"Really? Sure didn't act like it."

"That little baby . . . and the man in the bathroom . . . and those bad men at the store. . . ."

I swerved into the parking lot of a Jesse James convenience store, parked, reached out a hand and squeezed his shoulder roughly. "They couldn't hurt us," I said. "I wouldn't let them."

"I was scared."

I breathed deeply, searching for simple words. "What it is, Will, is there's bad people all over the place. Always have been, always will be. Don't ask me why, I'm not that smart. But what I do know is that if you're lucky enough to be big and strong and halfway bright, you got a duty—it's your job—to stop the bad people and help the good people. Because a lot of the good people aren't strong enough to be able to help themselves."

"I was scared."

I looked at him for a long moment. "Well, so was I." I grinned. "The important thing is this: Never let anyone else realize it."

†††

Carole, face dark and unreadable, met us at the door. We trooped past her into the living room. The game show was, of course, long over. And from the looks of the VCR it was clear that Carole hadn't taped the bonus round for me. Rats.

"So what's the story, fellows?" Carole asked finally.

"Had to get gas," I answered.

"Stuck by a train, too," the carefully coached Will said.

"You've been gone a whole *hour*, fellows," Carole said in her patented glasscutter tone.

"Just another boring errand," I said airily, and went into the kitchen to put the milk away. When I returned to the living room, Will was sitting on the couch next to his mother, holding his book. "Can you read this to me now, Ben?"

The Fly Went By again. "Read it? I feel like we just *lived* it."

"What?" Carole asked darkly.

"Later, Carole, okay? Later."

I sat down and read Will the book. After that we put Will to bed. Back in the living room, I assumed the position in the La-Z-Boy and stretched my legs and lighted a cigar, trying to get interested in a New York City private detective with no visible means of support. Carole disappeared into the kitchen, came back with a hefty shot of Jack Daniels Black, handed it to me then sat on the couch, crossed her legs, crossed her arms, smiled with utter certainty and said: "Spill it, Ben."

Here goes nothing. I began the story, keeping it light and casual, hoping she'd still be speaking to me when I finished.

Afterword

I love the team-up of Ben with Will Somers, his sort-of stepson. It prefigures Perkins's for-real fatherhood of Rachel and depicts him in a much more human light.

Even so, he gets plenty of chance to strut his hero stuff, while at the same time getting (and claiming) little credit. For all of that, he manages to use what Cathleen Jordan, *Alfred Hitchcock's editor*, called a "madcap" episode to teach the young man some things about life.

The Seuss books were the first books I remember reading. As my own kids came along, we provided them with unlimited books and reading experiences, and *The Fly Went By* was one of them. That's probably what triggered this story.

Not all of it is fictional. The cigarette-case wrestling match actually happened, but in Tennessee, not Michigan, and I was only a spectator. And I once saw a woman in a car ahead of me being smacked around by a male driver.

I hope she's okay.

Left for Dead

It wasn't a landing, it was a barely controlled crash. My ultralight hit on all three wheels of the tricycle gear simultaneously and, hurtling entirely too fast along the rock-hard, burned-out field, bounced from one wheel to another in rapid sequence as I fought the stick for control. A quiet voice in my head speculated quite impersonally that any second a viciously errant gust of wind would catch one of the wings, flip the aircraft over, and smear me into a long red stain on the ground.

But the voice, for once, was wrong. I rolled to a stop, throttled down the 350cc Zenoah engine, and cut the ignition, leaving only the sound of the driving wind.

I clambered out of the open cockpit, shucked off my wool hood and heavy goggles, unzipped my black snowmobile suit halfway, and paced a small circle under the influence of maximum adrenaline, trying to figure out where I was and what the hell I'd do now.

The first part was relatively easy. I was somewhere in the middle of the twenty-five-hundred-acre Southern Michigan Wilderness Preserve, located roughly halfway between Detroit and Sturgis, in Whitlock County near the Ohio line. What the hell I'd do now was, without doubt, wait. Wait for better weather. Even if I had to spend the night in this godforsaken place. I was lucky I'd gotten the aircraft down in one piece as it was.

I stopped pacing, zipped my suit back up against the October chill, and scanned the area. I was near the center of a large flat valley. Behind me was the westernmost fringe of the Irish Hills. Ahead was a mass of forest, as far as the eye could see. Nowhere were there people or signs of habitation. In a month or so the area would be covered with the first dusting of snow and peopled by blaze-orange hunters taking potshots at anything that moved, especially each other. A month after that there'd be snow on the ground and crowds of snowmobilers and skiers. Now was the dead time, nobody but little old me, an unscheduled visitor but pretty damn glad to be there, just the same.

The afternoon was wearing on, getting colder and windier by the moment. I grabbed the ultralight by the downtube and wheeled her along the hard ground till I reached the fringe of thick trees. I folded down the wings and, for extra measure, propped some rocks against the wheels. Then I ventured twenty feet or so into the woods and found a nice comfortable spot against a rock outcropping, the ground covered with a thick layer of leaves and humus, and tamped myself a place to rest. I lay down, propped my head against an old, rotting stump, and relaxed. Nothing to do but kill time till morning, maybe sleep if I could, later.

I had nothing to eat or drink, but I did have a handful of cigars tucked away, so the essentials were certainly taken care of. I extracted one, stuck it in my mouth then dug beneath the snowsuit into my jeans pocket in search of a light. Found a wad of bills. A dead Michigan Lotto ticket. Some coins. And a loose .45 caliber bullet. Pretty typical pocket inventory—but no matches. I was starting to panic when I found my kitchen matches in the other pocket, sighed in relief, and flared one. I was just getting the cigar going when I heard the far-off scream.

I jerked upright, listening hard. Nothing. Could have been my imagination, I thought. Or maybe an animal. But I'm not known to imagine things. And, though I knew there were no settlements within twenty miles, I felt certain the scream was human. Female, flat, atonal, not expecting to be heard.

I sighed, hoisted myself to my feet, tucked my cigar away, and hoofed into the vast clearing. Still deserted. I stood still for a moment, hearing the scream again in my mind then turned left and began to hike. I wasn't even sure the sound had come from that direction. I could very well have been wasting my time. But time was something I had plenty of just then, so I set out hiking.

The woods bent away to my left as the valley turned toward the west. I followed the curve down a gentle incline, and as the trees fell back I saw a cabin at the bottom of the slope, hard against a sudden, wooded rise.

I stopped for a minute and surveyed. The cabin looked small, maybe twenty by twenty, weathered planks topped by a rusted tin roof and a stone chimney, no porch. A gaunt wood-slat snow fence, bowed in sports, surrounded it. The dying grass had grown up tall here and was being whipped to and fro by the wind. Overall, the place looked like it had been built as an afterthought and not occupied much since then. Certainly it looked abandoned now.

I set out for it anyway. Even if there was no screamer to be found, a man-made shelter sure beat the hell out of a makeshift camp deep in the woods. As I drew nearer, I saw a narrow gap in the fence about twenty feet from the cabin, and a path beaten in the tall grass up to the door. To the right of the fence gap was a platform of rotting planks, probably the covering of an old disused well. Beyond that, in the corner of the makeshift yard, was a neatly stacked couple of cords of split, well-seasoned firewood. Back of the cabin I caught just a glimpse of a small, leaning, tin-roofed outhouse. Somebody had obviously put in some time here. How long ago, I had no idea.

I slowed my pace as I passed through the fence gap and ventured up to the door. Not a sound from anywhere, nothing but the wind. The rough-hewn plank door stood open a couple of inches. I looked at it for a minute then pushed it open slowly on groaning iron hinges.

The inside smelled of old wood and mold. A two-man folding cot stood open on the plank floor, covered with a nondescript pile of gray army blankets. To the right, a wood table hung against the wall with a broad ceramic sink built into it, into which an iron hand pump dripped. On the left-hand wall, between the pair of dirty, cobwebby windows, stood a makeshift cabinet, its twin doors hanging open like a dead man's jaw, its contents indistinct in the darkness.

Dead ahead, to the right of the back door, was a large cobblestone fireplace. Hanging above it was a dusty, rough-hewn mantel propped up by wrought-iron supports bolted into the plank wall.

And handcuffed to one of the iron supports was a woman.

Tall. Short blond hair. Thin, frightened, obviously exhausted. And completely naked.

Her face changed when she saw me, went into shock. "Who the hell are *you?*"

†††

Who the hell I am is Ben Perkins, and all I'd been trying to do that afternoon was get myself home after completing a quickie job for a client.

The night before, I'd been peaceably enjoying game two of the World Series when Tony Omaha had called all in a lather. While the rest of the nation was engrossed in the I-70 series, Tony was, as usual, competing in a top-secret, high-stakes poker tournament held annually at a lodge at Burns Point, down near the Ohio line. Normally, Tony does pretty well in those things. This time, he told me tersely, the cards weren't being too friendly. I knew very well what he meant—though I'm not in Tony's professional league—having held in my time plenty of hands composed of unmatched garbage cards.

But in today's session he'd felt the cards turning, he told me in all seriousness; all he needed was a fresh infusion of capital, and he'd be able to turn the thing around in the next day's session.

He wasn't putting the arm on me. All he wanted me to do was deliver some cash to him, cash that his wife had waiting and ready. I told him I'd get it to him the next morning, and went back to the TV to watch the Royals take it on the chin. I didn't give the errand a second thought. Private detective work isn't all sleuthing; I've sort of broadened the definition to include anything that turns a more or less honest buck.

I picked up the cash first thing the next morning from Omaha's suspicious, yet resigned wife, and headed back to my apartment, having decided to fly down to Burns Point rather than drive. It was pushing mid-October, stretching the ultralight season a little, but the weather outlook was good, and this could very well be my last chance to fly this year. Besides, Burns Point was an eighty-mile drive, but only a sixty-mile flight. Furthermore, just the weekend before, I'd completed the 350cc engine's five-hundred-hour rebuild, and a hop like this one would break in the work, securely reseating the components. Just the thing to do prior to putting the aircraft away for the winter.

And it worked out great, the flight down, anyway. I coasted down at two thousand feet on a due southwest heading, dipped south when I reached the village on Burns Point, then approached the resort from due east and landed on the golf course. My arrival caused something of a sensation—in my snowmobile suit, black wool hood and heavy goggles, I looked a little like a Michigan Ninja—and Tony Omaha, obviously regarding my mode of arrival as a good omen, gave me half a G and urged me to stay for lunch and sit in on a few hands. I accepted the lunch but passed on the poker, refueled the aircraft, and taxied to the number six fairway, a four-hundred-yard par three bearing due west, for takeoff.

Even as the aircraft left the ground, I knew I was in for trouble. The formerly clear western horizon had scudded up with dirty clouds, obscuring the sun. From the powerful lift I felt upon leaving the ground, I knew the wind had picked up. And, as I made the big banking turn to head northeast, I felt an ominous tugging at the aircraft's thirty-eight-foot, nylon-coated wings. Wind gusts, and strong ones. A storm front was pulling in from the west. Fast.

My first thought was to put about five thousand feet beneath me to try to outrun the sucker. But the wind was from the tail, reducing my lift, and I could tell from the way the engine was laboring that I was sucking up a lot of gas. And as I flew, the wind gusts got progressively worse, making it hard to maintain a heading. I was being knocked around in the sky, and try as I might to stay calm, I began to sweat in my snowmobile suit, my heart pounding, every muscle in my body strung tight and trembling. I knew very well that an ultralight is purely for pleasure flying in absolutely benign skies. Any kind of rough weather up there can crumple you up like a paper cup and send you fluttering down in a lethal embrace of aluminum frame and nylon.

Nothing to do then but take her in as best I could. I made a long, sweeping, banking turn till I was headed south, and began to descend in a series of abrupt jerks. The land below flowed away on all sides of me in densely wooded hills and valleys as far as I could see. A couple of miles ahead I could see a reasonably wide valley running east-west, ending at a lake to the east and a large hill to the west. Have to take her down there. As to which direction, there was no contest. Left was downwind; in this wind it was practically

210 | ROB KANTNER

impossible to land that way. So I began to swing to the right. Right for safe, I thought. Left for dead.

†††

I didn't answer, being slightly taken aback at finding a naked woman hand-cuffed in this shack in the middle of nowhere. She shrieked, eyes wild. "Who *are* you?"

"Perkins," I managed. I jerked a thumb over my shoulder. "I was forced down—I heard—uh—"

She rattled the handcuff. "Get me loose! Please!"

"Oh sure, right." It wasn't quite that easy. There were no tools to be found inside the cabin. I remembered the woodpile, trotted out there, and found an old, heavy, rusted hatchet. She cringed as I approached her with it. "Take it easy," I said. "Stretch the chain tight against that mantel there." She did so and covered her eyes with her free hand. I severed the chain with one hard chop. The woman took two steps, fell to her knees, bent her head nearly to her thighs and began to cry. I lay the hatchet on the mantel and examined the iron mantel support. It was scratched bright and deep where the cuff hung. There were corresponding scratches, livid ones, on her thin wrist. She'd been tugging at it for a while.

I looked at her. No point in questioning her till she'd calmed down. "How about I step out, and you get yourself dressed."

She tossed her head back, ran her hand through her blond hair, and got clumsily to her feet. "No—" she sniffed— "you just stay put, it's all right." She walked uncertainly to the cot, rifled the blankets, and found jeans and a heavy white ski sweater. She was utterly unselfconscious as she dressed, and gave me an occasional glance out of the corner of her eye, but said nothing. I leaned against the mantel and watched her. She was a long-limbed one, five-eight, one-ten, her hair a straight blond cap around high cheekbones, deep eyes, a generous mouth and snub nose. Relatively young, in years anyway. Twenty-five, max. Pretty tough, too, to compose herself so quickly after an experience like this. Whatever *that* was.

"What's your name?" I asked.

"Jill. Jill Evans." She slid her bare feet into a pair of worn hiking shoes and began to lace them up. "You're . . . Perkins, you said?"

"Ben." Finished with her work, she clambered to her feet, went to the pump, worked the handle till the rusty flow had passed, then bent under and drank deeply. Wiping her mouth once, she went back to the cot, wadded up a couple of blankets into a makeshift pillow, and lay back with her head propped on them. Though her face was slack with weariness, her light eyes were sharp and bright on me. "Oh God, that feels good," she sighed.

"How long you been penned up like that?" I asked.

"Two days, two whole days. I couldn't sit down, I couldn't sleep . . . it gets *cold* at night this time of year, and—"

"How'd you get here in the first place?" I interrupted.

"I was kidnapped," she replied. "They held me here till they got the ransom. Then they cuffed me there and split. Left me here, left for dead." She straightened vertical, forearms propped on her knees. "Hey, you got a car out there or something? I want to get the hell out of here."

For something to do, I ambled to the cupboard and peered inside. Not a hell of a lot there by way of food. Canned tomatoes, a couple of cans of Spaghetti-Os, a spilled jar of Folger's instant. Some plastic utensils. And four cans of low-alcohol beer. As a matter of policy, I avoid any beer that sends me to the can cold sober; but, any port in a storm. I popped the top, took a slug, and turned to face her. "No car. I was flying an ultralight, the weather forced me down." I gestured at the darkening window. "Day's about gone, no getting out of here before the morning."

She barely contained the shrillness in her voice. "I want to go home. My family's got to be scared sick worrying about me." She tossed her head. "Maybe I'll walk out. There's light left."

"Listen up, Jill, it's twenty-plus miles to the nearest phone, and after two days tied up like that you're in no shape to walk it, trust me."

Her face slackened with resignation. "You got that right. Oh well." Her eyes brightened above a narrow smile. "So it's just you and me here for the night, huh?"

"Sure do look that way." Every man's fantasy, I thought with sour amusement. The big heroic rescuer of a helpless kidnap victim, a natural blond and thoroughly female (both verified beyond dispute), young, yet exuding experience from every pore. To the victor belong the spoils. Ha. I said, "You must be starving. Menu's kinda thin here, but I can hack open a can of Spaghetti-Os for you if you want."

"Oh, not right now. I could use one of those beers, though."

I carried one to her. She popped the top and drank. I said, "Easy, now. Don't wanna lose your head or anything." She winked at me and drank some more. I glanced out the back window—sure enough, another woodpile back there, near the outhouse. I looked back at Jill. "Light's going quick. Think I'll fetch in some firewood and get something going. It'll be a cold one tonight."

Before she could answer, I was out the back door. The dead grass was knee high, and I waded through it toward the woodpile. The wind was strong and the temperature was dropping steadily; I began to feel a chill even inside my snowmobile suit. Got to get the fire going quick, I thought. Hope the wood's okay.

I didn't find out right away. Because, halfway to the woodpile, I stopped and froze, staring down. A man lay prone there, face down, inert. His suit jacket was jagged with an array of small, bloody holes, and he was quite dead.

†††

I used the hatchet to whack some thin strips of well-seasoned maple, built a pyramid of them in the fireplace, fired them up with a kitchen match then patiently began to feed the heavier pieces to the gaining blaze as Jill Evans watched me from the cot.

Finally she said, "Aren't you going to ask me about it?"

I carefully laid a four-by-four hunk of wood on the blaze then used a twig to relight my cigar, and faced her. "Ask you about what?"

"The body out there."

"Which body."

"The dead body."

"Oh, *that* body." I exhaled smoke and cleared my throat. "I figured you'd get around to it sooner or later."

The skin stretched taut over the good bones of her face, making her eyes look larger in the half-darkness. "He was one of the kidnapers," she whispered.

"How'd he get dead?" I asked.

"Some kind of argument with the other two men. I'm not sure what it was about . . . I was only half-listening. . . . Suddenly they hustled him out there and I heard shooting. . . . He never came back in. The others tied me up and left right after that. I assumed he was dead. I didn't ask. I was—I was scared they'd kill me, too."

"Might have been more merciful if they had, rather than leaving you tied up to freeze to death."

She got to her feet and walked over and sat cross-legged next to me in front of the growing fire. "You're probably right," she murmured. "But you know? All I wanted to do was live. For the next minute, the next hour, the next day." She leaned her head onto my shoulder and took my left hand in both of hers. "I had no way of knowing someone like you would happen along. But you did."

I squeezed her hand, broke from her gently, and stood. "Getting warm in here. Think I'll shuck the suit."

"All right." I didn't have to look to see her smile.

I unzipped my black snowmobile suit down to the crotch and, dancing awkwardly on each foot in sequence, tugged it off. Jill rose, too, and stood very close to me, watching me with her unreadable eyes, lips parted. As I tossed the suit away, Jill reached up and began to unbutton my chambray shirt, the handcuff clinking like a cheap bracelet on her wrist. I made no move to interfere, just reached behind to the waistband of my jeans and pulled out my .45 automatic. She stepped back from me suddenly as I hefted it. "I'd better secure this somewhere."

She laughed nervously. "Packing, huh? How come?"

"Private detective. Standard equipment." I went to the cupboard, laid the weapon down on the shelf, grabbed a large can of Spaghetti-Os, and began to wipe the dust off it with my shirttail. "Hungry yet?"

She exhaled impatiently then grabbed the hem of her sweater, shimmied it off over her head, tossed it toward the cot, and shook her head to loosen her fine blond hair. The firelight ran whitish-gold fingers over her smooth shoulders, her up-aimed, arrogant breasts. She threw her shoulders back and hooked her hands in the empty belt loops of her jeans. "This answer your question?"

It was indeed a transfixing vision: the young half-dressed woman, framed in the blaze of the fire which filled the cabin out in the middle of darkening nowhere with sweet-smelling heat. I grinned. "Look, it's been two days, you gotta eat. Get some of this in you then we'll sort out the other."

Long pause, then she sighed impatiently. "Oh, all right then." She went to the cot, sat, flung one leg over the other; then, for good measure, she pulled the ski sweater back on even though, by then, it was getting quite warm in there.

I cleaved the top of the Spaghetti-Os can with the hatchet, wedged a respectable opening then took it to her along with a beer. "Eat hearty," I advised. "Every bite now." She nodded glumly at me and began to eat, taking about four swallows of beer for every bite of cold spaghetti.

I took my time about stoking up the fire with fresh logs. It was roaring now, popping and sizzling, so hot that each fresh log fairly exploded into flames as I tossed it in. I sat down, leaning against the far wall, and smoked my cigar as Jill finished the spaghetti and tossed the empty can into the fire. She took a long draft of beer and licked her lips. Her eyes looked glassy as she said through numb lips, "Okay."

"Okay." I stood. "You get yourself ready, I got an urgent errand." She was unzipping her jeans as I went out the back door and pulled it shut behind me. The cold wind was steady and piercing as I loped through the tall grass to the privy. On my way back, I stopped at the body, fired up a kitchen match and, cupping it with my palm, lowered myself for a long look. Then I flipped the match away and walked slowly and deliberately back to the cabin.

Aside from the crackling roar of the fire, all was still and silent inside the cabin. Jill Evans lay sprawled on the cot, white legs spread, jeans hanging forgotten from one bare ankle. I walked softly to the cot and looked down at her for ten long breaths then gently lifted her legs onto the cot and covered her with two of the blankets. She muttered vaguely and curled into a fetal position and buried her face in the coarse mattress.

I watched her for ten long heartbeats then went silently out the front door. I was out there for a vigorous quarter hour, and when I got back I had to wash my hands in the icy pump water. Jill slept silently, almost invisible under the blankets. I tossed a couple more logs on the fire, shunted myself back into the snowsuit, stretched out on the hard plank floor by the fire and, using my hands as a wholly inadequate pillow, free-fell into inky black, totally dreamless sleep.

†††

The explosion didn't just rouse me, it sent me nearly to the ceiling. I came fully awake on knees and fingertips, back arched like a bird dog, heart pounding supercharged adrenaline to every nerve. As the sound replayed in my mind, I relaxed. It had been nothing more than a superheated knot exploding in the dying coals of the fire.

I sat back on my rump, breathing hard. Dawn shot hard bright fingers of light through the dirty cabin windows. Birds chirped outside. The drone of the wind, a natural part of the environment the night before, was gone. It was early yet, somewhere between six and seven, but with the full break of day I knew that flying weather would be back.

Jill Evans had not moved, but suddenly I realized her eyes were open, and on me.

She pursed her lips then licked them quite deliberately and rippled the blanket back off her. The ski sweater had bunched up under her breasts, leaving her bare from there down.

She said, "Come on now, Ben."

I got to my feet. "Better throw on a couple of logs. Getting chilly in here." Ignoring her skeptical look, I tossed on the last chunks of split maple, blew the coals, watched as the flames started their reddish-blue licks, then faced her.

She said in a hard voice, "Don't come near me with that damn snowsuit on."

"Oh. Certainly." I unzipped it, peeled it off, kicked it away then sauntered to her and sat on the edge of the wobbly cot. With a faraway look in her eyes, she wandered her hands up my shirt and began to unbutton it. I said, "Look, I got a confession to make."

"Mm-hm."

"I believe in honesty in relationships."

"That's your confession?"

"Uh-huh. I don't want to get involved with you under false pretenses."

"Ooh." She finished the unbuttoning and ran her hands over my chest. "I'm not as complicated as you. All I want to do is screw."

I bent and gave her a quick, brushing, teasing kiss, and said very softly, "I just can't stop thinking about my daddy."

Her hands had deliberately wandered to my pants and were busily unsnapping and unzipping. "What about your daddy?"

"What he used to say."

"And what was that?"

"My daddy used to say . . . he told me . . . 'Never lay down with a woman who has more troubles than you.' That's what my daddy always said."

She laughed, and prodded me gently, and I lifted myself just enough to enable her to pull my jeans down over my pelvis. "Sounds like good advice. But hey, Ben," she cooed, "I don't have any troubles. You fixed up the worst of 'em yesterday. And what troubles I have left," she breathed as I kicked my jeans back off one leg, and then the other, "I think you're about to take care of for me. Mm. Yes, indeedy."

I lowered myself onto her, slid my left arm under her neck, and we enjoyed a long kiss of tongue tips. I looked into her bright eyes. "But see, that's the point. I don't think your troubles are over. I think they're just beginning."

She traced my eyebrows, cheekbones, mouth and chin with just the lightest touch of fingertips, intertwined her ankles with mine, and laughed softly.

I kissed her again then raised myself on my palms and said in that same light, casual tone: "'Cause you ain't the victim, babe. You weren't the kidnapee. The kidnap*er*, more like. Or one of 'em, anyhow."

†††

She tried that laugh again, and though she was good, very, *very* goddamned good, it sent back a hollow echo in that little cabin.

I disentangled my legs, negotiated myself a sitting position on the edge of the cot, and began pulling on my jeans. Out of the corner of my eye I saw her frowning as she propped her head on the heel of her palm. "That's a nasty, ugly thing to suggest, Ben Perkins."

"Oh, yeah. I couldn't agree more. 'Specially since it happens to be true, now ain't it, little darlin'."

"This is starting to perturb me," she said, giving the blanket a deliberate jerk over her, "*totally.* You read me?"

I zipped and snapped my pants shut, stood, took a step toward the fire then turned and faced her. "'Member what you said when I first busted in here? You said, 'Who the hell are you?' Like maybe you were expecting somebody else. *Not* like you weren't expecting to see anybody at all. Dig it?"

Her face was a smoldering mask, God knows what churning behind her eyes.

"And then that stiff out back," I added, jerking a thumb. "For a helpless, innocent kidnap victim, you were awful casual about that. And how come he's all dolled up in a business suit? A kidnaper, knowing he was going to spend some time out here, wouldn't dress up in some fancy business suit. Nope, he'd've fixed himself up with jeans. And a sweater. And boots. Sort of like *you*, kid. . . . Then there was the way you reacted to my pistol. 'Packing, huh?' Not exactly civilian talk. And this seduction routine, that don't hang right with me either."

Her jaw was square and ugly. "I *liked* you, Ben."

"Oh yeah, sure. I don't think I'm completely disgusting to look at, but for a helpless, traumatized kidnap victim, you seemed awful anxious to get me between the knees. That old soften-up stunt insults my intelligence, kiddo; it's older than running water."

"I won't repeat the mistake," she said pointedly.

"Suits me just fine," I answered, picking up my shirt.

"Me, too," said the male voice from the window. I whirled as glass crashed in and saw twin shotgun barrels that were so large I almost didn't take notice of the muscle-bound grinner behind them.

†††

Jill Evans jerked upright on the cot. "'Bout time you got here, Darrell!"

He was young, burr-cut, and a weight freak, judging from the way the veins and muscles stood out on his neck and arms. He wore a sleeveless bright orange hunting jacket and a big grin. "Took me some time, Jill. This ape been molesting you?"

"No way," she said disgustedly, then skooched off the cot and began pulling on her jeans. "What kept you?"

I slid my right hand into my jeans pocket.

"Took me a while to get the drop on Edgar," he said, keeping the twin barrels fixed on my chest. "Got it done late last night and drove like hell to get back here. He the one with the plane?"

She snapped her jeans closed. "Yeah, so what."

"Saw it out there, so I circled around with the Jeep and drove cross-country and snuck in here. Figured you had company."

She ignored him. "You got the money then?"

I sorted through my pocket silently and palmed the loose .45 bullet.

"All hundred G worth, out there in the Jeep." He glanced at me. "What do we do with him, tie him up?"

Her look at me was venomous. "I've got bigger plans than that. Get in here, Darrell."

"He got a gun or something?"

"Yeah, wait a minute, cover him. I'll get it." She trotted to the cupboard and rescued my .45 automatic from the counter and swung around to hold it on me. "Okay. Come on in."

He gave us one appraising look then disappeared from the window. We heard a clank, a thump, a "son of a bitch!" and, as Jill glanced out, I tossed the bullet in the fireplace. It landed soundlessly, hopefully—for me, anyway—in the flames somewhere.

Darrell came in the door, shotgun at port arms, grumbling. "Tripped over a damn bucket out there. Can't wait to get out of this pigpen." He stood at the opposite end of the cot from me, shotgun hung under his arm and aimed half downward. Judging from the way he posed, he was proud of his body; every muscle seemed to stand out whether there were clothes over it or not. His grin was bright and giddy and humorless. "So this fella happened by and turned you loose, huh, Jill?"

"No thanks to you, Darrell. I'd given up on you. I thought I was going to die here."

"Well, hey! You shouldn't have wasted old man Simmons."

I said, "Oh, Simmons the stiff lying out back there? The victim?"

"Shut up, Perkins," Jill said.

Darrell beamed. "Yeah, that's him all right; big shot insurance man, richer'n God. You shoulda seen what Jill did to him. We'd gotten the ransom, we're all set to split; before Edgar and me know it, Jill opens the back door and shoves Simmons out. He starts to run. She's carrying this twenty-two target revolver, single-action job, and she draws down on him, and cocks, and *bang!* Cocks it again, just as cool as could be, and *bang!* All six shots, the last four after he's on the ground."

I glanced at Jill, who held the heavy .45 in both hands aimed at me, and wondered how long it would take the bullet to explode, and where it would go when it did.

Darrell continued, "Well, Edgar got madder'n hell. Wasting Simmons wasn't part of the plan. He grabbed Jill and slapped her around and said to me, 'We're leaving this gun-happy bitch here, teach her a nice lesson.'"

"And you went along with him," Jill said hoarsely. "You helped him strip me and tie me up and you drove away with him."

"Hey sweetie, I had to! He had the gun, and he'd of hurt me bad if I hadn't fallen in line." His smile became earnest. "You knew I'd come back for you, just as soon as I could."

"Yeah. I knew I could trust you, Darrell," she said sourly. She hefted the .45 and drew a bead on me, eyes narrow. "We'll argue about that later. First, a little target practice with our private detective friend here."

I took a deep breath, wondering *where the hell is that damn bullet,* and said, "Darrell, you better think about what she might do to you once you have your back turned."

He chuckled. "Sounds like one of them cute little private detective-type tricks. Divide and conquer and all that. No thanks." He looked at Jill. "Careful with that thing, babe. Aim low and leave some give in the wrists. That ain't no twenty-two that gives a snap and drills nice neat holes. That thing kicks like a mule. Built to stop, drop, and splatter."

"Good." I braced myself to jump, and then—finally—the bullet in the fireplace exploded.

I don't know where it went and I didn't take time out to check. I jumped as high as I could and came down with both feet on my end of the cot. The other end flew up like a runaway teeter-totter and caught Darrell under the elbows. The shotgun flew sideways and discharged both barrels, blowing out the front window. I had a quick sight of Jill leveling the .45 toward me, but I was nowhere around; I took a running, full-body leap at Darrell and plowed him back against the cabin wall with a crash.

There could be no Marquis of Queensbury niceties with this clown and, moreover, I had to keep him from grabbing me, or I'd be finished. Fortunately big muscle-bound guys like him aren't all that fast. I came up with a knee to his groin, jinked back and, as he drove at me I took him by an elbow, pivoted, and threw him across the cot onto the floor. Jill danced back toward the fireplace, aiming, trying to get a clear field of fire, but I was on the move again as she aimed for me, diving across at Darrell as he sprang to his feet.

"Hold him still! Hold him *still!*" she muttered as I piled Darrell against the pump. He gave me a shot upside my head with a bricklike fist, and stars spotted my vision as I fell back. I was aware of Jill frozen in place just behind me, aiming for true now, and as Darrell moved in for me I took a wrist in both hands and jumped on one foot with both of mine and flung him toward me as hard as I could, dropping to the floor as I did so.

Completely off-balance, he fell straight at Jill, who apparently had maximum pressure on the trigger of the .45. The gun went off and Darrell flew back over me, clearing me easily, and landed suddenly inert at the wall. Judging from the looks of his head, he'd only been six inches from the .45 when Jill fired. Like the man said: stop, drop, and splatter.

I heard the .45 hit the floor as Jill screamed. I turned to see her holding her right wrist with her left hand, bending and gasping, face twisted with pain. I started for my feet, but she saw me and charged the door and disappeared outside. I stood, in no particular hurry to chase her. From outside I heard a shriek. Then silence.

I took several deep breaths then put my snowsuit back on, trying not to look at Darrell as I did so. Then I retrieved and secured my .45 and trotted out the back door. It was a splendid Michigan October morning: pale blue sky, bright sun, just a hint of breeze. I had no trouble finding the Jeep back in the woods, and sauntered back to the cabin, carrying a vinyl carry-on bag under my arm. I circled the cabin to the front and walked up to the gap in the fence. The ground disappeared at that point, leaving a circle of black. I stepped toward the lip of the old disused well and looked down.

It was maybe fifteen feet deep, its walls old, rough discolored brick. At the bottom lay remains of the old rotted boards that had covered the top, and atop these lay Jill Evans, on her side, one leg twisted oddly under her.

Her eyes looked very large in her pale pinched face. "You moved the fence."

"Uh-huh. Last night, after you were asleep."

"You knew even then?"

"Let's just say I had my doubts."

"Oh, God." She squirmed and winced. "That was slick. Real slick, how you tricked me, Ben."

"Wasn't that much to it. All I did was move a section of fence, cover the well top with weeds, and tramp a new path up to it from the cabin door."

"I think my leg is broken," she said in a small voice.

"Doesn't surprise me a bit."

"How are you going to get me out?"

"Hadn't planned to, actually."

She swallowed and blinked and licked her lips. "You can't be serious."

"Am, too. You honest to God scare me, kid. I don't want you anywhere near me. Don't trust you, for some damn reason."

Her efforts to remain calm made her voice sound labored. "Is that—is that bag the money?"

"Uh-huh."

"A hundred thousand, cash."

"If you say so."

"We can—we can take it and go away—together, and—"

"Listen, even if I was the larcenous sort, no way am I going to spend the rest of my life with you in my backfield. Get real, here."

I started away. "Wait!" she shouted. I stepped back. Now, for the first time, her voice was crushed, despairing, completely lost. "How can you just leave me here like this?"

I considered. "Well, all I have to do is picture you standing at the door of the cabin, drawing a bead on that poor old man and putting six shots into him as he ran, four after he hit the ground. That's how."

"I'll *die* here!" she sobbed.

"You, die? No way. The cops'll be here by afternoon. You're a tough chick, you'll keep till then."

"Heartless bastard!"

"Takes one to know one."

As I began the long hike toward the ultralight, I heard her screaming obscenities. Gradually the voice faded and then stopped entirely.

As I powered the ultralight into the air and swung northeast, it idly occurred to me that I could, in fact, just keep the money and sort of forget to call the cops. No one would ever know that I'd ever been at the cabin.

Of course I did notify the police once I got home, but not because I felt sorry for Jill Evans.

Quite the opposite.

Afterword

Unlike "traditional" private eye stories, this one is not about a "case." It's another example of old Ben tripping over trouble and getting himself into quite a pickle. In this case he literally falls into trouble thanks to problems with his ultralight—a bit of an expansion on the use of the ultralight as a dramatic device; it opens the door to a situation rather than being a tool for resolving one.

Overall I feel good about this story from the standpoint of its unpredictability. Ben truly stays well ahead of the reader. He's significantly smarter than the villains, too. To prevail he uses his brains as well as his talent at physical violence.

(Of course, it's handy that he happened to have a .45 bullet floating amid his pocket change, eh?)

And to me it's especially interesting that Ben doesn't even come near to falling for the seductive Jill Evans. Let's face it, he could have done her and *then* done her in, with no kickback, just as certainly as he could have walked away scot-free with the ransom money. But Ben not only has a sense of honor, he lives it, and he does so without beating his chest. Just doing his job.

The setting for the story is wholly fictitious, but there are plenty of places like it in Michigan, particularly in the central and northern areas. Ironically, it's a lot like where I live now.

Duck Work

The two-sided billboard atop the low-slung cinder block building said H&C HEATING AND COOLING. An orange banner plastered across the front windows advertised FURNACE REPAIR AND DUCK WORK. A sign spray-painted on the curbstones said CUSTOMER PARKING ONLY. I wasn't a customer, but I parked there anyhow.

The dim showroom was crowded with model furnaces and hot water heaters standing around like stalagmites, but was empty of people except for a worn-looking salesman extolling the features of a Bryant unit to a prospect. From the look on her face, I didn't think he was getting anywhere, so I interrupted. "Where's Owney?"

"Back office."

I walked around the sales counter and through an open doorway into a small, crowded, paneled office. Owney Busbee hung up the phone and rose, a grin cracking his wide, flat, freckled face, and said in his razor-sharp Tennessee twang, "Man, that was quick, Ben."

"You said it was an emergency. What's cooking?"

Owney looked down and sifted absently at the layers of papers, pink callback slips, and other debris on his desk. He's a large, rubbery, pear-shaped man, small-eyed and bald except for a smear of long darkish red hair bisecting his pale scalp. To see him there at H&C Heating and Cooling, dressed as usual in baggy pants and tieless, colorless sport shirt, you'd make him for just another of Detroit's legion of smalltime, just-this-side-of-broke merchants.

But appearances are deceptive and assumptions are dangerous. Owney has at least two other offices. One's in a place in Wayne called Bullet Realty, which he also owns. The other is the front seat of his acre-sized Cadillac, where he spends some fifty thousand miles a year, crisscrossing southeastern Michigan supervising his businesses, making deals, adding steadily to what is probably a pretty substantial fortune. His tools are potent if intangible: salesmanship, an unerring instinct for getting the customer what he wants, an encyclopedic memory, and a roster of private guys peddling part-time skills. Guys like me.

He looked at me and I could see he was anxious. "I got a furnace down in one of my buildings over on Plymouth Road. One of my boys is away hunting, 'nother one's in the hospital, and the other one's on a job he won't get done till suppertime tonight. Meanwhile, tenant's bitchin' up a storm, and—"

"What's the address?" Owney gave it. Plymouth near Grand River, near west side. "Sure, I'll shoot over there right now."

"Wal, that's rat fine. I'm grateful." He fished through a fist-sized bundle of keys on his desk, detached one, and handed it over. "Utility entrance, back side." I pocketed it. "Hunnert do it?" he asked.

"Sure." A hundred would get me to day after tomorrow, the outer limits of my financial planning. "Kinda beast we talking about?"

Owney squinted. "Dunno. Gas-fired, I know that, and older'n God."

"Better take along some parts."

"C'mon." Owney led me out of his office and into an adjacent back room, lined with steel shelves laden with parts and a workbench dark with tools. I began filling a box with blower belts of several sizes, a selection of replacement generators, various thermocouples, tubes, and other bits and pieces. Owney stood beside me, large hands shoved into his back pants pockets. "Stayin' busy?"

"Just keeping the plates from hitting the floor."

He laughed. "You ever get wore out on that maintenance job out in Belleville, you come see me, hear?"

"Thanks, Owney."

He scratched his head as I closed the box and latched it. "How 'bout the detective work? Done any good?"

"Oh, yeah." I hefted the box. Heavy but doable. "Pay's not great, but the hours are long."

Owney chuckled. "Well, maybe have something for you along *that* line pretty soon, too."

"Any time, pal, just holler." I grinned dutifully, waved, headed out to my '71 Mustang, secured the box in the trunk, and drove away.

As I headed east on Warren toward the Southfield Freeway, I remembered what I'd said to Owney about the detective work. I hadn't been exactly honest. Fact is, there'd been a whole lot of ugly lately, and I was tired. I planned to go into coast mode for a few weeks and recharge the batteries.

That was one reason I took on Owney's furnace repair job. Another was the money. And the third was the fact that you do favors for people like Owney Busbee whenever you can because he reciprocates in kind. It's the coin of our realm.

†††

The utility door grunted open. I propped it with my foot and shunted my toolbox and the parts box inside, then hit the only available switch and pulled the door shut. A bare bulb on the wall lighted up the grim utility room and its typical accessories: set tub, mops and buckets and brooms, janitorial supplies, and a wood ladder running up ten feet to an open loft.

Just my luck, I thought. Furnace is up above. Figured. Even from the outside, I could tell the building was one of those strip jobs, built on a slab and subdivided by paper-thin drywall into three suites. A symptom of the era we live in. The Era of Cheap. Maximum return for minimum investment, meaning no basements or crawlspaces, and furnaces placed up above, guaranteeing hernias for aging maintenance guys.

I hoisted my tool and parts boxes up there then climbed up myself and, duck-walking low under the ceiling, dragged them through the dimness along a narrow two-by-four catwalk to the corner where presided the furnace: an old Kramer gas-fired job, swathed in dust and, as advertised, cold as a corpse.

I squatted in front of the furnace, opened my toolbox, strapped my battery-operated lamp on my forehead, and switched it on. The loft was stuffy and silent except for the chirping of errant birds and very distant, muffled voices. The ceiling struts seemed just inches above my bare head, and beneath me, below the cheap aluminum joists placed at twenty-four-inch centers, showed acoustical ceiling tile. Place is held together my chicken wire and spit, I thought. I aimed my face at the furnace and took off the access panel.

Obvious things first. Pilot light was out, but gas supply was okay. Emergency switch was inactive and manual shut-off valve was on. Electrical showed positive. Okay. Could be simplest hundred bucks I ever made, as in the pilot light went out. I fetched a wood kitchen match from my toolbox, flare it on my thumbnail then mashed the gas cock and lighted the pilot. It took. I blew out the match and held the gas cock down, watching the bluish yellow flame, counting seconds.

The bird noises were still indistinct, but the voices were clearer now, no doubt amplified through the ducts. Spooky-sounding but distinct. Distinct enough to inform me that the man was the boss; the woman, Ginny by name, was an employee. He was married, but not to her. They were alone in the office and having the very best of times down there.

Suddenly I realized that my thirty-second interval had passed several minutes ago. I released the gas cock and turned it to "on." The pilot stayed lit. The burners caught with a whoosh. I inspected them for a moment; then, satisfied, replaced the access panel, closed the tool and parts boxes, and dragged them back along the narrow catwalk.

I motored around the building to the Plymouth Road exit. A red Toyota Camry sat there, waiting for traffic to clear. Back in front of the building, by the left-hand suite, sat a dark blue Ford Escort hatchback. A tall, dark-haired woman was just climbing into it. The willing Ginny, no doubt.

So what. I'd done my job and pushed my tired ass a C-note ahead. To hell with the rest of it.

†††

Exactly twenty-four hours later, I was climbing back into that very same bird-infested loft.

My failing is, I guarantee my work. So when Owney called me that afternoon to inform me that the furnace still wasn't working, there was no point in arguing. All I could do was go back and try it again.

The furnace was deader than Hoffa. I popped the access panel and peered inside, aided by the light of my forehead lamp. Pilot light was out again. Okay, we're talking thermocouple here. I sorted through the parts box, found a replacement that was close enough for jazz, and went to work.

Once again, I heard voices. Male and female; Ginny and the boss, no doubt. I worked on, entertained by the voices. Almost as good as having a radio on up there.

Him: "... *tremendous* cash intake. You just wouldn't believe it, babe." Her: "Oo, yum." Him: "We're going to get *real* well on this one." Her: "Well, then ... how about it, Ron? Where's my bonus for last month?" Him: "I'll fix it, don't worry. Have to do some creative bookkeeping, you know?" Her: "I'd hate to think you're going cheap on me." Him: "Me, cheap? C'mere. I'll show you how cheap I am. . . . Wait a minute, make sure that door's locked. . . ."

Hoo-boy. In the new silence I completed replacing the thermocouple and went through the pilot lighting routine again. It took fine and, with a twist of the gas cock, the furnace kicked over and roared hotly. Terrific.

This time both the Toyota and the Ford were still out front, by the far-end suite, as I drove out. That interested me not one bit. Such off-to-the-side funny stuff betwixt boss and employee began at the dawn of time, if not before. What was harder to figure was the talk about tremendous sums of cash and bonuses and everything.

But I'd lose no sleep over it. My detective instinct was dormant. And I've learned that if you get through life understanding as much as ten percent of what's going on, you're way ahead, pal.

†††

The first thing I noticed when returning to the building the following night was that there were two cars there. One was the Toyota; one was a dark Buick Century. Not Ginny's.

Yeah, I was back. Yeah, the furnace was still fritzed up. Owney had called me that morning, downright apologetic this time. It's an old crock, Ben, he'd said. Sumbitch'll have to be replaced soon, he'd said. How 'bout giving it a look-see once more, Ben, he'd said.

So back I went. Into the utility room. Up into the loft. Across the catwalk, boxes in hand, to the Kramer, sitting sneering at me in the corner. I could hear the motor humming, accompanied by a weird thunk-thunk-thunk sound. It was running all right, but now I knew why none of the heat was getting downstairs.

I took off the access panel again and peered in. Sure enough, the belt between the blower and the blower motor was flopping loose. Snapped in half. Frayed and bound up in the pulley. Great.

I shut the furnace down. In the sudden silence all I could hear was the chirping of birds and, once my ears had adjusted to lower-grade sound, voices through the ducts. Both male, this time.

As I went to work replacing the belt, I tried not to listen to the conversation, but I couldn't help it.

You been what?

You heard me. I been doin' her.

Oh, man. Money, too, I suppose?

Yeah. Nickel-and-dime stuff. Just to keep her happy—

And now she's getting pushy, huh?

Yeah.

Just like Pittsburgh and D.C. You can't keep your hands off the young stuff, can you, Ron?

Hey, it's vice versa, too, bud.

So freakin' what. We only been in town here a month. We got three-plus months to go, guaranteed. *If* we play our cards right. Looks to me like you're creating problems—

Well, we better fix this one.

What do you mean, we?

I want you to waste her.

The wrench dropped from my hand. I leaned forward, squinting, the work forgotten, scarcely believing my ears.

Oh no, not me, not this time. You created this problem, you take care of it. Soon. Before she blows the whole thing.

For Chrissake, I—all right, I'll do it tomorrow night. I'll ask her to stay late and take care of it after everybody's gone. She'll just disappear—

Shut up. I don't want to hear about it. Just finish it and don't get into any more fixes like this, okay?

The voices faded and then vanished entirely. Operating on total automatic pilot, I finished replacing the belt and fired up the furnace. It worked. I closed up, packed my gear, lugged it outside. The Toyota and the Century were gone now, I noticed as I drove around front. I motored away, satisfied that the furnace repairs would hold this time, telling myself that I absolutely, positively would not be back.

†††

The left-hand suite?"

"Yeah, down at the west end there."

"I don't know for sure. I'm in my car, I don't have my records with me. How come you wanna know?"

"Come on, Owney, humor me."

"Um, wal, seems to me it's some kinda investment firm or something."

"Know anything else about 'em?"

"They pay their rent."

"Anything else?"

"That's *all* I need to know, Ben."

"Oh. Okay."

"What's going on? That furnace still acting up?"

"Working fine when I left there."

"Guess that solves the problem then, huh."

"One of 'em."

†††

"Let me see if I got this straight. You was fixing a furnace in the building, and you overheard some kinda garbled conversation that leads you to believe a murder's gonna get done tomorrow night."

"Right, uh-huh."

"I'm genuinely shocked at this news."

"Leave off the sarcasm, okay? I just figured as chief of the Detroit police homicide squad, you might want to head *off* a murder for once, instead of dealing with it after."

"Man, there's all kinda problems with this."

"Especially for the victim."

"Number one, maybe you misunderstood what you heard."

"Come on, Elvin, you know me better than that."

"Then there's a silly little thing called probable cause. We bust in there on the word of some nobody private detective and, if there's no stiff, who do we arrest? And what for?"

"Ron what's-his-name. For conspiracy."

"On the sole basis of your say-so. If we was to arrest everybody who talked ugly without a permit, you'da been in the Walled-Off Astoria *long* time ago."

"This was more than just talking ugly."

"And it's also less than a crime 'cept in your own over-heated imagination. We got enough to do down here—"

"Listen—"

"—bare handful of guys ridin' hard on a city full of teenagers killing each other. More'n two hundred of them shot down this year alone. Little babies, some of 'em, sitting peaceably on their porches only to catch a bullet in the eye—"

"Elvin—"

"—crack wars, racial incidents, plus the regular old garden-variety domestic disturbances that result in hair on the walls average of three times a week—"

"Look, I know you're busy—"

"Busy! He say I'm *busy!* Slick-o private eye sits on his **head ass out in lily-white Belleville an' call me BUSY?"

"Captain Dance."

"Yeah?"

"I'm reporting a potential homicide."

"Look . . . best I can tell ya, I'll send a squad car swinging around there sometime tomorrow evening, check up on things. Okay?"

"Okay."

"Okay. Happy to oblige. Say something nice 'bout Detroit, hear?"

"Doing the best I can, bro."

†††

As I passed the front of the building the next afternoon, I saw that the lot in front of the westernmost suite was crowded with cars, including Ginny's Escort and Ron's Toyota. That figured; it wasn't quitting time yet. Wouldn't be any action for a while, not till the other employees left. Plenty of time for me to get into position.

Instead of pulling into the rear lot, I took the first corner off Plymouth Road onto Ohio Street, went up about half a block, and parked at the curb. I locked up the Mustang and hoofed it back the way I'd come, hopped a chain-link fence, crossed the back lot, and used Owney's key to let me into the utility entrance once more.

I'd spent the night tossing in the twilight of half-formed sleep, unable to shut down my mind. All the arguments paraded before my reviewing stand in an endless circle. Could be you *did* misunderstand, and she's in no danger. And even if she is, it's not like she's your sister, or friend, or client, or even anyone you've ever *met*, for God's sake. It couldn't be less your business. There's *got* to be a place to draw the line, and this is it. And you're tired; too much work, too many cases rolling you along like a boulder in an avalanche; you deserve a break, could be exhaustion has weakened your judgment; how do you know you'll even have the right moves when you need them? Ease off, Ben. No one will know. Duck it.

Powerful arguments. Irrefutable logic. And, of course, none of it worked worth a damn.

I mounted the wood ladder into the loft. It was an easy trip this time; no toolboxes to tote, no tools at all except for two. Strapped to my forehead: the battery-powered light. Carried securely in the waistband of my jeans against my spine: my .45 automatic.

Bent nearly double, I stepped silently along the catwalk to the furnace, which was humming away merrily. Good job, Ben old son, I thought: quality work sooner or later. I hit the emergency shutoff—I was going to need silence up there—and all went quiet except for the distant muffled chirping of birds and the even more distant drone of voices down below.

Then, switching on my light, I backtracked along the catwalk to the beam that bisected the building longwise, and started my hunchbacked, teetering walk westbound toward the suite occupied by Ron and Ginny and friends.

I'd considered simply staking out the front of the building and awaiting developments. The idea had appeal—certainly better than the prospect of crawling around in a dark, dusty, bird- and spider-infested attic—but the problem was the word "awaiting." Putting myself in Ron's mind, I'd concluded that, if I was going to whack Ginny, I'd do it right there inside the building, once everyone else had left. Inside, there was no possibility of witnesses. The neighborhood was solidly commercial for blocks around; no one around to hear anything. If I was going to any good, I'd have to be on top of the situation. Literally.

Along the way I encountered two load-bearing cinder block walls, which defined the divisions between the suites below. Through each wall was hacked a small, just barely man-sized hole. I cleared these with some effort and pressed on. The voices below were fading. End-of-the-day sounds.

By my calculations, I was now over the westernmost suite. I stopped and rested and listened. Not much noise from below, now. A muffled male voice sounded from ahead. I moved on, listening hard. The top stringer of a drywall partition passed. I was nearly at the end now and over a corner office. The voice was louder, braying on in a monologue; sure sounded like Ron, probably on the phone. A corner office, as befit the boss. Made sense.

I lowered myself to a seated, cross-legged position on the dusty beam, propping my feet on a two-by-six joist that ran fifteen feet to the outside wall opposite me, bisecting the office below me and supporting, by means of wires, the aluminum grid which in turn held the white acoustical ceiling tiles and fluorescent light fixtures. The voice carried on with abrasive financial mumbo-jumbo. I was now certain that friend Ron was alone, talking on the phone. No Ginny. Not yet.

Fluttering and chirping came from the cinder block wall across from me. I directed my light there and saw the bright beady eyes and black shape of some kind of bird. Starling, most likely. It squawked and a chorus of peeps answered. A nest, a Goddamned starling nest. The mom-bird hopped and fluttered to the joist and sat there, a man's length from me, squawking, head pivoting jerkily. Beat it, lady, I thought anxiously; I'm not going to bother you or your little brats. Get lost.

She did no such thing. Instead she leaped and swooped straight at me with a kamikaze cry. I ducked and waved my arm, swatting blindly at her. She circled me and shot back over to her nest and danced there on one leg and then another, as if she had to relieve herself, screaming bird curses. I almost went for my .45—I don't take that kind of language from anybody—but decided that shooting her would be impractical. Instead I shut off my forehead lamp and sat as still as I could. She calmed down. Probably forgot I was there. No Rhodes scholar, that bird. Good.

Ron finished his call and immediately began another. Otherwise, all was dead silent. Fun should be starting any time, if it was going to start at all. Time to get into position. I edged and twisted myself onto the two-by-six joist and, carefully holding my feet above the acoustical ceiling tiles, slid along, an inch at a time, toward the center of the office. It was tight, tense, very delicate work, there in the pitch black, trying to keep my balance, moving my two hundred pounds as quietly as I could to the ideal position, directly over the center of Ron's office. The minute the trouble started, all I had to do was kick the tiles through and then drop down, ten feet to the floor or seven feet to the desk. Talk about element of surprise. Evening, folks!

Just as I reached the center, I heard a couple of muffled popping sounds. Sounded like Styrofoam cups being squashed, somewhere in the building. Ron hung up his phone. A woman's voice came, almost making me jump. "Hi."

"Well, hi there, Gin," Ron said smoothly.

"Got a little surprise for you."

"Oh yeah? What's that?"

"Here."

Then a loud flat pop. Silence, then I heard the creak of a chair. "Isn't this nice?" Ginny said gaily. Oh yeah, I thought. Champagne. Buttering up the boss, huh, gal? Well, good for you. Just be careful.

No more voices. I pictured them sipping, smiling at each other. I wondered what Ron was thinking. My arms began to ache from the strain of holding myself absolutely still on the thin joist. Could be this was all for nothing, I thought. Maybe I did misunderstand Ron and everything's going to go lovey-dovey down there, with me up here in the pitch black, sweating and snorting dust, when I could be home sipping a cold one—

A chorus of baby birds sent up a hymn. Their mother shrieked and I heard wings. I swung my left fist blindly toward the noise, ducking. She screamed from behind me, the wings huffed closer, and a sudden pain lanced my neck. She stuck me! The stinking bug-eatin' bitch *bit* me!

I bent and twisted convulsively, reaching for the injury. The joist moaned beneath me, and I heard the distinct snap and groan of aged wood. A shadow of wings cross my face. I swung ineffectually at the shape, the joist shredded and sagged and gave, and I tumbled forward, arms flung out, knees punching through the ceiling—wait a minute, this isn't the way I'd planned it—

†††

The first thing I saw was a man with three eyes.

I was flat on my side atop a large mahogany desk. My knees and palms had taken most of the impact and were flat-numb. I blinked at the man's face trying to banish the spots, which were floating in my vision, and realized that the man, who was leaning back in a large executive chair, had originally had the standard issue of two eyes. What looked like a third was actually a bullet hole punched neatly above his nose.

I turned. Across the office stood a tall, young, permed brunette. She had a canvas bag strapped over one shoulder and a silencer-equipped handgun in her left hand. Her other hand was invisible, her arm elbow-deep inside a wall safe. Her handsome freckled face was expressionless, her body still. I shoved myself off the desk as the woman, with deadly precision, swung her handgun toward me. *Pop.* Fire threaded my hair. I landed on Ron's lap, rolling him back on his chair, tumbled to the floor behind the desk, and scrabbled toward some kind of safety beneath it, groping at my spine for my .45.

Must have lost it.

I wedged myself beneath the desk, face pressed against the desk's privacy screen, which ran down the front side to six inches above the carpet. In my panic I realized four things: First, the desk seemed to be solid wood and would probably stop whatever she was shooting. Second, it wasn't really raining; what I felt was my own blood, dripping on me from the underside of the desk, where it was spraying from the scalp wound she'd given me. Third, my safety was strictly temporary, because I was also trapped. And fourth, she was moving toward the desk, intent on finishing the job.

Without thinking I stuck a hand below and beyond the privacy screen and swept out. Caught an ankle and yanked viciously. Surprised and off-balance, the woman left vertical and came down with a hard thud, a pained grunt, and the muffled dance of metal that must have been her handgun. Good. I kept hold of her ankle and dragged her toward me, playing her like a shark. Her shoe was a blue Reebok with white stripes, topped by a white sock. I locked both hands around her ankle and pulled as hard as I could, doing hand-over-hand up her calf, intent on drawing her, if I could, through the six-inch gap between the privacy screen and the floor. Blood, forced no doubt by terror and exertion, sprayed harder from my scalp wound.

That made me mad. I had her nearly to knee length now, and I forced my own knee under her ankle and bent her leg up the wrong way, pinching it with the underside of the privacy screen. She screamed and tugged and suddenly got some new and very powerful purchase. Despite my strength and fury, I felt her leg slipping away from me. I realized what was happening. She was bracing her other foot on the opposite side of the desk and pushing with all she had, using leverage that more than compensated for my superior strength. Much more of that and she'd get loose and get her gun and, if that happened, it'd be dead duck for yours truly.

Her calf was slipping and had just about gotten away when the idea came to me from nowhere. I shoved her leg down onto the carpet, squirmed myself up, and planted my right knee on her ankle. She grunted and gasped, pulling with all her might against my weight, but for the moment I had her pinned. My back was braced against the underside of the desk, and I drew my left foot in under me and dug it into the floor and began pushing hard, upward, with my strong back and stronger legs, trying with all my might to send the desk flying toward the ceiling.

It didn't quite do that. Instead, it pivoted as if hinged on its front legs and fell forward onto the woman with a crash.

I lurched wobbling to my feet, gasping, my right hand planted on my gluey hair. Ginny lay only half visible beneath the shipwrecked desk, twitching, freckled face pasty white. Lightheaded and breathless, I weaved a dopey circle, my head warm, wet and sticky under my hand. Nobody else around. No one but me and her. The floor was a chaotic landscape of shredded ceiling tiles and desk debris. I caught a glint behind me and saw, beneath the chair that bore Ron's lounging corpse, my .45 automatic. Big help you are, I thought drunkenly. I retrieved it then went to step over Ginny's torso and nearly tripped and just barely kept my feet. Her handgun—a .22 automatic, I saw now, tipped by that big bulky silencer—lay just a foot beyond her outstretched arm. I kicked it away to somewhere and was about to leave the office past the open wall safe when I swerved back and looked down at her gape-mouthed, panting face.

"I came here to save you. To *save* you!" I said.

She coughed and croaked something, but I was in mood to listen. I turned and stomped out, bound for somewhere, a phone, I suppose.

The conference room beyond Ron's office was empty. The office past that was empty also except for a middle-aged man sprawled across a cluttered desk, head blood-soaked. I eyed him curiously while passing and entered the foyer, where a woman lay on her back, her chair tumbled across her corpulent body, blood soaking the carpet blackly all around her. Her eyes were wide open and vacant, her glasses askew, and across her stretched a phone cord, the receiver still clutched in her hand. From it issued a metallic voice: *Please hang up the phone. Please hang up the phone now.*

I stood uneasily and stared down at her. Now I knew what those pops were that I'd heard before Ginny had paid her visit to Ron. She'd gotten tired of waiting for these people to leave.

I pried the phone from the woman's cool hand, hit the cradle button then dialed 911.

†††

The suite was all mutters, cigar smoke, snap of camera flash, professional feet trudging in and out, in and out. I sat in a chair, leaning back, my hand pressing a wad of paper towel against my throbbing head. Before me, propped against the edge of a desk, was the natty, stocky Captain Elvin Dance, chief, homicide squad, Detroit police. His three-piece suit was luminous green, his tie a smoldering red, his dark hair shaved close, and his clean-shaved skin the rich black of the best coffee. Next to him stood an anonymous mustached uniform braced in perfect parade rest.

Elvin was taking no notes. I had the feeling he'd remember this one for a while. "So, you staked yourself up in the attic, figuring on saving this chick, and meanwhile she whacks her boss and the two others, too. Right?"

"Uh-huh." I'd left out the part about the bird. Dance and his cronies had enough to laugh about that night. "Nearly got me, too," I said, not looking for sympathy, just wondering if he'd noticed my head injury.

"You done took care of that, though," Dance noted.

"Hero," the uniform said.

"Good thing there was a desk handy," Dance observed. "Interesting choice of weapon. I been in this business twenty years, first time I ever seen a perp get desked."

"Resourceful," the uniform said.

"May be a problem bagging it for evidence," Dance grinned.

A couple of paramedics strode by. The stretcher between them bore Ginny, blanketed, strapped down, and unconscious. Elvin asked, "She gonna live?"

"Looks that way," the lead paramedic answered. "Won't be walking for a while, though. Both knees are crushed."

"Pity," the uniform said.

Elvin whistled as the paramedics disappeared through the door. "You *do* got good taste, Perkins. You don't waste your time trying to save no ugly chicks."

"Pulchritudinous," the uniform said.

Elvin scratched his head. "You know, think I'll run her stats by the National Crime Information Center people. Betcha she's got a pro sheet."

"Had moves," I said, each word painful. "Didn't strike me as a typist who up and went berserko or something."

"PMS?" the uniform asked.

Elvin squinted. "Take the weapon. Twenty-two auto ain't unheard of, but silencers, you don't pick those up at your local Kmart while shopping for socks."

Another giddy rush passed over me. I shut my eyes and breathed hard, wanting to be gone. When I could see again, a detective was standing next to Dance, holding Ginny's book bag. "Looka this, captain. Looks like over a hundred grand here."

"Mazuma!" the uniform said.

"Whaddya think, Charlie?" Dance asked the detective.

The hefty man hooked the book bag over his shoulder. "I looked over some of the paperwork. Looks like they were running one of those commodity broker operations outta here. You know, wheat, soybeans, pork bellies, and stuff." He swaggered out, for the moment a rich man.

Dance grinned and eyed me. "Yeah. Makes sense. This is one of them boiler-room places. I've read about them. They make their sales, send couriers out to pick up the bread in cash. Most likely a scam. It's been done other places, never in Detroit, far as I know."

I licked my lips. "Ties in. I heard the boss and his partner talking about other cities they'd worked on before this."

"Yeah," Elvin drawled, "milk it dry then fold up and split before people catch on."

"Only this time, the boss had to start fooling around with the help," I said.

"And *this* help," Elvin said, jerking a thumb, "got wise to the scam, prob'ly had some experience of her own, and decided to cash in. Or out. Except—"

234 | ROB KANTNER

"Gumshoe," the uniform said.

"Exactly right, Mac," Dance answered. "They didn't know a Detroit private detective was lurking up in their attic. Ha ha, hee hee. Laugh's sure on them, ain't it, Perkins."

"I'm just convulsed, Elvin."

Elvin's dark eyes were on my speculatively. "How long we been tangling, Perkins? Fifteen years? You sure have a talent for tripping over crime."

"Kinda just sorta tends to happen," I said.

Elvin let the desk go and stood. "Well," he said, shoving his chunky hands into his coat pockets, "we'll round up the partner and have the fine-print boys go through all this paperwork, see what was going down. Betcha we'll find out they're from somewhere else, all right." He glared at me. "As if we don't grow enough crime of our own in this town."

I got to my feet very, very slowly. Brought my rag down from my head, inspected it, put it back. "Through with me?"

"Oh hell, yeah," Elvin said. "We through all right, you're clean and green. Just be in my office tomorrow morning at eight, so we can get your statement."

Eight tomorrow, I thought. Great. I licked my lips and started turning for the door.

"Hey," Elvin said, "you all right, Perkins?"

I looked at him. "Think I need stitches."

"You ain't gonna faint or nothing, are you?"

"No. I'll get it took care of."

"Bourbon," the uniform said.

"Definitely."

I trudged to the door. As I pushed myself through, I heard Elvin Dance say angrily, "Listen, Mac. I ever tell you you're too damn yappy? Work on toning down the motor mouth, it ain't professional."

The evening was inky black and, for November, bitter cold. I rounded the corner from Plymouth Road onto Ohio Street and pounded along, my shoes crunching broken glass and kicking litter. A mufflerless Camaro bayed smokily by. A woman screamed happily from an upstairs apartment across the street. A gaggle of bearded leather-jackets partied past me, exchanging a bottle and loud one-liners. A Detroit police cruiser swept over toward the curb, shined its spotlight on me briefly then roared away. I stomped along, concentrating on staying vertical, thinking about how sick I get of this work sometimes.

At Northwest Hospital on West Chicago, they shaved a spot as big as a grown man's palm off my head, cleaned the injury and then, prior to putting in the stitches, administered a series of shots.

The first one was agony, the rest just hurt like hell.

Afterword

I collect titles. At any given time I have maybe 100 titles available, each one looking for a story. Sometimes the right title finds its story after the story starts to germinate. Sometimes the title actually kick-starts the story.**

"Duck Work" was a case of the latter. On a furnace shop window, near where I once lived in metro Detroit, hung a banner that said "Furnace Repair and Duck Work." The malapropism stuck in my brain and presently spun out this story.

I believe Owney Busbee, one of the more colorful characters, first appeared here. Elvin Dance was a regular by this time, a delicate balance between aid and nemesis. (In Perkins's world, unlike the world of other private detectives, the police don't bend over backwards to be of assistance to Our Hero.) Capt. Dance, as good a politician and bureaucrat as he is a cop, faithfully mouths the Detroit city promotional slogan of the time—not that it did much good.

Normally, I plan stories out pretty carefully, with special attention to the ending. I don't start a story till I'm completely comfortable with the ending, and I aim the whole story toward achieving that ending. This was a case where the ending kind of snuck up on me. I remember writing that last line, and looking at it, and realizing: This is it! This is fine!

One other thought I've had while editing this story: This is an example of the random ways in which Perkins gets cases. Seldom if ever is he waiting around for someone to walk up to him and hire him. Cases, for Perkins, to quote him, "Kinda just sorta tend to happen."

** And sometimes titles kill stories. More than once, a promising story has withered away and died before fruition because the title assigned to it ultimately did not work. An example of such a jinx title for me was "The Thousand Yard Stare," which I swear killed off two or three (ultimately fruitless) stories before it finally found its book. This is indeed a spooky business.

Unfinished Business

The day I met Holly Norwood, I arrived at Under New Management around five, as usual. Took the third stool on the left, as usual. Eddie Cabla, the owner, was working the stick; Jimmie Joe Putnam, professional Vietnam veteran, was talking Detroit Tigers; Bob Stella, retired foreman out of Michigan Truck, was arguing with him.

All as usual.

I ordered a Stroh's beer and lighted a cigar. As usual, Jimmy Joe demanded my "expert" assessment, as a high-school vintage third baseman, of the Tigers' trade of Tommy Brookens to the despised Yankees. I was, as usual, about to trot out my Sparky Anderson imitation ("It don't matter none nohow"), when the door opened and a woman walked into the bar.

Unfamiliar, alone, and attractive.

*Un*usual.

"Help you, miss?" Eddie asked. His courteous tone turned heads, but then Eddie likes them low to the ground and soft and round, which this one definitely was.

She looked around the bar room, giving it more attention than it deserved. "Wasn't this Chip's Market once?"

Eddie's eyes widened. "Yeah, way back in the sixties, before I bought the place."

"And made it legit," Jimmy Joe added.

"Dressed up the neighborhood," Bob said.

"Historical plaque's going up next week," I put in.

"Shaddap!" Eddie snarled. He snapped his cloth open and began to buff the bar top. "You don't look old enough to remember that far back," he said to the woman.

Flattered by the fiction—for that's what it was; her fortieth summer was imminent—she drifted closer to the bar. She was five one or so, and heavier than she probably liked. She wore a sleeveless, blue-checked top and sky-blue slacks over white sneakers. Her deep red hair waved thickly down to her shoulders, and her dark eyes sparkled as bright as her even white teeth. "Why, thank you," she said. "So gallant."

The other men chuckled. We all knew that Eddie's gallantry was aimed at an early round at what Bob Seger calls the horizontal bop. "How about a drink?" Eddie asked. "On the house, how about that?"

"Lovely. White wine?"

"Coming right up. My name's Eddie, but you can call me Ed."

"Leah," she said. She pronounced it Lee, and I didn't know about the "H" till it appeared in the papers. "Leah Norwood."

Eddie nodded then scooted into the back as she took the stool at the opposite end of the bar from me, equidistant from Jimmy Joe to her left and Bob Stella to her right.

Bob's good-natured potato face split into a grin. "You're from around here, huh?" he asked hoarsely.

"That's right," she said. "Haggerty at Begley. My mother used to send me up here for bread and milk. When this was Chip's Market."

"Back for a little sentimental visit?" Jimmy Joe asked.

Her expression was dreamy. "More than that. I'm here to stay. I just bought our old house back. Moved in today."

Eddie delivered the wine with such flair you'd never have suspected it was no-name jug white in that jelly glass. Leah toasted the bar at large, took a sip, and seemed to find it tasty.

Bob Stella drummed his empty beer mug on the bar and, as Eddie took it, said, "Haggerty at Begley. That old tri-level?"

"No, no," the woman said. "Kitty-corner from there, the big three-story fieldstone."

Bob's bushy eyebrows arched. "That's old Duke Werden's place. I didn't know he sold out. Where'd he go?"

"Florida." Leah pegged back the rest of her wine. "And here I am, back home again. Except this isn't Chip's anymore. Now it's—what *is* this place called, anyhow?"

"Under New Management," Jimmy Joe said.

"The fastest saloon in the west," Bob Stella said, laughing.

"Western Wayne County, that is," I added.

She was shaking her head, half smiling, looking misty. "Things change so much," she said. "I've been away for so long, and—you know what? There's one person I'd really, *really* like to see again."

Eddie propped an elbow on the bar and leaned toward her. "Now who'd that be, honey?" he asked, all velvety.

"My first-grade teacher from Belsen School. Mrs. Anderson. Edna Anderson." She glanced around at us. "Any of you men know her?"

"Belsen's still there," Jimmy Joe said. "Never heard of no Edna Anderson, though."

"Twenty-five years," Eddie said doubtfully. "I'll put this gentle as I can, sweetie. The old broad could be croaked."

"But who could find out for ya, toot sweet," Bob said, "is old Benjy down there. He's a private detective. The best in Michigan."

"Metro Detroit," Jimmy Joe said.

"Wayne County. Maybe," Eddie said.

"Ben's definitely the best in this corner of the county," Bob insisted.

"Whenever Norris Johnston is away," Jimmy Joe amended.

Pals.

The woman's eyes were on me hopefully. "Can you help me?"

For once I wasn't terribly broke. And I had no special desire to take on a humdrum locate job. But my friend Carole had a week off coming, and I planned to take her and her son out to the Lake Erie islands before she was, as she put it, "too gross" to be seen in a swimsuit. Trip like that costs money if you want to do it right. "You want somebody found," I answered, "consider her found."

The woman slid off the stool and walked over to me, smiling. She put out her hand and shook mine with a surprisingly strong grip. "Benjy?" she inquired.

"Ben Perkins," I answered. "Give you a ride home, and we'll talk about it."

She smiled graciously. "I accept! What a gentleman!"

We started for the door. "Me? Oh, I'm no gentleman."

"Good," she answered, and took my arm.

†††

Her house was one of those well-maintained gems they put up a hundred years ago: gray fieldstone and brown beams rising three stories, held down by an ornate red slate roof. It sat on a couple of heavily wooded acres just west of Haggerty Road about a mile from the bar. I wheeled my '71 Mustang into the gravel driveway and parked next to a copper Honda Accord with Illinois plates. "From Chicago, are you?"

"Lived there a few years," she replied, unsnapping the seat belt. "But I'm a Michigan girl, through and through."

I shut off the rumbling motor. "Nice wheels."

"You should see me in a skirt."

"I meant your car."

"Oh. Well, I liked it fine, till it died on me. Rent-a-Jalopy's ferrying a rental up to me tonight to tide me over." She climbed agilely out of the Mustang, and I followed suit. The massive trees around the big house whispered softly, and Leah spread her arms in an all-embracing gesture, looked at the house and then at me with a rapturous smile. "Oh, it's so good to be back here! I spent the best years of my life in this house."

"Gorgeous old place." I rescued a short cork-tipped cigar from my shirt pocket and lighted up. "Your family been back to see it?"

She laughed. "Oh, there's really no family left. Come on inside, we'll talk business." I followed her up the meandering brick walk toward the front stoop. "My parents are both dead and my sister is in an institution. That's all there was, just the four of us."

"Sorry to hear that." We went through the screen door and into the foyer, which yawned up two full stone-and-wood stories. A massive oak staircase rose to the right, curving majestically to create a balcony on the second floor. I didn't have time to gape, because Leah guided me through an archway into a big, sunny country kitchen, all bright yellow and brown. "Married or anything?" I asked.

She threw me an intent look. "Not married," she said, smiling slyly, "or anything. I suppose you're single. Not that it matters," she said, laughing. While I tried to sort that one out, she went to the refrigerator. "How about a drink, Ben?"

"Beer, please, if you've got it."

She peered inside. "Beer . . . let me see . . . right. Here." She came out with the bottle and saw me looking at a big scattered pile of mail lying on the table. "That's all for the previous owner," she said. "Stupid post office messed up his forwarding order, I guess. Here you go." She opened a pair of Stroh's, handed me one, and clinked her own against it. "Cheers!"

I took a schlook and set the bottle down. Leah put away half of hers and licked her lips. "Well now, Ben! What'll it cost me to find my old teacher?"

"Depends on how much time I use. I get two-fifty a day plus expenses. I like to get an advance. I figure two or three days, tops—"

She was nodding her head vigorously. "That's fine, that's fine. I've got loads of money. I'm a clinical psychologist. I'll be signing on with the Reuther Center or Ypsi State in a few days. Wait here, I'll be right back."

She disappeared through the archway into the foyer. I smoked my cigar, paced the kitchen slowly, then pressed the smoke dead in an ashtray on the table amid the scattered envelopes. Being nosy, I couldn't help reading over the return addresses. Something felt vaguely wrong, but then I'm a private detective. To me, most everything feels vaguely wrong.

Leah bustled back into the kitchen and handed me a thick wad of currency: twenties and fifties, old bills, a half a grand worth. "Any objection to cash?" she asked coyly, leaning her plentiful rump against the edge of the table.

"God, no." Questions, yes; objections, no. I put the money away; Lake Erie islands, here we come. "You get half back if I only use one day. No refunds if the lady's dead."

I meant that mostly in jest. But Leah's eyes narrowed. "She can't be dead," she said.

"Hey, lighten up. If she's alive, I'll find out where she's at. If she's dead, I'll find out where they planted her. Fair enough?"

Leah's expression went suddenly sunny. "Oh sure, that's fine. Fast as you can, okay?" She rattled off a phone number.

I wrote it in my pad. "I'll get back to you," I said. I started for the foyer, and stopped at her touch. As I turned she came to me in a smothering rush, engulfed me with her arms, and teetering on tiptoe, kissed me hard on the mouth.

Her body was warm and vivid, her ardor evident in her heartbeat. And she was stronger than she looked. It took me a moment to ease myself loose. She stepped back, eyes alight, hands on my hips. "Come on, Ben," she said, half-breathless, "stick around awhile."

"Sorry, kid," I managed, "I got things to attend to."

"Oh," she said. For an instant she looked cross, then she beamed. "Okay. Some other time?"

"Sure." I made some kind of parting gesture—a nod or a wave, I don't remember which—and left.

Strange, I thought as I drove, that she hit on me so early, so forcefully. Stranger still that I turned her down. But the strangest thing of all was that I had felt no desire for her, not even the slightest bit.

Getting older, I guessed.

Scary.

†††

The G. Mennen Williams Residence is a retirement facility in Westland, that capital of the aged a couple of suburbs north of me. It's a single-story building shaped like an octopus, surrounded by lush lawns and groves of trees. A far cry from the typical nursing home and a very clear sign that Edna Anderson had made like the frugal little squirrel, storing away nuts against the coming of winter.

I arrived there after lunchtime the next day. The polite desk clerk found my name on the appointments list and had me escorted to a small flagstone courtyard at the back of the complex. The lady who rose to greet me there was in her mid-eighties and certainly a shadow of her former self: translucent wrinkled skin clinging to fine bones, stooped and trembling, her bluish-white hair so fine and thin you could see her scalp beneath. But she was well dressed in tan slacks and blouse. Her grip was firm and sure as she shook hands with me. Her gray eyes, behind heavy glasses, were defiantly youthful.

"Thanks for seeing me, Ms. Anderson," I said.

"*Mrs.* Anderson," she said, smiling. "And it's I who must thank you. It's not every day I get a handsome young visitor." She winked. "What I wouldn't give to be thirty again, just for this afternoon!"

"Hey, me too," I grinned. She sat down slowly in her lawn chair and I took one facing her. "I was hired by one of your former students to find you, ma'am."

"And you succeeded." She nodded. "Very resourceful. How did you manage it?"

"Well, Belsen School's long closed. So I called the school district, and they shuffled me to the teachers' union. They refused to give out the information. So I called back and said I was Inspector O'Gannon from the Social Security Administration and had to verify your current address. Otherwise, you wouldn't get your check, probably go on dog food or starve or whatever. That turned the trick."

She nodded, an admiring glint in her old eyes. "And why, may I ask, are you here? Why didn't you simply give my address to your, um, client?"

I shrugged. "I'm funny about that. I don't think everyone has the automatic right to find anyone else. I mean, God knows there are a few people around I'd rather never found *me*. So, in locate jobs, usually I let the findee have a say in whether he or she gets found."

"I see," she said. When I didn't go on, she said, "Now for the sixty-four dollar question. Which ex-brat is it?"

Her harshness startled me. "Brat?"

She waved a hand, a hard edge to her mouth. "Oh, most of them *were* little brats. Demanding, obnoxious offspring of demanding, obnoxious parents. I'm eighty-six and long retired. I no longer have to maintain the pretense." I had no answer for that. "Don't keep me in suspense," she said sharply. "Give me the name."

"Leah Norwood." The old lady's expression did not change. "First grade at Belsen School, nineteen—"

"I remember," she interrupted. Her expression softened and her eyes went very far away. "Little Leah," she murmured. She looked at me and her smile was self-conscious. "One of the good ones. Such a sad little girl. How is she?"

"Seemed just fine to me. I gather was living out of state for a while, but she just moved back into the area. Bought the old family home, matter of fact."

"That surprises me."

"Why is that, ma'am?"

"I would think that house had such awful memories for her, she'd never go near it again. Let alone live there." The old woman's voice dropped to a confidential pitch. "Her mother committed suicide there, you know."

"Oh, really?" I asked. Priming the pump, we call that.

"Jumped twenty feet to the foyer floor, right in front of the daughters. Officially it was called an accident, of course, so she could be put in consecrated ground. But everyone knew it was suicide."

I remembered the foyer and the majestic staircase that rose up to a long balcony, twenty feet above solid slate. The vision made me uneasy.

She sat back in her chair and gripped its arm with whitening knuckles. "The father died drunk in a car crash a while later," she said, almost in monotone. "No loss, frankly. Looking back on it, I think he abused his daughters—Holly for sure, and maybe even Leah. Why didn't we notice such things in those days?"

"Maybe it wasn't as common then?" I ventured.

"No," she said softly. "Everyone looked the other way." The old lady was silent for a moment, clenching and unclenching one hand. "After he died, Holly and Leah were split up and sent away. I never knew what became of them. I'd had Holly two years before Leah. An intense child. Very difficult. But Leah . . . a sweetheart. And such a sad little girl. I did my best for her. Down through the years I've wondered what became of her. I've thought of her as unfinished business."

"She seems okay now," I observed. "And you can see for yourself, if you want to."

"That's true," she said, brightening. Her smile had the glint of gold in it and her eyes, back in the present, shone behind her glasses. "Please, Mr. Perkins, give Leah my number and address and tell her I'd very much welcome a visit. What an occasion it shall be!"

†††

I got hold of Leah that night and gave her the information. She seemed thrilled, gushed her thanks, and invited me by for a beer. I begged off politely and didn't give her a second thought, then.

Late that night, Bob Stella's wife called my apartment, upset and anxious. Bob never came home the night before, no one had seen him all day, and he hadn't called. That was definitely unlike him. I promised to keep an eye out.

By two the next afternoon I had wrapped up the maintenance chores around Norwegian Wood, the apartment complex where I live and—sometimes—work. I sat at my desk, alone in the office, flipped paper clips at the wastebasket, and thought about Bob, about Leah, about Mrs. Anderson, and about how uneasy I felt.

Lived in. That was the problem; Leah's house looked too lived in. Though she'd just moved in, her kitchen was neat, orderly, *lived in* already. I'm not personally neat and orderly, but I've been an apartment maintenance manager for a lot of years; I know lived-in when I see it.

What all this meant I did not know, but no way could I let it go. When in doubt, check it out.

I called directory assistance and learned that there was no listing for Leah Norwood in Van Buren Township, Belleville, or anyplace else in metropolitan Detroit.

From the edge of oblivion I snatched back the name that Bob Stella had mentioned. Called directory assistance again and asked for the listing for Duke Werden. The robot recited the number that Leah Norwood had given me as her own.

I sighed, lighted a cigar, and began twisting a paperclip, working it till it gave up the fight and broke. Then I picked up the phone again and called Jon Paluzzi at the Belleville Post Office. He fussed and grumbled, as usual, but could find no forwarding order for Duke Werden to anywhere, let alone Florida.

This was starting to bug me a lot. I pawed through my desk drawer, rescued a tattered business card, and dialed Owney Busbee at Bullet Realty in Wayne. Owney, who keeps an up-to-the-minute multiple listing between his ears alongside a history of real-estate transactions going back to antediluvian times, told me that the Werden house had not changed hands the previous week, the previous month, or at any time in the past twenty years.

†††

The big fieldstone house sat silent beneath its tall trees, unattended except for the crippled Honda sedan. I parked the Mustang facing the road, got out, and walked with deliberate caution onto the stoop to the front door. A brisk knock netted only sore knuckles, so I tried the knob. The door opened easily, and I went inside.

The enormous foyer was empty of everything but long slender fingers of sunlight that glowed the airborne dust and splashed yellow on the gray slate floor. Before starting my search, I looked at the second-story balcony, and then straight down to where Leah's mother collided with the floor a quarter century before. The suicide explanation troubled me; most people jump from much higher places.

One investigation at a time, I told myself. With a profound sense of unease, I went to work.

And came up empty. I toured the house, top to bottom, and found no Leah, no Duke Werden, no anybody. One thing was obvious. The house's otherwise uninteresting contents had clearly been in place longer than two days. More like twenty or thirty years.

Evidently Duke Werden had had no further use for them when he left.

I went out back. A broad lush lawn, shaded to near darkness by towering pecan trees, ran back to virgin woods. To the left was a stumpy, squarish wood building painted bright white that was probably older than the house itself. I walked over, disengaged the simple metal hasp, and pushed the wood door open.

The interior walls were made of heavy wood beams caulked with mortar, suggesting that this building had once been a smokehouse, and a very well made one indeed, judging from the way it had bottled up the smell of two corpses laying on the concrete floor. Bob Stella lay in a lake of his own making, throatless. The other man, whom I guessed was Duke Werden, had lost a hand warding off the swing of a sharp instrument, most likely the machete lying in a pool of congealed blood on the floor. From the looks of things, his attacker had then stood over him and whacked at him as if his face were a tree stump.

Taking very controlled breaths through my mouth, I forced another look at Bob's corpse. Nosy old fart, poor sad sorry bastard. All he ever wanted out of life was his beer, his Detroit Tigers, his *America's Funniest Home Videos* on Sunday nights, and his friends. That's why he'd come looking, because Duke Werden was his friend, and had up and left, and that made no sense to Bob. So he'd come over and walked right into it.

I stepped back from the door and started to turn blindly, but changed my mind when a woman's sharp voice barked, "*Freeze*, asshole! Police officer!"

I raised my hands. "Okay," I said finally, "what now?"

"Back up, belly down, eat lawn *now*."

I complied. Suppressed a gasp when she stepped on my left ankle—no doubt to give me something to think about while she frisked me. After a moment the pressure on my ankle ceased. "On your feet. Turn around."

I complied. The plainclothes cop was maybe thirty-five, on the tall side and thin in the manner of a pro athlete. Her hair was brown and close-cropped around a freckled face that was pretty but all business. She wore jeans, an open-necked white-on-white shirt, two gold chains, and a white plaster cast on her left arm from armpit to wrist. All in all, the only dangerous thing about her was the Colt Mustang she aimed at my chest.

"Don't fuck with me," she said.

"I wouldn't dream of it."

"I want to know who you are and what you're doing here. Right now."

The shock of the corpses had worn off. The relays were clicking and things were falling into place. Certain things about this woman—the tilt of an eyebrow, the way she pronounced her Rs, stuff like that—set off faint echoes.

I said, "My name's Ben Perkins. And I have a feeling—just a wild guess, now—that your name is Leah Norwood."

She nodded abruptly. "So?"

"Which means the woman who's been running around here, claiming to be you, is—"

"Holly," she said, unsurprised.

"Your older sister."

"That's right. Where is she?"

"Don't know. I can tell you where she's been, though," I said, gesturing toward the smokehouse door.

Eying me wearily, Leah Norwood—the real one, this time—stepped to the smokehouse door and peered in. After a long moment she turned back to me, sickened and trying not to show it. "We've got to find her," she said grimly.

"And when we do," I said, lowering my hands, "I have a feeling we're also going to find a retired schoolteacher in a hell of a lot of trouble."

†††

As I fought the miserable late-afternoon traffic up Wayne Road toward Westland, I asked, "What department you with?"

"Matteson, Illinois. Fifteen-year veteran." She stirred uncomfortably on the bucket seat of my Mustang. "That's why what she did to me is so fuckin' embarrassing. I didn't even know she'd escaped from the institution. First I knew of it was when she ambushed me inside my apartment door and knocked me down the stairs and broke my arm. Guys on the shift laughed their asses off."

"Surprised she didn't whack you. Seems violent enough."

"I think she wanted to, but she'd made too much noise, she had to get away. She stole my car and took off."

"In the Honda."

She nodded. "I knew she'd head here. She always had a thing about settling accounts, paying people back, and so forth. When I saw my car in front of our old house, I knew I was getting warm. So I was extra careful and got the drop on you." She laughed without mirth. "I thought private eyes were supposed to be clever, Perkins."

I felt it would be tasteless and insensitive to remind her which one of us wore a cast. "Holly always been violent?"

She snorted. "Look at this and tell me what *you* think." She handed me an old faded black-and-white snapshot. It showed two pretty girls in bobbed hair and jumpers. The eyes had been poked out of each one. "Holly did that to all our pictures."

I gunned around a bevy of slowpokes and crossed into Westland. Five minutes away now. "Likes to cut things, huh?"

"Including herself. After her third suicide attempt I finally had her declared incompetent," she said in cop monotone. "I got custody and put her in the institution in Chicago. They told me she was getting better. They told me not to worry. They *didn't* tell me she'd get loose and go on a killing spree, and I'd have to track her down."

"Damned inconsiderate, I'd say."

She ignored me. "Hell, I'm using *sick days* for this."

"Life's a bitch," I observed.

"The things we do for family," she grunted.

I glanced at her as we swung into the driveway of the G. Mennen Williams Residence. "Yeah," I murmured. "The things we do."

†††

I'm sorry, Mr. Perkins," the receptionist said. "Mrs. Anderson has gone out for the day."

"Where to?"

Leah, face intent, silently flashed the tin. The receptionist looked startled. "One of her former students came by and took Mrs. Anderson for an outing. I don't know where. Is there some sort of trouble, officer?"

Leah ignored her. She locked stares with me. "Belsen," we said in unison, and bolted for the door.

†††

I two-wheeled the Mustang around the corner from Polk Road onto Belsen Road and punched the gas. Belsen is little more than a strip of heaved tarry asphalt, pocked with chuckholes; a real spine-mangler for a stiffly suspended car like the Mustang. The noise was such that I barely heard Leah's voice as she said, "I'm going to shoot her."

I looked at her pale, resolute face. "We can always whistle up the cops, let them handle it."

She glared at me. "No. She's my sister, my problem, and I'm going to handle it. I'll do what I have to do and I don't need the local yokels to take her. I thought we agreed on that."

We did. Holly Norwood had flimflammed me and killed one of my friends and I wanted to pay her back myself. If that meant standing by and watching her cop sister put a warning shot in her shoulder, that was just peachy.

Only three things bothered me. One, I was unarmed. Two, I was worried that we'd guessed wrong. Third, even if we'd guessed right, I was afraid we'd be too late.

Belsen School appeared on the left as we barreled up a slight rise. It's a single-story orange brick building, plunked down in a large, treeless, and very cheerless plain. A quarter mile away, beyond the school property, was a heavily wooded neighborhood of older clapboard homes, but there were no people about and no signs of life at all.

"I don't see a car there or anything," Leah said as we approached the school.

"Hang tight." I slowed and swerved left into the school's driveway. Now, down toward the end where the weedy, disused playground began, we saw a car, a white Chevy Monte SS. It was parked slantways to the curb, casually and as an afterthought, as if it had served its purpose. Which, I saw on further examination, it had; someone, presumably Holly, had used the car to bash open the two steel double doors, which had been secured with heavy chains.

I shut off the Mustang engine and let the car roll to a stop, about twenty feet from the door. Leah and I got out of the car with a minimum of noise, not even allowing the doors to shut, and walked quietly along the sidewalk and through the ruined doors, crunching over broken glass into the hallway of the abandoned school.

In the distance we heard an echoing female voice: "All those days when I'd sit here and watch you. Watch you lecturing us, and what I've always remembered and never forgotten is your silly little face. All those games you'd play, and those stupid parties. You'd put on dumb hats, and. . . ."

We walked down the hall practically on tiptoe. Leah held her Colt in her good hand, pointed down, ready for action; her face was tight, eyes narrow.

". . . tried to tell you what Daddy was doing. But did you listen? No. All you gave me was that silly little face. Remember the time with the shoes? When you made me walk around the room barefoot? I kept looking at you, and there it was, your *silly little face.* I wanted to . . . all I could think about was . . . I had to *do* something about that *silly little face*—"

The double doors of the classroom at the end stood open. We walked in. The large classroom was bathed in gray light from the dirty, blindless windows. Some evidence of the room's former purpose remained. ABCs in capitals and small letters were stenciled on the wall above the blackboard. A mobile of Winnie the Pooh characters hung limp in the ceiling in one corner. An old upright piano stood in the other corner, and some poignantly small kids' chairs were scattered around. At the far end of the room were Holly Norwood and Edna Anderson.

The retired teacher was crammed viciously into one of the tiny pupil's chairs. She was pale, limp, shoeless, legs twisted, eyes dead, and the rest of her nearly. Her spidery wrists were bound to the chair leg with tightly knotted clothesline—a wholly unnecessary cruelty, considering what was happening to her.

Holly Norwood stood just behind her former teacher. Her left hand had hold of a twisted fistful of the old woman's fine, bluish-white hair. Her right hand held a long chrome letter opener. Its shaft rested on Mrs. Anderson's right cheekbone, and its point shone between her glasses and her eyelid. I remembered the picture Leah had shown me, and I felt fear and fury all at once.

We all stared at each other for one long silent moment. Then Holly let the teacher go and stepped away from her, allowing her to sag in a dead faint in the chair, out of the equation. Holly's smile was a skeptical smirk below her dark dancing eyes. "Well, well," she said as she faced us and tapped the business end of the letter opener in her palm.

Which was *all* she'd have said, had I been the armed one. You don't play patty-cake with an armed nut case. First splat then chat. "Well," I said to Leah, "you said you wanted to shoot her. There she is. Shoot her."

"Yes, little sister," Holly said, beckoning with the letter opener. "Come on. Shoot me."

Leah held her pistol with her right hand. Her other hand peered uselessly out of the sling-borne cast. The little automatic was easy to aim one-handed; at this range it would take no marksman to knock the other woman down.

But Leah did nothing except stare glassily at her sister.

Holly's grin widened. She stepped forward, bent, put the letter opener on the floor and stood up again. "That better? I thought so. Go ahead, little sister. Shoot me."

"Take her out," I said roughly.

Leah stood motionless, as if engraved there.

"Can't do it, huh?" Holly said sympathetically.

"Well, I can." I took the pistol from the unresisting cop, turned on Holly, and drew down on her two-handed. Pick a knee, any knee.

"You wouldn't shoot an unarmed—"

CLICK

"—defenseless—"

CLICK

"—woman, would you?" she asked.

CLICK CLICK CLICK.

"Jesus Christ!" I bellowed. Holly began to laugh. I popped the clip release of the weapon. Nothing came out. "The hell's wrong with you?" I shouted at Leah, whose face was vacant, uncomprehending.

Her sister was still laughing. "That's just like you, baby sister," she said. "Big tough cop. Gonna track me down and arrest me. But you conveniently forgot to load your gun. You know what they call that at the drool school, my dear. Significant, is what they call it. You show definite signs of ambivalence, along with a big dose of denial. But denial is your middle name. It goes way back—back to when I killed Mother."

At first the words did not register on me. But they did on Leah. Her eyes were big and owlish, her mouth a hard pout. "You did *not* kill Mother!" she cried in a high, whiny voice, gesturing with a fist. "Don't say that! It was an accident!"

Holly rolled her eyes. "It was not," she said wearily. "She was standing on the balcony railing hanging balloons for your birthday party. I pushed her, and she fell. You were there, you watched me do it, but you always denied what happened. Denied that Mother's death was anything but an accident. Why? You felt guilty. Because you hated Mother, too."

"I did not," Leah wailed.

"You wanted her dead as much as I did," Holly said lazily.

Leah turned and ran blindly from the room. "Call the cops!" I hollered after her echoing footsteps. No reply. I turned back to the sister, who had not moved from her position six feet away from the unconscious teacher. "Just you and me, babe," I said, tossing the useless pistol aside.

"Yep. Uh-huh," she answered jauntily, bouncing on the balls of her sneakers. "It's only fair to warn you that I learned judo and karate in the giggle house. I'm very very good. Very very strong. And fast. I'll snap your neck," she said, snapping her fingers, "given half a chance." She beckoned. "Come on!"

I walked toward her, kicked the letter opener away into a far corner, then squared off, eyes locked with hers. Holly's face was knotted with concentration; beads of sweat stood out on her forehead, and I could hear her breathe. One hand was out, as if for balance; the other was down behind her leg. I decided to make quick work of her. I feinted right and charged, planning to take her down with a full body tackle. She dodged nimbly and, as I charged past, slashed at my face with her hidden hand, drawing a blasting line of pain across my eyebrows. Sliding to a stop, I gasped from the pain and felt with a hand that came down bloody. She'd cut me.

"Surpriiiise," she sang, now standing where I'd been, still bouncing on the balls of her feet. Proudly she waved a tiny little silver knife, no longer than my pinky. "Nice and sharp," she said. "I like sharp things, don't you?"

I mopped blood again. I didn't bother to tell her that I *hate* sharp things. I favor blunt things, like a ball bat or a piece of pipe. I'm also partial to implements that blow large holes in people. But I had neither. Time for some creativity.

Watching Holly carefully, braced to counter any move, I unbuckled my belt, slid it out of its loops and wrapped it twice around my fist, leaving twenty-odd inches of buckle-tipped leather dangled toward the floor. "Oh, interesting," she said. "Ready?"

She feinted, jinked, faked a jab. I was swinging the belt over my head, timing my move, and when she made hers I was ready. As she lunged and slashed at me I swung for real, whistling the air, and the buckle smashed Holly's hand squarely and sailed her knife across the classroom to clatter uselessly into a pile of old student chairs.

Holly bent, nestled her hurt hand between her ample thighs, and began to wail. "Oh God, oh Christ, that hurts," she gasped.

I mopped blood again, wondering what other tricks she had in store, like the ones she'd used on Bob Stella, Duke Werden, her mother, sister, and God knew who else. But there was no question about my next move.

If I were a gentleman, I'd have left her be, or perhaps tied her up with all decorum to wait for the cops. But, as I'd told her the day we met, I'm not a gentleman. What I am is a feminist. The best kind, the kind that treats men and women the same. I stepped in, hauled off, and coldcocked her.

†††

I hugged Bob Stella's widow, murmured some comforting words, and walked slowly away from the grave. Others did likewise in the brilliant sunshine, streaming across the lush lawn of Michigan Memorial toward cars stripped of their purple funeral flags. Bob, I thought, would have appreciated the turnout. The whole Under New Management crowd was there; even Jimmy Joe Putnam had forsaken his army field jacket and donned a blazer for the occasion.

Carole Somers, who'd preceded me through the receiving line, fell in beside me. She was tall-blond stylish as ever, dressed for court in a blue business suit modified to allow for the extra, temporary girth in front. "You all right?" she asked. "You look sort of peaked."

"I'm okay. 'Preciate your coming along, kid."

"*De nada.*" She sighed. "I need to get off my feet, though. Soon."

"Well, how's about a big steak over at—"

"Hey, Perkins. Wait up."

I turned to see Leah Norwood advancing on me purposefully. It felt odd, seeing the murderer's sister at the victim's funeral. But what happened wasn't her fault, I told myself. Any more than it was big, amiable Bob's fault. You make the wrong move, you get dead sometimes.

"I wanted to thank you," Leah said when she reached us, "for helping out and everything."

"No problem," I said. "Leah Norwood, Carole Somers." The women smiled coolly at each other and nodded. "How's Mrs. Anderson?"

Leah brushed hair from her forehead. "I stopped by to see her this morning. She's being released tomorrow. She's okay. Shaken up, but . . . well, they built women of iron in those days, and—"

"Still do, kiddo," Carole said.

Leah laughed. "Damn straight."

"Headed home soon?" I asked.

"Tonight." Leah turned and looked back at the expanse of cemetery with its flat brass markers. "I've taken care of my unfinished business. Time to go home. Looks like that silly bitch sister of mine will be staying here for a while, though."

"Oh yeah," I said. "You won't be seeing her out Chicago way anytime soon."

Carole gave me a reproving look, but Leah ignored my tone. "I'm really glad I got to visit Mrs. Anderson." She squinted. "She kept saying I was such a sad little girl. Isn't it funny what people perceive? I've never been sad a day in my life. Bad things happen, but you go on is what you do. You don't mope around."

"Sure," I said.

"You just take it easy," Carole said.

Leah smiled. "You don't have to worry about me," she said with just the slightest edge, then took my hand in a grip that was nothing like her sister's. "'Bye, Perkins. Look me up if you're ever in Chicagoland." She turned and walked quickly toward the lot.

Carole and I trailed along after her at a significantly slower pace. I found myself thinking about unfinished business, about Leah's offhand statement that she'd finished hers.

Brave talk, but unrealistic. I stopped, turned, looked over the expansive graveyard one more time. Business, even old business, is never finished till you take up residence in a place like this. . . .

"You going to spend the night here," Carole broke in, "or are you going to waddle me out to dinner?"

I turned to her and returned her smile. "Dinner," I answered, and we started for the car.

Afterword

The bar I called "Under New Management" actually existed, pretty much where I placed it, but under a different name. And, as related in this story, it was a small country grocery before it became a saloon. Otherwise the events of this story are wholly fictitious.

Eddie Cabla, the bar's owner, made regular appearances in the novels. The other denizens of the bar were pretty much the same. For Bob Stella this story was his sole appearance; ditto for Leah Norwood, Holly Norwood, and Edna Anderson—at least so far.

Of the stories in this collection, "Unfinished Business" is one of four to feature a pretty seriously whacked-out villain who happens to be female. Call me an equal opportunity writer.

This story also depicts a theme that has occurred in my work before: evil lives long and recurs and, unfortunately, when it flares up can cost innocent people their lives. Ben, though hardboiled as always, is soldierlike and heroic: resists the blatant sexual advances of the villain, follows up diligently on his intuition that things are not what they seem, and puts himself on the line at the end to save lives.

And yet, one senses, the tragedy of Leah Norwood is not yet over. . . .

Something Simple

The first Monday of the New Year found us still digging out from the first big storm of the winter. Four days before, an Alberta Clipper had blown through the Great Lakes region, gifting us with twenty-one inches of snow. Behind that, an Arctic air mass depressed highs to twelve at best. All this fouled up the roads, loused up New Year's Eve, and kept me on the clock all weekend long.

Well, that's what they pay me the big bucks for. And besides, this being metro Detroit, we expect such events. We welcome them, even. They give us a chance to be as tough as we talk.

Relieved to be back indoors, I trudged into the cozy warmth of the Norwegian Wood maintenance office. My people were deployed on the day's chores around the complex, dealing with busted pipes, tenants' gripes, and snow and ice or a combination thereof. Time for a smoke. Time for some coffee. Time for—

"Good morning, Ben," Shyla said.

She sat in my chair behind the plain, gray steel desk, slumped down so low I hadn't noticed her. "Morning," I said, not bothering hiding my surprise as I unbuttoned my pea coat. "You working this week? I thought you were back at school."

"Classes start tomorrow," Shyla said, straightening. I noticed that she had poured herself some coffee, smoked two cigarettes already. She had also switched my desk radio from 'ABX to one of those Ani DiFranco stations. That's our Shyla, I thought with a smile. "Got a minute?" she asked.

"Sure, kid." Grabbing a chair, I sat down facing her and dug a short cork-tipped cigar out of my shirt pocket. Shyla Ryan was slight but not short, five seven or so. Her blonde hair was a close-cropped cap around a pretty face graced with high cheekbones and striking bright blue eyes. She wore a light brown jacket over a snug, long-sleeved dark brown top. Her lipstick was the color of her top, making her look even paler than usual. Unlike many her age, she had pierced no parts, at least none I could see. She seemed restless and intense, which was typical of her, and worried, which was not. "What's up?" I asked.

"I need your help," she said.

"Sure," I answered. Flaring a wood match, I lighted my cigar. "What's the story?" I asked, thinking college problems, car problems, maybe boy problems. Here's the windup and now the pitch: a nice high slow one for old Ben to hit out of the park for her.

"My dad's disappeared," she said, fidgeting. "Can you find him for me?"

A few years before, I got asked that a lot. A few years before, the answer was easy. Now the question came rarely, and when it did, it threw up all kinds of red flags. Looking into Shyla's blue eyes, I realized how troubled she was. Damn, I thought. "I'd like to help," I said, exhaling smoke. "But that's really something for the police to deal with."

Her eyes flashed. "You sound like my mother," she said. "I already talked to the police, filed a report. They just shrugged at me." She leaned forward, slender hands knotted. "I'm sure something awful has happened to Daddy. You've got to help me."

Stalling, I asked, "Well, how long has it been since—"

"Thursday," she said. "He called me Thursday. Said things were getting fixed. He sounded really happy. But after that I heard nothing. Yesterday I went to his place. He hasn't been there. No one's seen him." Taking a cigarette out of her small purse, she put it to her lips, bending forward to accept my light. Nodding her thanks, she took a big hard hit and looked at me, exhaling. "I'm so scared, Ben," she said quietly. "He never goes away without letting me know. Never."

"'His' place," I said, waving out the wood kitchen match. "Your parents divorced?"

"Separated," she answered. "He moved out four months ago. My mother had been such a bitch to him." She took another drag. "So how about it?" she asked, brightening. "Will you help me?"

Hating myself now, I said, "Wish I could. But I don't do that kind of stuff any more. Been out of it for years."

"But you used to," she pressed. "I heard all about you. Marge has told me things, and Mrs. Janusevicius—"

"Be careful what you believe," I advised. "The stories get wilder in the retelling."

"I heard you were awesome," she said quietly.

I shook my head. "Work with the police, Shyla. This kind of thing, it's their job."

Now she was blinking, and I feared what was coming. "What they said— Marge, and Mrs. J, and the colonel and everybody—what they told me," she said, voice shaking a bit, "is that you always came through for your friends." She stared straight at me, blue eyes shiny. "Aren't I your friend, Ben?"

†††

The cell phone whistled just as I was wheeling my Mustang out of the parking lot. Bracing the wheel with my knee, I jammed the shifter into third with one hand and pressed SND with the other. "Perkins."

"You called?" came Carole's voice.

"Morning, Your Honor," I said, and braced myself. "About tonight."

"Yes?"

"Instead of picking up Rookie at the courthouse, how's about if I swing by your place later, around suppertime."

"Works for me," she answered. "But doesn't that take you out of your way?"

"Most likely not. I've got some running around to do up that way today."

Pause. "But it's only 9 A.M. now."

"I know," I said hastily. "So, is it—"

"Why don't you just pick her up at the daycare when you're ready? They're open until—"

"Be less pressure," I said, "if we do the handoff up at your house."

Long pause. "What are you up to, Ben?"

Damn. This is what happens, when they've known you for years and have clocked all your moves. I sighed. "I'm doing some checking up for a friend of mine."

"Now there's a phrase I haven't heard in awhile," she said. "'Checking up.'" From her tone you'd think I'd uttered a most odious obscenity. "What sort of 'checking up,' Ben?"

"Shyla Ryan, woman I work with," I said. "College kid. Temps for Marge in the rental office during breaks. Her dad's dropped out of sight, she asked if I'd do some looking around. I told her I'd help out."

The tension was so tangible I could almost touch it. "God, this scares me," she whispered. "All those familiar terms. 'Dropped out of sight.' 'Looking around.' 'Help out.'"

"Nothing to be scared of," I said. "It's something simple. Trust me."

"You promised to stay out of that work."

"It's not 'work.' I'm not getting paid."

"Don't fence with me!" she flared. "Back then you didn't get paid either, half the time. That didn't stop you from getting stabbed and beaten up and *shot*."

I shook my head. "Nobody's getting shot."

I heard her intake of breath, uncharacteristically shaky. "Is this Shyla person . . . *special* to you?"

Knowing what she was really asking, I replied patiently, "She's a kid. We work together. I know how you feel about this, but . . . I sat there and looked at her and listened to her. In my mind's eye she looked like Rookie twenty years down the line."

I heard her inhale. "How manipulative of you to drag Rachel into this."

"Happens to be the truth," I said mildly.

Another pause. "You won't forget to pick her up tonight," she said.

"I won't forget."

In the background I could hear a female voice. Carole murmured something. To me she said, briskly, "You did promise me, you know. And Rachel, too."

"I know. And I've been keeping the promise. And I know this nudges it."

"Just so we understand each other. No rough stuff. Promise?"

I took a deep breath. "Promise."

"All right." She sounded cheerier, if only a little. "At least you told me. That's an improvement."

"Yes," I replied. "It is."

†††

Randy Ryan's apartment building was in Bloomfield Township, well north of the city, off Telegraph and Long Lake. It was a long, low single-story brick structure capped with a massive layer of icy snow. The eaves were fringed with long, lethal-looking icicles stabbing downward. For Bloomfield, the place seemed low rent and highly transient. Might as well have put "Divorced Dads Welcome" on their sign out front.

The parking lot sported a white 'Vette and a blue Crown Vic, but no large black Ford Expedition with white fuzzy dice dangling from the mirror. I wedged my Mustang in a parking spot between the Vic and a mountainous pile of plowed snow.

Huddled in my pea coat, fists clenched in pockets for warmth, I crunched across the hard-packed white stuff toward the door of Apartment 3. Already I knew what I'd find. Secondhand mismatched furniture. Worn appliances. Neutral colors on the walls, the trim, in the carpet. TV and maybe a CD player. And few personal touches except—if Shyla's description of their relationship was any indication—a picture or two of her arm-in-arm with her dad, smiling at the camera.

Five minutes later I left, my expectations fully confirmed. Only there was just one picture, of Shyla alone, probably her high school graduation portrait a couple of years earlier. Her hair had been brown and longer. She looked younger and more innocent, one to whom less had happened. Same blue eyes, though.

Of Ryan himself there was no recent sign. As Shyla had told me, the sinks were dry, the bed was neatly made, and what looked like several days' worth of mail scattered on the foyer carpet. To the front storm door were stuck three yellow tried-to-deliver sticky notes, from UPS or OOPS or somebody like that. The earliest one was dated December thirtieth.

I'd knocked on the other seven doors. The two that answered claimed no knowledge of Randy Ryan, past or present. I reboarded the Mustang and, heat on high, headed south on Telegraph. Normally four lanes each way, Telegraph was down to two narrow lanes now. They were walled with high white drifts that were already turning gray-black from tailpipe crud. The traffic ran slow and sullen, the lights especially lengthy at Quarton and Maple.

Worst of all was the sprawling interchange where Telegraph intertwined with the Reuther and the Lodge freeways. There the cars, the SUVs, and the big rigs crept along in ten-foot lurches. They noisily merged and disengaged like icy, metallic, salt-encrusted lovers, tailpipes sending up thick streams of inky exhaust like plumy cats' tails into the frigid midmorning air. I just lived through it, smoking a cigar, playing Buddy Guy's latest on the CD, tolerant, patient. Downright tranquil even. Surely in no hurry to meet Randy Ryan's estranged wife.

†††

"Oh, you," she said, grimacing at me through the storm door. "Jennifer told me about you. Come on in, I guess."

Jennifer? I wondered. Then, as I stepped inside, it clicked. "Thanks for your time," I said. "I'm just wondering if—"

"I know why you're here," Virginia Ryan said, turning on me. Physically, she was quite different from Shyla, besides being older. Short and quite round, lipless and worn, she had short wavy dark hair and deep worry lines. Her eyes were as narrow and hard and colorless as shards of window glass. She wore dark stirrup pants and a light sleeveless shirt. Silver wedding rings twinkled as she gestured. This was, I sensed, a woman who liked to throw things, starting with words and moving on, as needed, to heftier items. "You're trying to find that sorry, sleazebag, soon-to-be-ex-husband of mine."

"No," came another voice as Shyla entered the room. "He's looking for Daddy. Hi, Ben," she added, giving me a small wave.

"Hey, kid."

The three of us stood, for a moment seemingly immobilized by tension. The living room of the small Redford Township ranch house was a kaleidoscope of beige: dark, medium, and light. The furniture and decorations were rounded, puffy, and plush. The scent was potpourri and sweetish, with the hint of recently baked bread and remote tobacco smoke. "Can we sit down?" I asked.

"Well," the mother said, "I'm going to. You do what you want." She went to the sofa and sat on its edge, facing me, and hovered over the coffee table. On it was scattered piles of what looked like mail. "As to Randy, I'll tell you the same thing I've told Jennifer." She ripped open an envelope, using considerably more force than needed. "He's taken that money he stole and run off with that hillbilly slut girlfriend of his."

Shyla, who stood in the archway to the dining room, scowled. "That's so unfair. You don't know anything about a girlfriend—"

"I have all the evidence I need," her mother cut in flatly, unfolding an ad.

"And the money thing, too," Shyla charged on, "you don't *know* that. You're just connecting the dots. It's what you always do. You sit around and stew about things and—"

"For God's sake!" Virginia snapped, slamming the ad down. "The police were here, Jennifer! Your father's *boss* has filed a *complaint!*"

"Did you ever get his side of it?" Shyla asked hotly. She was hugging herself, and her blue eyes were a tad glassy. "Of course not. Because you *want* to believe—"

"Whoa!" I interjected, making the T with both hands. "Hold the phone. Steady on, as we say." The women looked at me, expressions eerily identical in their annoyance. "One thing at a time, if we could."

"Who asked you?" Virginia retorted, head cocked at an angry angle.

"I did," Shyla said.

"None of this is any of your business, *Jennifer!*"

"I'm involved in it, too, you know," Shyla replied stubbornly.

"Please," I said, holding up both hands. "Let me get the information I need, and I'll scoot."

Virginia ripped open another envelope and huffed a sigh. "Whatever."

"Okay." I picked through the scraps of facts in my head, framing questions. Or trying to. It had been a long, long time. Surely this was easier years ago. "You mentioned a girlfriend and evidence. What can you tell me about that?"

Virginia gave Shyla a cold smile and a glance. "I found a greeting card she sent him. A sexy greeting card. Left nothing to the imagination."

"Because you went through his briefcase!" Shyla put in. "You always do that, Virginia. Snoop through people's private things."

"He's my husband," her mother answered. "He's not allowed to have secrets from me." Shyla, rolling her eyes, hugged herself tighter and looked away. "So I checked our phone bills, line by line." Virginia went on, opening another envelope. "There were lots of long distance calls to Georgia. Which makes sense because that's where Plant Two is, and Randy calls there a lot. But I found a lot of other Georgia calls, to just one particular number. Place called MO-tee-yay. That's how I found out about *her*."

"I don't buy it," Shyla said airily.

I looked at the mother. "Can you give me the woman's name and number? I'll need to touch base with her."

Virginia shrugged. "You want to waste your time, that's your business."

I looked at her again, seemingly engrossed in a bill of some kind. More there than met the eye. I was pretty sure Shyla was blind to it. To see what I saw, you have to have lived a lot of years, taken a lot of shots. "Now, on this embezzlement thing—"

"*Alleged* embezzlement," Shyla corrected.

"Yes, thank you." Virginia was ignoring me, but I talked to her anyway. "You said a cop came out here? What jurisdiction?"

"Farmington Hills, I think," Virginia said, setting the bill aside. "That's where the main plant is." She picked up a catalog-sized envelope and shredded the end open. "I don't remember the officer's name." She extracted some papers. "It was so embarrassing," she whispered, "that bastard putting me through this."

Then, staring at the papers in her hands, she froze. "Oh," she said, more to herself than to us, "for God's sake." Squinting at the papers, she whispered, "He sold it. The son of a bitch *sold* it."

"What?" Shyla asked guardedly.

Virginia looked at her daughter. "The farm!" she answered. "He sold the farm!" Looking at the paper again, she read: "'Please consider this formal acknowledgment of the sale of the property located at blah blah blah.'" In grim silence she skimmed further. "'Two hundred ** twenty-two hundred twenty-three thousand dollars, less our standard commission of.'" With a toss she skittered the paper onto the coffee tabletop and looked up at Shyla with weary anger. "This is your father," she said, tone deceptively mild. "He cheated on me, he stole from his company, and now he's stolen from *us*."

"I don't believe it," Shyla said.

"That was our estate," Virginia murmured. "I'm entitled to half of it as part of the settlement. Now he's run off with it."

"It was in his family," Shyla put in. "It was Daddy's before you married him. You aren't entitled to a dime of it."

"Oh, so you're a lawyer now?" Virginia sneered. "Grow *up*, little girl. *This* is him," she charged on, waving the letter. "*This* is your father. *This* is what he's about. He's a liar and a cheat and a crook. He betrayed me, and you just wait, he'll betray you, too!"

Raising her head, Shyla replied, "He's the best daddy a girl could ever want."

Though there's no such thing as good timing in a situation like this, to me it seemed like high time to leave. I rose. "I'd better get going," I told Virginia. "Could I trouble you for the info on that woman down in Georgia?"

After a moment's frozen silence, Virginia got wearily to her feet. "I suppose," she grumped. "Why are you even wasting your time with this? Can't you see what's going on here? Don't you have better things to do?"

Feeling Shyla's eyes on me, I shrugged. "Said I'd help out."

"I suggest," Virginia Ryan said, "that you just let it go."

With a glance at Shyla, who was watching me tensely, I said easily, "Thing about me is, once I get started, I don't quit. Not unless the client waves me off." Some things have changed, I thought. But not that. I looked at Shyla. "Do I keep going?"

"Yes!" Shyla said, fists thrusting upward, beaming at me.

†††

By now the traffic has eased up some. Even so, the massive drifts of snow made Telegraph slow as I motored north. To get to Farmington Hills I needed the Reuther freeway west, and it was once again stop-and-go through the metastatic cloverleaves of Reuther/Lodge/Northwestern/Telegraph. Turning off Buddy Guy, I used the opportunity to mash out Doreen Mason's 706-area-code number on the cell phone.

"Hah. This is Doh-reen," recited the high, breathy voice on tape some seven hundred miles south. "Ah cain't tawk now, but if you leave your name, an' your number, Ah'll—" Hitting END, I tossed the cell phone on the bucket seat and returned my full attention to my driving. I could have left a message, but some creaky old detective instinct told me not to. Better to try again later and catch her off guard.

†††

At the Farmington Hills police station I was kept waiting for a long time in the dim, stuffy, noisy visitor area. How well I remembered this waiting around jazz from way back when. Detective work, I recalled, was long stretches of boredom interrupted by extended periods of waiting. Interspersed, at the oddest times, with quick bursts of pure terror, which for me, back then, had been a diseased form of fun. Like the times I almost got garroted, and thonked in the head with a ball bat, and shot in the butt.

But that was then, back in those bad old days of seemingly endless Republican presidents. I'm too old for that now, I told myself. Besides, I swore an oath to Carole and Rachel, the women in my life. No rough stuff. Dragging myself away from the memories, I killed time scoping out the other visitors who drifted in and out of the cop house. Their grumpy demeanor was typical of involuntary visitors. I amused myself trying to determine which were perpetrators, which were perpetratees. And which were both (attorneys, natch), and which were that most dubious and threatened of species, the innocent bystander.

"Mr. Perkins?"

I glanced over at the plain steel door by the counter and nodded. The man, a short, well-built specimen in dark pants and a tieless white shirt, strolled toward me. No smile, I noticed as I rose. No greeting. No offer of a handshake. Just, "You're here about Randy Ryan?"

"Yes. Appreciate you seeing me, Detective—"

"Shanahan. So where is he?" the cop asked abruptly, hooking hands in his pants pockets.

That caught me off guard. I studied the lawman briefly. He had very curly dark hair cut quite short, a squarish, flat, cop face with just the faintest of age lines, gray eyes of Navy steel. He was younger than me, which was no surprise there being, I've noticed, more of those each day.

"That's what I'd like to know," I answered.

He blinked. "What's your interest?"

"His daughter asked me to find him," I replied. The cop said nothing. Remembering that to be a rather effective investigative technique, I made a mental note. "Talk to him lately?"

"Not since Thursday," Shanahan answered. "He was supposed to turn himself in. Never showed."

"So you're charging him?"

"Embezzlement. His employer swore out a complaint."

"How's it look?"

"Dead bang, man. Couple hundred grand. A slam-dunk." Shanahan seemed to relax just slightly. "Buzz is he's a bright guy, but no matter how hard I look, I don't see anything all that clever about how he worked it. Dumb stealing from dumber." *Typical*, he could have said but did not have to.

Poor Shyla, I thought. "So you talked to him Thursday?"

"Yeah, he called in. Surprised hell out of me," Shanahan added, looking anything but surprised. "I guess he sensed we were set to scoop him. Said he'd come in voluntarily." He shook his head. "Just a diversionary tactic. I waited till eight, got caught in the snowstorm, missed my kid's hockey game. No sign of Ryan, then or since. From that I am forced to infer that he has skipped."

Which of course made Virginia Ryan's theory look better and better. I thought for a moment. "So I take it you've posted surveillance teams at the airports and train stations and bus stations and—"

"Yeah, right," Shanahan said, with just the faintest smile. "We've put the word out. He'll turn up. He'll bust a red light or get ratted out by a friend or—hey," he said, squinting at me, "maybe you'll even find him. You're some kind of detective, I take it?"

"Used to be."

"Not any more?"

"Nope," I said, smiling. "Went legit."

†††

Next stop was Ryan's employer's place on Northwestern. Instead of heading there right away, I fired up the Mustang motor to get some heat into the frigid car, and hit SND on the cell phone to redial Doreen Mason's number. While listening to it ring, I looked idly at the phone bill Virginia Ryan had given me. Fully half the entries were highlighted in bright yellow and were virtually identical to the 706 number in a Georgia town called Motier, which Ryan had pronounced MO-tee-yay but was actually, I suspected, pronounced Mo-TEER.

"*Ah don't want any!*" came a loud female voice in my ear.

"Ms. Mason?" I asked.

"Will you *leave* me alone," she charged on, accent a foot thick. "I don't buy things on the phone, and I never will, and—"

"I'm not a salesman," I said. "I'm calling about Randy."

Her pause was just a tad too long. "Who?"

"Randy Ryan," I said, and took the plunge, no doubt a bit too precipitously. "Is he there?"

Cell phone static hissed in my ear for a moment. "I don't know who you're talking about," she said. "Who are you?"

"Name's Perkins," I said. "I'm calling from Michigan. I'm looking for Randy." An inspiration came, and I went with it. "His daughter asked me to find him."

"Yeah?" Doreen asked, tone challenging. "His daughter, huh." Pausing she asked abruptly, "What's her name?"

"Shyla."

"No. Her real name," she prodded cagily.

"Jennifer. And her mother's Virginia. And he works for Brighton-Leopold." Or worked, I thought but did not say. "I know the whole deal," I said quietly. "I got your number from Virginia." Doreen did not reply. I sensed she was not all that quick on the uptake. "What made you think I was a salesman?" I asked.

"Call ID said 'anonymous,'" she answered. "That usually means telemarketer." Static hissed again for a moment, and when Doreen spoke again, she sounded tired. "Randy's not here. I don't know where he is."

Of course she could have been lying. I did not need to hark back to my investigating days to recall that people frequently lie, even when they don't have to. But I decided to go with it for now. "Are you still . . . involved with him?"

"No. He broke if off."

"When?"

"Last week he called."

"When last week?"

"I don't know. Wednesday, Thursday, what does it matter? He called me and said it was over, done with. Said he was going away for a long time. Said it was the best for all concerned." With each phrase I heard the emotion welling up in her. Now she paused, and when she spoke again, she sounded steadier, and quite dull. "I told him it was all right. I told him whatever he wanted, whatever was best for him." She sighed. "I've always heard about 'if you have something, let it go.' What they don't talk about is how much it hurts."

I let a silence grow, thinking about what she had said. "So you don't know where he is."

"No, sir."

Keeping my voice easy I said, "Don't know if I buy that, Doreen. I mean, he's flown the coop and took a pot of money with him, and you were his sweetie—"

"Oh, don't get me wrong," she cut in, tone pointed. "If he'd asked me, I'd be with him this instant. He's the sweetest, kindest man. But I knew, somehow I knew all along, it would never end up that way. And I was right."

I believed her.

"If she'd ever been nice to him," Doreen murmured. "That's all the man ever needed was a little kindness. And love. And acceptance. That's all. If she'd ever given him that, he'd never have looked at me twice. I ain't no prize."

"Not to pick a fight with you, but you seem like a very nice person to me."

That brought a hint of warmth, a touch of playfulness to her tone. "Aw, what do you know from all the way up there? Listen . . . when you find him?"

"Yes?"

"Tell him I'm praying for him."

†††

Brighton-Leopold Corp. was one of those downsized, streamlined, New Age companies with no receptionist. The foyer of the large, flat, anonymous building was in fact empty except for a row of plastic visitor chairs and a table scattered with magazines and literature. A vacant desk bore a phone and a sign saying, "Please call the extension of the person you are seeing and have a seat."

With the sign was a helpful list of about fifty names and extensions. Randy Ryan's name was on it. But there were no titles or positions or helpful hints like, "This guy is Randy's boss." Then I noticed several names in a clump: LEOPOLD N., LEOPOLD P., LEOPOLD T. There being no Brighton listed, I did the next best thing and called the first Leopold.

"Yes?"

"Mr. Leopold?"

"He's in a meeting."

"It's very urgent. It's about Randy Ryan."

"Oh. Surely. Please hold." From the quickening in the young man's voice, I inferred that the mention of Ryan had struck a nerve. I waited. Almost at once the gray steel door buzzed and opened, and a short, roundish man bustled through. As I hung up the phone, the man wheezed, "Where's Randy?"

I stood and said, "Wish I knew, sir. I'm Ben Perkins. You're Mr. Leopold?"

"Neal." His black hair was a bushy black mop around a fleshy face anchored with thick glasses. He wore dark pants and a nondescript dress shirt unbuttoned at collar and cuffs. He had the look of a teddy-bearish absent-minded professor, but his eyes were steady and careful as he stuck a pawlike hand out for me to shake. "Have you seen him?"

"No, sir. His daughter asked me to—"

"He'd better move fast," Leopold said. "If you're in touch with him, tell him I can't keep the wolves at bay much longer."

"Wolves?"

"My partners." He looked wounded and anxious, hope fading in his eyes. "When Randy called and said he'd make good, I told my partners, look, he does this and we drop the charges, make it all go away." He sighed. "It's been, what? Four days now? And now you say he's missing?" He stared at me. "I just can't stand up for him much longer. My partners—"

"I understand," I said, which was not strictly true—it hardly ever is—but saying so usually quiets people down. "So he called you and offered to—"

"Every nickel," Leopold assented, bushy head bobbing. "That's what he said. 'Every nickel' he'd pay back."

"When did he call you?"

Squinting, Leopold counted back. "Thursday." Hm. Seemed to me that day had been mentioned before. Could this be a clue? Or simply what my friend Raeanne calls a "co-inky-dink"?

Leopold charged on. "He pays the money back, it's all forgiven, see? He keeps his job, it'll all be like it was before. That's what I promised him."

"Seems right generous of you."

Leopold made an it's-nothing gesture with shoulders, hands, a brief bow of his head. "He's like part of the family. We all make mistakes, we all do dumb things. Nothing is stranger that what actually happens. Life goes on—"

"Neal?" came a voice from the door. A mere clip of a young man shaved nearly bald and wearing white over tan seemed to slither in. He extended an envelope to his boss and whispered, "Excuse me. Thought you should see this right away."

Leopold took the opened envelope in his big hairy hands and shook out what looked like a business card. There was also an elongated piece of yellow paper. The owner's eyes squinted at the latter then widened behind the thick lenses. He positively beamed, holding the larger item up like a diploma. "He did it!" Leopold crowed.

It was a check. From where I stood, I could not make out the details. The young man said, softly and sibilantly acerbic, "What makes you think it's any good?"

Leopold flipped the check around and read. "'Pay to the order of Brighton-Leopold Corp. four hundred ten thousand dollars,' signed 'Randy Ryan.'" The man was positively glowing; I thought he might dance a jig right there. "Of course it's good," he said to the young man. "He said he'd come through, and he did. End of discussion." Turning to me, Leopold seized my hand. With a slight bow, he pumped it hard, as if I'd had anything to do with anything. "Thank you. Thank you so much."

"Well, sir, I—"

"And when you find Randy," Leopold commanded, letting go and pointing at me like the I WANT YOU poster, "you tell him it's time to come home now."

†††

But he was still missing. Which, in light of what had just happened, made no sense.

But then little in this work ever does. *This* part I remembered all too well.

I sat in the icebox Mustang, running the engine to warm it up. Flurries fell on the flat, snow-covered plain adding insult to icy injury. Just past the parking lot, beyond a mountain of freshly plowed snow, trucks crept along 10 Mile Road. Why? I asked myself. Why do I still live in Michigan? More to the

266 | ROB KANTNER

point, why am I out here in the bitter snowy cold, twisted around a mental axle trying to figure out this Randy Ryan mess? Where I should be is back in my warm, pleasant, Norwegian Woods maintenance office. In full control of my own little world. Listening to 'ABX and drinking coffee and smoking cigars.

But . . . I had promised.

So get on with it, stupid.

Now. The central theory had been that Randy Ryan had absconded with a pile of embezzled money, perhaps into the arms of his girlfriend in Georgia. That theory was now inoperative. So where was he?

At times like this, when your Big Theory goes poof, the only thing to do is start over with what you know for sure. In sequence. Think orderly for once, I told myself. When did Shyla last hear from her dad? Thursday, she had said this morning. I was sure of it.

On Randy's apartment door, the oldest UPS delivery sticky note was dated . . . December 30th, which was . . . Thursday. So he had not been back there since.

Then there was Doreen Mason. I was pretty sure she had told me it was Thursday when Randy called her to break off their affair. What about Shanahan, the detective? He'd said Randy had promised to turn himself in on Thursday. And when Randy called Neal Leopold to tell him he was making things right, that had been last Thursday, right? Correct.

Thursday, Thursday, Thursday. All these things in one day, this was not just a "co-inky-dink." Back there in Leopold's office I had heard a tinny little ringing in my ear—that long-dormant detective instinct saying, *this is something important, pay attention, idiot.*

And every one of the contacts he had made had been by phone. The logical question was from where had he called? How could I find out?

Ah, yes.

Clenching the smoldering cigar in my teeth, I picked up the cell phone and mashed SND. Ringing, then *click*, and the taped answering spiel started. I overrode with "Doreen, pick up, please? It's Ben again."

Click. "Well he*llo* there," she purred. "I was hoping you'd call back."

Nice as it is to be come on to, I had no time for flirting, or interest in it, either. "Well, I need a bit more information if you don't mind. About Randy."

"Uh-huh," she replied, resigned.

"When was it he called you? To, uh—"

"To dump me?" she supplied, tone patient. "Um. Let's see. Thursday, that's right. I know because I went to a New Year's Eve party, and—"

"This is important. Where did he call you from?"

"I don't know. He didn't say."

"Doreen, please," I said patiently. "You have Caller ID, right?"

"That's right!" She seemed surprised to hear this. "It's in the kitchen, that's why I didn't see it when he called."

"Can you check it for me now and tell me where he called from?" I asked.

"Okay." Fumbling noises and then she said, "Hope it's still in here. I get a lot of calls, it might have . . . let's seeeee. . . ." Long pause, silence. "Well, this must be it," she said. "It's the only one I don't recognize from Thursday."

"Read it to me," I said, groping paper and pen out of my glovebox.

"*Redemp Eee See*," she said slowly and then recited a phone number in the 248 area code. "What the heck is that? And where the heck is 248?"

†††

Redemption Episcopal Church is on Quarton Road in Bloomfield Township, several blocks east of Telegraph. I got there during lunch hour but luckily found the lone office worker eating a sandwich at her desk. I hadn't gotten half my question out of my mouth when she started shaking her head. "You'll need to see Father Dave about that," she said, not unkindly.

"Is he here?"

"He should be free." She put down her sandwich. "Come along."

I followed her down a narrow hallway to the end office. It was all glass on one wall, bookshelves on the other. Its occupant rose to greet me as we entered. He was evidently a person of the cloth. But you would not have known it from his dark Dockers pants and open-necked pale blue polo shirt. He also looked way too young to be a priest. "Dave Collins," he said, shaking hands with a very firm grip and a very direct look in his eye. "How can I help you?"

"Ben Perkins," I said as the office worker stepped out, clicking the door shut behind her. "I'm here about one of your, uh . . . congregation people."

"A parishioner?" Collins asked, eyebrow arched. "Please, have a seat."

Okay, I was nervous, as I always am around people with a direct line to God. I sat on a sofa under the light of a floor lamp. Had it not been on, we'd have both been in deep shadows. The light from outside had dimmed considerably in the darkening sky. Looked like another storm, I thought.

"Yes, a parishioner," I said as Collins sat down in his desk chair, facing me. "Randy Ryan."

"Mm," the reverend said, expression placid, not at all wary.

Not knowing how much to tell him, I stuck to the essentials. "He's missing. Hasn't been seen since Thursday."

"Oh no."

"Unless, of course, you've heard from him."

"No, I have not."

"But you saw him that day, right?"

Collins considered that. "What is your interest, if I may ask?"

"His daughter asked me to find him."

"You're a detective?"

"Not hardly. Just a friend helping a friend out."

"I see."

He said nothing. Neither did I until it occurred to me that he had ducked my question. "You saw Randy last Thursday, right? I know he was here, he made a phone call from here." And maybe more than one, I realized.

"Thursday, Thursday," Collins murmured. "Yes, of course. The day of the big storm."

"Whatever." I felt that incomparable rush that you get when you're on to something. "What was he here about?"

The priest tipped his head back a bit, watching me, expression kind, perhaps even a bit amused. "You know I can't talk about things like that, Ben," he answered. "And besides, it's not really what you need to know."

I wanted to retort: Look, you be the preacher, and I'll be the detective, okay? But that would have been impertinent. I did my best to smile back. "Then what is it I really need to know, Father?"

"Where he was headed when he left here. And I can tell you that." He smiled. "Home."

†††

Another fond hope blown to bits. I mean, after seeing Neal Leopold I thought I had figured out what Randy's deal was. I hoped, upon meeting Father Dave, that he would confirm it. Instead he felt obliged to play coy and send me ricocheting back into the icy outdoors on yet another wild goose chase. "Home," my Aunt Lizzie's butt. No way did Randy go home last Thursday after seeing the padre. He had not been back there. I was sure of it.

Even so, I wheeled north toward Randy's Long Lake apartment. Might as well check it out again. Nothing else to do. I felt fatigue in my legs and back, a numbing of the spirit, the sour taste of having been laughed at. This was such a joke. I never liked going over the same unfruitful ground a second and third time. It always meant that I'd missed something. Had been less than brilliant. Had been, as Raeanne likes to say, "a mere mortal."

Feeling sour, I smoked a cigar. I went over Randy's chronology again, probing for soft spots. Propelled the Mustang north in the thick Telegraph Road traffic, piloting along between the high walls of plowed blizzard snow. Did the litany, each time ending up with "home." Which made no sense.

Unless.

What if home did not mean Randy's apartment? What if home meant

Redford Township, where he'd lived with Virginia and Shyla?

Well, now. This was more interesting. And it made all kinds of sense, given the other things Randy had done that day. But if he had gone there, Virginia would have mentioned it. Wouldn't she?

But she had not. Why not?

Perhaps because . . . because something really bad-ugly had happened?

Availing myself of a median crossover, I switched sides to southbound Telegraph and motored along, Redford-bound. I made fairly good time despite the old snow, new snow, and traffic. I thought about Virginia's flinty eyes, the set of the scowl on her face, the tone of utter contempt and loathing in her voice as she spoke of her errant husband. The sense I had had that this was a woman who threw things with grim purpose and deadly aim. I remembered how she had tried repeatedly to wave me off the case. Oh, my imagination did all kinds of things as the big Mustang wheels ate up several snow packed miles. I pictured Virginia aiming a pistol. Randy going down. Blood splattered a beige wall. His body wrapped in plastic, entombed under a snow-covered pile of boards behind the garage. . . .

Of course the scenario was dumb and obvious, but most real-life murders are just that. I played around with different elements as Tel-Twelve Mall approached. This was always one of the worst traffic choke spots in all of metro Detroit, and today was no exception. As the traffic lurched along in its stop-and-go fashion, I wound back the tape in my mind and replayed how it might have gone down. Randy leaving the church, inspired, fervent, anxious to get to her. Motoring south on Telegraph, just as I was doing. Except that this had been Thursday afternoon when the blizzard hit, the big Alberta Clipper, right? So he was in a hurry, trying to get there before everything shut down. He had come flying along here, and—

And just as I was doing now, Randy had approached the interlocking cloverleaves where Telegraph met Reuther Freeway/Lodge Freeway/Northwestern Highway.

But Thursday there had not been snowpack on the macadam and lines of crawling cars and walls of plowed snow on both sides and flurries flying in the air. Thursday had been, as Father Dave had said, "the day of the storm." The Alberta Clipper had struck right about the time Randy barreled south on Telegraph. There had been a howling wind and snow pouring down like porridge. The pavement had slickened up, and there'd been nothing on the sides of the road to stop him from—

And that's when it came to me.

Leaning forward, gripping the deep-dish Mustang wheel, I stared through the windshield. I thought about angles and distances and timing, the vastness of the cloverleaf. The great expanses of open land with its slopes and gullies and blind spots. I thought about Virginia Ryan again, too, but this time there was no gun in her hand, as I knew in my heart there had never been.

Hitting the brakes, I halted the Mustang in the left-hand lane, right in the middle of the cloverleaf. Traffic continued to pass on my right. I mashed the four-way lights, shut off the engine, and got out.

Instantly the wind tried to bite me through. I turned up the collar of my pea coat and buttoned it tight and jammed the cell phone in my back pocket. The wall of snow rose eight feet or more, a slanting slope of grayish white interspersed with big black icy chucks. Bracing myself, I began to climb up the wall of icy snow, virtually on all fours, freezing my hands as I clambered up, shoes slipping, fingers freezing as I fought for purchase.

I was halfway up when a male voice hollered from down below, "Hey, moron!"

Looking down, I saw a big beefy guy leaning through the window of his **whole [white?] Olds Intrigue. "What're you doing parking there, ya idiot? Jamming up all the traffic here!"

"Got business," I called back. "Possess your soul in patience. Jackass," I added, just for his information.

"You move that damn car," he bawled, "or I'll rearrange your face for ya!"

I hesitated. From inside came that dark chuckling feeling I remembered so well, the feeling of *all righty then, let's party*. And I thought about going back down there and dragging him through the window and using him for a pogo stick or something.

But "no rough stuff," Carole had said.

And I had promised.

And all the man wanted was a clear ride home.

So I grinned and waved. "Back in a minute," I called and, with final scrambling effort, propelled myself over the summit of the snowdrift and down the other side.

Stretched out before me was a rising snowy plain, truly tundra as far as I could see, unmarked by anything, manmade or otherwise. I was calf-deep in the icy white stuff, but down here it was loose and wet, biting like frozen fingers through the soles and sides of my utterly inappropriate shoes. My enthusiasm for my brainstorm began to wane. I mean, there was no evidence here, none that I could see. Unless you looked a certain way at the surface of the snow. Was there an unnatural unevenness there? Kind of like faint ruts, way way down? Hard to tell, especially in the gray light with flurries angling down. We'd gotten, after all, twenty-one inches of snow on Thursday. Plenty enough to cover tracks if he'd come skidding through here early enough.

But where would he have ended up?

The slope rose and then crested. From here I could not see what was beyond it. Quelling one more urge to turn around and get back into the nice warm Mustang, I trumped uphill through the knee-deep snow. It packed its way up under my shoes, causing my feet and lower legs to dampen and then numb. Hugging myself, I forced myself ahead, eyes on the prize, the crest of the slope. Beyond was a whole lot more white nothing. But this was a downslope, with several intermediate mounds, leading to what looked like a gully and another hill beyond. Amazing that this vast open area could exist here in the heart of a cloverleaf. Invisible to anyone passing by, especially with those walls of plowed snow alongside the roads.

Following the path of least resistance, I marched down the slope, aiming for the halfway point between two of the intermediate mounds. My legs were now numb from the knees down. The wind had picked up and was waging a serious attack on my coat. I hunched as I tromped along, hands fisted in the coat pockets. My chin was buried in the collar, mouth muttering monotonous oaths on the general theme of *the things I do, the things I do*. The snow fell thicker and dusk did, too. I did not realize how bad my vision was getting until I was barely twenty feet from the thing.

It was the first manmade object I'd encountered. It was a large, slanted rectangle—white, of course—being covered with snow except for just a black tip up high, the right angle of what appeared to be a rear fender.

My breath caught in my throat. Incipient hypothermia forgotten, I spread my arms and ran, high-stepping. The vehicle was nose-down, thrust like a blunt spear into what had to have been a sharp depression in the ground. Of course I could not tell that for sure, given the drifts of snow. As I drew nearer, I could see the whitish faint outlines of a rear wheel and a roofline. The ghostly silhouette of an urban assault vehicle, perhaps of the Ford Expedition variety.

Panting, I thrashed to a stop at the vehicle and brushed at the window. Peering in, I squinted long and hard. As my vision adjusted to the deeper dimness, I could just barely make out the interior white fuzzy dice hanging crazily from the sideways rearview mirror and, on the passenger side, the faint, crumpled outline of a body.

†††

So, it's true then," Shyla murmured, eyes downcast. "He did do all those things Virginia said."

"'Fraid so," I replied.

We stood in a hallway of the emergency room at Metro Detroit General. Around us bustled orderlies and nurses and people pushing gurneys bearing bodies, not all of them animate. The closed door in front of us said EXAM ROOM 2. NO ADMITTANCE. I was finally starting to thaw out and was leaving little puddles of melted snow on the linoleum floor around me.

Shyla shivered in her coat and hugged herself, half turned from me. "But why?" she asked softly.

I shrugged. "He's just a man. People do bad things sometimes. It's what happens." I could relate. I thought, but did not say, that Randy Ryan had shown all the signs of a man who had gotten just so sick of himself. I could relate to that, too.

"What's important," I added, "is he was turning things around, trying to make things right."

The young woman's pale face crumpled, and she tottered to me, engulfing herself in a big hug. "It's just so unfair!" she murmured into my neck through sobs. "Now he won't get the chance to finish the job."

I patted her back. "Don't be too sure of that, kid. Doc says he's got a fighting chance of—"

"Is this the room?" came a voice from behind me. We turned to see Virginia Ryan approaching, hatless, wearing a dark winter coat, short dark hair askew, lipless face pale, eyes icy as the outside. "Where is he?"

"What are you doing here, Virginia?" Shyla asked, disengaging herself from me.

"Your detective friend called me," the mom said. "Which is only right, since I'm still your father's wife, Jennifer. Surprised?"

Shyla's eyebrows arched. "Not that Ben called you," she said. "Surprised you'd care enough to show."

Virginia stepped closer to us and glanced at the door.

"How is he?"

"He's in a coma," I answered. "Was dehydrated. Core temp is low. But in a way the freezing cold actually helped him. Retarded the bleeding from his crash injuries."

"Will he live?" Virginia asked evenly.

"They won't say for sure, naturally," I answered. "Even if he does, he might lose some—"

The exam room door opened, and a nurse looked out at as. "Ms. Ryan?" Both women stepped forward. "Only one at a time," the nurse commanded.

Shyla shot her mom a look. "Can I go first, Mother?" she asked.

"Very well, Shyla."

The daughter went inside and closed the door. For long moments the mother and I just stood there. I could not help wondering if they were giving up on him in there, if I had been too late, with all my banging around and rookie mistakes. What Virginia was thinking was anyone's guess. Presently she asked with the usual abruptness, "Well, are you going to tell me?"

"Tell you what, ma'am?"

"What he was doing up there. How he got in this fix."

"Well, before the crash, he'd been to see his priest."

"Confessing all?" Virginia asked, trying to sound hard and cynical and not quite succeeding.

"Don't know about that," I answered easily. "I do know about some of the other things he did while he was with Father Dave. If you're ready to hear."

She stared at me. "Well?"

I looked at her. Ready or not, I thought, here it comes. "Well, from Father Dave's office he called his lady friend in Georgia and told her it was over. He called his boss to tell him he'd be making restitution for the money he stole. He called Detective Shanahan to tell him he was turning himself in. He called Shyla to tell her everything was getting fixed." Virginia's expression did not change. I thought my words were just bouncing off her, bouncing off the armor of her preconceived notions. "I know these things for a fact."

"And then," she said, "he took off from there, headed for the airport. He was blowing town. He did all that stuff to throw everyone off the scent—"

"That's one way to connect the dots," I cut in. "But there's another way."

She was looking at me intently. "Yes?"

"Number one, if he were headed for the airport, he'd have turned west. Instead, he kept going south. You know where he was bound for, Virginia. You know it in your heart."

"Where?" she asked, voice small.

"To your home. To see you. My guess is, to beg for your forgiveness."

Just then came Shyla's voice from inside the exam room. "*Yes!*"

Virginia blinked. Her throat worked. She cupped her mouth with a hand that trembled. I reached for the doorknob and opened the door. With a last glance at me, Virginia dashed through, and the door eased shut again.

Suddenly alone, I stared at the closed door. Reached out for the knob again, hesitated, let my hand drop. Under these circumstances the last thing they needed was me hanging around. I had never felt so suddenly useless. For a moment the unfairness of it blazed in my mind. Over already? Where was the applause, the admiration, the attaboys? Where were the simple thank-yous, for heaven's sake?

But this too I remembered from the old days. The better the job you've done for a client, the less you exist for them when the job is over. Once they're out of the woods, clients make haste to forget how desperate they were for your help. It's just human nature.

But that was okay, I thought, as I headed for the exit. I had, after all, promises to keep and better things to do. Such as go home and change out of my wet clothes and then pick up the girl of my dreams from her daycare.

Afterword

Thing is, something like this really happened. I swear. A few years ago, a metro Detroit newscaster disappeared after leaving his home to drive to work one morning. It was quite sudden and very mysterious. It took several days for someone to figure out that he'd lost control of his car, veered into that very same interchange (which is, as Perkins describes it, quite mammoth), and crashed in a way that rendered his vehicle invisible to anyone driving through.

This was in the *summer.* I changed the time of year to winter, convinced that, otherwise, readers would not find the proposition credible. (And if there's one thing I try not to mess with, it's suspension of disbelief.)

Otherwise, the tale is fiction from start to finish. Most of the characters are unique to the story. Having been on break from Perkins for five years, I had to decide what to do about the passage of time. My decision was and is to do, basically, nothing. We pick up right where we were, with Rachel not even a year old yet.

Still, things have changed. Carole Somers, Rachel's mom, is a judge (in Plymouth, if it matters). And old Ben is feeling the passage of time . . . but then, who isn't?

Sleeping Dog Lies

"Well," Darlene said brightly, checking her watch, "time for me to scoot, I'm afraid."

She rose, and George did also. "Too bad," I said, standing. "Night's young yet."

"Duty calls," George said, beaming proudly as he gave Darlene a hug.

"Should never have signed up to do these seminars," she said, round face mock-grumpy under the flowing red hair. "Especially right now, with the weather getting good." Darlene bussed me, hugged Raeanne, slid an arm around George. "Walk me out, honey?"

"Sure. Back in a minute," he tossed back at us. Arm in arm they strolled toward the restaurant exit.

Grinning, I sat back down. Our booth, semi-secluded, was candlelit and cozy, a comfortable distance from the noise of the crowded restaurant. Raeanne looked quietly radiant in the soft light. "So what's your take?" I asked her, lighting a cigar.

"They're very nice," she answered. "Her especially."

"Yeah, she's a regular sweetheart. He's a good guy too."

"Factory rat?" she asked.

"Years ago." I looked at her. "Good eye."

"Well, I'm an authority on the breed," she said, offhand, "being as I am in love with one."

"And who might that be?" I asked.

"Do you have to ask?" she said slyly.

"Oh. I getcha. I'm just not used to having a term like 'breed' applied to me," I explained.

"I said breed. I didn't say *good* breed," she said sweetly.

I looked at her. "Why do I even start with you, sweetheart?"

"Yes," she drawled lightly, "one would think you'd eventually learn." She steepled her thin fingers in front of her face. "And they're so *cute* together," she went on. "Both forty-somethings, well-seasoned, a bit on the stout side."

"Meow," I said, grinning at all about-120 pounds of her. "Plus both have red hair," I added. "Though most of his is gone."

"Meow," she echoed, giving my coarse black hair a rough affectionate tousle. Resting her hand on mine, she looked closely at me, amused. "I've never known you to socialize with clients."

"Mainly because they seldom invite me," I replied. George still had not come back into the restaurant. Suddenly I wished I had tagged along. I don't know what brought that thought on. He'd never needed protection, or asked for it. This was Ann Arbor's Depot Town, early Saturday evening, not exactly a hotbed of crime. And anyway my rough-stuff days were long gone. "Clients are not usually inclined to hang out with me, kind of things I get paid to do."

"What do you do for George?"

"Nothing heavy," I answered, exhaling smoke upward where the ceiling fan could catch it. "Mainly background checks on prospective employees. The odd skip trace. Fetch and carry. Whatever he wants. I'm what my daddy used to call George's 'hey-boy'. . . . Oh good, here he comes."

George Remmert returned to our table in his bounding, energetic gait. He was hefty, good-living, apple-cheeked, with a just-been-kissed smile on his large sunny face. Seating himself, he took a healthy belt of Burgundy, the dainty wine glass incongruous in his large knuckly hand. "God, I love that woman," he said expansively.

"Congratulations on your engagement," Raeanne said.

"Pretty nice rock you gave her there, old son," I observed.

George, beaming, nodded just once, and then looked at me. "I want you to check her out, Ben."

I blinked. "Whuh?"

"Check her out," George repeated. His smile was still there, but the gray eyes had gone shrewd. Purposeful. Presidential.

Raeanne's hand tightened on mine. I took a drag of cigar and laid it in the ashtray to go cold. "You suspect something, George?" I asked quietly.

"No no no," he said, waving my words away like gnats. "Darlene's a wonderful gal. The sweetest, most loving person I've ever known." The waiter, ever observant, scooted over and slid the leather check holder to George's elbow. Flipping it open, George scanned the check as he went on. "A: She's smart. B: She's educated. C: She's got ideals, she walks the talk. Could have had big jobs making big bucks, but she's worked for that substance abuse clinic since college, for Chrissake. Why? Because she believes in it."

"That's wonderful," Raeanne said quietly. "And D?" she prompted.

"D," George went in all seriousness, "she's active in her church. E: She works at the Crossroads soup kitchen once a week. She does these freebie seminars, like the one tonight. For parents of addicted kids. She even—she puts flowers on her mother's grave once a month. Drags me along."

"Okay," I said carefully. "So after four years—and now you're engaged to her—why do you—"

"Prudent step," he answered briskly, dealing twenties onto the bill. "Cheap insurance, that's all."

"Cheap?" I asked, smiling. "You don't know what I charge for this kind of thing."

"What I do know," he replied, smiling back, "is the size of the retainer check I write you every month."

Ten-four, and giddy-up. "Yes, sir. I'm on it."

"Good," he said, flipping the check folder shut.

I picked up my expired cigar and studied it. "Just one thing. Could be you'll have to hear things you'd rather not hear. You need to be prepared for that, sir."

"I don't expect anything of the sort," he replied, leaning back in his chair. "But thanks for the heads-up."

"And," I went on, "these things have a way of taking on a life of their own. Once I start poking around, information starts to flow, and it can be very hard to shut off."

"Wouldn't want to," he answered evenly. "Information is power. It is in fact what I am paying you to get."

"Yes, sir. So. What level we talking? Whole nine yards, or the quick sniff?"

George considered that then pushed his chair back and rose. "Quick sniff to start with," he decided, "and then we'll see."

"Whatever you say."

†††

Gunning the Mustang's 302 motor, I blew away a couple of trucks as we roared onto M-14. "So what do you make of George's assignment?"

"Surprised," Raeanne said after a moment. She always thinks before speaking. A rarity. "Not very trusting is he."

"Guess not. Thing is, he had that bad marriage. The bruises still show."

Since it was still light out—we'd had a very early dinner, thanks to Darlene's seminar—I could see every detail of Raeanne's delicate oval face. "So," she said deliberately, "were we invited to dinner out of friendship, and to celebrate their engagement? Or because he wanted to expose Darlene to you again before sending you into her backfield?"

"The first one, I'm sure." I glanced at her. "Got an issue, darlin'?"

She shrugged. "My problem is him turning you loose on Darlene's past without her knowing about it."

"Happens all the time in this work."

"In business things, I understand it. And in legal affairs, sure. But this is a matter of the heart, Ben."

I glanced at her. "It's not something I would recommend," I told her. "But I'm just the pointy end of his spear, so to speak."

"I know." She considered. "Thing is, when you dig long enough and deep enough, you're bound to find things. Darlene's forty-something, she's been around, there's gonna be dirt. Count on it."

"Not to worry," I assured her. "This is only the quick sniff. My guess is, she'll turn up roses, and then on to the next thing."

I bore east at the U.S. 23/M-14 split. The greening trees on the flattish landscape started to redden in the glow of the setting sun behind us. Raeanne was looking out her window, her tall slender form in absolute repose. I felt a surge of affection for her, this quirky enigmatic young woman, quietly loyal, confident, centered. "What're you thinking about, darlin'?"

"He said he doesn't suspect anything," she replied.

"Right."

She looked at me. "That's not true. No," she corrected herself quickly, "I don't mean that the way it sounds. He suspects something, but he doesn't *know* he suspects something. See? He senses something wrong about her."

"I get you."

"He's just too rational to admit it. Too hardheaded to acknowledge, even to himself, that he has that intuition."

"Which means—"

"There's something to find. Something she's hiding," she said quietly.

"Could be."

We drove for a bit in silence. Raeanne was worked up about this, more than I'd have expected. "Know what he should do?" she asked, turning to me. "He should just drop her right now."

"Really? Why?"

"Because he already doesn't trust her. Or he wouldn't have asked you to do this."

"Sweetheart, it's just a precaution—"

"Either you trust," she said with great precision, "or you don't. Trust is such a strange thing. Robust yet fragile, too. It's not renewable. Once you stop trusting, there's no getting it back. And he's stopped trusting her."

"I think this comes under the heading of 'trust, but verify.'"

"Shame on you," she said quietly, "spouting such a tired Republican wheeze. And a self-contradictory wheeze, at that." She turned away. A mile or two went by. Sometimes," she murmured, "I'm not such a big fan of the work you do."

"Me neither," I answered.

†††

I'd met Darlene Helms before. George had introduced her to me at his office, when she showed up late one workday just as George and I were wrapping up some business. Another time the three of us went out for a beer after work. And a few months earlier, George had connived with me to host a surprise 40th birthday party for her at my apartment while Raeanne was away on *Good Will Hunting.*

So I knew some things about Darlene already. Born and raised in Ecorse, a downriver factory community. Graduate of Eastern Michigan. Devout Episcopalian, some kind of lay minister for them. She was a substance abuse therapist and counselor for Lighthouse Home in Ann Arbor. Light wine drinker, junk food addict, passionate Detroit Pistons fan. No kids, never married.

Fairly routine, as was the quick sniff I did over the following week. Credit bureau turned up a clean Visa, a paid-off loan with Ford Credit, a mortgage on her modest house in Ypsilanti, and no derogatory. A consult with my mole on the state police revealed an intriguing failure on her part to observe NO RIGHT TURN ON RED signs, having racked up three such violations over the past couple of years. Nothing else.

Since she knew my mug and my car, too, I could not safely tail her. So I put Darryl Rockecharlie on the case. Though a big guy driving a not-exactly-unobtrusive mint-green '69 Caddy Deville, he is surprisingly deft on the shadow, and I'm sure Darlene never noticed a thing. Darryl tracked her to work, to the grocery, to client's homes, and to dates with George. He followed her to church and saw her suited up, helping the priest pass out communion. He kept a meticulous list of times and places in blocky pencil print.

"All places she was supposed to be at," George confirmed, sliding the list along the bar back to me.

"That's good," I ventured.

"Yes, it is." George drained his dark, and Gail, the barkeep, served him up another. "What's next?"

I shrugged. "That's your quick sniff."

"I see."

We were sitting at the bar. Aside from Gail, no one was near us, it being barely noon. I waited out George's blank stare as long as I could. "What do you want me to do, sir?"

"What's the next level?"

I wanted to advise him to give it a rest. But, I reminded myself, he's the boss, and this is your work; *this is what you do.* "Get into the history. Job, education, family, all that jazz."

280 | ROB KANTNER

"Prior involvements?" he prompted, sipping his beer.

"I imagine she has some. I haven't turned up any so far."

He set his glass down. "Only one serious one," he said briskly. "Guy named Ed McNabney. Lives in Canton, sells cars for Winston Auto in Wayne, remarried now. Darlene lived with him nine years."

I smiled. "Sounds like you know more about him than I'm likely to find out."

He shrugged. "She's told me a lot about him. They still talk from time to time. She says she's still friends with everyone she's ever been involved with."

"No reason to doubt it," I said. I could not resist the temptation to steer him. "Look, George, if she's been that open about that kind of stuff, what could she be hiding?"

George got out his wallet and sifted bills. He spoke so softly I could barely hear him. "You know what she does, she keeps her eyes open when we kiss."

I groped for a response, and came up empty. "I'll do whatever you want," I said. "Just tell me—"

"Check McNabney out," he cut in, throwing a five on the bar. "Take it to the next level," he added, heading for the door. "Get back to me," he requested, and left.

†††

I had to wonder about George. Which was not unusual. Detective work is a process of focused wondering. It's easy to get carried away and start wondering about the client instead of the case.

But the more you do that, the longer it takes to get done, and, more to the point, paid. So I soldiered on to the next level. There was no job history to research, since Darlene had been with Lighthouse Home for 20-odd years. I did check out her educational credentials: Master of Arts at Eastern Michigan, Magna, '79. Pretty impressive, I thought, graduating college at the tender age of 20.

Next back was high school. On the way there I stopped at Winston Auto in Wayne. Ed McNabney, they told me, had left there a year before to go move iron at Car Town in Dearborn Heights. I found him there, working the lot. And, once he got past a half-hearted effort to trade my '71 Mustang for a Dodge Durango, he was willing to talk. I don't think my glib insurance investigation cover story even registered.

"Good kid, Darlene," he said, lighting a cigarette. He was whip-thin and a bit bug-eyed, as if jacked on a quart of joe. He wore blue Banlon and tan slacks and more hair on his arms than his head. I don't think he ever once looked at me. Instead he monitored the lot, watching pedestrians walking the busy Michigan Avenue sidewalk and cars slowing down to look at the gaily decorated vehicles for sale. "Long time we were together."

"From when to when, about?" I asked.

"Till what, four years ago now. I got married last year," he added, flashing his ring.

"Congratulations. Now, some of these questions, they may get uncomfortable for you. I know you and Darlene are still friendly, but—"

"Makes you think that?"

I looked at him. "You still chit-chat back and forth, it says here."

He shook his head slightly. "No. I bumped into her at Fairlane one day, I don't know, year or two ago. Aside from that, no contact at all."

Hm. I decided to cut to the chase. "Why'd y'all break up, after all those years?"

"Thing just ran out of gas."

"Outta gas, huh?"

"Mm-hm."

He seemed content to leave it there. I was not. "No other girlfriends for you."

"No."

"Or for her."

He smiled briefly. "Nope."

"Boys either."

"Not for either of us." He smiled briefly, flicked ash.

"Well, what happened? Did she snore? Clip her toenails during meals? Smack you around? Drink your last beer?"

"No," he said softly. "It just all dwindled out."

Clearly, if he had any dirt on Darlene, he wasn't about to dish it to me. But I pressed him anyway trying to get, through him, at least a sense of her. A peek at what she had been like pre-George. I started out by laughing. "Hell, man. Last time I had one go down, she threw all my clothes out the second-floor window. Without opening it first."

That brief smile again, on-off. "Yeah, well, I've had that too. But not with Darlene." He sighed. "I figured, it was her personal stuff hitting right along then, triggered it."

Getting somewhere finally. "What personal stuff?"

"Well, she hit the big four-oh. Rough time. And then her dad died a couple weeks later. I guess that was the last straw. We came home from the funeral, and she told me it's over."

Wait a minute. "This was when?"

"Four years ago, about."

"When she hit forty."

"Yep." He stiffened abruptly. Out in the lot, a young couple was circling a relatively clean Dodge Intrepid. Evidently he saw something in their body language that I didn't. "Gotta go," he said, with a glance at me. "Anything else?"

"No, not right now. Thanks for the help."

"You're welcome." He hesitated. "Always thought it was odd. Our time together ended with a funeral, her dad's. And it started with another one. Her mom's."

"Yeah," I said. "Odd."

†††

Darlene Helms was turning out to be more interesting than I'd thought. I mean, not everyone turns forty years old twice.

Who would want to? Two rounds of death jokes, black balloons, hearses at the curb, all that jazz.

What we have here, I thought, could be just a simple case of vanity. She shed Ed and sheared a few years off her official age, it being a handy time, between guys and all.

But still.

I motored on down to Ecorse and paid a visit to Ecorse Edsel Ford High School. It's an old four-story granite pile, a broken-bat squibber from the river, its steep peaks, towers, and turrets sooty from decades of factory pollution from nearby River Rouge, Wyandotte, and Zug Island. School was in session, and the principal's office was busy, but they started me on the expected sequence of hand-offs. I wound up in the counselor's office, in the detention carrel, feeling right at home, the 1974 yearbook in my hot little fists. Flip-flip-flip and there was Darlene, in the senior section under the aitches. She had been round-faced back then also, but wore her hair long. The cheery smile looked just a tad forced, as it often does when you're sitting in a hot studio for what seems like days.

Activities showed nothing for her. Her beam did not appear in any of the group shots for the Honor Society, cheerleaders, French Club, or track team. Didn't trouble me greatly. Maybe, I thought idly, her activities were, like mine way back when, not precisely yearbook fodder. I returned it to the student-employee and was halfway out the door when another thought made me stop and squint.

If you're gonna do a job, do it right.

So back I went and rescued the yearbooks for '73, '72, and '71. Sat back down in the carrel and flipped the '73 to the juniors section.

No Darlene.

Checked the whole rest of it. Nada.

Just to be thorough, I checked '73 and '72 also. No joy.

Now this was curious.

I handed in those books, got the '74 again, turned to the aitches in the senior section and wrote down some names.

†††

"And that's not all," I ended, and paused.

You sling the revelations too fast, and the client usually stops hearing them. So it's good to take an intermission, let the client's brain catch up, absorb, or, to use Raeanne's term, "process." George was quicker than most. He gestured wordlessly, fingers flicking toward himself in a silent "Come on," and eased back in his big executive chair.

"She never graduated," I said.

That made George blink. He stared at me intently, brow furrowed, jaw set. "She didn't?"

On the floor at my feet, Rachel ceased her inexplicable organizing of George's pencils, gathered them up, and flung them across the office with a triumphant "Ah-ha!" I picked her up and held her squirming in my arms. "Not from Edsel Ford, anyways," I added. "It's the only high school in Ecorse. So who knows. Could mean anything, or nothing."

Rachel's struggles were getting vigorous and vocal, so I set her back down on the floor. She scooted to the scattered pencils and began picking them up, chanting unintelligible things. George looked thoughtful. "So there are three difficulties," he said. "A: Instead of going to Ecorse High all the way through, she transferred in for her senior year only. B: She never graduated from high school."

"Right. And Number C is—"

"She's forty-four instead of forty."

"Apparently. Not that big a deal."

"Makes her older than me," he said matter-of-factly. Gazing at the backs of his big hands, he mused, "Maybe I misunderstood her," he said. "About graduating from there."

Not likely, I thought. "Could be," I said.

From elsewhere in the building, I could hear loud repetitive grinding sounds as machines bent, shaped, and formed metal.

"She told me she was sixteen," George murmured. "Child prodigy type." I did not answer. He looked at me. "What would you do?"

I'd been asked this many times, over the years. In my experience, clients usually did the exact opposite of whatever I advised. Still, George was the boss and entitled to an honest answer. "I'd sit down with her and say 'Look, darlin', there's some things that are confusing me, and we need to clear the air.'"

George's intent squint softened, and he smiled. "That's perfect, Ben. That's exactly what I'll do."

Well, well. "'Kay. Let me know. Hey Rook!" Rachel, seated cross-legged and organizing her pencils in various arrays on the floor, looked up at me with a preoccupied scowl. "Let's go. Uncle George is busy."

"No," she proclaimed, blue eyes big and certain.

"That's right, honey, stick around," George said, grinning at her as he reached to his phone console. "We'll just deal with this right now." He mashed the speaker button, got a dial tone, and hit a speed-dial. It must have been Darlene's private line, because she answered it herself. "Hi, love," he said.

"Well hi!" she said, so pleased at his call that she more sang the words than said them. "What're you doing?"

Looking at me, George placed his index finger to his lips, frowning at me until I nodded understanding. His voice, when he spoke, was much cheerier than his expression. "Opening my mail. Guess what I got."

"What's that, sweetie?"

"Invitation," George said, "to my 25th high school reunion. September at the Pontch."

George's desktop was absolutely clear except for implements. No mail of any kind.

"That sounds wonderful!" she said. "Are we going?"

"I suppose, if you'd care to."

"I'd love to!" came her voice through the speakerphone.

Rachel, still cross-legged on the floor, continued sorting her pencils. George seemed to sigh and cast his gaze toward the ceiling. "What about yours? That'll be coming up next year, won't it?"

"Sure will," she said. "I don't think I want to go, though. Ecorse is so different now."

George eyed me. "But you must have a lot of friends from those days. Four years of high school, lots of fond memories."

"You'd think so," she said, very matter-of-fact. "But it was more like a four-year jail term. Graduation night was my discharge, and I don't look back."

George looked bleak, but his words were brisk. "Whatever. I'll put us down for mine. See you later?"

"Sure. Bye-bye! I love you."

"Same here."

George mashed the phone button, folded his big arms, eased back in his chair, gray eyes on me all the while. I gathered up Rachel, returned his pencils, gave him a salute with my free hand as I went out the door. George didn't say a word. He didn't have to.

†††

"George Remmert."

"Your duty sleuth, reporting in, sir."

"From where?"

"Oakland County courthouse. Evidently she was not born up here."

"Why check up there? She said she was born at Women's in Detroit. That's Wayne County—"

"I checked there first. No record of her there."

"I see."

"Not for '59 or '54 or any other year of the Eisenhower administration."

"Did you check in—"

"Yep. No record in Macomb or Washtenaw counties either."

"You've been moving around."

"It's a livin'."

"Mm-hm. So not only did Darlene not graduate from Ecorse High, she's not even from this area."

"Well, her family was here, I know that. I checked city directories, found her dad's address in Taylor."

"Sure it's the same one? Helms is a pretty common—"

"Robertson Clifton Helms was the name she gave as her father's, on her app at Eastern. I found record of him in Ecorse Township."

"Very good."

"Evidently the Helms lived at the Ecorse Township address from the early fifties till '95 or so. Which ties in with when Ray said her dad passed on. Went over there and did a door-to-door, but nobody remembers them."

"Neighborhood turning over?"

"Big time."

"So what now, Ben?"

"You tell me. I'm tapped out."

"I need it all now. Chapter and verse."

"I can understand that, George, but I'm just a tad lacking in leads at the moment."

"Wish I could help. But this is your skill set, not mine."

"'Skill set'? That's what you call this that I've got?"

"Yes."

"Skill set. I'll be damned."

"It's just a term, Ben—"

"No, what I mean is, I just thought of something."

"A lead?"

"More like a thought. You said you visited her mom's grave, where's it at?"

"Woodmere. Fort Street at—"

"Oh, I know that bone yard real well. Better than I care to."

"Can't imagine what you'd find there."

"I think of cemeteries as 'clues in marble and granite.' Where's the grave at, in there?"

"How would I know?"

"You said Darlene dragged you there bunch of times."

"Yes, but I wasn't—"

"Paying attention, okay."

"It's a stone's throw beyond a kind of medium-sized hill. Near a pond. Sort of to the right."

"Thanks. I'll just jot that down."

"No need for sarcasm, Ben. Woodmere's a fruitless idea, trust me."

"George. Please. This is my skill set, not yours."

"So it is."

†††

Woodmere Cemetery is officially in the city of Detroit, but it crowds the Dearborn line like it's dying to get out. It's several hundred acres of well cared for meadows, ponds, and wooded bluffs. From the highest of these you can see the smokestacks of Mr. Ford's River Rouge vast factory complex—what we call simply "the Rouge"—and the infamous overpass on which Mr. Ford's thugs beat up Mr. Reuther and friends during the troubles.

Over there looked busy. But the cemetery, on this regular working day, was deserted.

And of course the cemetery office was closed.

Logical.

Lacking any other plan, I drove around a little, glancing this way and that, hoping for luck-lightning to strike. And I thought about Raeanne. In the days since our Ann Arbor double date with George and Darlene, things had been a tad strained between us. I knew why. This George/Darlene case was jostling old baggage. Neither Raeanne nor I had ever gotten the relationship thing right. We were both walking wounded, limping out of histories about which both of us were guarded. She'd told me some things, I'd told her some. But we were, by unspoken agreement, making our way slowly, refraining from going what old H.R. Haldeman called "the full hang-out route." This case of George's, involving truth, lies, and trust, cut way too close to the bone for the early and gingerly state of our relationship. She didn't want to discuss it, but felt compelled to ask. I didn't want to lay it all out for her, but felt required to share. It was like we were having two conversations: one spoken, the other sensed. And it was not comfortable.

I wanted to take her and hold her tight and whisper things in her ear—

The cell phone screamed. I grabbed it and was mashing the ON button when I came around a steep curve and nearly collided with a riding lawn-mower.

I screeched, he swerved, we halted with inches to spare as my phone flew to the floor. The mower driver, a burly African-American in twill and Tigers ball cap, gaped, grinned, and put his big hands on his head. "Wow!" he barked over the engine noise. "That was close. Good reflexes, man!"

"Sorry," I hollered back, "I wasn't paying attention. When does the office open?"

"By and by," he called.

I knew what that meant. They operated on the Detroit version of what Raeanne calls "Texas time." I had a brainstorm. "Looking for a grave."

Idling the riding mower engine, he answered, "Lots of 'em around."

Everyone's a comedian. "Particular one," I modified. "Helms."

"Helms?"

"I know there's a blue million graves in here—"

"Helms, oh sure," he said, dead serious. "U-turn right where you're at, bear left at the fork, all the way to the bottom of the hill. They're on the left, second plot in."

"Seriously?"

"What's the problem?" he retorted, mock-serious. "Can't follow simple instructions?"

"Certainly. It's most definitely part of my skill set."

"Then have a nice day." He smiled, actually doffed his ball cap, revved up his engine and roared on.

†††

And I found it.

Sort of.

The plot was right where the lawn man said it would be. The stone was a black and high polished rectangle, about the size of a double-bed headboard.

It grew out of turf that was deep, green, and well cared for, under the protective arms of a big oak. It said HELMS in big capital letters.

The rest of the engraving was spare, to say the least. Like the majority of stones in the cemetery, it listed two people.

The name on the left was the one I recognized:

Barbara Hoyt Helms

1925—1986

Darlene's mom. Name and death date fit my information. The other name, the one on the right, was the head-scratcher.

Mary Hoyt Yats

1928—1969

I stared at it for quite a while. Walked back to the Mustang, brooding, and picked up the cell phone. Whoever had called had left a voice mail; I'd check it later. I walked back to the grave and lighted a cigar.

Who the heck was Mary?

Probably Barbara's sister, the birth names being identical. But even if so, why was it Mary doing the big dirt nap beside Barbara instead of Robertson Clifton Helms, husband of Barbara, father of Darlene?

And where, by the bye, was Robertson, anyhow?

On a whim, I roamed the section in the immediate vicinity of the Helms grave. And by golly I found him, about thirty feet away, under a stone of his own. Robertson Clifton Helms, 1922—1995. Ka-ching.

Back I went to the Helms grave. Besides its occupants, and the mysterious name Yats, something else was niggling at me, and after a moment I had it.

The side of the plot under the name of Barbara, Darlene's mother, was empty.

The other side, beneath the name of Mary Hoyt Yats, was adorned with a fairly fresh arrangement of flowers in a glass vase. And next to it stood one of those blue-and-white statues of Madonna. The saint, not the singer.

The grave of Mary Hoyt Yats, whoever she was, obviously got regular loving attention. Not so Barbara's. And Robertson's, I verified with a quick return visit, clearly hadn't been visited or cared for in years, if ever.

†††

"Might I ask, Mr. Perkins," Father Spencer inquired, "how you traced these people to our church?"

"According to the death notices in the paper," I answered, "Mr. and Mrs. Helms both were buried out of here. Were they parishioners?"

"They were," the neat little priest said quietly.

Well, he could have said that ten minutes before, when I told him why I was visiting St. Eligius Church. But this was not the prototypical hail-fellow-well-met Irish type of priest, the sort who, as in the cozy mysteries, supplies the sleuth with oodles of info. Father Spencer was more of a real world sort: one whose default reaction to even the most innocent approach was suspicion.

A hesitant, if not hostile, witness. Meaning I'd have to ask leading questions.

"Did you officiate at Mr. Helms's funeral?" I asked.

"I did."

"And Mrs. Helms?"

He smiled briefly. "That was a long time ago. I've quite forgotten."

I nodded. From the priest's tidy wood, book-lined office, I could hear a kids' choir rehearsing elsewhere in the church. They were struggling with a particular melody—start and stop, start and stop. Sort of like detective work.

"What about Mary Hoyt Yats?" I asked.

"I cannot help you there," Father Spencer said, folding his hands neatly in his lap. "I was not here in 1969."

"Maybe there's records, though," I ventured.

"Maybe there are," he observed.

I waited, and when he did not add anything, I said, "I need all the information I can get on anyone in the family. Could you do some checking for me?"

"I could."

"Um . . . soon? As in today?"

He was motionless except for his eyes. "I'm not quite certain I understand the urgency."

I sighed. "The inheritance, if still unclaimed by Labor Day, will be escheated to the state. That would be unfortunate for Ms. Yats's heirs."

The priest's eyes were unimpressed. "As well as for you," he observed. "Because you no doubt collect a percentage of the inheritance for your trouble."

So that was his beef. At first I was irritated, then I was amused. It's not every day I'm accused of being greedy for a nonexistent commission from a nonexistent inheritance. "We must all make a living," I answered humbly. "But my principals are generous. I'm sure they'd recognize your assistance with a contribution."

Though he did not respond with a chorus of alleluias, he did become visibly more comfortable. "How do I reach you?"

"Be glad to wait, Father."

"I'm afraid that's impossible. I conduct our healing service in just a few minutes."

290 | ROB KANTNER

In this work you learn when to push and when to ease up. I smiled. "Here's my card," I said, extending it. "Let me know as soon as you can, will you?" He took it and nodded. "On Mary," I added, "and anyone else in the Hoyt, Yats, or Helms families."

†††

It was noon already, and I had not been to my real job yet. On my way west I did a bunch of reaching out, and touched no one. George Remmert was out on the shop floor. Raeanne, who was temping on afternoons that month at National Steel, was in some kind of quality circle meeting. Carole was in court. Rachel couldn't come to the phone. I had just mashed END for the last time when the phone whistled in my hand. "Mr. Perkins?" came an unfamiliar male voice.

"Ben here."

"Joe Hass. I'm sorry about the phone tag, I've been running WFO."

I squinted. "WFO?"

"Wide, uh . . . wide open. What can I do you for?"

The fog cleared, if only barely. "Oh, yeah. Are you the Joseph X. Hass that attended Ecorse Edsel Ford High?"

"That's right."

Ooh. Rush. "Graduated in '74?"

"I did. How do you know that?"

"Found your name in the yearbook. Got a question for you."

"Shoot."

"Do you remember a girl named Darlene Helms?"

After the briefest hesitation, he said, "Sure. How'd you know?"

"Your name and hers are close in the alphabet," I explained. "I figured, you know, kids often get seated alphabetical, maybe—"

"Yeah, we knew each other. Same homeroom senior year," he told me.

"What can you tell me about her?"

"Oh, man. Long time ago." I had the sense that he was stalling. "What's this about?"

What the heck, you come up with a good con, stick with it. "Inheritance, maybe."

"Big bucks involved?"

"I really can't go into it," I said self-importantly.

"Well, I'm in investments," he said. "I could do her some good, put that dough to work for her."

"I'll pass that along," I promised. "What can you tell me about her?"

"Um . . . not much." He paused. "She was a good kid. I didn't know her all that well. She was new that year."

"Where from?"

"I don't know. Transferred in from somewhere. I don't remember."

Shoot, and *shoot*. "Can you try to remember?"

"I don't know, I really don't." Pause. "Took her out a couple of times. Just casual, you know. She was real bright, real cheery. I remember that. Is any of this helping?"

Not really. "You're doing great."

"It's about all I know, Ben." He really did seem regretful. "I don't think I ever saw her after graduation. She wasn't at the reunion back in '94, I know that."

"'Kay. If you think of anything else, will you call me?"

"Of course."

Not, I added.

Well, I admit it was a long shot. Of the six people close to Darlene Helms in the alphabet, I'd tracked down two now. The previous one didn't remember Darlene at all. I got the sense that she had been a sort of "stealth" student . . . slipped in her senior year, slipped away without graduating. And then constructed an Ozzified facade to cover it all up.

The question was: Why?

†††

Fortunately, things were as under control at the Norwegian Wood maintenance office as they ever were. Half the job tickets were completed and back in my box. The remaining ones were ongoings that wouldn't get done that day anyway. I did my "management by wandering around" to make sure there wasn't too much smoking 'n' joking going on. Upon return to my office I found Shyla Ryan, our college intern, waiting for me. She was smoking a cigarette and had Ani DiFranco on the boombox.

"Fax for you," she said, indicating a sheet that she'd placed on my chair, my desk being, well, a tad cluttered.

"Good, thanks, kid," I answered, picking it up.

Shyla stubbed out her smoke and drifted toward the door. "Marge said to tell you you're not supposed to get personal faxes at the company office."

I looked into her sunny knowing face and said kindly, "Tell Marge for me that she'd make a great dominatrix if she'd lighten up a little."

She laughed, waved, left. I switched the box back to 'ABX and then looked at the fax. It was on St. Eligius letterhead and began with an address to which my "principals" could send the promised donation.

Approximately eighty-two seconds later I was in the Mustang, headed north.

†††

"Sister Bay?" George repeated.

"Yep. She ever mention that to you?"

"No," he said definitely. "Never. Are you certain?"

"Priest at St. Eligius dug up some records," I said. I steered with one hand, held a cigar in my teeth, braced the phone between shoulder and ear, and picked up the fax with my other hand. I'm no throwback; I can multitask with the best of 'em. "Found out Darlene joined his church in late '73. For bona fides, she displayed a baptismal cert, dated January 1956, from St. Elmo the Worker Church in Sister Bay."

At the other end I heard a long exhale. I felt badly for him. After a moment he said, "So you're headed there."

"Just getting on 96 now. I can be there before the offices close."

"Good work, Ben."

"Thanks." I hesitated. "No joy in this, sir."

Pause. "Get it done."

"You da man."

I mashed END and tossed the phone onto the other bucket seat, overly hard. Father Spencer's fax had gone on to say that there was no information about Mary Hoyt Yats, the mysterious grave-mate of Darlene's mother. I put all wondering on hold for now and focused on driving—I wanted to get back by suppertime if I could—

The phone screeched. I mashed SND. "Ben."

"Yeah hi, it's, uh, Joe Hass."

And somehow—somehow—I instantly knew that I'd been expecting this call. "Sure, Joe, what's cooking?"

Dead silence. It dragged on so long I thought we'd lost the connection. "Is that a joke?" he asked then, tone strangled. "Someone told you about the fire?"

"No. Just an expression." He was a full sentence ahead of me, but I caught up. "What fire?"

He steadied on. "This goes no further," he began.

How many times have I heard that. "Sure, no prob."

"And I don't *know* anything for sure—"

"Joe," I said patiently, "could we just skip the disclaimers and get to it?"

"All right. Back then," he said softly, "I took Darlene out a couple of times, like I said. What I didn't tell you was that she got . . . *interested* in me. More so than I was in her. Anyway, I finally told her, hey, this isn't going anywhere, let's just be friends—"

"To which she did not take kindly?"

"Well, that's not it exactly. She seemed okay. But. . . ."

"But what, Joe."

"Week or two later," he said finally, "it was late spring, I remember that—our garage burned down. Kennel too, and all of the—"

"I get the picture," I said faintly.

"There was no way we could get to them in time," he said shakily. "They were sleeping in there, and the whole place went up—"

"Joe, please," I commanded. "was it Darlene who—"

"I don't know!" he said. I could hear the echoes of that old anguish in his voice, even now. "It was written up as mysterious causes. No suspects. But I just . . . I just had this . . . I went to her, and I took her aside. And I asked her straight out."

"What did she say?"

"Oh, she denied it. She seemed shocked. Then she got mad. And then she cried and cried."

"Uh-huh."

"I felt bad," he said, sounding tired now. "I told her, let's just forget it."

"Okay."

"Just thought you should know. For whatever, I mean, whatever."

After a moment of careful thought, I asked, "So now, these years down the road, Joe—what do you think about that fire now?"

When he answered, I could barely hear him over the cell phone distortion. "There was something scary in her eyes. Something . . . not . . ." He cleared his throat. "She is not someone that I have missed."

"And the fire?"

"I don't *know*. I'm not *sure*."

I did not report that to George. At least not then. Give him time, I told myself. Go easy with the revelations. I did call Raeanne. We had a nice talk. She asked me how the case was going. I said fine.

†††

In Michigan we like to name our towns after geographic features, Detroit ("the strait") being the best example. Unfortunately, in some cases we've let our imaginations get the better of us and named towns after geographic features that don't exist.

Sister Bay, for instance. It's smack dab in the middle of the mitten, with not a bay to be seen for hundreds of miles around.

But for an out-state outpost, Sister Bay looked like a right pleasant place as I rolled past the city limits on U.S. 270. They even had helpful signs directing me to the Ferdinand County government offices, which struck me as a good place to start.

"You're welcome to search," the clerk told me, "but you'll have to do it yourself. We're short-handed here."

"That's fine," I answered. "Just give me a tube, and I'll—"

"Tube?" she repeated blankly. "We're strictly manual. Everything's in ledger books: births, deaths, marriages. You may need a while."

I needed, it turned out, just one hour.

The newspaper office, on the other hand, was fully computerized. I was in and out of there in a half.

And headed for home as the red sun dived for the horizon.

†††

After a long, long pause, George eased back in his big executive chair. "Tell me how you pieced it all together," he said quietly.

That's our George, always curious about process. There was a larger reason for his request too, a deeper reason, I felt. Hearing about the process would give him time to absorb the information I had just presented to him.

And, maybe, to decide what to do about it.

"I went up there with Mary Hoyt Yats's name and 1969 death date," I told him. "And I had Darlene's baptism date of January '56."

"Right."

From George's dim office I could hear the sounds of his plant's second shift in action: overhead cranes, hi-los turning, and boring machines shooting sparks. The sounds of things being made: parts, money, livings.

"I figured if Darlene was baptized in one of fifty-six, she must have been an infant," I went on. "I mean, she says she's forty, the dates point more toward forty-four, I figured she can't be much older than that. So I checked the births for the months prior to one-fifty-six, and I found her."

"And you found her mother, too," George said quietly. "Mary Hoyt Yats."

"Yep. Darlene was born Darlene June Yats. Daughter of Mary, and of Ertman Yats of Sister Bay."

"So the woman we all thought was Darlene's mother—Barbara Helms—"

"Was her aunt."

George was so motionless I could barely tell he was breathing.

"Checked the death records then," I went on. "Went to the ledger books for 1969. And I found her. Mary Hoyt Yats deceased June 8, 1969."

"Yes," he said softly.

"And of course because it's a ledger book system, the deaths are listed in chronological order," I told him. "So besides Mary, there was Ertman Yats, June 8, 1969. Ertman Yats, Jr., June 8. Duane—"

George held up a hand, dropped it wearily. In the dimness of his office he looked whiter than pale, his burly form somehow frail, as if he had just been worked over with ball bats.

"That was it for the county office, pretty much," I went on. "The only other thing I could find was a probate court proceeding, in re Darlene June Yats, for the fall of '69. But they wouldn't let me see the file. Said it was a juvenile action and sealed."

"So you went to the newspaper then."

"Yes, sir. They had the rest of it. They were very helpful."

"I can just imagine," George murmured. "Did you tell them where she is?"

"No."

"Why?"

"To protect you."

"How does that protect me?"

"I'm sure they'd love a follow-up story, all these years later," I explained. "If the media machine comes down on her head, could drag you into it too."

"Right," he said, sounding distracted. "You're right. Thanks."

I lumbered to my feet. "I'm really sorry, old son."

He looked away. "Not your fault. You helped me. I'm grateful."

I could not tell if he wanted company, or to be alone. I asked, "So what are you going to do?"

He did not answer or move so much as a muscle, for a long, long time. Then he turned toward me, swiveling his whole body. His grin stretched across his round, normally jovial face, so tight you could almost see the skull beneath. "I'll review it all with her," he said overly loudly and with cheer that sounded brittle. "It won't be a problem. A: I love her. B: We're engaged. C: All that was a long time ago." He nodded. "We'll put it behind us." He took a deep breath. "And we'll go on."

†††

Darlene Helms showed up at my place three nights later.

I was out on my deck, fixing to barbecue for the women of my life. The younger one was there already, sitting in her highchair, noshing on potato chips, guzzling at a Barney Rubble juice bottle. Kicking her bare feet, dark blue eyes alight under the explosion of curly blond hair, she chanted "Muh-MA" over and over. Carole, Rachel's mom, had told me Rachel's chant when at her house was "Dad-DEE." It seemed the absent parent was one of her favorite topics.

I was just lining up the barbecue tools and fixing to start up the charcoal when I saw Darlene come around the corner of the building. The ground was much lower there, plunging from the apartment building down a grassy slope toward a grove of trees that backed the property. "Hi," she called, tone friendly. "I thought you were here. I buzzed but you didn't answer."

"Been out back here," I said. I was surprised to see her. Then I wasn't.

My guess was that she had had a talk with George.

"Can I come up?" she asked.

"Why not."

I watched her ascend the wood stairs the eight feet or so from the yard up to the deck. She looked nice in light slacks, a sleeveless white shirt, and sandals. A small handbag hung by a shoulder strap. Her thick red hair was bunned up high in back, accentuating the good lines of her round face. Her smile was fixed, perhaps too fixed. Her eye contact, while kindly, seemed to me glassy and forced.

Or maybe, knowing what I did, I was reading into it.

Though an inveterate hugger, she did not offer me one. I did not think to offer her a drink.

"Well, hi, baby," she cooed, reaching out to caress Rachel's cheek. That's when I noticed that the engagement ring was gone. My daughter pulled back, giving Darlene what looked to me like a hard unafraid stare. "Grumpy girl today?" Darlene sang, turning to me with a laugh.

"Just metcha," I said. You sure could tell Darlene had never been a parent. I took and squirted charcoal lighter on the pyramid of coals. Flaring a wood match on my thumbnail, I fired the pyre. Darlene paced the deck briefly, looking around, beaming. "What a great place! You're so lucky, Ben."

"Thanks. Comes with the job," I shrugged, lighting a cigar with the match.

She leaned against the railing and crossed one leg over the other. Just another chum dropped by for a neighborly chat. "I talked to George," she said. Glanced at the flames.

"How's he doing? Haven't seen him lately."

"He dumped me," she said evenly.

I puffed smoke. "Sorry, kid."

She looked at me closely, saw what she expected to see, and nodded understanding. "It's just . . . you have to understand. I'm different now. A whole other person. It was so long ago."

Darlene's expression, normally cheery, was a mask of hurt now, bravely bearing up. I saw her glance at the charcoal flames again. Stepping to the grill, I closed the hood. "Is that what you said to George, when he first confronted you with this?" She looked away in silence. "Don't tell me, let me guess," I said presently. "You tried to deny it."

She took a deep breath. "Yes. I admit that. When he . . . when he first brought it up to me, my response . . . my responses . . . what I said to George did not comport with reality."

Nineties for "I lied."

"But that's not the point," she went on, deliberate, reasonable. "The point is that the sad little girl back then . . . she is not the me that I am now."

"Well, that's good," I answered.

"And I've worked so hard on myself," she went on, more assured now. "My life . . . my whole *life* has been about healing, and growth, and making amends."

"George has said." Rachel had gone quiet. Forefinger in her mouth, she was watching us intently.

"And anyway," Darlene said, "I don't know how much about the story you know—"

"Enough."

"Then you know about . . . about the abuse, right?" she tumbled on. "The physical and the mental abuse. And what my—what my dad did to me—and . . . so many *years* of it. My life was such a dangerous and ugly and awful place." She nodded at me, eyes bright with furious certainty. "And I know, I know, yes, I did things, hideous things. The drugs, the alcohol, the violence. But I was a kid, Ben. A *kid*. I was not in my right mind. And you know what else? I don't even remember setting the fire. Not a glimmer. I admitted it finally because they had evidence—I mean, I know I *had* to have done it—but I don't remember any of it. That's how far gone I was."

"It's a sad case," I replied. By the smoldering grill, the sharp tines of the meat fork glinted in the sun. I ambled over there, as if to check the grill.

"But then I went to Harbor Springs Center," Darlene said. "And I got straightened out. And they gave me a clean bill of health. So I'm not *her* any more," she said urgently, and thumped her upper chest. "I'm not *her*."

As she glanced away, I flicked the fork off the grill, down to the grass. "And then, when you got out," I prompted, "they sent you down here. To live with your aunt in Ecorse."

"My mother," she corrected, visibly softening. "I mean, *technically* she was my aunt. But she—she took over as my mother—she truly gave me life—she was more of a mother to me than anyone."

Then why, I wondered, did Darlene so elaborately adorn the grave of her real mother? But I did not ask. If I started working all the threads of this thing, it would be like a land war in Asia—I'd never get out.

And speaking of which. "What do you want from me?" I asked.

She nodded. "I'd like you to talk to George."

"And say what."

She gestured. "Explain to him. How it was with me."

"How would I know how it was with you?"

"Come on, Ben," she said, looking closely at me. "You have a past, too. I know you do." I did not reply. "I love George," she said softly. "And I understand him. He's such an innocent. Nothing really bad has ever happened to him. You're a man, you've been around, you know how things are. And he respects you."

"And I respect him," I replied. "But George is no innocent. And I can barely run my own relationships, let alone someone else's. And this is his decision."

"No," she countered. "Don't pin it all on him. You're responsible, too. You got him the information."

"Which was my job."

"It's your fault," she murmured. "It was going *so well.*" She seemed to have gone back, way back, in her head somewhere. I found myself wondering what was in that handbag. And noticing, as if for the first time, the size of her, the obvious strength in those arms and shoulders. Plenty enough to hoist a highchair and hurl it, occupant and all, out off the deck—

"I wish you hadn't lied to him," I said, going to Rachel and pulling her out of her chair, into my arms. *Holding you tight. Never letting you go.* "That's probably what tore it."

Darlene's face crumpled, eyes runny as a tear trail shot down one round cheek. "You're just like him!" she said. "You blame me too. You just can't let sleeping dogs lie."

She started for the stair. I should have just let her get, while the getting was good. But I could not resist. "About Joe Hass's garage and kennel," I said. "Was that you?"

She stopped, turned, faced me. Face frozen, eyes fixed. "For God's sake," she said softly. "On an average day in the city of Detroit, ninety buildings burn down from natural causes!"

"Okay," I answered, rocking Rachel gently, surprised at how quiet and still she was. "Just asking."

Darlene thumped down the steps. At the bottom she stopped and faced me once more, brows clenched above her frown. "Why did you do that just now?" she asked.

"What."

"Pick up the baby."

"Wanted to hold her."

She scowled. "You actually thought I'd do something to hurt that child?"
I hesitated. "No."

She gave her head one hard shake. "*Liar!*" she hissed, and walked away.

†††

"Once," I said, "I got a job wrecking a barn. Teenager visiting my grandparents down in Georgia. Guy wanted the weathered siding. So I was stripping it off. Not paying much attention, just doing the job. All of a sudden the whole barn started to sway. I scampered off just in the nick of time. The whole barn just twisted and collapsed on the ground. Pretty awesome sight."

Raeanne glanced at me, her face half in shadow from the setting sun. "This is an allegory, I take it."

"No," I said, a little ticked. "It's the truth."

"Ben—"

"Turned out the siding gave the barn rigidity and strength," I explained. "Well, that siding was like George's trust. Take it away, and the whole relationship collapsed. Under the weight of Darlene's lies."

We sat side by side on lawn chairs. Beyond the deck the advancing darkness cast shadows on the trees.

"So," she said quietly, "for four years they were together and happy, with the lies. Now they're apart and sad, with the truth. I don't honestly know which is better."

"I don't know either," I said.

From inside I heard Rachel murmur something. Never fully in repose, even in sleep.

"She could be on the level," Raeanne observed. "It could all be true, about the abuse and so on."

"It could also be a con," I answered. "Look at all the lies she's told. And there's that Joe Hass business."

"Did you tell George about that?"

"I did."

"But it may have been—"

"I know, I know. But I have a rule. What I know, the boss knows." She said nothing. "I think, for George," I added, " it came down to choosing what he felt most comfortable believing. And then acting on that."

She wore a snug denim dress from shoulder straps to mid-thigh, and brown high-heeled sandals. Looked like something she'd just slipped into before coming over.

"Lies, and damned lies," Raeanne said quietly. "So destructive. What's ironic is that lying can also be used for good. You're a detective, I'm an actor.

300 | ROB KANTNER

Lying is part of our—"

"Skill set," I cut in.

"Yes. Good term."

"Thank George."

"So," she said, "did we learn to lie because of the work we do? Or did we choose our work because of our ability to lie?"

"Lot of questions," I answered.

With that she turned to me. "Questions," she said. She took a deep breath. "You've told me a lot about your . . . past," she said. "I know you have questions about me. I'm ready to come clean." She smiled tightly. "Brace yourself."

"Let me say something first." I leaned over, took her in my arms, held her to me hard. "I know there's things about you," I murmured. "Just as there's things about me. Nobody gets by without making messes somewhere, sometime. What matters to me is who and what you are right now. Whatever the other stuff is, it's just details. Whatever the other stuff is, it's automatically good, really. Because it helped make you the you, the *precious* you, that you are right now. Whatever the other stuff is, it's your business. Tell me if you want, if it helps you. But I feel no need to know."

She let out a long breath, warm on my neck, and relaxed in my arms. Then she kissed me with considerable intensity and pulled back. Though the light was dim, I could swear her eyes were damp.

"My goodness, she drawled. "Quite the speechmaker tonight."

"Hey. Been practicing."

We sat there hand in hand for a long time, watching the darkness of night complete itself around us. Presently, Raeanne said, "It really is true what you said. About Darlene. It really does come down to choosing what you want to believe."

"Yep."

"So which is she? Wicked killer or abused innocent?"

"What do you think?"

Here we learn a bit more about Ben's career these days. He's very much the freelance corporate investigator, avoiding—per his promise to Carole—"the rough stuff." But in this story he brushes against danger, for Ben gets sucked into a situation in which the past not only lives on but has the capacity to cause some present-day harm.

This story marks the first appearance of Ben's daughter Rachel in a short story. I think her entry into Ben's life went a long way toward humanizing him. Though still plenty tough, Ben has finally met a female against whom he is helpless. "Rachel *owns* Ben," was the observation of Carolyn Marino, who edited the Harper novels.

I see Darlene Helms as a sad, borderline tragic figure. We know she did terrible things, but it could very well be that she has fully rehabilitated; we'll never know. George Remmert had never appeared before, but he's a keeper; he'll be back. The opening scene takes place at Ann Arbor's Gandy Dancer restaurant. Woodmere Cemetery, which was a factor in *The Quick and the Dead*, is a real place. Not true for Sister Bay, though anybody familiar with the middle of the mitten can figure out where I'm talking about readily enough.

My Best Fred MacMurray

Chick was never what you'd call smooth, back in the day, and the years in between sure hadn't taught him much. Because when I appeared, the smart move would have been for him to hide his surprise, but he didn't.

Not that he wigged out or anything. He was standing out on the patio, towering over those around him, elbows sticking out in that odd way. Drinking and chatting and making that percussive laugh of his, he caught a glimpse of me over his right shoulder. Of course it had been some years, and he could not be sure it was me, and he obviously needed to check. But the smooth move would have been to wait. Not Chick. He had to know, *right that instant*. He did as I expected, as if I'd scripted it: turned to his left and shot a glimpse at me over his *left* shoulder.

Like I said: not smooth. He might as well have faced me and cupped his hands around his mouth and shouted *Yes, Ben, it's me, Chick Hafer and, yes, as usual I'm up to no good, no good at all. . . .*

That anything like this was about to happen I was blissfully unaware, two hours earlier as we sped up a long, fine U.S. 13 hill. After all, I was on a vacation of sorts. To one of the remote reaches of the state, far from the saloons and dark alleys and smoky factories of my Detroit stomping grounds. In the most pleasant company of Ms. Raeanne, whose considerable acting skills could not smother her excitement as my Mustang flew over the crest of the hill.

She let out a whoop. "There it is! My town, my town, my *town!*" she enthused, in her excitement shaking my gun arm.

"Welcome back, darlin'," I said, downshifting as we passed the city limits of Hope Springs. Though there were, as far as I knew, no springs to be seen, there was plenty of water. From our vantage point on U.S. 13 we had a postcard view of Lake Michigan, a deep bay, a river, and at least two lakes. The town of Hope Springs, bisected by a river, clustered on gentle hills that rolled along the bay. "Pretty place," I said.

"It sure has grown, though," Raeanne said, squinting. "I hardly recognize anything. Look at this road! It was just a two-lane when I used to visit here." Which had been, I knew, during the Nixon administration. "Guess I never realized the sprawl would make it this far north."

"So many strip malls," I observed, "so little land."

"Well," she answered confidently, "this is just the typical edge-of-town Wal-Martville," she noted, just as we passed one. "In a few minutes we'll be in the *real* Hope Springs. I'm taking you to the Gas Light District, and the marinas, and the parks. And the *best* thing is seeing the sunset at Bayfront Park. I can't wait to show you that."

"Looking forward to it," I said. I was eyeing the commercial strip as we rolled north.

"Can't wait," Raeanne mused, lost in memory. At that moment she looked half her 30 years. I got a glimpse of that long-lost teen face, oval, even more delicate, but with, I was sure, more hair and less assurance. Just then I saw what I needed, and wheeled us into a driveway of a big new Pit 'n' Git. Raeanne glanced at me. "Stopping?"

"Taco salad dressing."

"Oh, right," she said, and touched my hand. "Thanks for remembering."

"Hey, I was the one left it on the kitchen counter," I replied, grinning. I eased the Mustang into a parking place. "Anything else you need?"

"No." Raeanne's hand tightened on mine. "Sure you're okay with all this? New town, new people, family stuff?"

"Hey," I said cheerily, "twice in my life, guys tried to garrote me. This I can deal with."

"Why," she breathed, smiling, "you're fairly bubbling over here!"

I smiled back. "I'm good. Really." I shut off the engine. "Back in a flash." Disembarking the Mustang, I sauntered toward the Pit 'n' Git. A bright orange sign on the door caught my eye as I pushed through. THIS PREMISE UNDER ARMED SURVEILLANCE, it read. OFFENDERS WILL BE MET WITH DEADLY FORCE. Seemed a bit overdone to me. Obviously lawyers on overtime.

I found the salad dressing and walked it to the busy checkout counter. I was feeling good. Oh, I knew it'd be a bit tense, meeting Raeanne's family, what was left of it. But I knew what to do: stand around, avoid bumping into furniture, smile a lot and, in general, do my best Fred MacMurray. And enjoy watching Raeanne reconnect to what she still fondly thought of as her world and her people.

Outside, I saw that she was no longer alone. A man stood by her side of the Mustang, leaning against the roof, chatting companionably with her through the open window. I recognized him right off—hell, you don't mistake guys his size, even 200-odd miles from where you expect them to be. "What's shakin', Hammer?" I asked as I approached the car.

Hammer Lane straightened and favored me with his flat, gray-eyed smile. He wore black jeans and a sleeveless leather vest over a white tee shirt. He was still muscled like a weight lifter. Not that I'd ever seen him lift weights.

304 | ROB KANTNER

Never seen him exercise. Matter of fact, I never saw him ever break so much as a sweat. "Just chattin' with your friend," he said, voice a deep gravel-rumble. "Takin' some time, Ben?"

"That would be correct," I said, as easygoing as I could manage. I'm not exactly little, but he made me feel puny. He unleaned himself from my car without being asked, though. "You?"

"Workin'." He bent down to the window and gave Raeanne a tiny salute. "Enjoy your visit, Ms. Brennan." Then he strolled into the Pit 'n' Git, a big family parting like a sea to make way for him.

I slammed my door, handed Raeanne the dressing, and started the engine. "Hammer Lane?" she drawled as I backed out of the parking space. "Please tell me that's not his real name."

"Haven't a clue," I said, scooting us over to U.S. 13. "Some people think he was a long haul trucker once. Truckers call the passing lane the 'hammer lane.' Somebody once told me he ran a drop forge at a hammer factory, about the nastiest most dangerous job there is. Heard tell elsewhere he was in the fight game, got the name that way. Another guy claimed Hammer was drummer for the Syndicate of Sound band. There was even a wild tale of him playing pro ball. And then there's women that describe Hammer as being—"

"Thank you," she cut in sardonically. "That image I can live without." She eyed me. "So how do you know him?"

"Um, him and me did union together."

"Oh."

I flung us out onto the road, merging smoothly into a small gap among the campers and RVs. I'd tell her anything she wanted to know, but there were parts of my past about which she hesitated to ask, and my policy was not to push. "About me being comfortable doing this?"

"Yes?"

"Remember back Easter, when my sister invited us to her house? You told me you were happy to do it. That not everything we did had to be about you."

"I remember."

"Well, darlin'," I said, looking into her light eyes, "I'm happy to do this. Not everything we do has to be about me."

Impulsively, she reached over and kissed my cheek hard. "I'm grateful," she whispered. "More than you know."

"Pleasure." Almost at once our motel came up on the right, and I swerved us into the parking lot. "Just surprises me," I said, "running into a Detroit mope all the way up here."

"Doesn't surprise me," Raeanne replied. "Everybody around here is either from around here, or from Detroit somewhere."

†††

Two Detroit mopes, as it turned out. Three, if you count me.

But I was still ten minutes from spotting Chick, as we motored up the driveway of Raeanne's uncle's property north of town. It looked like a nice spread: rolling hills, dense woods, miles of white fence, a glimpse of the bay way to the west. Raeanne supplied excited narrative as we made our way, images from her adolescence: a tire swing, a creek, a pond, and a pig near which she said she and her cousin made mud pies as little girls. I looked real hard, but saw no pigs. Which did not surprise me. Earlier, as we'd neared Hope Springs, Raeanne had twice spotted deer near the road, but try as I might I could not see them. "City eyes," she'd called me, laughing.

The house was a sprawling, dark brick, low-slung affair. It needed new shingles but was otherwise quite nice, with big windows looking at odd angles out at all that woods. The vast apron of asphalt driveway was parked solid with vehicles, with emphasis on red, silver, chrome, shiny, and huge. Among them my '71 Mustang looked small and quaint and "then," to use Raeanne's term.

Getting out of the car, I saw that the party had taken over the whole place. The double front doors stood wide open, as did the windows and the doors to the triple bay garage. Inside there, tables stood in rows covered with bright table cloths and dishes and containers of food and beverages, which were being fluttered over by people, mostly female. From inside boomed music, big band stuff, overlaying a steady but perceptible drone of loud cheery conversation. On the concrete stoop stood a flock of men, smoking cigarettes and drinking beer from cans and watching us speculatively. At our appearance one ducked into the house. "Ready for this?" Raeanne asked, getting her big covered salad bowl out of the back seat.

"Into the breach," I answered cheerfully, shutting the car door.

Raeanne waited for me to join her, and we walked toward the garage together. "I hope they like my salad," she said nervously. "It's what Aunt Barb told me to bring."

"It'll be fine."

"It's just . . . there's nothing more depressing than taking most of your uneaten potluck dish back home with you."

"They'll love it, sweetheart. They'll eat every bite and lick the bowl clean, if need be at gun point."

"Now stop it . . . oh!" she said tremblingly, spotting movement in the garage, "here she comes . . . *here she cooooomes!*" Thrusting the salad bowl into my arms, she ran toward the garage as a woman shot toward us, red hair flying in the wind. Colliding, they did a hugging circling dance, seeming to cry and laugh at once, the blended sounds almost musical. As I approached, Raeanne broke free, but held both hands with the much shorter woman as she turned to me. "Ben, this is my cousin Shay. Shay Hatrick. Soon to be Shay—"

"Wardwell," Shay supplied, beaming.

"It's so exciting!" Raeanne enthused.

"I know, I know!" and they hugged again. Then Shay's eyes found me. "You must be Ben!"

"Perkins," I answered, grinning. "Glad to meetcha."

"Same here," she said, and the look she gave me was more a checkout than a glance. Which was okay. I clean up pretty good when required. I wore slacks and sneakers and some sort of golf shirt. I'd trimmed my thicket of coarse black hair back to something like civilized. Back in the room I'd even shaved—violating Commandment One of "time off."

Shay seemed to find me acceptable. "Come inside, you two, Mother's dying to see you." She led us through the garage. Greetings were exchanged, introductions made. I stayed what athletes call "within myself," nodding and smiling and murmuring pleasant inconsequentials. When directed, I placed the salad in what appeared to be a plastic kiddie pool full of ice. Then I followed the women into the house.

The family room was sprawling and all glass at the south end, with a large wood deck just outside, a concrete patio beyond, and a swimming pool in the next township. Children cavorted, teens bunched in suspicious murmuring clusters, and adults stood in clumps, outside and in. From the nearest an older bright-blond woman turned and, spotting us, shouted: "So *there* you are!"

Shay led us over. That was when I saw Chick out on the deck, and he did his ridiculously obvious *yes I see you, no I don't* act. Raeanne hugged the older woman, who as it turned out was Aunt Barb, Shay's mom. "So nice to meet you," she said, giving me just her heavily ringed fingers to shake. She looked a little like a blond Lauren Bacall. "You're from Detroit somewhere?"

"Belleville, ma'am. Congratulations on marrying off the kid here."

"Well, it's about time!" the mom boomed. "I told Shay, I said, by the time I was your age I'd already *had* my starter marriage." The mother's sharp eyes found Raeanne. "I told her, I said, whatsa matter with you? Even gawky Rae's had *one* marriage already, even if the best she could do was a man as poor as a church mouse."

"True," Raeanne said equably. "So, where's the lucky boy?"

"Oh, out on the deck with Mike," Shay replied, tossing her red head that way. "Wanna meet him?"

"Are you kidding?"

"Ben," Mrs. Hatrick commanded, "you need to meet my boys over here. Get your quota of man-talk out of the way."

"Back in a bit," Raeanne said, giving me a *good luck* wink. She and her cousin headed off arm in arm toward the deck—and Chick Hafer. I wondered again what the heck he was doing here.

Mrs. Hatrick introduced me to several men of varying ages: her husband, two of her sons, a male in-law. Don't ask me their names; they flitted across my brain and skipped right out again. The dad was bald all over; one of the sons had a badly bruised face; the other son was small-eyed and portly, and the in-law had a goatee.

Introductions done, the mom churned noisily away. I really wanted to go out on the deck and check up on Chick, but—*this is not about you*—it would have been rude to just walk off on these guys. There was an interval of awkwardness, as the group adjusted to my sudden appearance. Then the dad said, watching them, "Rae and Shay. The Bobbsey twins."

"Twins? More like a study in contrast, Dad," the portly one said. He was right. Raeanne was a good half-foot taller than her cousin, with a willowy build, short dark brown hair, and a loose-limbed way of walking. Shay was solid and freckled with longish, brilliantly red hair, a small pursed mouth, and a strut for a walk.

"From Detroit somewhere, Ben?" asked the bruised one.

"Belleville. Thirty miles west."

"What's this rumor Rae had a part in *Good Will Hunting*?" the dad asked me.

"Yeah, what was she, an extra in the bar scene?" the bruised one put in. "I played the whole tape in slo-mo, never saw her."

"Her scene was cut," I put in. "It's on the DVD, though."

"So've the dizzy spells stopped?" goatee asked the bruised one.

"She had a whole scene?" the dad asked me.

"Yopp, I'm doing better," the bruised one said.

"Her and Ben Affleck," I answered. "She got to kiss him. Many times."

From out on the deck I heard Chick's hard, percussive laugh. My daddy would have growled: *That boy couldn't sneak up on a war.*

"When do you start back?" the portly one asked.

"What kind of work do you do, Ben?" asked goatee.

"Monday week I'm back there," the bruised one said.

"Manage maintenance for an apartment complex," I answered.

"Light duty?" the portly one asked.

"Not much money in that, is there," goatee said to me.

"So," I said to the dad, "I hear you've got pigs on the place?"

The dad laughed. "Only pig I've got is the propane gas tank out past the garage."

"Yuh-huh," the bruised one said, "till they figure out about the dizzy spells."

"What happened to you?" I asked him. "Bar fight?"

"Deer," the dad said.

"Hit a deer," the bruised one told me offhandedly and added "Button buck," as if that explained anything.

"With your face?" I asked.

"Nuh-uh," the man answered. "My car. Deer came cartwheeling over the hood and crashed through the windshield feet first and got stuck half in, half out. I'm swerving all over the road, can't see for the deer in my face. And he's hurt and mad as hell, just kicking the bejeepers out of me."

"Whyncha just shoot him?" I asked.

"Outta season," the dad said, fetching a laugh.

"Woulda been poaching," the portly one chortled.

"Hey," I shrugged, "if a deer is kicking the crap out of me, where I come from, shooting him wouldn't be poaching, it'd be self defense."

Goatee, whom I made as a lawyer, said, "To do that, you'd have to have a loaded gun on your front seat. That's illegal."

"It is?" I asked blankly.

"Ben!" came Raeanne's voice. I turned. Smiling, Raeanne said, "This is Shay's fiancé." Sticking out my hand, I looked way, way up into the beaming face of Chick Hafer as Raeanne said, "Meet Bill Wardwell."

†††

The Hatrick elders convened the family in the garage to say grace. People trooped through the potluck line, paper plates in hand, and loaded up chow. Then everyone sat down to eat, grouped by family unit at picnic tables and elsewhere on the property.

Raeanne and I drew a picnic table on the driveway with Shay, her brother Mike, and Chick Haf—excuse me: Bill Wardwell. Much of the conversation was carried by the women, chattering about the wedding the next day and the reception afterward and the "fabulous" (Shay's term) Las Vegas honeymoon impending. Mike and Chi—Bill, Bill, *Bill*—talked about the family machinery business, which Mike evidently ran now, his father being pretty much retired. Mike was an older and heavier version of his redheaded sister, unlike her a bit on the sweet and dreamy side. He was obviously great pals with you know who, judging by the way he listened to him, deferred to him, hung onto his every word.

Speaking of Chick—for that's who he was; to me he was no more "Bill Wardwell" than Winston Churchill—he really had not changed much in the dozen years since I'd seen him. He'd always dolled himself up, and today was no exception. I had to admit he looked great in white open-neck shirt and shorts, with loose gold chains at neck and wrists. He still had that athletic build and squarish head and those eager questing eyes. His sharklike mouth wore the constant smile that he learned by watching other people and then practicing in the mirror. His laugh was an aural version of a drive-by shooting, an assault on the ears that made you want to duck for cover. When his talk was not about money and things—talk in which he was eagerly joined by his blushing bride—it was about his exploits in business, politics, finance, high-stakes gambling, and playing semi-pro basketball in Greece. He held the table rapt as he spun his glib glowing sentences, maintaining eye contact with each of us, even looking me innocently in the face as he reeled off one whopper after another.

I was getting fidgety. This wasn't about me, and I was supposed to stay within myself here. But I found it hard to just be still and, as if signing off, listen to his blizzard of B.S. At the same time, I marveled at his ability to act as though he didn't know that I knew exactly who he was, what he was, where he'd been, what he'd done. I wondered why others did not see the truth of him as clearly as I did. I wondered how he wormed his way into the confidence of this obviously affluent and successful family. I wondered how he survived his 18 months in Jackson. I wondered if he ever made restitution. I wondered why someone had not, long hence, shot him through the head. Just in the interest of nuisance removal.

But I kept a lid on it. Not my issue, not my problem. And not my family. And not my occasion. *Not about me.*

After a while Chick, or Bill, or whatever, who had managed to empty his plate even during his virtual nonstop talking, got up to get seconds. Without thinking about it, I got up also and carried my plate over to the buffet tables. I found him by himself, towering over the array of food, serving himself some Jell-O. "So Bill, hey. Tell me," I said, scanning the serving dishes. "What's the crime situation in these parts?"

Chick said, "Oh, there's no crime here. Not like—you're from Detroit somewhere, right?"

"Yeah," I said, watching him.

"I'm sorry," he beamed down at me.

I saw that Raeanne's taco salad was about half gone. I served myself two big heaps of it and started to eat as we chatted. "Nothing to be sorry about," I said. "Aren't you from Detroit?"

"Me?" he snorted. "Oh hell, no. Petoskey." He seemed to shiver. "I wouldn't go anywhere near that hellhole down there."

"Uh-huh," I said, eating. "So you're working for Mike, I gather? What do you do for him?"

"Executive VP of marketing administration," he crowed, glancing over the rest of the dishes.

"Oughta try the taco salad," I said offhand. "You didn't eat any before."

"Sure I did!" he boomed. "It was great! But I'm just—"

"No, you didn't. I was watching," I said easily. "But okay, let's pretend you did. In that case, it's time for seconds. Help yourself!"

He looked down at me, grin white and wide. "Oh, I don't know, I should leave some for—"

"Take some more," I suggested. He just looked at me. "I really think you should." His mouth moved, but before he could emit words, I said softly, "It's highly advisable."

"Well," he managed. "Sure! Sure, why not. Ya twisted my arm!" Laughing percussively, he piled a couple scoops of taco salad on his plate. With a glance at me, he added one more. Then, having suddenly and mysteriously run out of achievements to trumpet, victories to lord, or toys to brag about, he scooted back over to our table, where he sat next to Shay, closer than before. I finished my plate, tossed it in a trash barrel then resumed my place beside Raeanne. I found myself rubbing my hands aimlessly on my pants, as if to ease an itch for Chick's neck. I did not know how Fred MacMurray would have handled this. What I did was go into one-minute-at-a-time mode. Let Chick finish Raeanne's salad first, I told myself. *Then* you can strangle him. . . .

†††

"Wow," Raeanne said, warmly pleased. "My salad got wiped out!"

"They loved it, babe," I said, guiding the car down the driveway. "It was great."

"I didn't make enough," she fussed, placing the bowl in the back seat.

"That's right," I said, grinning, "keep digging, you're bound to find a defeat in there somewhere."

She laughed. "Yeah, yeah. You're right." I swung the car right onto the main road headed back into town. "So are you going to the bachelor party?"

"Doubt it. You wanted to show me the sunset."

"Ohhh, yes."

"Besides, I think Mike invited me because he felt he had to."

"Mike's a sweetie."

"I'm not in the least opposed to an alcohol-soaked debauch," I told her.

"Just not with people I don't know."

"Then don't go. It's fine with me. I'm piggy. I want you with me." I felt her hand on mine. "Now, are you going to tell me about it?"

"'Bout what?"

She looked at me, and I looked back. The late afternoon sunlight angled the delicate features of her oval face. Her expression was calm, expectant. "Why you're in such a state."

"Well—"

"Please, Ben. I can tell. You know how this works. When you love someone, you pay attention."

It was not that I had decided not to tell her. I was learning I could tell Raeanne anything—anything at all. I just hadn't figured out the right time. Looked like she'd decided that for me.

"Wardwell's not his real name," I told her. "It's Hafer. Chick Hafer."

"Oh," she said presently. "You know him?" Then she interrupted herself. "*Chick??*"

"Short for Charles," I said as we passed the Hope Springs city limits. The road four-laned there, following a high bluff over the expanse of bay stretching out to Lake Michigan. "I knew him, sort of. Years ago."

"A case, I take it?"

"Yep. He was the perp."

"Oh, boy," she said. Crossing her legs under her skirt, she braced her chin on her fist, and let out a soft sigh. "What kind of case."

"He stole some antiques from my client, an elderly woman, from a house she owned," I explained. "Years ago now. She was renting the place to his girlfriend, it's a long story."

"So he ended up—"

"Prison," I told her. "Caught five to eight, did eighteen months. The girl flipped on him and got probation. My client got some of her stuff back. Not all of it. Chick was supposed to make restitution, but who knows."

We paused at a traffic signal at the center of town, signaling to bear left on U.S. 13. Raeanne looked thoughtful. "And this was when?"

"Wanna say twelve years ago," I answered, lunging the Mustang onward.

"Long time."

I knew what she was thinking. I was having the same thoughts. But there was more information she needed. "Thing is, I learned a lot about him. I had to testify, I was in and out of it for months—anyway, this wasn't just a one-shot. Chick's been grifting and scamming and pulling fast ones since he was a kid. Got a sheet as long as your arm."

"What kind of offenses?"

"That's the thing, nothing really big. Consumer fraud. Credit card scams.

He was always kind of reckless, he got caught a lot. Like the antiques case—he knew he was suspected, went right on stealing anyways." I realized I was overshooting the motel just as it happened. Banging the shifter into second, I gunned us into the Pit 'n' Git driveway and U'd back over to the road. "This ain't no evil genius, this schmo," I said, looking at Raeanne. "He's not so much evil as pathetic, with these scummy little scams of his."

"Just the same, sounds like he's hurt a lot of people." She drew a deep breath. "Could be he's reformed since then."

We motored back to the motel driveway. "Hey. Maybe. Anything's possible." To that my instinct said a loud and clear no, but I kept that to myself. "It's been twelve years," I added. "My information is a tad dusty."

"I just . . . feel so bad for Shay," Raeanne said. "I wonder if she knows."

We parked, got out, walked toward the motel. "Well, we know she knows him by a wrong name," I pointed out, taking her warm hand in mine. "And look at all this other stuff he told us today, stuff she obviously believes. MBA from Michigan? Born and raised in Petoskey? Father a heart surgeon? Crewed for Ted Turner in the America's Cup race? Pro basketball in Greece? All false."

I don't know how much of that she heard, because her head was somewhere else. "She's *marrying* him, Ben. Tomorrow."

"I know."

Inside the room, Raeanne sprawled on the lone double bed. I opened a window to get the good lake breeze and lighted a cigar, leaning, watching her. Eyes shut, she massaged her forehead with her slender fingers. "Please don't be insulted at this question," she said to the ceiling, "but . . . is there *any* possibility of mistaken identity?"

"Babe," I said quietly.

"It's been *twelve years*," she said, emphasizing the words with small clenched fists. "You've seen a lot of people, done a lot of—"

"Sweetheart," I said, "in this work, you remember the wrong guys a hell of a lot longer than the citizens. And Chick, in my humble opinion, was about as wrong as they come. Back then anyways," I amended, extending benefit of the doubt in which I did not for one moment believe.

We sat there silent for a long, long time. I smoked, being sure to vent out the window. I felt bad about this. Raeanne had looked forward to Shay's wedding for so very long. She so badly wanted everything to work out all right. It just made me angrier at Chick—*still* messing up people's lives, after all these years.

And speaking of which. "But if he's reformed," I ventured, "I might know how to find out."

"How?" she said, looking at me.

"Fella down home. Knows all the scam artists around town, he's a walkin' NCIC database. If Chick is still scamming, T. Tommy'll know. Same if he's gone straight."

"Know what?" Raeanne said, getting up lithely from the bed, "I think I'm going to take a walk down to the marina and back. Try to clear my head."

"Sure." I stood also. "Want me to make the call?" She said nothing, just walked pensively toward the motel room door. "I'll do anything for you," I said. "All the way out to everything, and all the way back to nothing at all. Your call."

She looked very directly at me. "Call," she answered, and left.

†††

Unless you do business with him regularly, which I do not, there is never any way to reach T. Tommy Fledderjohn directly. You have to know people that know him. These need to be people who not only know you—and know that T. Tommy knows you—they must also know he is willing to talk to you. So it gets a little complicated. On top of that you're dealing with people who lack, besides abstractions like morals and ethics, fixed addresses, voice mail, family, secretaries. So I had to work my way through a thicket of hand-offs and no-answers and *the-number-you-have-reached . . . is-not-in-services* to get to T. Tommy.

Who came on the phone, voice deep, bubbly, rich as always. "Why Mistah Benjamin Perkins!" he boomed, his mellow tones harking back to his Mississippi Delta upbringing. "What brings you into my den of iniquity?"

I pictured him in that huge executive chair behind the desk on the second floor of an East Grand Boulevard mansion. Of course that place had to be long gone by now—for all I knew he was in a doublewide in Melvindale. But my guess was he still wore big thick black-framed glasses on his large round face, and had quadruple chins and a whalelike physique. "Got a name for ya, maybe you can help me out with," I said.

"Happy to be of service."

"Chick Hafer."

"Aaugh!" he barked shortly. If I wasn't mistaken, I thought I heard pain in his voice, if briefly. "Hafer, sure, I know of him. You can take *that* to the bank. Truly a *pitiful* little snot, Ben."

"This is what I hate about you, T., the way I have to drag information out of ya."

"Why," T. Tommy said, "he had a score going perhaps two, three years ago, something to do with the Internet. I don't recall all the details," he said, which by definition was a huge lie. "Bottom line is that things 'somehow' went awry. Several good friends of mine, his ostensible partners, were incarcerated, my best intercessory efforts notwithstanding."

"He set them up?"

"You know, I had that very same quite uncharitable and un-Christian thought," T. Tommy boomed. "And were I a man given to violence, such as yourself, Ben, and of a similarly unforgiving nature, I might have been forced to exact physical retribution. Why, I almost called you, my friend, I truly did. To perhaps arrange for you to provide Mr. Hafer with one of your nigh legendary face-first staircase slides. But—"

"Heck, T, it's been decades since—"

"But then I had a moment of clarity," T. Tommy said. "And realized that Mr. Chick Hafer doesn't have the intellectual horsepower to carry out a con within a con. He can, however—and has proven on many an occasion—screw up a perfectly good con. You can take that to the *bank*. So I let him live, digits intact."

"What I need to know is, is he in the business, or out of it, or what?"

"On the fringes! Like always! He works the low rent crowd, the elderly and infirm, for nickels and dimes. Not that he doesn't continue to have grander ambitions, but—"

"But not real lately, am I right?"

The big man hesitated. "Matter of fact, it's probably been a year, year and a half since I've heard tell of him. He was working the smack at the airport then, I know that. Got a little obvious—which at six foot seven wasn't hard—and that idiot laugh of his, he's been ticketed for violating *noise* ordinances. He drew 90 days for loitering, which we found to be hilarious. Since then nothing."

"Well, I know where he is," I said, and told him. "What do you think?"

"You're thinking perhaps he's gone straight," T. Tommy said shrewdly.

"Just wonderin'."

"Ben," he said gruffly, "please. Bent Hafer was born, and bent he'll always be. Till he's three days dead, that is. I'll tell you what he's doing, and *this* you can take to the bank. Your friend Chick has always thirsted for the big con. Wants to be a master of the universe, so to speak. What he's doing—and I guarantee this is true, even in a place like—where the hell are you again?"

"Hope Springs."

"Oh, Ben," he moaned, "a Godforsaken backwater like that? I'll send my car for you at once."

"My sweetheart's family is here, we're—"

"I might have known!" he boomed. "That was always your failing. Skirt. When *will* you learn."

"When I'm three days dead," I answered, thinking of Raeanne with a smile. "But what about Chick?"

"My bet is he's got a mark," T. Tommy said, "A rather substantial one. And he's working him. Maybe not so much for the dough, but to prove to the rest of us that—"

"Any way you can get a line on exactly who he's doing?" I asked, not that I didn't have a theory.

"Not way out there, not any time soon."

I found myself believing him, not that it mattered. "Okay. Appreciate the insight."

"Remember," T. Tommy said. "Chick Hafer is two things. No, three. Greedy, stupid, and impulsive. The first two I could live with—hell, they make my business possible! It's the third that makes him dangerous. You just never know when he's going to fly off in some direction."

"Thanks, T. I'll keep that in mind. And thanks for leveling with me," I added, not sure that he completely had. Raeanne returned just then, looking lovely, sober and thoughtful as she eased into one of the club chairs by the window. I fielded some questions from T. Tommy about certain Detroit area figures, and we signed off. To Raeanne's arched eyebrow I responded by filling her in.

"So he's still, uh . . . what's your word for it? Dirty?" she asked.

"Yep. Dirty."

She shook her head slightly, expression bleak. "It's just awful. So awful for Shay."

"I know. What do you want to do?"

She glanced around the room, as if seeking an escape route. "I could sit down with her. Tell her what's up."

"Yeah, you could. And there's something I could do, too."

"What's that?"

"Talk to Chick. Convince him to back off whatever he's up to."

"How would you do that?" I just looked at her. "Oh."

"Again, it's your call," I said, relighting my expired cigar, swiveling on the sill to vent out the window.

"You mean," she said, with a very small smile, "you'd actually go do *enforcing* for me?"

"I'll do anything for you."

Smile fading, she slouched in the chair, spraddle-legged, fingers drumming the chair arm. "There's another whole way to look at this."

"Yes?"

"It's not our problem." She studied her hands as she spoke in a soft certain voice. "All we have are strands of things. We don't know the whole story. Not really."

"True."

"And," she went on, looking at me, "it's not like Shay and I are boon companions. Since we were kids it's been Christmas cards and a phone call here and there. Why, she didn't even come sit with me when my dad died."

That did not surprise me given the low-key disparaging remarks I'd heard about Raeanne's dad back at the potluck. "You're under no obligation," I told her.

"What right do we have," she asked rhetorically, "to come blazing into town and upset everything and everyone on Shay's wedding weekend?" She held her hands out, palms up. "This is not about us."

"Right. Not about us."

"So," she said, clapping hands once and standing, "let's go eat and watch the sunset."

†††

Which we did. And it was great. But Raeanne seemed to be at most half with it. The only time she became fully engaged was during Sean Ryan's performance at the Elbow Room. He spotted her in the crowd and called her over between sets. After much giggling and whispering she strapped on his 12-string, and the two of them opened his second set with a killer duet of "She Came in Through the Bathroom Window." The crowd loved it and demanded an encore. Raeanne obliged with a solo of "When All Is Said and Done," which got hearty applause also, though no one but me had heard it before.

A while later we walked silently, hand in hand, up Lee Street toward the hotel. I could sense the percolation of her thoughts. When she spoke, though, she asked a question I did not expect. "Did you have a good time at my uncle's today?"

"Yeah. Sure. It was all right. You?"

"I don't know," she said vaguely. "I guess. It's just . . . they're not the way I remember them."

"People change."

"Some," she said distractedly. We walked a bit more, crossed a busy street, homed in on the hotel. That was when she got down to it. "You know?"

"Yeah," I agreed.

We looked at each other with complete understanding. "I have to at least tell her what we know," she said. "She deserves that."

"And I need a word with him too," I answered. "If I can do some good, I gotta at least try. It's what I'm about, if anything."

"I know," she said, voice small. "God knows I don't want to bring it up to her. But I love her, and this is the loving thing to do, even if it's such a very hard thing."

"Don't envy you," I told her. "I've got the easy end of this."

She let go of my hand as I gave her the room key. Kissing me lightly on the lips, she said, "Don't hurt him, okay?"

"Just a little chit-chat," I assured her, and headed for the car.

†††

I arrived at the bachelor party just in time for the obligatory stripper bit.

The meeting hall of Hope Springs Chapter 1957 of the Amalgamated Brotherhood of Standpipe, Spigot, & Stopcock Fabricators, Fitters, Formers, & Threaders was a small dim building in the town's tiny Colony Street industrial district, well uphill from the bay. The gravel lot was parked solid with muscle cars and pickups all parked nose out. Hard rock pounding through the open windows sounded coarse and brutalizing after listening to an hour of the lilting ballads of Sean Ryan. But that was okay. This place, this situation, felt familiar, comfortable. For the next little while, I thought, feeling myself smile, I would be back in my own world.

No one noticed me as I went through the door. The room was a large low oblong, fluorescent-lit with a portable bar to the right and padded folding chairs scattered around. Blinded windows spotted the walls. A hallway ran off the room way to the left. Two-dozen men packed the center in a dense smoky huddle, making appreciative noise against the blaring music backdrop. The object of their adoration was a tiny nude blond woman, just finishing her athletic dance on the lap of the sweating, beaming Chick Hafer.

The bartender, who doubled as the DJ, was engrossed in the action. Finally I stepped around and drew myself a glass of beer, being familiar with the technology. He glanced at me and started to express himself, but thought better of it. I strolled over to some chairs by the wall beneath the big blue and gold union banner, drank some beer and waited. I did not light up; the secondhand smoke was doing me just fine. Presently the song ended, and the blond sprang from Chick's lap. She bussed his cheek and ruffled his hair as the men clapped and whooped and bayed. Then she slipped his roaming mitts and dashed barefoot out of the room down the hall for the johns, G-string and pasties in hand.

The men flooded toward the bar, flushed and animated and chattering loudly. Mike Hatrick, Shay's brother, spotted me and veered over. "Hey, Ben, glad you could make it!" he said, shaking hands with me unsteadily.

"Thought I'd stop by," I said. "Good of you to invite me."

"Oh, it's the best!" Mike said for some reason. He was having trouble focusing on me, and his lips and tongue seemed rubbery. "Y'know I wouldn't of blamed you for not coming, not with Rae to be with. Any man she cares for is best friends of me. She's the greatest, I just love her swilly—stilly—*silly.*"

Chick was on his feet and headed toward us, elbows out. I had my plan and knew it was just a matter of time. "She loves you, too, Mike," I told Hatrick.

"Bill!" Mike said to Chick. "Look what the cat drug in!"

Hafer drew up and beamed down at us with his big oblong grin. His white golf shirt was dampish and he had a liquor glass in hand, but I was certain he was cold stone sober. All to the good. "Hi, Ben," he said.

"Bill!" Mike said, bumping against his much taller colleague. "About the fight later! What do you say, let's ask Ben along. Bet he's got a big Detroit wad on his hip, and—"

"No-no," Chick said, clapping a big hand on Mike's shoulder. "You just, uh . . . go fetch me a refill, huh Mike?" he asked the company president, thrusting his glass into the smaller man's hand. "I gotta go squirt." Wheeling on his heel, he strode across the room toward the corridor.

Mike smirked at me and gestured helplessly with Chick's glass and headed over to the bar. I let Chick disappear down the dark hallway to the right, then set my glass down and ambled along. Halfway down the hall, a string mop leaned against the wall. Handy. Liberating it, I swung into the men's room.

It was a three-holer, painted green and thick, two stools inside enclosures and an honest to God trough. Chick towered over the latter, just buttoning up. When he saw it was me, he flashed a deer-in-the-headlights look. Then managed to replace that with a fairly sincere leer. "Pretty well-made young lady out there, huh Ben?" he asked, going to the sinks.

Without answering, I snapped the mop handle in two, tossed the string part over into the corner, and leaned against the door, tapping the splintered end in my palm. "Chick," I said, making it a statement.

He froze in place, staring at me as the water ran over his hands. "What the hell," he said.

"Can we talk," I said, making that a statement also.

"Whaddya mean 'Chick?'" he said, mimicking my tone.

"Please!" I said, rapping the handle overly hard in my palm. "Everybody's not dumb."

He blinked once, twice, three times, and then grinned. "So you do remember me." He seemed flattered.

"Chick. My man. You're six foot seven. You got elbows stick out funny. Your laugh could knock over a Brink's truck. Plus you stole antiques and family mementos from a helpless old lady. Guys like you I remember."

"I did my time," he said, voice low. "I'm on the square now."

"And got yourself quite a nice deal here."

He started washing his hands, and his eyes flickered to me. "You putting the arm on me, Ben? To, uh, buy your silence?"

"I got a transaction in mind, all right," I answered. "But not that kind."

He shook his hands over the sink. "Things are good for me here," he said. "My straight gig, and Shay and . . . you can't mess that up for me. It's not fair. I did my time."

"'Straight gig.'"

"With the company. You know. Working for Mike." He started to dry. "So what kind of 'transaction' you thinking of?"

"Very simple. You pull the plug, and I go away."

"The plug? On what?"

"The game."

"I don't know what you mean."

"Aw, jeez." I gestured at him with the mop handle, and he stepped back, clenching wadded towels, wary eyes worried despite himself. I said, "I don't care about your job, and Shay—all that you can keep. But the game you're running? That stops. This instant."

"I'm not running a game! I told you! I'm—"

"Do you remember when I first saw you? At the house you were living in with Gretchen Philbrick? The one with the antiques you stole?" I could tell he remembered very well. It was all he'd thought about, probably, since seeing me at the potluck. "The minute I saw you, I knew you. I knew what you were about, what you were doing. I knew it all, chapter and verse. And I was right. And why was I right, Chick?"

He swallowed hard. "I don't—I'm—"

"Because I OWN you!" I shouted. "I see right through you. Right through the blather and the B.S. You're an open book to me, Chick. I knew what you were up to then, and I know what's going on now. And I'm saying to you: Pull the plug on it. Forthwith."

Looking me over from his greater height, Chick gnawed his lip. "Okay."

"Okay what?"

"Okay, it's off." Turning to the wastebasket, he jammed the paper towels into it unnecessarily hard.

Hiding my surprise, I pointed the jagged mop handle at him. "You got the message then."

"Yeah, sure." He looked at me earnestly. "Nobody was getting hurt. Not really. They got plenty."

"And they're entitled to keep what they have," I said, winging it like crazy.

"Spare me the lectures," he said quietly. "You're no angel either. Can I leave now?"

We stared at each other, and then I stood back. "Sure, why not." He left. I threw the mop handle into the corner, went to the sink and washed my hands. The black-haired gent with the deep blue eyes staring at me from the mirror looked troubled, and I knew why. I had the uneasy feeling that I'd been finessed. But then, what I'd come to do was to deliver a message. Beyond that all I could do was hurt him, which Raeanne in her own offhand way had commanded me not to do. Besides, he'd given me no reason to.

Damn.

†††

Inside our motel room, Shay and Raeanne were sitting on the edge of the sofa, knee to knee, four hands clasped. Raeanne, I could tell, was on the verge of tears. Shay was trying not to look annoyed. "Oops," I said. "Bad timing. I'll come back."

"No, stay," Shay said rapidly, and let go of Raeanne. "Rae says you've—"

"I just told her," Raeanne said, tense and expressionless. "I'm so sorry about this, Shay."

The redhead crossed one sturdy leg over the other and folded her arms, bright blue eyes never leaving me. "You're the one found this out?"

"Yes, ma'am. I really didn't want to cause—"

"I thought you were just a janitor or something."

"That, plus I do a little detecting here and there. Met him way back in—"

"Don't bother," she said, a shrug in her voice. "I know all about it."

"Oh," Raeanne said.

"He told me a long time ago," Shay said, tossing her head, sweeping her long red hair back over her shoulders, watching the middle distance. "Bill and I don't have any secrets from each other."

"That's good then," Raeanne said and gave Shay a hug, which was not returned. "I've been so worried."

"Well, don't be," her cousin answered, standing. "It's quite all right, it's all in the past." She walked toward me, Raeanne, hands twisted together, trailing. "So all your research was for nothing," she told me.

"Just a phone call," I answered, giving her room.

She swept past and sang cheerfully, "Well, kids, I've got to fly. Big day tomorrow."

"Sleep tight," I answered, going to the sofa. Raeanne escorted her cousin to the hallway. I heard murmuring from there then the click of the door. Presently Raeanne came back into the room. Her long arms, down at her sides, ended in small fists. The set of her oval face reminded me of her portrayal of Clara, the scorned wife in *Life, Part 2*. She did not say anything, just stood by the TV staring off into space.

"What," I said.

"Why," she said quietly and with great precision, "that sneaky little lying sack of shit."

"What," I repeated.

"She didn't know."

"You think?"

"I *know!* She *didn't* know! She didn't have a clue! It came as a total surprise to her!"

"What makes you so sure?"

"Hey," she answered, "I know acting when I see it."

†††

The wedding was held the next afternoon, and it went fine. The radiant couple, wearing all white like John and Yoko, pledged their troth at the front of a banquet room at the country club. The officiant was a district judge; the attendants members of Shay's family; the witnesses a packed mob of well-dressed people seated on folding chairs. Having had experience at appearing before judges, Chick was stiff and formal. Everyone else was quite cheery. Shay in particular could not conceal her exuberance. Even from where the ushers had seated Raeanne and me, toward the back of the hall, a long way away from the family, I could hear her gleeful tones. At the end of the recessional ("Trumpet Voluntary," what else), as Shay and her new husband swept out the back, I distinctly heard her say, "Hey, that wasn't so bad!"

The reception was held in a separate banquet hall equipped with two buffet lines, bandstand, dance floor, and several eight-rounds clothed in white. The bride, groom, and family sat at a long table at the front, dominated by the triple-tiered wedding cake. Raeanne and I were assigned to an eight-round about as far from the food as you could get. During dinner Shay and Chick made the rounds of the tables. They never bothered to come by ours.

I couldn't tell if Raeanne had picked up on any of this. She cheerily chatted with our tablemates—some distant relatives of Shay's mother, and a couple of Mike's machinery firm customers. I just stayed well within MacMurray mode as the conversation swirled about me. They discussed buck poles, mud bogging, and bed races, whatever those were. They mentioned Snigniss, which seemed to be a town, and Nuck Muck, which I believe was a school. The couple beside Raeanne said they were leaving for "up north" the next day. I just barely caught myself before telling them that they were *already* up north.

By the time dinner was done, Shay was so drunk I could have bitten her hand and she wouldn't have felt it. Her voice, shrill and high-pitched, was audible all over the room, offset by Chick's hammer-hard laugh. She about

knocked him down with hugs and kisses every time somebody did the obligatory cling-cling-cling of spoons on glasses. While cutting the cake she dropped
the first piece and, with the second, clean missed Chick's mouth. During their
bridal dance, under the single spotlight, it was clear to me he was as much
holding her up as dancing with her. Somehow she got through the garter toss,
bouquet toss, and dollar dance, of which I did not avail myself. Chick shot
me a couple of glances, I noticed, looking determinedly triumphant.

Raeanne and I slow-danced. Back at the table, the topic turned to my alleged "city eyes." In defense, I pointed out that I *had* clearly spotted a herd
of turkeys during our drive up to the country club. Raeanne felt compelled
to inform me that it was a flock, not a herd, and was blocking the road at
the time. The good-natured laughter was interrupted by a piercing shriek of
electronic feedback, and then Shay's amplified voice: "This thing working?
Hello?"

"Oh Lord," Raeanne murmured, but shifted in her chair to watch as the
room noise dimmed. Shay stood by the bandstand, cordless mike in hand.
She seemed unsteady, as if wearing skates for the first time, and bleary-eyed.
Her white wedding outfit was looking a tad rumpled. Her bright red hair,
previously so meticulously done up, now looked done in. She gave a rambling
blurry lecture of thanks, interrupted every so often by polite applause. At first
I was only half listening, but presently she got my full attention.

" . . . My cousin Rae. From Detroit." Shay held the mike close to her lips,
blinking and staring, as if trying to spot Raeanne through the bright lights in
her face. "I just *know* you'll have all this someday, y'know, Rae? Just don't
be mad at me 'cause I didn't put you in the wedding party. 'Cause I was doing you a favor. 'Cause it costs money. Not a *lot* of money, of course, but—I
know how tough things are for you these days, kind of things you must have
to do to get by." Now the silence was complete. I glanced at Raeanne; she
was blank-faced.

Shay rambled, "Too bad about the movie—that's got to've been *so* humili-
ating. To be cut completely out of it, oh my God. We watched the DVD last
night, and I could see why. Just don't worry, you'll make it someday, you'll
make it, you're cute enough." A kind of mass exhalation rose faintly from
the crowd. I thought Shay would stop then, but she charged right on. "I just
wish you weren't so jealous—but did you have to—have to try to *spoil* things
for. . . . Was it because you blew it your first time out, with that loser? Not a
hard act to follow! So what do you do? You fall into bed with some disgusting mutt from Detroit somewhere! What the *hell* is up with *that*, Rae? I just
don't. . . ."

I was aware of an embarrassed stirring and shuffling that rippled among
the watchers. In my vision Shay's father appeared and took the microphone

from her and escorted her back to the head table. My ears heard the band strike up some kind of Dixieland. But my mind, my thoughts, had gone utterly blank. I did see Chick, sitting with his wife—he looked out at me, pointed at me once, and winked. My chest seemed frozen, my lungs incapable of getting enough air. Consciously I uncoiled my hands, one finger at a time. It's not about you. *Not about you.*

Then Raeanne was on her feet and faced the crowd in profile to me, stock still. She wore but a simple navy chemise. She had no spotlight and no microphone. She did not tap her glass, raise a hand, make a sound. Yet almost at once she became the focal point of the room. The voices dimmed and trailed away. The band quit abruptly. I had seen her on stage, on screen, and before groups large and small. But I had never seen her project such star power, so effortlessly take over a room like that. As the last sounds faded, she folded her hands at her abdomen and spoke.

"I'd like to thank Uncle Ray and Aunt Barb for all those great summer visits. You extended to me a lot of love at a time I really needed it. I really loved being here, wanted to be part of it, fantasized about someday being one of you. Since getting here yesterday I've learned how skewed my perceptions were, how naive I've been. Well, we're all human. Bottom line is that you're still family. And I'll always love you."

Someone started to clap. Raeanne did not notice. "In my work I've learned to accept being the target of the cruel and thoughtless things people say. Goes with the job. As long as it's me on the receiving end, I can deal with it. But—" she looked toward the head table, directly at Shay— "when you're landing them on the man who saved my life, who puts himself on the line for me, who I love with all my heart—well." She smiled, eyes shining. "That will not do. Goodbye."

We walked out hand in hand, without looking back. As we exited into the darkness of the summer-warm parking lot, Raeanne said, "I'm so sorry."

"Nothing to apologize for, sweetheart."

"Yes, there is. Let me get this out." She looked at me. "From the bottom of my heart, I'm sorry I made you leave before the hokey-pokey."

"Oh well," I answered. "Ya turned yourself around."

"That's what it's all about," she sighed.

†††

"I wonder if there was any bell ringing for Shay and Bill?" Raeanne asked as we rolled up the motel driveway to the road.

"What's bell ringing?" I asked, looking both ways. Not much traffic on Route 13, that early in the morning.

"Tradition up here," she said. "You go where the newlyweds are staying their wedding night and make some huge noisy racket, to wake them up. Know what they did for mine?"

"I'm afraid to hear."

"My cousin Mike got a pass key to our motel room," she said. "Snuck inside at 3:00 A.M. and fired up a power lawnmower. Hey," she interrupted herself, pointing, "think we could hit the Pit 'n' Git? I need serious coffee."

"Chunky coffee, coming right up," I replied, wheeling us into the parking lot.

"Just hang the I.V. bottle on the window here," she said drearily, "and plug me in."

"Gotcha." I shut off the engine and headed inside, barely noticing the orange warning sign on the door. I felt good. Sure, it was early, and sure, it was a six-hour drive home. But I was glad to get shut of this place. In the end, I'm a city guy, a city of Detroit guy, and that was where I needed to be. What's more, I thought as I fixed four large coffees—two black, two double-double—my Fred MacMurray act had gone threadbare. Best leave it to the professionals.

As I approached the checkout counter, I saw the elderly sales clerk staring my way, goggle-eyed, hands half up. Between us stood a figure with his back to me. He was very tall. His elbows stuck out at an odd angle. He had something in his hand. And he seemed to be wearing something over his head—something soft and blue. A stocking mask.

"Chick?" I said.

"Hand it *over!*" he said to the counter clerk. I realized he was repeating himself, that he'd said that just an instant before, but it hadn't registered. "Now. Gimme the money *now.*"

I hesitated then stepped closer, keeping space between us. The thing in his hand, I now saw, was a chrome revolver, a .32 or .38. My mouth went dry. The cardboard tray of coffees felt enormous in my hands. "Chick, for Chrissake, what're you doing, man?"

He glanced at me. Through the ski mask holes his eyes looked wild. "It's not me!"

"You done gone funny-turned, boy," I said, watching the snout of the pistol, which remained pointed in a more or less safe direction. "Put the *gun* down and—"

"Get back," he shouted, and the gun veered toward me, "or I'll blow you away too! I'll whack the lot of ya!"

The gun seemed real enough, but oddly, I was not scared. Even armed, Chick was not scary, only pathetic. "Whaddya want to do something like this for?" I asked gently.

"I need the money!" he yelled. "You shut down my game, I need the scratch for Vegas—Vegas takes serious moolah, I can't take Shay out there without—"

"So you were working her brother," I interrupted, hoping to distract him, buy some time. Setting the coffee tray on the checkout counter, I faced Chick. "What a nice family thing to do. What was it," I asked, guessing wildly, "a fight store?"

"Something like that. And it'd've worked fine, nice an' easy, if you hadn't butted your big fat nose into it."

"Put the gun down, Chick," I said quietly. "It's over."

"No!" He veered the weapon back toward the clerk, who stood as he'd been, hands half up. "Pop the drawer and fork it over. *Now.*"

"Chick," I said, as gently as I could, "in case you haven't figured it out yet, you're made."

"That's right," came another voice. Glancing to my left, I saw Hammer Lane by an open door next to the restrooms. On the wall to his right was a big mirror, which I realized now was a one-way security window. The shotgun, a Remington pump, looked like a toy in his big hands, but was anything but. It was 16-gauge at least, maybe even 12, and loaded, no doubt, with buckshot.

Now I was scared.

"Who're you?" Chick asked, annoyed.

"Put it down," Hammer answered conversationally.

I knew what was next. I could get in between and complicate things. Or I could play smart and step back.

I played smart.

Even through the ski mask, I could see Chick's leer. "Go ahead and shoot, bitch!" he yelled, waggling his pistol.

"Please!" I said.

Without a word, or any sort of movement, and almost casually, Hammer fired. The *boom* walloped my eardrums as the load of lead caught Chick's upper body. The impact sent him rocking backward, in a clumsy knock-kneed dance, into a wire rack loaded with huge colorful bags of fat-free chips. Arms flailing, he took it all down with him, a long, long fall, the handgun bouncing away, chip bags popping and flying. I scrambled over and crouched over him, swatting bags away, and nearly got nailed by a spurt of arterial blood shooting from Chick's ripped neck. His breathing was hard and wet, and he was convulsing the very life out of him. Taking his hand, I felt him tremor once, twice, and a third time. Then he was still.

Presently I realized that Hammer Lane was standing behind me, weapon shouldered, looking down at us, his expression dark and thoughtful. I got clumsily to my feet and said, without looking at Hammer: "He just got married yesterday, man." Then I went to the door and caught Raeanne just as she came flying through it.

†††

It was four hours before the cops let us go. By then Raeanne was wrung out, so drained and listless that I thought I'd have to fasten her seatbelt for her. As I backed out of the parking space, she stirred and straightened. "Well," she said, "we tried to help. She ignored us. So now, this."

"Yep."

"Is this what always happens?" she asked me. "When you try to help people? Is this how it always comes out?"

"Sometimes," I answered. "Especially when they don't ask for the help in the first place. And sometimes even when they do."

"Oh, God," she murmured. Leaning over, she buried her face in my shoulder. I wheeled us out onto U.S. 13, geared up to high then put my arm around her. "You know what," she said, voice muffled, "we need to go up there."

"Where?"

"Shay's mom's house. I know, I know," she said, as if to override me. "She said all those mean things—but she couldn't help it. She's silly, and she's sick. Desperate for money, desperate to be married, desperate to look good in front of her family."

"Uh-huh."

"But I have to go sit with her now," Raeanne said. "I'm a Brennan, and it's what Brennan's do. We take care of family . . . so turn around please?"

"No need. We're headed that way already."

"We are?" She straightened, looked around quickly through red eyes. "Hey, we are!" she drawled. "How—"

"Turned that way to begin with, coming out of the parking lot."

She looked at me, cleared her throat. "You knew?"

"When you love someone," I said, "you pay attention."

Letting out a sigh, she took my hand. And held it very tightly as we roared north.

Afterword

This was one of those stories whose title drops in on me during the writing. Till then the working title had been "Detroit Somewhere"—who knows why I thought that title would ever work!

In 2000 I bought property in central Michigan, 150 miles north of Detroit. I started keeping company with a native of the area, Deanna Heath, whom I married in July 2001. In the course of that I became acquainted with some of the local customs and traditions. Much of that influenced "My Best Fred MacMurray," and some of it drove elements of the plot, dialogue, and characters.

But the main impetus of this one came from some study I had been doing of the art and science of the confidence man. I was (and am) fascinated with that. The characters of Chick Hafer and T. Tommy Fledderjohn emerged from my research of that world. Chick's fate is based loosely on the end met by a man of my acquaintance who, the day after marrying, stuck up a liquor store (evidently to get cash for his honeymoon) and was shot to death.

For me, what works best about this story is the interplay between Perkins and Raeanne. It flows seamlessly from where they left off in the previous story and that, in turn, flowed from the end of the ninth novel, *Concrete Hero*. For the first time, Perkins has a serious and reasonably mature relationship with a woman—and just one woman at that. Who'd a thunk it.

Hope Springs does not exist, but places very much like it do, up in the knuckle-country part of our state. Aside from Raeanne, most of the characters are one-shots, and wholly fictitious—all except for Sean Ryan, who still ably plies his folkie trade at, among other places, The Noggin Room in Petoskey. And the "Finally!" award for this story goes to Hammer Lane, a character I've been trying to work into a story for 25 years now. He may never appear again, but at least he made it in this once.

Sex and Violins

Jail's a place I skip when I can. In this I've been less than 100% successful. A brief time or three, I've been a guest. Every so often I visit chums. And once in a while my work takes me behind bars.

Like today. My client: Micheline Quick, attorney at law. The defendant: Sal Vavaglia, #102557. His residence: Wayne County Jail. Way down deep, where they park murderers.

Unlike most, Sal was no kid. Forty-four, according to the file, but looking not a day over fifty. Squat and square-headed, his thick salt-and-pepper brilliantined hair contrasted stylishly with the blaze-orange jumpsuit. His squarish, unworked fingers fiddled on the smooth vinyl table, making his wrist chains jingle. This, at the moment, was the only noise aside from the occasional metallic door-slam, profane shout, shuffling footsteps, muffled scream—the sounds of the feeding of appetites, for justice and otherwise.

"You're innocent," I echoed him, careful to conceal my skepticism.

"You seem skeptical, Ben," Micki said. She was short and blond, smooth white skin, dressed in red, glasses hovering in front of guileless blue eyes. Thirty-and-change, her good looks were a bushel under which she hid razor-sharp smarts—to the dismay of many an opposing counsel around Detroit. "If he weren't innocent, I wouldn't bother to hire you. I'd just plead it out."

"Gee, thanks, lady," the suspect said sourly. Micki shrugged. Face flushing dark, Sal turned to me. "I didn't kill her, Mr. Perkins. I swear to God, I swear on my mother. I know I'm no angel—"

"As it happens, Sal," I cut in, "I've read the reports. During your marriage, the cops rolled on domestic violence calls six times. On three of these, they saw fit to cool you off in the can. After your wife left you, she beefed you twice for stalking and telephone harassment. Just the day before her death, her co-workers saw you trailing her—"

"I loved Holly," Sal murmured, dropping his forehead into his palms.

"So," I went on, "the cops knew just where to go after Holly's housemate found her at the bottom of the stairs, head bashed in. By a brass candlestick," I went on, overriding his lawyer, "that came from *your* house."

"Brass candlestick's not the big problem," said Quick. "It was wiped clean of prints. Our big problem is Sal's being alibi-challenged."

"Our big problem," I countered mildly, "is Sal's penchant for violence."

I wished Raeanne could have heard me pronounce it *"paw-shaw,"* just as she'd taught me. If she ever comes home from her film shoot in Canada, we'll continue our tutorial on *"li-berry."*

Sal said dully, "At the time she was killed, I was out for some air. I *told* you."

Looking at him made me want to ease up. For some reason I always pity penned-up people—even those accused of whacking their wives. Call me a softie; I've heard worse. "Any idea who might have wanted her dead?"

"None," he said.

"So I got nothing to go on?" I asked Micki. "This is a problem."

"You have a clean slate," she said brightly. "This is an opportunity."

"Yup. Well, what's needed from me here? ID of the real killer, complete with full confession?"

"That would be nice," she said, missing my jest, if that's what it was. "But let's not overtax your talents, shall we? I'll gladly settle for some reasonable doubt." She showed me thumb and forefinger, close together. "Just a smidgen will do."

"I'll get back to you," I said, rising.

Just past the outer sally port the attorney caught up with me. "Business slow?" she asked cheerily, bouncing along at my shoulder.

"Not hardly," I said. "Why?"

"'Cause I really didn't think you'd take the case. Johnston and April turned me down flat."

"I'm not first on your dance card?" I asked. "Micki, Micki, Micki."

"Johnston has a good rapport with the police. April finds it unnecessary to get smart-alecky at the most inappropriate times. *But,* both think Sal is guilty and I'm wasting my money. What's your story?"

"As it happens," I said slowly, glancing down at her, "I think Sal's telling the truth."

"You do?" Micki asked, shooting up an octave. "Why?"

"The brass candlestick," I explained, holding the door for her. "I'm not saying, friend, Sal's any rocket scientist. But we're to believe the killer was smart enough to wipe the murder weapon clean, yet dumb enough to leave it at the scene." We emerged into the brilliant Michigan fall sunshine. "It's so amateurish, it's like putting up a billboard that says PLANTED WEAPON."

†††

The other thing about it—I thought, but didn't share with Micki—was how hokey a candlestick, brass, pewter, or otherwise, was as a choice of weapon. I mean, in this era of mines, spores, fertilizer bombs, and 767s, who this side of Agatha Christie picks a killing tool so low-tech, labor-intensive, and lacking in elegance?

But to quote my daddy, you dance with them whut brung you.

And, hokey or no, the B.C.S. admittedly did an efficient job of knocking off Holly Czarnick.

Who had died where she lived, in a big ark of a house on Randall in the west side Detroit community of Biltmoor. This is one of those yo-yo neighborhoods that started off swanky in the 1930s, went slummy in the 60s and 70s, and then, with the turn of our shiny new millennium, yo'd upward again, its architectural charms, proximity to downtown, and dirt-cheap prices having been discovered by a new generation better equipped with cash, and less burdened with racial prejudice, than earlier ones.

I rumbled my '71 Mustang up the narrow slope of driveway and parked to the side. The house was two-story white brick with black hip roof, quietly stately, trimmed with copper downspouts and black wrought iron, and window boxes over-spilling floral greenery. There being no garage—my sense was that a detached one had vanished years before—vehicles sat in a line along the drive: a dark blue BMW convertible whose license plate read YIPPEE; a tanklike gray Toyota Land Cruiser; a beige Dodge Intrepid showing the beginnings of rust around the fenders; and a sleek black-and-chrome Harley Sportster, the real-deal road-ready muscle machine, not the yuppified midlife crisis model. My eyes lingered over the latter the longest, till the front door of the house opened.

"Yes?" asked the woman, tone more *no*. Slim, bright watchful eyes in a very dark pretty face, untucked plaid shirt above painted-on cutoffs.

"Ma'am, I'm Ben Perkins. Micheline Quick hired me to ask around about—"

"Oh yeah, you," she drawled. "We heard. Jeremy?" she called behind her, pushing open the door.

It gave directly into the living room, an expansive space in every dimension, brightly lighted from big windows on two sides. To break the ice a little I said to the woman, "I'm sorry about what happened to your housemate."

She was barefoot, arms folded, pensive (or is it "*paw*-sive"?), her distance from me marked. Her dark brown hair was unfashionably straight and pulled back to a short tail back of her head. "Housemate?" she snorted. "Oh no, not me." She jerked a thumb. "Him."

Who, trudging down the wide creaky stairs toward us, was a tall gent in his mid-40s, sleek and lanky, with longish brown hair and pale eyes in a soulful catlike face and a cycle helmet under his arm. He gave off an air of profound, centered calm. This can reflect a highly evolved level of inner peace and serenity. It also comes from long stretches in solitary. "You're the detective," he said, voice low.

"Private."

"This case don't rate even a corporal?" he asked, slanted smile, hand extended.

"Ha-ha," I said politely, shaking with him. "You're Jeremy, I take it."

"Warmbold." No sign of nervousness despite the arrival of the private eye. Damn, I'm losing my touch.

"And you're?" I asked, facing the woman.

"Uninvolved."

"Come on, Shurice," Jeremy said easily.

"Pribbernow," she completed, through pressed lips.

"And you," I said to the man, "were the victim's housemate."

"That's right." He wore a white dress shirt and sky blue jeans. Casual—he oozed the stuff. "Holly and I bought the place together two years ago."

"You were a couple?"

"No, no. We worked together. Just friends." Shurice made a quick quiet hiss of air. Jeremy smiled at her. "What?"

"You did boink her, Jer."

"Well, that was—"

"I know, I know. 'Way back when,'" she sang, "and 'just a flang thang.'" Turning to me, smile stretched over-wide, as if in apology for making me witness her snipe, Shurice asked, "Care for something to drink?"

"That'd be good, thanks."

"This way," Jeremy said. The living room spilled through a wide archway into a dining room with a beautiful oak table; just past that the kitchen peered through an open door. Our path took us past the mouth of the wide wood staircase. "This is where I found Holly," Jeremy said, hanging his helmet on a newel.

An oval rag rug covered the hardwood floor at the base of the stairs. I had a feeling it had not been there when Holly landed—at least not that particular one. Shurice looked strained; Jeremy thoughtful. "She'd been dead quite a while," he murmured.

"Must be hard on you, dealing with this," I commented, following them into the kitchen.

Jeremy shrugged lazily. "I've thought about selling out, moving on." Shurice busied herself getting sodas and ice out of the refrigerator and arraying them on the large chunky butcher block that stood on thick wood legs in the kitchen's center. Jeremy and I stood on either side of it, Jeremy's back to the sink and counter and the large window above. "So what exactly have you been hired to do, Mr. Perkins?"

"Number one, call me Ben," I said lazily. "Number two, there's the feeling amongst Sal Vavaglia's defense team that the cops have got the wrong man. So here I am!"

Shurice put out drink glasses and gestured to me in invitation. I poured root beer. Jeremy helped himself to a diet, drinking right out of the can, which I'd have done myself had I been in my own house. "So what's your plan?" Jeremy asked. "Pick someone to be guilty then hunt up evidence pointing only that way? The Ken Starr approach? Or start with evidence, and follow it till it points credibly at someone other than Sal."

I grinned. "You clearly have me mixed up with someone who's organized. I just bang around kicking at things, jarring stuff loose, discuss here, percuss there, fisticuff as needed. Whatever it takes to bring to light clues that point toward someone, anyone, other than Sal Vavaglia."

Jeremy sipped. "I see."

"It's the investigative equivalent of throwing Jell-O at a tree," I explained, "till some of it sticks."

Shurice leaned against the counter. I noticed she was closer to me than to Jeremy and didn't look at him at all. Her lover—if that's what he was—said mildly, "Since I'm hearing nothing about presumption of innocence or due process, I take it you're willing to cast suspicion even on someone entirely innocent."

"Sorry, mister, I just work here."

Shurice smiled briefly. Jeremy's next words were quite placid considering the deep breath he first took. "I did not kill Holly. Sal killed her. I'm sure you've heard how violent he can be."

"Sure, to all appearances he's the most likely. That—and the absence of alibi and the most conveniently arranged brass candlestick—is the reason he's in the pokey. But after him, the next most likely suspect, sir, is you."

"Well, I'm innocent. I liked Holly. She was a good woman. We were close."

"All the more reason. The closer you are, the more likely. That's statistical," I said importantly.

"That's cynical," he countered.

"Whazzat mean?" I asked Shurice. "Same thing as 'experienced'?"

Shurice just smiled again.

Still calm, thoughtful, faraway, Jeremy said, "I was at a concert that night."

"Could have hired it out."

His pale eyes flickered. "Sure."

After a silence I said, "Well?"

"Well, what?"

"Pretend I'm Phil Donahue," I said and, bulging my eyes, waved my hands: "'help me out, help me out!'"

"I don't know what you—"

Rapping sounded from the front of the house. Jeremy leading, we drifted that way. Obscured by the screen door stood a tall blond woman in worn jeans and black boots and a slinky red sleeveless top. If I said she was 35, she'd never object. "Could we talk?" she asked Jeremy by way of greeting, elaborately not noticing us.

With an eye-roll for me, Shurice turned back toward the kitchen. I hung back a bit, watching. Jeremy said quietly, "You know there's no point. We both just need to move on."

"I want to be friends," she said tightly. I could see that she had dark brown eyes, intent on him.

"Sure," Jeremy said easily. "But I'm busy just now."

She pursed her lips then spun and marched down the drive. Jeremy guided me back toward the kitchen, leading with his slanted smile. "My ex," he confided.

"In *your* mind," Shurice put in. "Clearly, Gloria has yet to read the memo."

To me, the sexual tension in that kitchen seemed thick. Of the three of us, only Jeremy seemed oblivious to it. "So what were you asking me before?" he asked.

"Who else?" I asked. "Who else might have wanted to do Holly in?"

"Everybody loved her," Jeremy told me, picking up his drink.

I considered. "How about boyfriends?"

"She dated," Jeremy said. "Nothing serious."

"She was happily divorced," Shurice commented, rattling her ice. "That's why the YIPPEE plate."

"Uh-huh. Work trouble?"

"Nothing I can think of," Jeremy said.

"No way," Shurice chimed in.

I paused a beat. "Oh, you all work the same place?"

"Ad agency," Jeremy said. "Shurice writes, Holly was an account manager."

"And you?"

"Art."

"You're an artist?"

"Right."

Looking at him fresh, I could see it, if barely. "Okay, well, tell me about this concert."

"My friend Key is a doctoral candidate in composition," Jeremy said. "He put on a concert of his work. That's where I was."

My brain had stuck, as it often does, a phrase or two back. "'Key'?"

"Key Brown is his name."

"A musician. Named 'Key,'" I mused. "That's what my girlfriend would call 'way too weird.' How do I find him?" Jeremy told me. "And you?" I asked Shurice.

"Me what?" she asked, pouring me some more root beer.

"Where were you that night?"

"Well," she chuckled, "sure as hell not *there*."

"Why?"

The phone rang over by the eating area, and Jeremy wandered over to answer.

"That kind of concert is so not my thing. I like *songs*, man," Shurice answered me, and ticked fingers: "you know, like, with a beginning, and a middle, and an end, you know?"

"So where were you then?" I asked. "Here at the house, by chance?"

She beamed and pointed at me once, and again. "Nice try! That's a subtle detective trick, isn't it, to kerfuffle me into a self-incriminating disclosure. *Very* good."

"Obviously not so good," I grumped, "since it apparently didn't work. Unless of course you'd care to confess."

"Inconveniently for you, no. For one thing, I have no motive," she said. "I liked Holly, and she liked me. Besides, I was at my mama's that night with about 42 of my kinfolk. I can give you a list, Mister Perkins," she added helpfully.

"Not just now, thanks." I looked over at Jeremy, who was huddled on the phone. He caught my eye and gave me a wave. I nodded and gestured to Shurice. "Care to do the hostly thing and see me out?"

"With pleasure," she said primly. We walked through the dining room and living room toward the front door. "He didn't do it, you realize," she said quietly.

"I do, huh? Just when did I realize that?"

"Well, you ought to, is what I'm saying."

"Why for?"

"Trust me," Shurice said, dead serious. "Whatever mean Jeremy ever had in him, it's been gone a long time."

So he *had* had, as she put it, some "mean" in him once. I'd caught just a whiff of that; how and from where, I couldn't begin to tell you. "Where do you figure in this whole thing?" I asked her.

She faced me at the door. "Me? I'm just the latest love of Jeremy's life."

Spoke volumes about him. And maybe her, too. "Okay, so—"

"And the reason I didn't go to the concert," she cut in, "was because Gloria let it be known I was not welcome."

"Hold the phone. Gloria? The memo-less blonde at the door just now?"

"The very one. Jeremy's ex. My immediate pree-decessor," Shurice said, with no lack of irony.

"Why'd she have a say in whether you could go to the concert?"

"She performed in it," Shurice told me. "Fiddle player. She told Jeremy that seeing me with him there would throw off her concentration. So he asked me not to go."

"Well, weren't they broke up by then?"

"Long before. But Jeremy complied. He's such a sweet guy. Doesn't like any upsetness around him."

We stepped out the door onto the concrete stoop. My blue Mustang looked an oddball at the end of the yuppie-line of vehicles, from the YIPPEE-Beamer up to the raked, chopped Harley, which I eyed again, thinking about its owner. "Sounds to me," I observed, "that friend Jeremy has trouble breaking off things clean with folks."

Shurice nodded. "Surprising, huh, given how much practice he's had."

"Busy boy?"

"His whole life. The support group you'd need Ford Field for."

I looked at her, conscious of a double and maybe triple message. "He given you the hand-shaker?"

"Not yet. That I know of. It's sometimes hard to tell, with him."

A guy, I reflected, too kindhearted to be an efficient dumper is hardly likely to bash a woman's head in. Without a really good reason.

I'd already thought of one.

"I know I'm not right for him," Shurice said softly. "He'll never admit it, but what he really likes is girls like Gloria—nail-hard factory manager-types, super full of themselves, who enjoy wiping their feet on men's backs."

"Well," I commented, "it ain't none of my business, but you need not settle for being a link in *anybody's* chain."

Her eyes lit up. "I know," she said, smiling briefly. "But thanks."

On the way to my car I glanced back at the house. I really liked it. I was partial to its occupants, too, especially Shurice, and even including Jeremy. But that didn't mean I'd hesitate an instant to wipe up Holly Czarnick's murder with him, given half a chance.

†††

Though it usually takes 20/20 hindsight to notice, most every case has just one major turning point. And here it was: Had I taken Randall south to Fenkell, the whole business would probably have puckered out eventually. But instead I went north, toward McNichols, thereby encountering a rust-blue

Chevy Celebrity, Bush I vintage, slantways to the curb. Wrestling with the hood was the tall blonde visitor to Jeremy's house, the persistent ex, Gloria somebody.

I parked behind her, mashed the blinkers, and approached on foot. Her look at me was narrow-eyed at first. "Oh," she said. "You were at Jeremy's."

Surprising she remembered. "What seems to be the trouble?"

She had the hood half-unlatched. "I already called Triple A."

"Let me see." I fiddled the stubborn latch loose and raised the hood with a metallic moan. Beside me Gloria stood, bare arms folded, everything about her—boots, jeans, blouse, expression—tight, except for the blond hair that flowed in waves to her shoulders. Her top was particularly snug, a ruffled silk number in burgundy: fetching, teasing, quite the feminine billboard aimed no doubt at Jeremy's eye. "Mm-mm-*mm*," I said appreciatively, "an engine I can understand. What's the story?"

"Just stopped by to say hello to Jeremy," she said. "Not that it's any of your business."

"I meant with the car."

"Running real rough. Keeps conking out."

I squinted in at the works. "No wonder. Your two and six are switched."

"'Scuse me?"

"Plug wires backwards. Allow me?" Before she could answer, I popped the offending wires off the plugs, switched them, and secured them. In the process my hands got super-grimy; clearly car maintenance wasn't Gloria's top priority. "Fire her up," I suggested, stepping back.

Looking sour, Gloria got behind the wheel and hit the ignition. The engine started rough, quaked violently on its mounts, spewed blue then smoothed. I was relieved being, as an old Ford Motor man, not entirely sure of this GM product's firing order. As I closed the hood on the third try, an enormous green wrecker hissed to a stop beside us idling in high diesel drone. It said JAKE'S SERVICE in big letters and 24 HOUR TOE below that. The driver, in gray twill, bustled around to us. "'Sup?"

"Too late," Gloria called dismissively, "he fixed it already. 'Bye."

The wrecker driver bridled. "Need to sign the paperwork anyways," she said, "or I don't get paid."

"You snooze, you lose," Gloria said, starting her door shut.

I caught it and pulled it open. "You need to sign off," I told Gloria, who looked highly displeased. "It's only right."

She rolled her eyes. "Perfect," she said, biting off the word.

The driver went to her truck. Back at my Mustang I cleaned my hands with a shop rag from the trunk, and waited and watched as the two quickly transacted their business. When Gloria finally pulled away, I cruised up beside her and glanced over. Behind her window she was smoking a cigarette and singing soundlessly. It took a block or two for her to notice me. When she did, she gave one brief wave—all five fingers, though my sense was she had to think about it first.

†††

As a former factory rat of the union enforcer persuasion—genus automotive, species Ford Motor Company—I had no truck with computers till the mid-nineties, and then only kicking and screaming. Since then I've become acquainted with them enough to know that what works best for me is to have and to keep friends who live and breathe the things. Which is how I obtained, through the expert exertions of Shyla Ryan, keyboard commando, copies of the deed and mortgage of the Randall Street house out of some Wayne County database. Even better, I had Micki Quick ready, willing, and eager to interpret them for me.

"Ooh," she cooed over the phone as I motored east, "isn't this interesting. Jeremy and Holly owned the house jointly. Both names on the deed. Mortgage in both names also. Everywhere is stipulated full right of survivorship," she charged on, "which means Jeremy automatically inherits Holly's share of the house."

"Shyla pulled some comps," I replied, wheeling the Mustang east on Jefferson. "They bought the place for fifty gee, today it'd fetch close to a hundred large."

"And going up all the time," Micki agreed. "You're saying there's a motive here? Financial?"

"Three reasons for murder," I replied. "Sex and money."

"On both counts Jeremy's interesting," she said thoughtfully. "Keep me posted."

Yes, ma'am. First order of business was to check out, like a piece of ripe fruit, Jeremy's alibi. Conveniently, by doing that I'd be checking out Gloria's alibi too. Not that I thought she needed one, and not that I thought it wholly logical for her to knock off the nonromantic housemate of her ex. But I've been around enough scorned women to know not to put too much past them.

The Sanford Rosen Institute for the Fine Arts campus occupied the site of a former tire factory along the Detroit River not far from Chene Park. Its series of low, ultra-modern circular brick buildings rose at odd angles from grassy, well-manicured hills. The School of Music department receptionist directed me to Rehearsal Hall A, where Mr. Brown, he said, was preparing for a recital.

The modest hall, on several levels rising in circles around a podium, was packed with people, dark with music stands and chairs, glittery with instruments in use. Most of these were violins and the bigger fiddles, but there was also a weird looking oversized bongo drum set, and a pipe contraption on strings, and some kind of wood xylophone deal being beat on from time to time. The racket they made was persistently random and determinedly tuneless, the kind of thing you stood back from rather than listened to. At first I thought they were just tuning up or something. Then I saw they were reading sheet music and being directed by a gent in the center whom I took to be Key Brown.

The song, if that's what it was, went on for a while. Scanning the musicians, I was surprised to see Gloria there, in the front row, blond head tipped and face intent as she sawed away fiercely at her violin. She seemed to be holding her own. Without warning the sounds stopped and the instruments went to rest. The gent in the center started to say things, which after the initial "Pretty good," I could make no sense of. Through it all the musicians listened attentively. Except Gloria. Bored, she fidgeted, smothered yawns, stretched out her arm palm down to inspect her glossy nails.

When Brown finally announced, "It's lunch," conversational babble broke out as the musicians, mostly young adults, began moving about. I trailed toward Brown but, seeing he was busy with two musicians, I angled over in the direction of Gloria, who seemed to be headed for an exit.

"Hey," I called, and she turned toward me, slowing. She wore a silver-gray sleeveless halter dress that snugly slimmed her nearly to the knee. Her hair was tied back today and, overall, her look trim and businesslike. "Car running okay?"

"Indeed," she said, and squinted at me. "And you are?"

That's right, we were never introduced. "Ben Perkins. I was thinking," I went on. "Plug wires don't just switch themselves. You ought to be careful where you have your car worked on."

She started to answer, held up, looked away, back again, and smiled. "Okay!" she said. "Gotta go!"

I watched her walk briskly out, and turned slowly back into the rehearsal hall. As is so common in this work, I was in a midnight of confusion. By Gloria's reaction, you'd almost think we'd never met before. Quite the blow to the old ego. But, I reflected, it's also a tactic used by women who are keeping the fences way, *way* out.

†††

Key Brown was a large man in his mid-forties. Comfortably dressed autumn-casual, he had thick iron-gray hair, a sunny disposition, and the easy demeanor of a man who loves what he does. He had an even rarer quality—the contented aura of a person free of secrets. "I heard about you!" he boomed. "Jeremy mentioned you were over there. Share my lunch?"

"I ate already, but thanks," I answered. He led me to some scattered chairs and music stands in a corner, fetched a sack, and took out an apple and sandwich. "Enjoy the performance?" he asked, unwrapping.

"Ah, you can't go by me," I replied. "If it don't start with 'woke up dis mawnin' I sort of zone out." Key nodded. "Let's start with the big question," I said. "Where was Jeremy the night Holly was killed?"

"Recital hall upstairs," Key answered promptly. "Attending my graduate composition recital."

"Here the whole time?"

"Absolutely. Stayed for the afterglow even."

Which placed Jeremy eleven miles away from the scene at the time Holly was killed. "How do you know Jeremy?"

"Oh, we go way back," Key said, still smiling. "Since we were six."

"And Holly?"

"Well, not as long. But ten years at least. I do music for the ad agency."

"And she and Jeremy had a thing?"

"Well," he said precisely, "more like a thing-let."

"Bought a house together though."

Key shrugged. "Yeah, go figure."

"What do you mean?"

"Well, it made financial sense. But I just thought. . . ." I let the silence drag. Key looked at me and sighed tolerantly. "They insisted buying the house together was strictly a business deal. But to me it looked like Jeremy was walking into a trap. Holly had her hat set for him. And everybody knew it."

"Maybe not Jeremy though?"

"At some level, maybe. But he's like a great boxer. Good hands, sharp eye, keen instincts, knows how to stay that critical thirty-second of an inch out of reach."

"So you're saying he didn't feel pressured?"

"Not that I could see. He went about his business. Socialized all he wanted."

"Like with Shurice now."

"Nice girl."

"And Gloria, before."

"Yes," was all he said, squinting at me as he chewed.

"So what's *her* story?" I asked.

"Well," he said, "we're not friends exactly. She was part of the circle, while she was with Jeremy. High-achiever type, runs the roll mill plant out at RackMasters."

"And plays the fiddle."

"Violin."

"Good at it?"

"Excellent, or can be. Erratic lately though."

Pause. "I hear," I said, studying him, "that Gloria had a hissy about Jeremy bringing Shurice to your concert."

Laughing, shaking his head, Key said, "Yeah, that's Gloria. She's curious, all right."

"What do you mean?"

"Can't ever tell with her. While she was with Jeremy she was disdainful toward him. After the split, she went all needy and clingy and demanding. At the same time, she's making runs at Jeremy's friends."

"Like who?"

"Well, Sal, for one."

"Sal? Vavaglia?"

"Mm-hm."

"Holly's ex. In the pokey, charged with whacking her."

"Right."

Fitting that one into the picture about gave me a headache. I started with the obvious. "Since when were Jeremy and Sal friends?"

"Since we were six," Key said patiently.

"All y'all?"

"Absolutely."

"I don't get it. Sal's a known wife-abuser. Not that nice a guy. And—"

"What are you saying?" he inquired.

"I'm surprised," I clarified, "that reasonably pleasant gents like you and Jeremy could be buddy-pals with somebody like Sal."

"Hey," Key said equably, "nobody's 100% likeable. Sal has his darker impulses. Jeremy runs with that Ypsilanti biker crowd. And me, well, I'm sure Sal and Jeremy have gripes about me galore. But the three of us, we've always been tight."

"Ypsi? You mean Willow Run?"

"Somewhere out there, who knows from the west side."

Me, for one. And I knew that crew. I squinted into middle distance, thinking. Plenty of knuckle-dragging freelance day-help for hire out there. "So Sal did Gloria."

Key was nodding. "Yeah. Bragged about it, too."

"Really. How was Jeremy with it?"

"Well, he and Gloria had been split for a while. But I could tell he was ticked."

"This was when, in relation to Holly's death?"

Key thought. "Not sure. Month, two months before."

God, I needed a cigar. Squirming, I fetched my little notebook out of my pocket, and a stub of pencil, and started a list. "Let's see if I've got this straight," I said. "Holly and Sal were married, and then split. Then Holly and Jeremy had a thing."

"Thing-*let*."

"Yeah, whatever. Jeremy had a thing with Gloria, which then fell apart, though she's still digging at it. During that time Gloria had a thing with Sal, who'd been stalking Holly, who had dumped his butt."

"You catch on fast."

"And now Jeremy's got a thing with Shurice."

"Bingo."

We sat in thoughtful silence. I sketched in my little notebook, names and lines. People were drifting back into the rehearsal hall. Presently I looked at Key. "I've worked a lot of cases," I said. "But this is the most tangled rat's nest of sexual complications I've seen since, as we say, I dined here alone."

Wadding up the lunch trash, Key lazily shrugged his large shoulders. "Be that as it may," he said, rising, "Jeremy didn't kill Holly. Nor," he continued mildly over my attempt to interrupt, "did he get someone else to do it for him. And," he squinted down at me, as voices from returning musicians started to build, "here's a clue for you. Sal didn't do it either."

"Then who did?"

"When you find out," Key Brown replied, winking, "be sure to let me know."

On the way out I passed Gloria again. Now her color was high, there was spring to her step, her eyes sparkled, and at the sight of me she brightened. "See you around, Mister Mustang Man," she sang, smiling, leaving in her wake the scent of tobacco smoke.

†††

Whoever claimed criminal detection is a neat, clean linear deal has his or her head up too many episodes of *Law & Order: SUV*. Out here on the street, sports fans, we sometimes jink, or swerve, or go back to the beginning.

Which explains my return trip to that Wayne County Jail interview room. Same cast of characters. Pretty much same apparel, too, except Micheline Quick wore blue.

"Yeah, Gloria and me did the dance," Sal Vavaglia said. "What about it."

"'What about it' is, you didn't mention it before," I answered.

He shrugged. "Slipped my mind."

"And you didn't ask, Ben," Micki put in.

Details. "So what about it?"

"What about what?" Sal mimicked. "Plumbing exercise, pretty much."

I glanced at Micki, frowned at the suspect. "Man, you're really making me want to keep on trying to help you."

"Whassat mean?"

"Never mind," I sighed. "This went on for how long?"

"Week, maybe."

I stared at him. "And?"

"And what?"

"Could we have a little *detail*, please?"

"You want detail?" he glowered. "Here's a detail, Mister Detective. On her back, down low, she has this big tattoo of a sunflower blossom, saucer size. Ain't *that* something, on the backside of a chick like Gloria, young yup business tycoon type."

Micki had her hands up, palms out, eyes shut. "*Must* we be so clinical? What *is* this in aid of?"

"Look," I said. "I have to tug at every loose end I can find."

"Gloria's loose, all right," Sal said.

Micki winced. "But what does Sal's, um, dalliance, with Gloria, have to do with anything?"

"By itself, probably nothing," I admitted. "But Gloria interests me. I've met her twice now, and something about her don't exactly square."

"Got that right," Sal said. "That little girl is *bent*."

At that Micki flushed, but maintained her trial lawyer poise. "Whatever she may be," she said, "Gloria performed in the concert, right? Up on stage, in front of everybody? So she couldn't have killed Holly."

"That *does* cloud the chances of a conviction," I conceded. "But something about her just don't set right. Where's she live?" I asked Sal.

"Never knew."

"Her last name?"

"Beats me."

"RackMasters is where?"

"Dunno."

"Well," I said, patience wearing dangerously thin, "during your hit 'n' run with her, how'd you reach her?"

"Beeper."

"And the number is?"

"I forget."

Micki Quick was silent all the way out of the jail till we reached the parking lot. "So you don't know Gloria's last name," she said. "And you don't know where she lives. And you have but a scant idea of where she works."

"The first half of any investigation," I said confidently, "is figuring out what you don't know."

"Well then, so far you're doing a hell of a good job."

"Thanks, boss."

"I await the second half, eagerly."

"Me too."

"Just so you know, for my money Gloria's not much of a suspect."

"You gotta wonder."

"And I *do* wonder," she said earnestly. "I wonder lots of things. I wonder if it's true that two-thirds of the world's eggplant is grown in New Jersey. I wonder why my name doesn't rhyme with Buick. But mostly I wonder why I'm working so hard to put a jerk like Sal back on the street."

"Because it's our job?" I ventured. "Because it's the right thing to do? Because—dare I breathe it—he could be innocent?"

†††

Next morning I got Rachel up, bathed her, diapered her, dressed her, and had breakfast with her. I'm making it sound easier than it was for, at one, she was already the sort of self-willed, high-powered, independent little cuss that reminded me of her mom. Even so I got her to daycare on time, and from there repaired to Free Beer Tomorrow to drink coffee and smoke cigars and try to sort sense into my dog's breakfast of a case.

There I confronted, and not for the first time, the twin questions of detection: What's up? And what now?

First, Sal. He'd certainly shown animosity toward Holly. And I could not put murder past him. But I was not sure that this was the type of killing he'd do. As a threatener, a screamer, a thrower, and a smacker, he might kill on impulse. But this was a planned, lying-in-wait type of killing. Didn't seem to fit him.

Jeremy Warmbold was Mr. Nice Guy with the hint of a dark side. He might want Holly dead for her half of the house, but there was no sign he was inordinately greedy or financially strapped. He might have whacked Holly if she had in fact been pressuring him to commit to her, but there was no sign of that, either. He'd rode some tough streets once, but evidently had gentled out. And his alibi worked.

How about Shurice? The only reason she might want Holly dead would have been to get rid of her as a competitor for Jeremy's, um, affections. But there was no evidence Holly actually was a rival, and there was no evidence Shurice saw her that way. Plus, though I had not yet confirmed it, Shurice too had an alibi.

Then Gloria Whosis, the scorned woman. Certainly she too might view Holly as a rival. Her resentment of Jeremy's other love interests was on record—she'd succeeded in barring Shurice from attending the concert. Based on my encounters with her, she seemed to be an odd duck. That didn't make her a killer, and besides, she too had a solid alibi.

But still. . . .

I sat there mulling. There were things about Jeremy I needed to check out. Shurice's cover story could use a look, too. I might even decide to poke around in Key Brown's backfield a bit. But, I concluded, of the frail leads I was dealing with, the one to move on first was the one about which I knew the least.

†††

RackMasters, once I found it, turned out to be a sprawling factory complex in the Mound / 8 Mile Road area. The small lobby was spare and empty except for some vinyl sofas and chairs, old *Manufacturing Engineering* magazines, a reception window, and a desk with a phone. Beside the phone was a stand-up laminated sign with a list of maybe 75 people—last name, first initial, and extension—and the advice to "Please call the extension of the person you are here to see."

Eight names had the first initial G. Big help.

The young woman behind the reception window was on the phone, poking at a computer keyboard, and sorting flimsies. She rewarded me with the last available eight percent of her attention span. "Gloria who?"

"I don't know. I do know she's an executive here."

"Well, we don't just give out employee names. Do you have an appointment?"

"I just want to talk to her."

"Sorry, you need an appointment. We have new security rules. Nine eleven, you know."

"Certainly. Can you at least tell me Gloria's last name?"

"Even if I knew it," she answered, "I'm not allowed to."

I went out into the autumn gray day, punching my cell. No answer at Jeremy's house; I left a message. No listing for Shurice Pribbernow. "Doctor" Brown, the Rosen Institute department secretary told me, was not expected in today; I left word for him too. Micheline Quick was in court, but would call back when she could. I thought, if nobody else cares enough about this case to be available when I need them, I'll just go back to the bar and this time drink beer, in large quantities. But the wave of self-pity receded when another notion burbled from the murk. Gloria's car, that old rattletrap Chevy Celebrity—could that be an angle? The name I wanted eluded me, but I recalled another clue, and I called my old pal Bill Scozzafava, Romulus bump-shop owner. I knew he'd know.

And he did. He gave me the name and laughed. "You know how that happened," he said. "They painted their first truck that way by accident, back in the 60s, and it got so many comments and chuckles, they just kept on doing it."

†††

JAKE'S SERVICE / 24 HOUR TOE, said the big sign on the blue-brick garage building on Central near the Edsel Ford. I parked plenty clear of the bays and walked in, luxuriating in the metallic clattering of tools, hissing of hydraulics, and scents of gas and oil and grease. The wrecker dispatch area was at the south end. I went into a small lunchroom cluttered with tables, chairs, soda machines depicting dead drivers, and several less-famous but living ones in blue twill jumpsuits, sitting around smoking cigarettes and waiting for their next runs.

Including, miraculously, the driver I needed, eating a sausage biscuit and reading *Waiting to Exhale*. She heard me out and shook her head and laughed. "I can't do that. Don't be ridiculous. That's confidential information."

I leaned down toward her, lowering my voice. "Do you remember me?"

"Yeah."

"The chick driving that Celebrity was fixin' to boogie on you without signing the paperwork. I got in her face, made her do right. Remember?" She nodded again. "I did for you that time, now I need you to do for me."

Back the wrecker driver came, halfway through my cigar, and handed me a slip of paper. I scanned the scrawl. "Can't be," I said, looking up at her.

"What it says," she shrugged, sitting back down to her book.

"The woman's name is Gloria," I pressed. "Not—" I checked the sheet again—"Cynthia."

"What it says," she repeated.

"And now I have to chase all the way to Port Huron?" I groused.

"Not before I get my thank you. Didn't your mama teach you?"

"Well, thank you."

"Well, you're welcome," she beamed, and went back to her book.

†††

Port Huron is about ninety minutes northeast of Detroit, where Lake Huron meets the Black and St. Clair Rivers. The address in question was in an older neighborhood, a cluster of high narrow wood-frame homes and scrubby swatch yards and curbs parked dark with clunkers. Halfway up the walk I could hear family noises from inside, kids yelling and TV and the honk of a clothes dryer alarm. The front door swung back at the hand of a shortish balding middle-aged man in tan slacks and a wife-beater tee-shirt. I asked, "Gloria here?"

He shook his head. "Must have the wrong address. Sorry."

Yessir, I just *knew* this was a wild goose chase. "Wait," I said, and the door opened back. I consulted the paper. "How about Cynthia Brooker?"

The man's placid every-guy face clouded. He blinked, squinty eyes boring in on me. "What do you know about Cindy?"

"Well, not much—"

"Are you from the Internet?"

"Huh?"

"You better come in." He pushed the door back and allowed me through. The living room was a chaos of dark heavy furniture, brightly colored toys a-tumble, generalized cacophony from the TV and some kind of children's cassette player. Three little kids were in evidence, a girl and two boys, the oldest maybe four. With an absentminded sweep of his foot, the man cleared a toy trail for me and uncluttered a chair for me to sit in. "So who are you?" he asked.

"Ben Perkins. Private detective. From Detroit."

"Orthal Brooker," the man said, and shouted: "Mom! Visitor." He sat down across from me. The little girl, cute, blond, and naked from the waist up, ran to him and he scooped her up onto his lap, strong, protective, sure of himself. "Do you know where Cindy is?" he asked me, brow furrowed, honest face intent.

"Point of fact," I said, "I'm not certain it's even Cindy I'm looking for. You sure you don't know any Gloria?"

"Positive," he said. "Matthew, don't beat on your brother now."

"Five nine or ten, blond, dark brown eyes, about thirty-five?"

"Nooo," he said hesitantly. "Matthew, no. No. *No!*" He blinked at me. "What makes you think this Gloria person was here?"

"Well, she had a Triple A call down in Detroit. The Triple A account she used came back to here. Name on the ticket was Brooker, Cynthia, though. Blue Chevy Celebrity, '89 or '90."

Unconsciously he hugged his daughter. "Ninety," he said, and hollered, "Mother! Get in here! Matthew, please do *not* twist Jimmy's ear." A sixty-ish gray-haired lady in a pink housedress puffed in, eyes just visible over a mound of laundry in the basket she carried. "Mother," Brooker said, "this man saw Cindy in Detroit. When?"

"Thursday."

"Oh my God," the woman said. She dropped her laundry basket, pried the youngest boy loose from the hammerlock of the one I presumed to be Matthew, and knelt on the floor next to Orthal. "What was she doing?" the woman asked.

"That's a long story," I said. I hardly knew what to say, where to start. "I know her as Gloria. She works for RackMasters. She plays violin."

Mother and son glanced at each other. "Cindy played violin in school," Orthal said. "That's what she told me. What's RackMasters?" I told him. "Can't be Cindy," Orthal said, shaking his head. "She *never* goes down there."

"But the car, this Celebrity, that's hers?"

"Old beater I bought her," Orthal said. "So she could go to work and bingo and bowling."

Information exploding every whichaway; I had to back and fill. "I take it Cynthia's your wife?" Orthal nodded. "And she's vanished, then?" Twin nods. "When?"

"Month ago now," he calculated.

Well, that didn't work. Gloria had been associated, if that's the word, with Jeremy Warmbold and Key Brown and the others for several months at least. Were Gloria and Cynthia Brooker the same person or not? I felt like I was trying to shovel smoke. There's order to everything, and there had to be order to this, but I sure as hell could not see how. I asked the good old standby fallback question: "What happened?"

"Her and her Internets," the woman said, holding the squirming Matthew securely in her strong arms.

"I bought her a computer for Christmas," Orthal said.

"And she got obsessed," I guessed. By now an old story. Technology's gift to the detective profession: business for everyone.

"Orthal bought her things," his mother said, absently rocking the baby. "Anything she wanted, he let her have. Jewels and flub-dubs. Weekends away alone." Her eyes burned. "So she rewards this good man by running *off* on him!"

"Yes, ma'am," I said. "Where'd Cindy work?"

"Scale operator at the scrap yard. Don't bother asking," Orthal added, waving a hand. "They ain't seen her either."

Well, I'd have to check that for myself. Maybe. "Cynthia have any sisters?"

"Only child," Orthal answered.

"And no family," his mother put in. "I told you, Orthal—girls with no family is bad news!"

"Mother, please," he said wearily. The spindly, worn woman drew herself up short at the sight of her son, whose eyes were welling with tears. "Mr. Perkins," he said, "please tell me what's going on."

I looked around the small, cluttered living room, the din of the TV and the toys and the kids reverberating, the dad whispering calmly to his squirming daughter as he brusquely wiped his eyes, the grandma perched awkwardly over a basket of clothes, and shook my head. "I don't know. A lot to sort out. You got a picture of Cindy handy?"

Orthal puffed to his feet, handling his daughter with easy confident affection, and pawed with his free hand through the clutter on a hutch. Back he came with a creased eight by ten. It was a color studio head shot, crisp and vivid: bright smile, luminous brown eyes, red lips, healthy pink skin, hoop earrings, bushels of blond piled high in a Nashville saloon big-hair look.

And unmistakably Gloria.

"Picture goes back quite a ways, I take it," I said.

"Last year," Orthal said. "Cindy." His eyes softened. "Gorgeous, ain't she."

"It's Gloria, too," I said. "With a different 'do." I stood and handed the picture back. "Curiouser and curiouser," I commented. "Twins. Gotta be."

Orthal wasn't listening. "Can I pay you? To find Cindy for me? Whatever you want."

"No. Absolutely not." I clapped his shoulder. "But when I find her," I told him, "you'll be the first to know."

†††

"Ben? Key Brown, returning your call. Capitani is Gloria's last name. I don't know where she lives. I can dig up her phone number if you need it. Call me back."

"Hi sweetheart. It's awfully c-o-l-l-d up here in Yellowknife. Can you please come snuggle with me under my down comforter? Love you. Bye."

"Hey Ben, Gloria's last name is Capitani, she works at some factory in Center Line, I think, not sure. Lives in Fraser right off Groesbeck Highway someplace. Seeya, bye. Oh yeah, this is Jeremy. Warmbold. Seeya."

"Ben, Carole. Rachel's appointment is next Wednesday. Pleasant Ridge office. Thanks for covering it for me. Take care."

"Mr. Perkins, this is the law office of Micheline Quick, J.D. Be advised that the case file shows 'Gloria's' last name to be Capitani: C-A-P-I-T-A-N-I. No home address on record. The police interviewed her at her place of employment, RackMasters Sport Systems in Sterling Heights, Michigan. If you need further assistance, please do not hesitate to inquire. Bye-bye now."

All righty then. I returned Raeanne's call, cleared the rest of the messages, and aimed the Mustang back south toward Detroit. The cigar I smoked did nothing to clear the fog. I now knew Gloria's last name. I knew that Cindy Brooker had been banging around Detroit, pestering Jeremy. And I now knew, almost for sure, that Cindy and Gloria had to be twins. Were they interacting, acting together, acting in opposition? Did Jeremy and the others know anything about Cindy? Did Scorned Gloria have anything to do with Holly Czarnick's death? Did Cindy Brooker have anything to do with anything? Or had my simple garden-variety murder case been sideswiped by an otherwise unrelated Port Huron deal? The answer-to-question ratio, I thought, was seriously out of whack. . . .

A furious 90-minute drive later, I consulted the RackMasters lobby directory, dialed 1418 for one Capitani, G., and she answered right away: "Gloria."

"Ben Perkins."

"Who?"

I repeated the name, drawing out the syllables. "We met at the Rosen Institute last week, at your rehearsal."

"I meet lots of people." Good thing, I thought sourly, I already have a girlfriend. This being disremembered by pretty women could get depressing. "What do you want?"

"To chat about the murder of Holly Czarnick."

"You a cop?"

"No. Worse. Think of me as a stubborn little terrier, chomped down on your pants leg. Bounce me off the wall, I *still* won't let go."

Her chuckle surprised me. "Well, then. Can you meet me at my office tomorrow?"

"As it happens, I'm out in your lobby right now."

"Tomorrow would be better. Or next week."

I turned my back to the others, lowered my voice further. "Listen. Lady. I have chased all over hell's half acre today, from Detroit to Port Huron and back, and I am officially in no mood. Do I make myself clear."

The receptionist buzzed me through without asking for my name, ID, business, signature, or loyalty clearance documents. So much for security, but then, Tom Ridge can't be everywhere. Gloria Capitani's office was halfway down RackMasters's "admiral country" hallway. It was a nicely carpeted space, single window, muted colors, the traditional large mahogany desk cluttered with cartons, a purse, and a pack of Winstons with matches tucked in the cellophane. Gloria wore jeans and running shoes, blue Sylvester tee-shirt, and a red bandana over her mop of blond hair. "So you're the detective," she said coolly, reaching out her hand.

It was warm and strong. She clung just an instant too long, checking me out. I liked what I saw, too. She was rangy and vivid, a type I knew well: shop rat who'd worked her way up from the floor, ultimately earning the large mahogany desk. I gestured around. "Relocating?"

"As of today, quitting," she said, scooping books off a shelf and jouncing them carelessly into a box.

"For something better, I trust."

Folding the box lid shut, she fixed me with a brown all-business stare. "Let's get to it," she said, tone clipped. "You mentioned Port Huron. I take it that means you found my twin."

"Cynthia Brooker?"

"Only twin I've got. What'd you think of her?"

"Didn't actually see her. What's she got to do with this?"

"Not a thing," Gloria said, opening a desk drawer. I leaned against a visitor chair, waiting, watching, listening. "Just my personal pain in the neck."

Not sure she was being fully truthful; not sure which direction to push this; not sure of much of anything. "Was told she split from her husband up there," I said.

"Really? So that part of her sob story was true?" Straightening, she dropped more junk into a box. "I didn't even know she *existed* until a few months ago. She tracked me down through some Internet adoption search service."

"You were adopted then."

"Obviously."

"So Cindy tracked you down. What happened then?"

She sighed impatiently, folding the carton shut with quick sure hands. "I let her stay with me a few months. It didn't work out so well. She ran up bills, gobbled down food, trashed my house. What is it guests and fish do after three days?"

"Stink," I ventured.

A muted musical tone sounded from her desk. Gloria opened her purse, checked a pager without expression, and put it back. She looked at me, expression conflicted. "Cindy was *family*, my *sister*, I *wanted* it to work out. But things got worse and worse. She brought home strange men. Embarrassed me in front of my friends."

"And went around pretending to be you?"

Fetching herself a fresh carton, she fixed me with a look. "That, too. Said it felt kinky. What it was, was creepy. When did you see her?"

"Last week, at Jeremy's."

She snorted. "Really. That's funny. I kicked her out weeks ago. Thought she was long gone."

"To where?"

"Who cares?"

"Her husband. I promised him I'd find her."

"That loser? Well." Bending, Gloria dragged out the lowest desk drawer, hoisted it on the desk, and began unloading files into the carton. "Cindy said she had an Internet lover, a one-eyed guy in Newfoundland—odds are she'll hook up with him. Good riddance." Boy oh boy, I thought, and not for the first time: For hundred-proof venom, nothing tops siblings gone sour. "Is there anything else?" she asked. "I'm really busy."

"Well, there's the murder."

"Oh yes." She beamed. "Ask away. Brace me, beat me, make me confess all."

Saucy dame, one of those tough Detroit chicks, like half the women I grew up with. My feelings were an unhealthy brew of uneasiness and interest and speculation. It would, I thought, start out really really good, and end up really really awful. But that part in-between—Lord have mercy. To quote my mama: O Death, where is Thy sting?

I ran down the routine questions and got the expected answers: At the time of Holly's death, Gloria was playing violin at Key Brown's concert, with Jeremy in very obvious attendance. "What do you think," I asked, "about the cops's theory that Sal Vavaglia did Holly in?"

"No opinion," she said, transferring files.

"Hm. I kinda thought you'd be a bit more definite."

Her desk phone rang. She snatched it up, said some monosyllables intermittently, hung up. "What makes you think I know from Sal?" she asked innocently.

"Well, you did sleep with him."

I don't know what I expected, but whatever it was, I didn't get it. "Who says?" she asked, amused.

"Sal."

"Well," she said, still smiling, "I have just a *lit*tle better taste than that. For example, *you* I'd do in a New York second."

"Yeah, I'm sure," I blurted.

"Shut the door," she said. "Try me."

I freely admit, my heart pounded. The dirty little schemer-boy inside me started a-calculating. But then the thought of Raeanne, far away but never really, came clear, fading Gloria, moist lips, bright eyes and all, to a cardboard cutout.

She smiled. "Of course," she went on smoothly, "if I had really *good* taste I'd never have gotten involved with Jeremy." Ouch. She dumped the rest of the drawer contents—paperclips, junk like that—into the carton. "Word to the wise, Mister Detective. Check Jeremy out carefully."

"Meaning what?"

She returned the drawer to its place. "He's got a mean streak. Did time for assault, years ago. Ran wild with a biker crowd, still hangs out with them weekends." She slid her firm jeaned fanny onto the desktop and, making a fist, studied her nails thoughtfully. "That's why I ended it with him. I got this creepy-crawly feeling that I'd best not stay too close."

"*You* ended it? What I heard was *he* gave *you* the buh-bye, and you were upset about it."

"Playacting, that's all." In her averted look I caught what felt like fear, way back. "I didn't want Jeremy feeling rejected. Hurt his fragile masculine ego. I was afraid it would make him mad. You don't want to make Jeremy Warmbold mad. Not ever."

†††

Which sounded mildly interesting. So I turned my attention back to Jeremy.

Or tried to.

Saturday I went out to Tattoos, Boots, & Motorcycle Parts in Willow Run. The autumn day was warmish and sunny. The saloon's vast asphalt parking lot was parked dark with Harleys, attended by beefy gents clad in leather and spikes, accompanied by their similarly adorned babes. Grizz, my main man, wasn't around, but I found Drano in his usual spot, holding down a corner booth. He wore a BABY ON BOARD tee-shirt with an arrow pointing down at his massive gut. He knew Jeremy quite well. And liked him, even though Jeremy had long since gotten a straight gig. Drano, straight-faced as ever, told that there was no way either Jeremy or Drano's crew had anything to do with Holly Czarnick's death. Between the lines I inferred that crank distribution was the cash crop; nobody out there had need to dabble in contract murder.

Leaving there for dinner with Rachel and Carole, I should have been sifting through everything Drano had told me. Evaluating the words, trolling for clues, trying to scope out the truth. Instead I found myself thinking about the sight of Gloria—who turned out to be Cindy Brooker—at Jeremy's door that first time.

Made me uneasy. No idea why.

Next stop, early the next week, was Admetco, the Southfield ad agency where Holly had worked with Jeremy and Shurice. From the start it was clear that the cops had worked this turf down to the nub. Holly's boss, an arthritic curly-hair with a beer-nose and suspenders, was sure that no one there—for sure not Jeremy—was a valid suspect. But he had lots of stories about Sal Vavaglia's stalking, threats, and abuse of his ex-wife.

On my way to my weekly poker game at the Judge's, I tried to filter what I'd seen, heard, and felt at the agency. Looking for disconnects, contradictions, disparities. What kept elbowing in was the memory of Gloria at the Rosen Institute rehearsal hall, bopping out, bopping back in.

Felt edgy. Didn't figure. Plus I lost big.

Along in there I'd put full court press on digging out Jeremy's paper trail. Credit report showed no evidence of financial distress. Criminal record was just as dull. Only item of interest was a no-contest plea back in '83 to a single count of disorderly conduct. That stemmed from what sounded to me like a biker brawl at the Christmas Café in Ann Arbor. Far cry from the "assault conviction" mentioned by Gloria.

Whose face kept floating to the forefront of my thoughts: Gloria in her RackMasters office, Gloria packing boxes, Gloria trying to hop on my bones, Gloria trashing Jeremy. Gloria who, when I'd called her from the lobby phone, had suggested I come back next week, only to tell me ten minutes later she was quitting as of that day.

It gnawed at me. Something there—but *what?*

Wednesday afternoon I was pulling out of the daycare lot in Royal Oak, talking on the phone, when call-waiting beeped. I punched it to get Micki Quick. "Busy?" she asked. "Took you a while to answer."

"Was talking to my travel agent."

"Headed somewhere?"

"Newfoundland, if I can get there from here."

"Why, pray?"

"Promised a guy." I gunned the engine, roaring into traffic. "What's up?"

She sighed. "Well, 'fraid I have to whistle the play dead."

"Not surprised."

"It was worth a shot," she said. "So we goose-egged. It happens."

"Just don't feel right."

"I know. But you did your best. And of course we'll pay you anyway. Through today."

For once that wasn't what mattered to me. "What're you going to do? Plead it out?"

"If we get a good offer. If not we'll go to trial. The case against Vavaglia isn't all that strong. Listen, I've got another call. Catch you later."

"'Bye, Micki," I said, and she hung up before I could thank her for the work. I felt sour. Unfinished business—it happens, but I don't have to like it. What's that overused term? Closure? There you go, I needed some closure. After a moment I figured out how to get me some.

††††

This time Jeremy himself answered the door. "Oh, hey," he greeted with his slant smile, stepping out onto the stoop. "Guess you been busy."

"I have," I answered. "But I'm here to tell you, it's all over."

"Oh yeah?" Jeremy wore a navy University of Michigan sweatshirt and jeans, and was barefoot below, ponytailed up top. "What's up?"

"I owe you an apology," I said.

"What for?"

"I took this case to try to cast doubt on the guilt of Sal Vavaglia. To do that I went the extra mile to find dirt on you. Bottom line is, you're in the clear. And if my banging around has caused you discomfort, I'm sorry."

He looked sheepish, hands hooked in back pockets, facing away. "It's all right. Just doing your job." Looking back at me, he smiled. "Come on in, why don'tcha. Buy you a beer."

"Hey, sounds good. Thanks." I followed him inside, glad I had come here, not just for the beer, but for the satisfaction of squaring things with him. "Saw Drano the other day," I commented as we made for the kitchen.

"I know. He called me right after."

"Pretty tight with him, huh?"

Jeremy, traipsing into the kitchen, answered something, but I didn't hear it. Turning from the sink, hands soaked below rolled-up sleeves, was Gloria Capitani. "Well, hi, Ben," she said cheerily. "What brings you here?"

Jeremy, semi-oblivious as ever, was digging in the fridge for bottles. I said, after a pause for equilibrium, "Just saying hi. I'm, uh—it's good to see you."

Jeremy came out with a fistful of beer bottles and put them on the butcher block. Gloria was drying her hands, smiling a smile of immense satisfaction. "Oh," she said lightly, discerning the unasked question, "Jeremy and I are—"

"We're back to hanging out," Jeremy said with a wink, gesturing at the bottles.

I took a Stroh's dark longneck and twisted her open. Gloria, down-homey in tan cutoff bib overalls over a white tee-shirt, was quite the chatterbox. "We never really were finished," she said. "I realize that now," she added, with a private smile for Jeremy.

A silence settled briefly on the kitchen. Gloria leaned against the full kitchen sink. Jeremy stood silently to my right, sipping beer. I was in that midnight of confusion again, could not figure out why. "How about the job? That finished now?" I asked.

"Oh yeah," she shrugged.

"You quit?" Jeremy asked, surprised. "RackMasters?"

"It was stupid," she said.

"But Christ, you been there fifteen years."

I took a sip of beer. No time to be hammering it. "Quit the orchestra too?" I asked casually.

"Absolutely," she said sourly. "Who's got time for that, all that practicing."

"What're you going to do for work, babe?" Jeremy asked easily.

"I'll find something. Not to worry."

Again the silence. The kitchen counters were jam-stacked with dirty dishes, glasses, utensils. Evidently Jeremy, who did not strike me as an overly domestic type, had been between roomies for some time. Gloria showed miles of gorgeous pale leg below the cutoff bibs. Her blond hair was tied up and back. She wore little if any makeup. Even her nails, which she was inspecting at the moment, were plain.

And that was what triggered it. Not the plainness of her nails, but the way she looked at them. Her hand was a fist, nails up. Back at the Rosen Institute, during the rehearsal break, Gloria had inspected her nails too. But palm down.

Jeremy said something, Gloria answered, I put in a comment. Don't ask me what; I was otherwise engaged. Like fuses, questions hissed in my head, and then went off, pop pop pop, like firecrackers. Things were lining up now. About time. The beer bottle warmed in my hand. I needed a cigar. "Excuse me," I said, interrupting Gloria. I looked at Jeremy. "I need to see a man about a horse."

"Out by the stairs, hook a left down to the end," he said.

With a wave I went out. But not down the hall; out the front door. A cigar was to hand and smoldering before I was off the stoop. Besides my blue Mustang, only the gray Land Cruiser sat on the driveway. Jeremy must have picked Gloria up somewhere. Quite the rekindling they're having, I thought, extracting my cell phone and notebook. Too bad I'd have to bust it up. Too bad for Jeremy and too bad for Orthal. But good news for Sal, and only fitting—it was things he'd said that broke this open for me, things he'd said that I'd discounted before. My mistake. One of them.

After barely a ring, Orthal answered. "Hey," I said, "it's Ben."

"Been wondering, man. Any luck yet?"

"Dunno. Cindy have a beeper?"

"Yeah, why?"

Thought so. I'd seen it. "Give me the number."

He did so. "Not much point, I try it every day."

Made no nevermind. "One other thing. Tell me about the tattoo."

Five minutes later, nicotine-stoked and content, I went back into the kitchen. Gloria and Jeremy abruptly disengaged. Her color was high, lips moist.

He was smiling, with an aura of swagger. They had it bad; you could cut it with a knife. But like idiots they elaborately went about separate businesses, Gloria back to dishes and Jeremy flipping through mail on the counter. I picked up my beer, not that I lacked things to do, and said, "Hey, Jeremy, tell me about Gloria's tattoo."

"What tattoo?" he asked, glancing up at me from an Episcopal diocesan newsletter. "Doesn't have one."

Back to us, Gloria just hesitated in her dishwashing. I said, "I didn't think her the type, myself."

She turned, drying her hands. "What're you talking about?" she asked, with perfect curiosity.

"You know," I said pleasantly. "Sunflower. Saucer size. On your spine, down low."

"Where you get this?" Jeremy asked me curiously.

"Don't worry, I haven't done her," I said. "But then, neither have you."

Missing that, Gloria said to Jeremy, "It was going to be a surprise for you," rushing her words a little.

"Where I got this," I continued to Jeremy, "was from your old buddy Sal. He saw the tattoo during his time with Gl—I mean, with this woman. Which," I went on to her, saying it like I hadn't just this second thought of it, "had to have been when you swiped the brass candlestick."

Her expression, the very picture of perplexity—*damn* she's good, I thought—changed. She checked her pager, which must have been on vibrate, and squinted at it. "I told you," she said, and looked at me a bit stern now, "I never had anything to do with Sal."

"One oh two five, five seven," I answered pleasantly.

"Huh?" Jeremy asked.

The woman squinted at me, and though she said nothing, had to know I had her. "Sal's prisoner number," I told her. "I'm sure you were wondering why it's popped up on your beeper." Jeremy was watching me with a mix of suspicion and curiosity, for once fully engaged in here and now. "Just now on the porch I called the pager number of a woman named Cindy Brooker," I told him. "Gloria's twin. And that pager in her pocket is what went off. Which makes this woman Cindy. And leads to the question," I went on, looking at the woman: "Where's Gloria?"

"*I'm* Gloria," she said sharply. "Cindy left her pager behind, and I took it over."

"You took over *Gloria*, you mean," I retorted. "And I even know when you did it. At that rehearsal, at the Rosen Institute. I talked to Gloria before the break. Only time I ever saw her, come to think of it. She didn't know who I was, even though I'd supposedly met her out here. She left for lunch. But the woman who came back—same looks, same clothes, similar hair—well—that woman, *you*, saw me and said, 'Hey, Mustang Man.' Which Gloria could not possibly have known."

Wearing down, steel belts showing, Cindy was blinking, eyes darting to Jeremy and back—you could practically hear the whir of her wheels spinning. "But I was *here* when you were here, I saw your car then."

"Gloria didn't do that," I said patiently. "*Cindy* did that. See? Even you can't keep it all straight."

Cross now, right on schedule, she said, "You been smokin' wacky tobbacky, old man."

"What happened to Gloria?" I asked. "What did you do to her?"

"I think you need to talk," Jeremy said mildly.

"*You* need to throw this son of a bitch out of here," Cindy told him. "Right now, if you want me happy."

Turning her back on us, she went back to washing dishes, loudly splashing water, clattering utensils. I looked at Jeremy. "Be my guest. Throw me out."

Clearly conflicted, Jeremy said, "There's a lot of this I don't understand. I—"

Whirling, bare arms snapping, Cindy flung at us, knives—long steak knives—five of them, the cops counted later. No aim, no science, but deadly enough if she got lucky. As I dropped, one nailed me on the neck. Handle-first, luckily, but it stung plenty. Plunging her way, I slammed into the butcher block and drove it on its four chunky legs across the linoleum with a loud rasping sound and into Cindy's legs, trapping her against the counter. She shrieked, struggled, then started hammering at me with an iron skillet, two-handed like Billie Jean. But I was down low behind the block, wrapping my arms around a leg, as the thing thonked harmlessly on the wood. Feet under me, crouching, I braced my shoulder on the underside of the block and lifted. Knowing Cindy might squirm loose, I turned and propelled as I hoisted. Sure enough she broke free, but the butcher block tumbled forth and over and caught her leg on its way down, slamming her to the floor, coming to rest on her ankle, splintering bones and pinning her in place as sure as a shackle.

Panting, I rose. My throat ached, my shoulder too. Moaning, Cindy thrashed on the floor: "Get this thing off of me. Please." As I got my phone out I realized she wasn't the only one moaning. Jeremy was on the floor, leaning against the far wall, busted glass everywhere, legs spread, face so chalky his eyes looked black. Red spread darkly on his Michigan sweatshirt, and from his shoulder emerged the black hilt of a steak knife. Cindy gasped louder: "You've got to help me. Please. I'll do anything."

I made the 9-1-1 call, went to Jeremy, knelt by him. "Hang in, man," I told him softly.

"I'm numb," he said softly. "Can't move."

"Take it easy." I look over at Cindy, who'd stopped trying to thrash herself loose and just lay there, panting. "I take it Gloria's the one who tracked you down, not the other way around."

"Yes!" she said promptly, voice dry and cracked.

Stepping around the mess, I got a cold cloth for Jeremy, and knelt by him again, applying it to his forehead. His breathing was labored, and he was clearly in shock, and the blood puddle was spreading. "Which one of you played in the concert?" I asked, "so that the other could knock Holly off?"

"I did," she said. "It was Gloria's idea, all of it."

Using a steak knife that happened to be handy, I carefully cut Jeremy's sweatshirt away. I stripped off my shirt and applied it to the wound, being careful not to disturb the knife. "Because she wanted Jeremy for herself," I commented. "But then you got a taste of Gloria's lifestyle, and got the hots for Jeremy yourself, and decided to do in your sister," whom the cops found three months later in a 55-gallon drum at the Port Huron scrap yard.

Having passed out, or pretended to, Cindy didn't answer. I adjusted Jeremy's cold cloth and the compress. His breathing was steady, and there was no blood bubble. Relieved, I patted him gently on the shoulder. "Well, old buddy," I said, "looks like there's such a thing as being too attractive."

about the author

Born in 1952, Rob Kantner spent early days in Ohio, teen years in north Georgia, and moved to the metro Detroit area in 1972. He served a Vietnam-era hitch in the U. S. Navy as a journalist, and was honorably discharged from the Naval Reserve in 1977. In 1978 he graduated from Eastern Michigan University.

Rob spent early adult years in middle-management marketing and advertising posts, later times in general management for small manufacturing/service firms. Since 1995 he has operated his own small business management consulting firm.

Rob's first published fiction appeared in *Alfred Hitchcock's Mystery Magazine* in 1982. Subsequently he published nine Ben Perkins novels and several dozen short stories.

These days Rob knocks out the occasional short story, historical fiction, and crime novels. His short story "How Wendy Tudhope Was Saved From Sure and Certain Death," published in 2003 in *Alfred Hitchcock*, appeared in **Best American Mystery Stories 2004** (Houghton Mifflin).

Rob is dad to Meaghan, John, and Robert. Meg is mom to the terrific Brenna and Evan. Rob lives with his wife Deanna on their rural Michigan horse farm, with Deanna's daughter Adrienne, plus two cats, two horses, and the dog.

Printed in the United States
34802LVS00003B/42